THIEVES' WORLD™

is a unique experience: an outlaw world of the imagination, where mayhem and skulduggery rule and magic is still potent; brought to life by today's top fantasy writers, who are free to use one another's characters (but not to kill them off . . . or at least not too freely!).

The idea for Thieves' World and the colorful city called Sanctuary™ came to Robert Lynn Asprin in 1978. After many twists and turns (documented in the volumes), the idea took off—and took on its own reality, as the best fantasy worlds have a way of doing. The result is one of F&SF's most unique success stories: a bestseller from the beginning, a series that is a challenge to writers, a delight to readers, and a favorite of fans.

Don't miss these other exciting tales of Sanctuary: the meanest, seediest, most dangerous town in all the worlds of fantasy. . . .

THIEVES' WORLD
(Stories by Asprin, Abbey, Anderson, Bradley, Brunner, DeWees, Haldeman, and Offutt)

TALES FROM THE VULGAR UNICORN
(Stories by Asprin, Abbey, Drake, Farmer, Morris, Offutt, and van Vogt)

SHADOWS OF SANCTUARY
(Stories by Asprin, Abbey, Cherryh, McIntyre, Morris, Offutt, and Paxson)

STORM SEASON
(Stories by Asprin, Abbey, Cherryh, Morris, Offutt, and Paxson)

THE FACE OF CHAOS
(Stories by Asprin, Abbey, Cherryh, Drake, Morris, and Paxson)

WINGS OF OMEN
(Stories by Asprin, Abbey, Bailey, Cherryh, Duane, Morris and Morris, Offutt, and Paxson)

THE DEAD OF WINTER
(Stories by Asprin, Abbey, Bailey, Cherryh, Duane, Morris, Offutt, and Paxson)

SOUL OF THE CITY
(Stories by Abbey, Cherryh, and Morris)

BLOOD TIES
(Stories by Asprin, Abbey, Bailey, Cherryh, Duane, Morris and Morris, Offutt and Offutt, and Paxson)

AFTERMATH

Edited by
ROBERT LYNN ASPRIN & LYNN ABBEY

ACE BOOKS, NEW YORK

AFTERMATH

An Ace Book/published by arrangement with
the editors

PRINTING HISTORY
Ace edition/November 1987

CONTENTS

1. Sanctuary
2. Old Ruins (First Settlement)
3. Ranke (Capital of Rankan Empire)
4. Ilsig (Capital of Old Kingdom)
5. (6) Contoured cities, now in Empire
6. Death's Harbor
7. Scavengers' Island
8. The Forgotten Pass

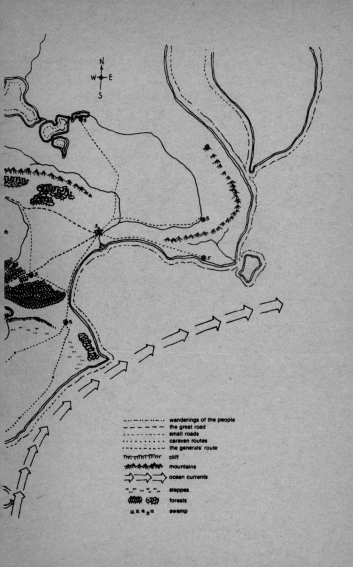

. _ . _ . _ . _ . _ .	wanderings of the people
_ _ _ _ _ _ _	the great road
- - - - - - -	small roads
· · · · · · · · · · · ·	caravan routes
- · · - · · - · · - · ·	the generals' route
ꟷꟷꟷꟷꟷꟷ	cliff
♠♠♠♠♠♠	mountains
⇨ ⇨ ⇨	ocean currents
ᵐᵗᵗ ᵐᵗᵗ ᵐᵗᵗ	steppes
🌳🌳 🌳🌳	forests
⚘⚘ ⚘⚘ ⚘⚘	swamp

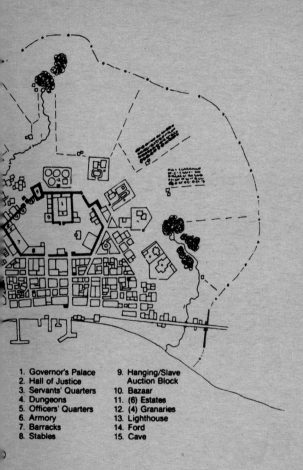

1. Governor's Palace
2. Hall of Justice
3. Servants' Quarters
4. Dungeons
5. Officers' Quarters
6. Armory
7. Barracks
8. Stables
9. Hanging/Slave Auction Block
10. Bazaar
11. (6) Estates
12. (4) Granaries
13. Lighthouse
14. Ford
15. Cave

← ~1 mile →

AFTERMATH

Dramatis Personae

The Townspeople

AHDIOVIZUN; AHDIOMER VIZ; AHDIO. *Proprietor of Sly's Place, a legendary dive within the Maze.*

AYE-GOPHLAN. *Captain of the palace guard before the arrival of Prince Kadakithis. Now he is one of three men charged with keeping the peace in Sanctuary.*

LALO THE LIMNER. *Street artist gifted with magic he does not fully understand.*

    GILLA. *His indomitable wife.*

    GANNER. *Their middle son, slain during the False Plague riots of the previous winter which signaled the end of severe civil unrest in Sanctuary.*

    VANDA. *Their daughter, employed as nursemaid to the Beysib at the palace.*

HAKIEM. *Storyteller and confidant extraordinaire.*

HORT. *Son of a fisherman and now Hakiem's sometime apprentice.*

JUBAL. *Prematurely aged former gladiator. Once he openly ran Sanctuary's most visible criminal organization, the hawkmasks; now he works behind the scenes.*

MASHA ZIL-INEEL. *Midwife whose involvement in the destruction of the Purple Mage enabled her to move from the Maze to respectability uptown.*

MELILOT. *Owner of a scriptorium where letters can be written or translated.*

MRADHON VIS. *Nisibisi adventurer and sometime spy. He has betrayed almost everyone and been betrayed in return, but he is a consummate survivor.*

MYRTIS. *Madam of the Aphrodisia House.*

SHAFRALAIN. *Sanctuary nobleman who can trace his lineage and his money back to the days of Ilsig's glory.*
> ESARIA. *His nubile daughter.*
> EXPIMILIA. *His wife.*
> CUSHARLAIN. *His cousin. A customs inspector and investigator.*

SNAPPER JO. *A fiend who survived the destruction of magic in Sanctuary. Now employed as a bartender in the Vulgar Unicorn.*

ZIP, *Bitter young terrorist. Leader of the Popular Front for the Liberation of Sanctuary (PFLS). Now he and his remaining fighters have been designated as officials responsible for peace in the city.*

The S'danzo

ILLYRA. *Half-blood S'danzo seeress with True Sight. Wounded by PFLS in the False Plague Riots.*
> DUBRO. *Bazaar blacksmith and husband to Illyra.*
> ARTON. *Their son, marked by the gods as part of the emerging diety known as the Stormchildren. He was sent to the Bandaran Islands for his education and safety—and to remove him from Sanctuary.*
> LILLIS, *their daughter, slain in the False Plague riots.*
> TREVYA. *A newborn orphan girl placed in their care by Walegrin.*

MOONFLOWER. *S'danzo seeress of remarkable obesity who was slain by Beysib guards who had mistakenly attacked her husband.*

THE TERMAGANT. *Oldest of the S'danzo women practicing her craft in Sanctuary.*

The Magicians

ENAS YORL. *Quasi-immortal mage cursed with eternal life and a constantly changing physical form.*

ISCHADE. *Necromancer and thief. Her curse is passed to her lovers who die from it. Her rivalry with Roxane drew her into the murky realm of Sanctuary's politics from which she has yet to extricate herself.*

ROXANE: DEATH'S QUEEN. *Nisibisi witch. Nearly destroyed when Stormbringer purged magic from Sanctuary, she is trapped inside a warded house and a dead man's body.*

> HAUGHT. *One-time apprentice of Ischade who betrayed her and is now trapped with Roxane.*
>
> TASFALEN. *The disolute Rankan nobleman, one of Ischade's lovers, whose body has become Roxane's prison.*

STRICK: TORAZELAN STRICK TIFIRAQUA. *White Mage who has made Sanctuary his home. He will help anyone who comes to him, but there is always a Price, sometimes trivial and sometimes not, for his aid.*

> AVENESTRA: AVNEH. *Once a preteen prealcoholic barfly at Sly's Place. Now Strick's very young receptionist with a sweet tooth.*
>
> FRAX. *Former palace guardsman, now Strick's fiercely loyal guard.*
>
> WINTSENAY: WINTS. *A down-and-out young Ilsig whose life has improved immeasurably since he began working for Strick.*

Visitors in Sanctuary

JARVEENA, *A woman, once Melilot's apprentice, who, with Enas Yorl's help, unveiled a plot to assassinate Prince Kadakithis shortly after his arrival in Sanctuary. In the intervening years she has been employed as Melilot's trading agent, and her many hideous scars have been slowly fading.*

SAMLOR HIL SAMT, *Trader from the north. His sister died in Sanctuary and his business sometimes brings him back to the city.*

STAR, *His seven-year-old niece. A single lock of white grows amid her black hair. The Beysibs claim this is the mark of the favor of their gods and the child does seem to have some strange abilities.*

The Rankans Living in Sanctuary

CHENAYA; DAUGHTER OF THE SUN, *A beautiful and powerful young woman who is fated never to lose a fight. She is the prince's cousin and is working to raise an army of gladiators which will place him on the imperial throne.*

PRINCE KADAKITHIS, *Charismatic but somewhat naive half-brother of the assassinated emperor, Abakithis.*

KAMA; JES, *Tempus's daughter. 3rd Commando assassin. Sometime lover of Critias, Zip, and Molin Torchholder.*

MOLIN TORCHHOLDER; TORCH, *Archpriest of Sanctuary's wargod (whichever deity that is at the moment). Architect for the rebuilt walls of Sanctuary. Supreme bureaucratic administrator of the city.*

> RANKAN 3RD COMMANDO, *Mercenary company founded by Tempus Thales and noted for its brutal efficiency.* GAYLE, *A member of that company.*

STEPSONS; SACRED BANDERS, *Members of a mercenary unit loyal to Tempus. Their years in Sanctuary have been among the worst in their history and they are eager to leave for anywhere else.*

> CRITIAS; CRIT, *Longtime mercenary in the company. An intelligence gatherer and assistant to Tempus. Also the partner of Straton, though that pairing has been in disarray for some time now.*
> STRATON; STRAT; ACE, *Partner of Critias. Injured by the PFLS at the start of the False Plague riots. He has been Ischade's lover and though her curse has not killed him, most of his former associates count him among Sanctuary's damned.*

TEMPUS THALES; THE RIDDLER, *Nearly immortal mercenary, a partner of Vashanka before that god's demise; commander of the Stepsons; cursed with a fatal inability to give or receive love.*

WALEGRIN, *Rankan army officer assigned to the Sanctuary garrison where his father had been slain by the S'danzo many years before. He is now one of three officers responsible for the peace in Sanctuary. He is also Illyra's half-brother.*

The Beysib

SHUPANSEA; SHU-SEA, *Head of the Beysib exiles in Sanctuary; mortal avatar of the Beysib mother goddess. Lover of Prince Kadakithis whom she wishes to marry.*

    CHABOSTU; CHA-BOS, *A daughter born before Shupansea was driven into exile.*

INTRODUCTION

Robert Lynn Asprin

Military units have never been noted for their punctuality, and the Stepsons were no exception. Even though their departure was originally planned for shortly after dawn, it was nearly noon before the first pair actually swung aboard their horses and headed off amid waves and good-natured catcalls from their comrades. This was not a regular army unit, but a free company of mercenaries, so the formations and columns one might expect in a troop relocation were nowhere in evidence. Rather, the men set out on their journey in pairs or small groups as they were ready, with no thought to waiting for the others. Indeed, it was doubtful they would even all take the same route to their new posting. However disorganized or leisurely their departure might be though, one thing was clear. The Stepsons were leaving Sanctuary.

Relatively few townspeople had gathered to witness their passing, but the first pair waved at them anyway as they set off. No one returned their salutation.

Of the watchers, two men were notable if only from the diversity of the pair. One was old, his hair more silver-white than gray, while the other was a youth barely out of his teens. The younger was dressed in the humble garb of the town's lower class, while the elder man's finery marked him as one who moved in richer, perhaps even royal, circles. That they were together, however, was never in

1

question. Not simply because they stood together and exchanged comments, though that would have been sufficient evidence for most. Even more apparent was their manner. While they conversed freely, their eyes never met, but instead remained focused on what was going on around them. Close attention was paid to the departing pair of Stepsons as if attempting to memorize their appearance and gear, then switched once more to the preparation of the remaining mercenaries.

Were they not so open in their scrutiny, the two might be mistaken for spies. As it was, they were ignored, for neither was unknown around the city. The younger was Hort, a lowly storyteller; the older, Hakiem, once a talespinner himself and mentor to Hort, was now adviser to the ruler of the Beysib.

"Well, it actually looks like they're going."

"Of course," Hakiem replied without looking at his friend. "Did you doubt it?"

"Yes, and so did you." Hort smiled. "But that didn't keep us from being out here at dawn. We should have known that even if anything happened, it wouldn't happen until later."

"True enough. Still, if we had slept in and they had decided to get underway on time, we would have missed it completely."

The younger man snuck a sideways glance at Hakiem.

"I can see where that would affect me," he said, "but why should it make any difference to you? Your storytelling days are behind you now."

"Call it habit," the old man grunted. "Besides, an adviser needs information as much as a storyteller, and the best information is still that which you gather yourself."

The men fell silent as another pair of Stepsons rode by.

"Well, it actually looks like they're going," Hort repeated, almost to himself.

Hakiem hawked and spat noisily in the dust.

"Good riddance!" he declared with sudden vehemence. "The sooner they're clear of the town, the better it will be for all of us! There has been nothing but chaos and death in the city since they arrived. Maybe now things will return to normal!"

Hort struggled, but lost his brief bout with silence.

"As I recall, Hakiem, there was chaos and death in Sanctuary long before the Stepsons put in their appearance. I don't see where they've been any worse than Jubal's hawkmasks used to be . . . or your pet fish-eyed friends for that matter. It's wrong to try to blame the Stepsons for all our problems . . . and dangerous to think things will return to normal when they've left. I don't think I even know what normal *is* anymore."

Hakiem turned away, his eyes avoiding both Hort and the departing Stepsons.

"You're right, of course," he admitted. "Though the Beysib have been far gentler with our town than the Stepsons, who were supposed to be guarding it. Water does not flow upstream, nor does time run backward. Sanctuary will never be what it was. Hawkmasks, Stepsons, Beysib . . . they've all had their impact on the town, and their presence will never be completely removed. Even the new laborers who are here to work on the walls will change our lives, though in what ways we have yet to find out. All we can do is what we've always done: watch. Watch and hope."

"Speaking of the new laborers," Hort said with an almost forced casualness, "have you heard anything of people disappearing?"

"I assume you mean dropping out of sight without turning up dead later," Hakiem retorted drily.

"That's right." The youth nodded. "Able-bodied men you'd think would be able to take care of themselves. I've heard of three so far."

"It's news to me. Still, I'll keep my ears open."

A group of Stepsons walked their horses by, not even looking at the assembled watchers.

Though he would never admit it openly, the withdrawal of the Stepsons as well as the Rankan 3rd Commando from Sanctuary concerned Hakiem much more than the disappearance of a few common laborers. He wondered how much of what was happening in town Hort was aware of and simply not commenting on and how much he was actually oblivious to.

There was a fight brewing. A contest of wills, if not swords, between the town and the Rankan Empire. He did not for a moment believe that it was coincidence that the Stepsons were being pulled out of town just when the tax issue was reaching a head. The question was, would they be back? If the empire tried to enforce its orders by force, would the Stepsons be the whip for the empire or the shield for the town? Or would they stay away, maintaining a mercenaries' neutrality, and not return until the matter was resolved . . . if they returned at all?

The old man studied faces, but could not find a clue to the future written anywhere: neither a hint of the future in the faces of the mercenaries, nor a glimmer of realization of the stakes that were being played for in those of the townsfolk.

CADE

Mark C. Perry

In another time, in another place, he could have been something else. He could have been a hero, or a general, a priest, or a king. But he was born in Sanctuary and that made him a killer.

Cade stood on a low hill looking down on the city. Sanctuary. He turned his head and spat. Sanctuary, the capital of hell. He had left the city eleven years ago, after killing a man, his first. Now he was back, to kill again. Somewhere in that cesspit his brother's body lay rotting, all his bones cracked by some torturer. It was that someone whom Cade was going to kill.

The wind shifted and the stench of the city assaulted him. After the long ride through the clean desert the smell was a physical force, full of wet decay, the smell of man at his worst. Victim and hunter were all the same in Sanctuary. The evil of his birthplace was alive, active, infecting everything that came into contact with it.

The sun was going down; dusk slowly covered the decrepitude of the city's ancient buildings, but the shadows could not hide it all, even from this distance. Cade was surprised to see a new wall going up around the town but it hardly helped the view, for surely that wall was not so much to keep enemies out as the inhabitants in. Even a madman would see there was no gain to be had by conquering Sanctuary.

Cade smiled to himself at the thought. Attack Sanctuary—
better to fight for a beggar's bowl. He turned to face west.
A house or something burned sullenly there, ignored by
the inhabitants of Downwind, the worst part of the whole
place. Downwind . . .

And that, he told himself, *is a place and a name you
promised never to have anything to do with again.* But of
course he knew promises meant nothing in hell . . .

If Sanctuary could be called the place of his birth, it was
Downwind that had created him. There he had lived between the age of six and sixteen. There he had learned
about the world, the real world, the truth behind all the lies
that men blind themselves with. He had learned about fear,
fear in his poor brother's eyes, who had always tried to
protect his younger sibling, even though it was Cade who
was the real protector. He learned of despair, as the money
became scarcer and the food rarer, and their mother did
anything, anything, so that she could keep her little family
together.

He remembered her tears when she heard he'd joined
the gang; she was dead by the time he became their
warlord. His time with the Demons taught him the most
valuable lesson of Sanctuary. He learned about blood, and
death.

Cade was so talented then, talented in the harsh passion
of the violent. The street brought out the blood in all its
miserable inhabitants, but some like Cade were born for
blood and shed it and lost it with equal calm.

He called it the waterfall, though he was eighteen before
he ever saw a real one. It was the moment when you either
let go and hit until you fell or you were pulled off and fear
never entered into it at all. That was the mark of the
talent, because some could do it when they were backed in
a corner, all could do it sometimes, but Cade would do it
every time.

He wondered if any of the Demons were still there:

probably not; they were either dead, or they had gotten out and would never come back. What did it matter? They were all punks anyway. Still, some of them might remember him.

He laughed thinking about it, but there was no humor in that sound. Wouldn't they be surprised to see him again? The local boy come back in triumph. He had made good by Sanctuary standards: He was rich beyond most men's imagination, and powerful, very powerful.

He had turned his talent into a very profitable art. The art of death. For a fee he killed. He was more than an assassin and less than a murderer. For he did kill with passion, but never pleasure. He killed in the name of mankind to free his victims from lies.

For Sanctuary had taught Cade the most valuable of all lessons; it had taught him the truth. In all its pain and agony, poverty and despair, was written the LAW, in iron-clad runes of blood.

And the LAW was one simple word. Hell . . .

For the world was not *a* hell, he knew that, it was *the hell*, the only true *hell*. A man lived a life of pain, no matter who or what he was; the punishment was daily. When he died, he either went somewhere better, or his spirit was annihilated for all time. It was simple really: the good, they went to their just desserts; the evil could sink no further, so they were destroyed.

All this ran through his thoughts as he stared down at the place he hated most. He was little concerned. He believed he had only killed the genuinely good or the genuinely evil, never those in-between. Now he was going to kill his brother's murderer and he was worried. What if the killer was neither good nor evil? What if he had not made the final choice—could Cade kill him then? After all, he was no soldier like his unknown father, butchering because someone told him to. He was very careful in accepting contracts, very careful in his death-dealing that whomever he brought the final moment to was either good or evil, either free or doomed. What if . . .

"Enough!" he cried out loud. Somewhere in the Maze Terrel's family waited in fear, in fear for their lives and in agony over the dead man they had loved so much. Cade would protect them. Terrel would have wanted that, but Cade would do more; he would use them as he had always used anyone he needed. Use them to find the murderer and for the first time in his long career he would not kill cleanly or quickly. No matter who had to die, or why, this time Cade would have vengeance!

He knelt down and cleared a space on the ground at his feet. He withdrew a dagger and began to make marks in the dirt. Here a slash for Tempus; there a curve for Ischade, others for Molin Torchholder, Jubal, Chenaya, the Stepsons, the PFLS, the Rankan 3rd Commando, Enas Yorl . . . He had run out of room. Sanctuary had managed to become the most dangerous place in the empire. It was truly hell's own capital. And all its demon princes were fighting for its bitter rule.

His information was incomplete. He could barely believe Tempus would stay here with the whole empire falling apart around him. And if Tempus went . . . he scratched out the marks for the Rankan 3rd Commando, and the Stepsons. He shook his head; it helped, but not by much.

Then he scratched in a fish eye. Beysibs. Now what the hell were they? Were they like other men? What happened when *they* died? Too, too many questions.

If it had been just magic, or men . . . but there were gods here now. All sorts of godly manifestations had taken place here, though his people had claimed that things had quieted down of late. Hardly a comforting thought.

He gripped the handle of the dagger tightly. It was all too unclear, too many random factors. Even Cade could not keep himself hidden from the gods, frauds though they were. Still, part of him hoped the trail would lead to one of these gods. He had only ever killed one obscure demigod. To cast down one of the great ones, those masters of the great lie, ah, now that would nearly make Terrel's horrid death worthwhile.

There was no point in going in quietly; this town was a catastrophe just waiting to happen. Why, any of these—he ground his foot into the dirt erasing the names—could be his target. Or all of them. Many of them would have the ability to find him: some would certainly know his name, others would be intelligent enough to make the connection between him and Terrel. *No*, he would simply advertise his presence and let the killers come to him, or others approach him with information. He stood up.

"This is going to be messy," he said to the empty land around him. But he would slip into the city later tonight and check in with his people before he revealed himself.

"I'm coming home," he whispered.

Cade took another sip of the wine, his black eyes searching the face of the man across from him at the oaken table. Targ was a good man. He had never failed a mission, but he was dangerous. Cade would have to be very careful how he used this one, very careful.

"So," Cade said, "I was right about Tempus and the others. Still, there are quite a few with power remaining."

"The streets are safer than even a few months ago," Targ answered, his thick hand digging in his beard. "The coalition seems to be holding, at least for now."

Just then the door to the house was opened. A young woman dressed in a fine gown and a dark shawl walked in.

"I told you not to go out at night," Targ said, though his voice carried no concern.

"I was just checking on Sarah," she answered, staring unabashedly at Cade, who simply stared back. Targ waved a hand at Cade.

"Our employer," he said. Marissa stood by the door, a little unsure of how to react.

"Sit," Cade said, watching as the woman seated herself, near Targ, but not too near. *So*, Cade thought to himself, *she fears him. I wonder how much she knows*. "Targ," he said aloud, "says you have done well. My brother's wife trusts you."

"Yes." She nodded. "She and I have become friends, lord." Cade smiled slightly at the title but he didn't correct her.

"She doesn't know that you work for me."

"No, lord, she waits for you, knowing that you will, ah, help."

"Understand one thing." Cade's voice was harsh. "I have come for revenge, nothing more."

"I think Sarah understands, lord."

"And tell me how does it feel to be the Lady Marissa?"

"Better"—she smiled—"than it did to be the slave girl Donan." Cade did not answer her smile. Disguised as an old merchant, he had bought the girl's freedom. Then two months ago he had sent her here with Targ to set up a base for him. It was no accident that the house next to this was his sister-in-law Sarah's.

He tasted the wine while the other two waited for him to speak. Cade nodded his head once. Good, they had done well, the girl in particular. She hardly resembled the anemic creature he had freed so many months ago. She had been a find, that one. Able to speak court Rankene, and read and write: a rare find.

And she was strong. He could sense that in people. After what this girl had been through it was surprising she retained her sanity. Cade had seen the scars that covered her back and thighs. He liked her; she was good and if he didn't need her he would free her from life's black curse, but first . . .

"Some here might still know me," he said. "Terrel did

not hide the fact that it was I who bought his house, and his shop.'' He stood up. ''Therefore I see no reason for further subterfuge on my part.'' He picked up his sword belt and buckled it about his waist.

''Tomorrow,'' he addressed the two, ''I will ride into town at dawn. I will go straight to Terrel's home. Let those who might care know that I am here. You two must remember: You do not know me, I do not know you. Since Lady Marissa is a friend of Sarah's, and I will be staying at her house, we will have plenty of opportunity to get to know one another.'' He smiled and turned to go.

''Ah, one last thing, Targ.'' The mercenary just looked up. ''Tomorrow, go to the guild. Get a few guards for this house, especially a good bowman. From now on I want both houses under constant surveillance.''

''You expect someone to make a move?'' Targ asked. Cade shrugged.

''If they do not, I will.'' And with that he was gone. Targ got up and locked the door. He could see no trace of Cade in the night, and if he couldn't, no one he knew could.

''Well, what do you think?'' he said.

''I don't know. He's strange,'' Marissa answered, ''scary.''

Targ snorted. ''He is a fanatic, a madman.'' Targ sat down and reached for the wine. ''And probably the most dangerous man I have ever met.'' There was fear in Targ's gray eyes, and that made Marissa shiver. Whatever could scare the strange mercenary was nothing she wanted to deal with. What had that old merchant gotten her involved in?

Targ opened the trapdoor to the roof, climbing up the ladder with silent agility. His sensitive nose welcomed the fresh air. The roof was flat, and a thin three-foot wall surrounded it. Targ moved to the wall, peering over at the

house next door. The two-story building was cloaked in
shadows; no light showed from behind the thickly shut-
tered windows. Targ stared at the dark shape for a long
time, trying to spot any figures that might be concealed in
the shadows, but he could detect nothing.

His thick hands fondled the pommel of his sword. His
eyes burned red in the night. Even if Cade was hidden
somewhere in those shadows, Targ knew from long experience that he would be invisible. Cade. He swore under
his breath. *Cade*.

He knew Cade was uncomfortable with this job; it wasn't
their usual sort of job. This wasn't for money, or for the
great war he always spoke about; this was for Cade. Targ
looked over the roofs of the town; somewhere out there a
murderer, a torturer was hiding, but it wouldn't do any
good: Cade would find him and Targ refused to even try to
imagine what that madman's vengeance would be . . .

No, this wasn't their usual sort of job at all.

Targ shifted nervously, sniffing at the wind. The air
carried its own messages, its own secrets, and the scents
spoke to Targ, as they never could to an ordinary man.

Sometimes Targ wondered if Cade was a man. What
really went on in his mind? Who could say? Only Cade,
and he wasn't talking.

But together the two had shared much. If killing and
blood could be considered sharing. How many had the two
killed? Ten? Twenty? A hundred? Targ had quit counting
long ago.

Cade hated this place, hated Sanctuary. Only his brother's death could have brought him back. Targ knew Terrel
had been the only person Cade really cared about and now
he was dead.

"Gods," Targ mouthed. He heard a cry. It sounded like
a woman. The lonely sound was lost in the wind. Was it
fear in that sound, or madness? In Sanctuary it was hard to
tell the two apart. Perhaps he should go and see, perhaps

. . . but no. His illusions of being the great hero were long gone, lost in that same night that had taken his ordinary mortality away.

He would help Cade as he always did. First because Cade only asked him to help kill those who deserved it, the real bastards. And second because Cade knew, knew of his curse and never showed fear, or disgust . . . or much of anything.

How could he explain to Cade that he liked Sanctuary? There was something here, something that soothed and calmed the curse. He had only needed to kill twice since he came here. For two months he had lived with the slave girl and successfully hidden the truth from her. And both of the kills had been ones who deserved it . . . Targ growled softly in his throat, remembering the screams and the blood. Murderers and rapists both, they had deserved it. They had.

He had heard there was a vampire here, Ischade. A vampire. In all the years he had been fighting the great war, never had he met a real vampire, or for that matter a real werewolf.

Cade watched the sun rise slowly, its light defining the harsh edge of Sanctuary. He reached back and slowly braided his long hair. It was an Ilsigi warbraid, something not seen in Sanctuary in a long time, something Cade had to do. He was returning, but he wouldn't do it quietly, or simply. He was back and the braid was his way of making one thing clear: No one and nothing would make him bow. He was not the same boy who had run away so long ago; run with the blood of a merchant on his hands, blood he had never meant to shed. But one thing was still the same. He had left as a killer and he was returning as one.

He gently stroked his horse on the nose, smiling as it tried to take a nip at his new braid, then lifted himself smoothly into the saddle and took a moment to settle his weapons.

He was no warrior, not in the normal sense. He did not fight in great battles, riding for honor and glory. He'd just as soon use a knife or a garrote in the dark as swing a sword, but that didn't mean he wasn't a dangerous swordsman. Indeed, only the best could match him in bladework, and even fewer were as adept with no weapons at all.

He had always known he would come back, though until this moment he had denied it. He had taken the gifts of Sanctuary and now he would bring them back . . .

He kicked the horse, heading it toward the main gate that pierced the half-finished wall. He sat straight in the saddle, comfortable with the gait of the horse. His cloak was thrown back to reveal the rich armor beneath. His sword alone was worth more money than most Sanctuarites could ever hope to see in their lives.

He smiled. It appealed to him, coming back like this, flaunting his wealth and his scars. The scars covered his hands, crisscrossed his features. His face was smooth-shaven; his hard smile emphasized the strong chin. The horse's steady pace brought him closer to the wall.

It loomed above him, beckoning him on, down the road into the ugly maw of hell. The other passengers of the road made room for him to pass. They knew trouble when they saw it. Maybe it was the tight muscles they sensed moving beneath the armor, or the sharp weapons that he carried. But maybe it was something else.

He had come home, to Sanctuary. He is Cade, here to return the city's gifts. He is Cade and he is riding into hell, with death his only follower.

Sarah walked about the main room in aimless circles. Her hand darted out to touch a chest here, a wall hanging there. There was no thought behind her motion; she tried not to think too much. She stopped, staring at a blank wall, fighting the urge to just cry—no, not cry but shout, scream, pound, and break things.

He's gone . . .

That was what it always led to, the thinking, that he was gone. Terrel, her husband, her love, Terrel, he's gone . . . She always tried to stop it there, but it continued, relentlessly, the memories still so fresh after almost half a year.

They had killed him right here in this room, while she slept. She heard nothing, nothing. Waking up, he wasn't beside her and she was always up first. Small annoyance, walking about, the children still asleep, going downstairs. Gods, she'd almost walked right past it. Even with all the blood.

His blood.

It had covered everything, the wall, the floor, even the ceiling and there in the middle, his skin so pale. His naked body looking tiny in that immensity of red horror. Spread out, bent at odd angles, the bones; the embalmer said they had broken all his bones. All his bones. How could they do that? There were so many bones. How could they break them all?

He's gone . . .

Those dark eyes, so kind, so full of pain. His gentle touch, warm breath on her neck. He's gone and she didn't even know why they had killed him.

"Gods, have mercy," but there were no tears to punctuate her plea. They had dried up in the horror of the last months. If he had fallen, or gotten sick, if he had even just died, but this . . . that pale body. Sarah knew the memory would never leave her.

"He's gone," she said aloud, slumping down in a cool corner. Thank the All-Mother for the Lady Marissa. She had taken the children to the Bazaar with her. If they saw their mother like this . . . She shook her head violently. If it would just go away for a while. The harsh visions scarring her memory like blood staining the walls, drying slowly, covering everything, everywhere . . .

Sarah was startled by the loud *thump thump* of someone banging on the door. She got up, adjusting her clothes. But it wouldn't be Marissa; she had just left. Carefully she opened the door.

The sun was bright that morning and it streamed through the doorway, leaving her visitor in backlit shadow. He was tall, with broad shoulders, his armor glinting. For a minute she thought it was the guard captain Walegrin. He had actually been kind to her, almost gentle. Her thoughts jumped. News, did they have news? Who did it . . . ? But no, Walegrin was even larger than this man, taller, more muscular.

"Sarah," he said, and his voice was full of strange emotions. But there was something about him. Something. He stepped farther out of the shadows and she felt a sharp pain.

Terrel, she almost said. It was there in his face, though Terrel had never had such scars. This man's skin was tanned, weathered, hard like his armor and body.

"Cade," she whispered. He had come. He was here. For a moment he seemed at a loss. He seemed to retreat into shadow, but there was the memory of Terrel in that face.

"I wish to come in," Cade said.

"Oh, of course, please come in. I'm sorry, I was so startled, I mean, please come in." He moved past her, his weapons and armor jingling slightly.

"You should look to see who is at the door before you open it," he said.

"Yes, I should, I suppose, I mean. Do you want anything? To drink, or . . ." Her voice trailed off, her confusion overwhelming her. He turned to look at her.

She was attractive in a way. Her face was round, but thin. Her features seemed somehow disjointed, as if a thin veil covered them. Her eyes darted about, not meeting his gaze. But they were her best feature. Brown in an ordinary way, now filled with knowledge and taut pain. She was pretty, her bare shoulder showing in the disarrayed dress. She was pretty. The thought surprised him. It was the sadness, always the sadness. When he saw it in women he could never turn from it, never ignore it; it always made them so pretty. He hoped his vengeance would cause her no more . . . sadness.

"I'm sorry," he said quietly. They both knew what he meant.

"Wine?" she asked, letting the moment pass.

"Wine." He followed her into the dining area, seating himself at the scarred wooden table. She handed him a goblet, the best she had. He poured the wine; the sound of the goblet filling reverberated loudly in the room. He put the decanter down, not looking at her, not touching the drink.

"You said in your letter," his voice was husky, "you said that Terrel was involved with the PFLS."

"I, Terrel . . ." She bowed her head. "I, yes. He . . . helped."

"Money?"

"A little. He didn't like the Rankans"—her voice got softer—"but he wasn't really involved, not in a . . . he didn't deserve . . ." but it was too much and she could say no more.

"I'm sorry," he said again. "Neither of us like Rankans. Mother always said they killed our father. He wore this,"—he touched his warbraid—"my father did."

"Cade." She dared to look up, but couldn't meet his steady gaze. "Terrel, he—" She stopped. Could you talk of love to such a man?

Cade stood up. "I will get my things. You have a room for me?" She just nodded. "Good. Sarah, we will talk later. I am here. I cannot take away what has happened, but I am here. You need never fear.'' With that he was gone. She sat there staring at the goblet. She should get up, show him the room, the room she had prepared, prepared months ago, but he would find it, know it was for him.

The dim light from the window glinted off the enamel overlay of the goblet. He was . . . Terrel had never said much about Cade, not Cade as a man. He was full of stories of their childhood, of the slow decline into poverty, of the family holding itself together fiercely, as all around them melted into the grayness of despair. Terrel had said that Cade was the stronger. A fighter. Nothing could beat Cade.

But who was this man, this man with his weapons and armor clanking about him, his ridiculous warbraid—who wore those anymore? She knew so little of him. Terrel had said he was some sort of warrior, but rich. She knew that. He had set Terrel up in business, bought this house. Money, yes, but . . . a shiver caught her by surprise.

His eyes, that's what it was. Not the scars of the sword, or even his strange way of talking. It was his eyes. She could see them clearly, reflected in the odd light of the goblet, framed by the hard lined face, the thick heavy brows, the impossibly black hair. His eyes. They were black, black like Terrel's, but . . .

She reached out and grabbed the goblet. His eyes, they were like weapons, spearing her, attacking everything they focused on, jabbing about, terrifying. She put the goblet down in front of her. It was bent, imprinted by his fingers when he had crushed it, unknowing. But Sarah did not see that. All she could see were those two black eyes.

Several days later Cade sat on a stone bench in the small courtyard behind Terrel's house sharpening his sword. With one hand he steadied the blade while with the other he held the whetstone, slowly smoothing out the minor imperfections in the razor-sharp edge. The sun light danced across the blade, hurting Cade's eyes, but he ignored the discomfort. The slow, grating scrape of the whetstone on the blade punctuated his thoughts.

Things were a lot more complicated than they had appeared on the surface.

Scrape.

Terrel must have been much more involved in the PFLS than Sarah thought.

Scrape.

He had been killed, tortured because of this.

Scrape.

Somehow, Terrel had crossed someone in a major way.

Scrape.

Damn them all!

Cade threw the whetstone across the courtyard, against the far wall. Damn. Why hadn't he come to me?

And that was what kept eating at him, demanding an answer. Why hadn't Terrel asked Cade for help? He knew what his younger brother was, what he did. Cade had always protected Terrel, but this time Terrel had chosen to do it on his own. And he'd paid the price. Whom had he crossed and how?

Cade ran over the information he'd uncovered so far. Terrel had stayed late at his pottery shop, remaining after his workers had left. He had done that for three months before his death. Why?

Then there were the shop accounts—confusing. During the worst period of chaos in the history of a town always on the edge of collapse, Terrel had shown a profit. By selling pottery? It made no sense.

Why did he stay late? What had he been doing? Cade reached into his tunic, pulling out several receipts. There was something else that bothered him about them. All the buyers had come to pick up their pottery at the shop, no deliveries. Fine. The orders had increased last fall. Terrel naturally ordered more clay. Everything had been paid on time, all for the proper price. Damn, it was here somewhere, he knew it; it had to be.

Why had he been staying so late?

Cade mulled over the receipts for another half hour, getting more exasperated by the minute. He knew the answer was here, not on the streets. Targ had covered Sanctuary up and down, Cade had followed in the last five days retracing all the likely leads. All had led nowhere. Terrel was liked, respected, not known by anyone who shouldn't know him. His work was good. People were satisfied. None of it made any sense. Even with Terrel giving money to the PFLS, he hadn't given enough to make a real difference. Half the town had been contributing to one faction or another at that time, although not always voluntarily. So why pick on Terrel? An example? Not likely; a bigger target would have served better. Besides, the murder had hardly been public. No, something else . . .

Why had he been staying late? How had he been making a profit? How much money could he have given? Money. Late. Money. Late.

That's it. Terrel had been working to make more money. No. Something else. If it was to increase profits, why had he let the workers leave? Why not have them work with him? What had he been doing that he didn't want the others to know about?

Cade rifled through the receipts again, singling out the purchases.

"You fool," he said aloud, but whether he meant himself by it, or Terrel, even he didn't know. It was all right there. Terrel's orders for clay had increased, but some of the clay was cheaper, much cheaper than that he usually used. And Cade was sure that when he checked on it, he would find the new clay totally inappropriate for making good pottery. Something not made to last, something made to break easily, something made for one purpose only: to conceal . . .

What was it, Terrel? he thought. *What was it you were hiding for your zealots? Weapons? Money? Drugs? All three? What went through your head, brother, staying in that little shop, everyone gone, the light fading, the wheel spinning, your deformed hands forming the cheap clay, changing it. What was it you made—false bottoms, sides? Probably bottoms.*

You little fool, did you think you were going to change things? Bring about a new Sanctuary, a new world? Make things better? Depose the Rankans you always despised so much? Ah, Terrel, don't you know, revolutions always fail in hell.

Cade stood up, sheathing his sword. He had the scent now. All he and Targ had to do was ask a few discreet questions, drop a few coins into sweaty palms. *This* trail would lead them to the truth, to the reason behind Terrel's horrid end. This would lead them to his brother's murderer.

Cade smiled. He had them now.

Sarah sat on the same bench Cade had used earlier that day. She watched the shadows sliding down the wall as the sun set and Sanctuary began its nightly ritual of madness. It was time to go inside, bolt the doors, lock the shutters. But why bother? That hadn't saved Terrel. In Sanctuary death followed you wherever you tried to hide. If it weren't for the children . . .

Toth was a good boy; he tried. He understood what had happened and tried to help. Little Dru had no idea what was going on. She was always asking where Da was, and no matter how many times Sarah had explained to her that her father wasn't coming back, she refused to understand. And now, with Cade in the house, they were that much more confused. He had turned their lives upside down.

Sarah couldn't decide whether she hated or feared Cade or if it was both.

He ordered everyone around like he owned them. Sarah still shook with anger when she recalled catching him teaching the children to fight with a knife.

Gods, they were still her babies.

Cade had accused her of coddling and smothering them. He had called her a fool and said that fighting was the only way to stay alive in a cesspool like Sanctuary.

But how could she explain it to him? Terrel was his brother—surely Cade knew about his brother's crippled hands. How could Cade forget? How could he continue to embrace violence? She and Terrel had consciously rejected it, and rejected it for their children.

She wasn't stupid, though. She knew he continued to teach Toth whenever she wasn't around. The bastard.

Toth worshiped Cade. For him, his uncle was a great warrior from one of the tales he'd once heard Hakiem tell in the Bazaar. But Sarah knew better. She had an idea now what Terrel had meant when he'd said Cade wasn't really a warrior. The man was a killer as sure as the sea is blue.

It was all so confusing. As much as Cade scared her, still he was kind in his own way, but not as Terrel had been. It wasn't gentleness; he was always grim. But he seemed so sad. Last night Dru had cried in her sleep calling for her Da; and when Sarah had gone to check on her she found Cade there soothing the child. He had held her, cooing soft words, unintelligible, but they calmed the child. She fell asleep in Cade's scar-ridden arms.

The door behind Sarah burst open and Toth ran into the courtyard.

"Ma, Marissa's here," he gasped out. Sarah looked at him for a moment. He wasn't tall, but his shoulders were beginning to broaden out. He had the Ilsigi hair and eyes of his father's family, but it was her nose and chin that defined his features. The boy shook the hair away from his eyes and beamed at his mother. She smiled back faintly. This last week he actually seemed happier; Cade at least seemed good for the children, for some strange reason.

"Tell her to come out here," Sarah answered.

"Out here? But it's dark. Cade says—"

"Never mind what Cade says," she interrupted. "Tell the Lady Marissa to come out here."

He shrugged and did as he was told.

Marissa came out moments later, holding a lantern and a goblet of wine. She handed Sarah the drink.

"I thought you could use it," Marissa said in her soft voice. Sarah smiled. Marissa was so thoughtful. At first Sarah had been put off by the other's title and light, Rankan good looks. Now she wondered if she could have made it this far without her friend.

"Thank you, Marissa. I think you're right." She took a sip of wine, letting the liquid numb her mouth, enjoying the sensation of it sliding down her throat.

"Cade's really getting to you, huh?" Marissa said with a raised eyebrow.

"Oh, that man. I don't understand him." Sarah's voice dropped to a whisper. "He frightens me."

Marissa laughed. "He frightens everyone," she answered, "even Targ."

"I can't believe that." Sarah considered the notion that anyone or anything could frighten Marissa's strange mercenary and found it ludicrous. As ludicrous as, well, as thinking anything scared Cade.

"Oh, it's true," Marissa said. "Targ snorts and struts around every time Cade walks into a room." She smiled though Sarah thought it looked a little strained. "I swear his hair stands on end." Sarah laughed at that. Targ's excessive hairiness had been a running joke between the two for some time. The thought of all that red hair standing up straight was amusing. "Just like a little porcupine," she said, and the two laughed again.

"Marissa," Sarah said, her voice losing all trace of amusement, "why have you hired more mercenaries?" Marissa was quiet. She hated this. She liked Sarah and longed to tell her the truth, all of it. The lies between the two of them kept them apart, but she owed people and she had always paid her debts.

"Well, I'll tell you, Sarah," she said. "This town, it is so dangerous, I just feel safer. Gods know I have the money to spare."

"How many did you hire?"

"Three, not counting Targ, of course." Marissa bit her lip. "I'll tell you a secret." She looked around. "I've told them to keep an eye out on your house, too. So that . . ." She left the rest unfinished. Sarah looked away, but her hand patted her friend's knee briefly.

"Thank you, Marissa." She turned back. "But I don't think anyone is going to bother us with Cade around." She took a large swallow of wine. "You know why Cade is here, don't you." It was a statement, not a question. Again Sarah was struck by Marissa's odd unease at her words. Marissa was hiding something, but Sarah did not intend to pry, respecting the other's private pain.

"Yes," Marissa said, "yes, he's here to find Terrel's, uh, murderer."

"He is going to kill whoever is responsible, Marissa."

"Well, Terrel *was* his brother."

"I know, but it all seems"—Sarah shrugged—"so dramatic."

Marissa laughed. "Oh, really, Sarah, that sounds so silly."

"No, I'm serious." Sarah turned to her friend. "Six months ago I was the wife of a potter. I had"—she swept her arm in an arc behind her—"a nice house, nice things, two wonderful children, and a man I loved dearly." Marissa laid a hand on her friend's shoulder. "And now . . ." Sarah shook her head. "Now I don't know.

"My husband has been murdered, tortured to death in

that same house, while my children and I slept. Why? I
don't even know. Then this man shows up. This strange
man. My husband's brother, but the two are not anything
alike. My mysterious brother-in-law shows up. With his
words and his armor, his dark looks, and dark ways.
Suddenly, suddenly I find myself in the middle of a con-
spiracy, a piper's tale of murder and revenge.'' Sarah
drank deeply again from the wine cup. ''I don't understand
anything anymore, Marissa, and I'm tired of being afraid.''

Marissa had no answer for her. No words of comfort to
offer. She knew all too well what it was like to fear, what
it was like to have the world change overnight; to go from
a warm, safe place to a world of sudden threats and
shadows. What could she say to this woman? What comfort could she give, she who had no comfort in her own
life?

''Sarah,'' she said aloud, ''Sarah. I don't know what
anyone can say or do to help. But I'll tell you one thing.''
She almost flinched when Sarah turned to face her with
those dark, sad eyes. ''I think there is more of Terrel in
Cade than you think. No matter what happens, he will do
everything he can to help you and I don't think it's only
because his brother would have wanted him to.''

It was cold comfort, but in this new world it was often
the only hope Sarah was allowed.

It took two more days for Targ and Cade to put the rest
of the pieces together. That Terrel had been running something for the PFLS was definite; what he had been running
was another thing. Why was still a mystery. But Cade now
had the most important answer. The contact was in Downwind. Downwind—the one place in Sanctuary Cade had
avoided, though in his heart he had known, from the
beginning, that it would be his destination.

But first he must talk to Sarah again. He wasn't looking
forward to this conversation. The woman was half terri-

fied, half fascinated by him. He was afraid he would have to reveal too much to her. There were things he might have to say, show, things he could never take back. But he had to find out what she knew. Accordingly, after dinner he ordered the children to bed. This earned him a dark look from the woman, but he ignored it. He faced his brother's wife across a table still covered with the remnants of the meal.

"Sarah, we must talk."

"Indeed we must." Her voice was firm. "You can't order my children around like that. You have to—"

Cade interrupted. "No, Sarah, not now. We have to talk about Terrel." She grew quiet at that. "Sarah, Terrel was involved much more deeply with the PFLS than you thought."

"What do you mean?"

"He was running contraband for them."

"I know he gave them some money, but everybody was supporting one group or another."

"He was doing more than contributing a few spare coins." Cade sighed, his hand drumming against the table edge. "When Terrel stayed late, he was making pots, special pots."

"Cade, that is what he did for a living."

"I know that." Cade leaned over the table. "But these pots were built to hide things."

"What sort of things?"

"Who knows?" Cade shrugged. "Weapons, money, messages, even drugs, whatever it was doesn't matter now. What matters is that he did it for the PFLS. He was not just paying them; he was one of them."

"I don't believe it."

"Believe it." Cade leaned back, staring at her. "I've discovered a whole underground organization, very well coordinated, slipping all sorts of things through the different control zones of the town. Terrel was part of it, and it's because of that he was killed."

"Why?"

"I'm still not entirely sure. Could have been a lot of reasons—one of the other factions found out, one of his own people betrayed him, perhaps even the PFLS themselves were the killers."

"But why? If he was helping them, why would they kill him?"

"Lots of reasons: a shipment got lost, an internal upheaval." His voice was bitter. "Sarah, this town was a mess, insane. No one knew who was in charge of what. The control areas changed daily, hourly. Somehow, someone decided Terrel had broken a rule, and they made him pay." Sarah's face was pale and her lips trembled, but she could think of nothing to say.

"Well," he continued, "there are a few things we can infer." He waited but she was still silent. "Okay, they didn't torture him for information."

"How do you know?"

"Because he was killed here, while you were sleeping. Yet you and the children never woke. Why? Magic— possibly. A sleeping draught—less likely. No one, anywhere, heard a sound the whole time Terrel was dying. I think magic, a spell to contain any sound he or his torturers made." He shook his head. "A lot of effort. Why not just kidnap him, take him somewhere else, interrogate him there? But, no, they did it here, therefore it had to be for one of two reasons: to set an example, or to exact revenge. Probably revenge."

"I don't understand."

"If he was killed as an example, well, there were other ways they could have done it, less hazardous ways, and more obvious ones. Besides, as I said, lots of people were doing what Terrel did. He wasn't a big enough fish to go to such lengths for. No, it has to be vengeance." Cade ground his teeth together, the skin of his face pulled tight, making his scars stand out in high relief. "They broke every bone in his body, Sarah. Think about it. That's not a normal torture, and as far as I can discover no one else has been killed this way. He was killed that way because . . . because someone knew."

"About what happened, his hands," she said.

Cade looked surprised. So Terrel *had* told her. "Yes." He said no more.

The two sat, lost in their memories. She recalled a warm night, a storm coming in, her new husband sitting on the bed telling her the tale of his deformity in a monotone. He, his mother, and Cade had come to Downwind; forced there because, with the death of their father there was no money, and there was no family to help them. Terrel's mother found what work she could, buying Terrel a slate, working hard to find the chalk. It had made it all livable for him, given him a hope for another way of life.

Then one day, four years after they had moved, a gang jumped him, breaking the slate, the chalk, and the fingers that loved to draw; maiming him for life, so he could never be the artist he dreamed about . . .

But Cade had other memories. "Sarah." She looked up at him, now with a tear in her eye. "Terrel told you what happened. Do you know the rest?"

"The rest?"

So, Cade thought, *he never knew. Well, that's something, I guess.* Cade had never told anyone before, kept it to himself. Now he could not hold it in, though he could see no purpose in his honesty.

His voice was harsh. "He came home that night, his lip cut where he'd bitten it through, trying to hold back his cries. His hands—if he had come home sooner, maybe we could have set them. I don't know. They were ruined." He looked away from her. "He was in such pain."

"Mother—" He sighed. "Mother tried to heal those

hands. Every night she held him, crying on the bent fingers, as if her tears could really take the pain away.'' He could still see them. Lying on the cot, the ragged cloth that divided their one-room shack tattered and frayed, not hiding the scene from his young eyes. She had rocked Terrel to sleep every night. He slept with her because of the nightmares, about the sound of the snap of bones that just wouldn't go away.

"I had nothing, we had nothing to give him.'' Then Cade turned to her, his eyes so fierce she looked away. "But then, I knew, I had one gift . . . Sarah, I had vengeance.'' His voice shook as he relived that time. He told her how he had found the rope in an alley full of mud and refuse, how he had pulled the brick from one of the few real buildings in Downwind. How he tied the brick to the rope and then waited.

"For three nights I waited,''—he stood up, his muscles taut with the memory—"until they went to sleep. Then I took my rope and brick, and one by one I found those who had done it.'' His eyes were wild. "I found them.'' He sighed. "I caught them and I smashed them with the brick.'' His hand pounded the air. "I smashed them over and over and over.'' He took a deep breath, then stood still.

"I found them. I didn't kill them. I found them and afterwards they never drew either.'' He sat down, not looking at her. "Terrel was thirteen. I was eleven . . .''

The room was quiet. Sarah stared at Cade, but he would not look at her. She realized he was embarrassed. He had told her something that he hadn't had to, at least not that way. He had showed her his secret. In it she knew was the real Cade, the answer to all his riddles, but she could not see it. All she could think of was Cade. He had only been about Toth's age . . .

"Sarah—'' Now his voice was soft, and he hadn't used

that tone with her before. "Whoever killed him knew; knew what had happened to him; knew of his fears."

"He still had nightmares," she answered.

"I thought so. They *knew*, Sarah, and I don't know how. But I do know the anwser is in Downwind. And it's there I have to go . . ."

Cade stood at the end of the decrepit bridge. Across its rotting length lay his goal—Downwind.

The smell from the slow-moving White Foal River was noxious, full of refuse and dead things. Cade ignored it. After all, it should smell like home to him.

He wore old riding leathers with a weather-stained cloak thrown over them. He carried his sword openly, though several other weapons were concealed about his body. He looked like a down-and-out mercenary, between jobs, but one who knew his business well. Tough enough looking that the dregs of Downwind would leave him alone, obscure enough not to draw attention, except from those who noticed the warbraid and knew what it meant.

The answer was here in Downwind. At first Cade thought he would have to find Zip, the leader of PFLS, and now apparently one of the military officers of Sanctuary. Cade didn't want to deal with the powers of Sanctuary if he could help it. There were several he'd rather not have to tangle with if possible. Take that madwoman Chenaya, building an army of gladiators. He smiled at the thought. Gladiators! Gladiators made poor soldiers, and were hardly equipped for the streets of Sanctuary. Everybody was insane here . . .

It seemed Zip had made several mistakes, and the PFLS had fractured into at least three recognizable factions. The hard-core stayed loyal to their charismatic leader, but some of the less patriotic and more power-minded had gone their own way. Cade followed the trail that led to money, and in a town like Sanctuary there were three quick ways of making money: prostitution, drugs, and slavery. The whore-houses were well controlled here. They were an important part of Sanctuary's economy. And the slavery, well it seemed Jubal used to control that, probably still did, but there were rumors on the streets of a new organization.

But whoever they are, they weren't in business yet when Terrel was caught, so the answer was drugs. That's where the faint trail became as clear as a paved road. Whatever Terrel had run first, he had ended up running drugs, something Cade doubted his brother had been too pleased about. That didn't fit into his image of a revolution. But the goals of the revolution had been revised, and the new rules were made here, in Downwind.

The many gangs of Downwind had become more en-trenched in the last few years, less like youth gangs and more like organized crime families. The largest, next to the beggar king's, was a gang called the Sharp Side. A gang that ran a good portion of Downwind, a gang that controlled Cade's old turf and it seemed, much more. A gang that had originally been part of the PFLS, but had re-formed in the last months, re-formed to take control of some of the contacts once run by Zip. A gang that now ran a third of the drug trade in Sanctuary.

So. It had all been there, easy to read, once you saw the pattern. Now Cade had to find the Sharp Side, and find out who had given the orders. Why they'd given them. And then he'd make them pay.

Casually he strolled across the bridge, giving no out-ward sign of the fast beating of his heart, his disgust and agony, his despair.

Slowly he headed toward his old house, his inmost self creating an ineffective shield against the world that passed before his eyes. Downwind was pain, for its inhabitants and for any with the eyes to see. All about him, as he wound his way through the filth-strewn streets, the night-mare was acted out. The adults were empty husks of aimless motion, the children dirty and mean. The toddlers plodded about, unwatched, their distended stomachs seeming to lead them about in their desperate search for anything remotely edible.

But that wasn't the worst. There were the carcasses of shacks, like decomposing animals, in which the inhabitants played out their desperate lives. The little girls, and boys, offering their bodies for a piece of bread. And of course the blood. Everywhere apparent, drying on the walls, spilling fresh from ragged wounds, and behind the eyes of every poor bastard who walked the empty streets. Every one of them seemed to carry an ugly scar, a reminder of some time when a blade met their flesh . . . or a thrown rock . . . or a fist.

He shuddered. Worse? What was worse? The term was meaningless. The blood? The hunger? No, the disease . . . the corruption in everyone's veins. Scales and shingles covering thin limbs. Eyes oozing mucous, coughs racking whole frames. Their slow descent toward uncaring death.

That was it, of course, the heart and soul of Downwind. Death. Coming at them from so many angles, attacking them, and they had no chance to defend themselves. Like his mother: the hard work she'd endured, the food she'd denied herself so that her children could have one more mouthful. What was it that finally killed her? Was it one of the many diseases ravaging her? Was it the fear? No, she was past that in the end. Past desperation. Past hope . . .

For her, as for so many, it had been the humiliation. The constant unending shame of being trapped, of having failed. The self-hatred for all those things she'd had to do just to survive. Cade still remembered the first night she had sold herself to a man. How she had bathed afterward in a decrepit washtub borrowed from a more fortunate neighbor. How he had stumbled upon her naked. The water red with her blood as she scrubbed and scrubbed, her skin floating like bits of dried leaves in the soft pink water.

He sobbed once at that memory, but he didn't cry. He had only cried twice in his lifetime. The first time when poor Terrel came home with his broken fingers, the pieces of his slate clamped between two swollen and useless hands. The second time . . .

His mother had been thirty-one when she died. She had looked much older. He could remember it so well. Her once thick black hair was gray and thin, the skin wrinkled with grime caught in the folds, her eyes dull and empty as they had never been in life. He remembered the hollow thump as her hardened corpse was tumbled into the shallow pauper's grave. He heard the sound all the time, every day—*thump-thump-thump*—as he waded through hell, his hands red with the blood of those he set free, to one fate or another.

It was agony to remember it all. His sensitive nose twitched at the familiar hateful smells. The harsh odor of human waste warming in the sun, the tang of sweat and urine, the thick reek of corruption. The sights, the smells. even the sounds. They built up about him, surrounding him like a vast sea of mud.

He moved through Downwind like a great black shark, swimming through the slime and seaweed of an ocean floor. About him were the remains of a thousand dark meals, bits of flesh and bone, floating in the silt-filled waters. Occasionally he bumped into a half-eaten corpse. And all around him were the unvoiced cries of the damned.

Finally he came to the end of his nightmare, to where it all began. He stood before a broken wall, four feet high. It outlined the remains of a building, the mud bricks cracked and decaying in the sun. This had been his home, so long ago. The home he still dreamed about at night, in the dark, alone. This pathetic shell was all that was left of the passion and terror of his childhood.

He walked through what had once been the doorway, though there had never been a door, just a ragged piece of blanket. Standing in the middle of the room he was surprised to see how small it was. The house had been a single room, a shack. But it had seemed larger somehow.

There had been no windows; the heat of the summer had been a living thing, latching on to him, drawing his strength out in a shuddering gasp. The winters were cold. He remembered choking from the smoke that never seemed to find its way out of the hole cut in the canvas roof. What monster conceived this? What had man ever done to earn such a payment? How could there be any being alive that enjoyed such perverse cruelty! Was there no one he could make pay for this? Nothing, no one he could attack? Must this sickening non-life be reenacted for eternity?

"Hey mister, you all right?" a voice intruded, calling him back. Cade was surprised to find that his two hands were held high above his head, making futile grasping motions in the air . . . searching for a neck to grasp? Or begging for relief from pain? He couldn't understand what his actions meant. He didn't care, not anymore. He dropped his arms to his sides and turned to face the speaker.

It was a boy, young, barely into his teens. He wore little more than a stained loincloth. His ribs were sticking out, though he had large shoulders, and his legs were well-muscled. He also wore a wicked-looking knife at his side.

"What do you want?" Cade asked. It came as another shock to realize he had been wandering about for several hours, his mind caught in its mad reverie, a dangerous thing to do in Sanctuary.

"I, I just wanted to know if you were all right," the boy answered. Cade looked at him again. He was Ilsigi, dark, dark. His thin chest had several scars, but he seemed in good health, if underfed. And he met Cade's eyes.

"Kindness?" Cade asked. "Or are you looking for something, boy?"

"Neither, who knows. Just asked." The boy's voice turned hard. "Sorry I bothered you, pud," and he moved away, not quite showing his back to Cade.

"Wait!" Cade said. "Wait." He moved to catch up to the boy, but the youth kept his distance. "Who are you?"

"What's it to you?" The boy crouched a bit, his body tense. Not worried yet, but definitely wary. Cade threw the boy a silver piece which the lad caught deftly.

"I don't sell myself, pud," he said.

"I don't want your body," Cade answered. He pointed at his head. "I want information." The boy looked interested. He bit the coin with stained teeth and then made it disappear.

"Some information costs more than others. What did you want to buy, pud?"

"How much can I buy about the Sharp Side?"

"Shalpa's cloak," the boy swore, "you trying to get killed, friend?"

"You were no colors, you're an independent," Cade said. "You must have been smart to survive that way. You have to know things. I want to know those things."

"Why?"

"Because they killed my brother." Cade knew he should have lied, but he could always kill the boy later. The boy was dead meat anyway; an independent wouldn't last very long around here.

"My name's Raif," the boy answered. He looked Cade up and down. "Can you use that sword?" he asked skeptically. Cade reached down, searched the floor for a moment, then pulled up a small piece of wood four inches long, half an inch wide. He handed it to the boy.

"Hold it out." Raif did so, holding it in his right hand. Making no sign of his intention Cade drew his blade right-handed and cut the wood in half; simultaneously his left hand withdrew a hidden knife and threw it—all at a blinding speed. The knife pinned the two-inch piece of wood to the ground. Raif just stared at the other half in his hand. Cade smiled.

"I do all right."

"Shit." Raif shook his head. "I'll tell you what I know, if you pay me another silver, then keep your mouth shut that I helped."

"Give me what I want, boy, and I'll put you under my protection." It was a lie, of course, but the boy's look was so open, so full of hope, and fear of that hope, Cade almost felt guilty about it.

"Follow me," Raif said. "I'll take you to a place we can talk." Cade followed, shaking his head at the lad's foolishness. Someone was bound to see the two of them together and Raif would pay for Cade's revenge. The boy was truly desperate. Maybe he could use him. He shook his head again. No, the boy was a dead man. Of course, it could be a trap, but not likely. Cade silently padded after Raif. He kept his thoughts off his face: a dead-eyed shark in the sea of hell.

Raif moved fast, avoiding all contact with anyone on the street. He led Cade through a series of winding alleys and unused paths. Eventually he stopped at a blackened wall at the end of a blind alley. Quickly he scampered over the wall. Cade followed warily.

On the other side, Cade found himself in a walled space about ten feet long and three wide. Raif went to his knees and dug through the garbage, revealing a small passageway. The two worked through the rank-smelling tunnel. Cade realized it was the remains of some sewer lines built in better times. For about ten minutes they crawled through the mud, taking several turns along the way. Finally Raif called a halt. There was a burst of light.

The light came from the sun. Cade was in a small brick-lined room. Raif had removed one of the bricks to let in a shaft of sunlight. The place smelled like a rotting corpse.

"This is my best hideout," Raif said. Cade smiled, acknowledging that the boy meant this as a gesture of trust. He looked Raif over again. The boy's face was lost in shadow but somehow those dark eyes gave the impression of giving off light, a silver light.

"Why do you hate the Sharp Side?" Cade asked.

"What makes you think I hate those punks?" Raif answered, but he couldn't hide his surprise at Cade's question.

"You want to help me, not just because you might get something out of me. You want to hurt the Sharp Side." Cade squatted down; the boy mimicked his movement slowly. "Besides, you're not stupid. People would have seen us together. If I hurt the Sharp Side they'll know I talked to you. They'll get to you." Again Cade surprised himself. Why was he being so honest? Raif was quiet for a moment, digesting Cade's words.

"You, do you know Downwind?" Raif asked, playing with his knife.

"I grew up here."

Raif nodded his head. "You have the look." The boy shifted uncomfortably. "You can tell, the ones who don't know, but those who've been here, lived here, it marks you. Can't ever hide it." Cade just waited.

"Born here," Raif grunted, looking past Cade's shoulder. "Father's a drunk, mother's a drunk. They sold my sister to a caravan last year. Father hits mother, raped my sister. Mom will do anything for another drink. Sometimes works at Mama Becho's. But my brother . . ." Raif said no more.

Cade understood. His family, destroyed by Downwind. He was an independent in more ways than one. He wasn't beat yet. And . . ."

"What of your brother?"

"Old Ilsigi family." Raif's voice was quiet and small. The place, his "best" hideout, was cool, but Cade could

smell the sweat on the boy. "That's why I talked to you."
A pale hand waved in the strange light of the room. "The
warbraid, I know it. I remember what it means. Not many
left who do."

"Your brother."

"PFLS. Thought, well, we're an old family." The boy
shrugged. "He beat up my father real bad when they sold
my sister. He and I left. He didn't make anything fighting,
but we were fed. I ran errands. We worked Downwind,
but my brother was due for a promotion." The light
reflected off the boy's knife as he shifted to make himself
more comfortable.

"The Sharp Side broke off when the Rankan god-warrior
pressured Zip. Things split. My brother stayed loyal. Sharp
Side slit his throat." He leaned back on the wall behind
him and waited.

Cade could think of nothing to say. How old was this
boy? Fourteen? Fifteen? They aged fast in Downwind;
Cade knew that well enough. His whole story told in
quick, short sentences. No explanation, no anger, no nothing. Just a story. The same story as always. The tale of the
damned.

"What was your brother's name?"

"No name. They're all dead." And Cade knew that the
boy included all his family in his statement. Cade sat
unmoving. Behind him he heard the slow drip of water,
the sound loud and monotonous. Time. It was time. Melting this pathetic refuge away. Until the boy was left
standing in the sunlight. Alone. Sacrificed to the madness
men thought of as life.

"Have you killed?" he asked.

"No."

"Have you raped?"

"No."

"Have you tortured?"

No answer. So there were things here, deeds here.

Cruelty. If he killed the boy would he free him? Or consign him to annihilation? Cade watched him for a moment. A choice must be made. It was so hard with the young. Kill them in their innocence and they are freed. Or are they? Is innocence ignorance? Mustn't they be given the chance to decide, to choose their path and therefore their destiny? Cade felt sorry for the boy, but then again he felt sorry for all men.

But this one had no chance. *And he was so much like* . . . but leave that thought. Still, one day Cade would die. Who would take up the war then? Who would defy the lords of hell when Cade finally fell and went to the emptiness? For of course Cade knew that there would be no better world for him. Madness can be a fine thing. Cade knew he was evil.

Still, he could give the boy the chance.

"Raif," his voice soft, "this is hell, do you understand?"

The boy just stared.

"In hell, all choices are hard." He took a deep breath. "We will sit here, you and I, in your best hideout. We will sit here and you will tell me of the Sharp Side. Then we shall leave together. And together we shall kill them all."

"All?"

"All. We might kill those we shouldn't, but we must kill them all, or they will retaliate, against you, against me. The burden is mine. I exceeded my allowed debt long ago. You shall have a chance." And then he laughed. Laughed truly. For Cade would do it. He would free this boy of Sanctuary's chains, let him roam and fight hell on his own terms. Give him a chance to be a hero as poor Targ was always dreaming of. Yes, that was it. He would do this as so long ago at the same age he dreamed of someone saving him. And Cade laughed harder. The sound reverberated in the dank tunnels, but somehow it was a comforting sound. It had power, and passion. But it was a gentle sound.

"Now"—Cade's laughter ended abruptly—"tell me of our enemies, young warrior."

It took nearly a week to set up. Raif acted as intermediary. They accepted that. Targ acted as the buyer, Raif his connection. Cade wandered about, following aimless leads to throw off any interested parties. The final act was almost ready to begin. He had the long-sought answers.

The why? Simple. The Sharp Side took over many of the operations of ther PFLS, including Terrel's. It had taken Terrel a while to figure it out. When he did he had tried to warn Zip. The Sharp Side had caught him.

Who? Well, one of them was known as "The Beast," an interrogator for the PFLS, now for the Sharp Side. A mysterious man, little was known about him. But it was rumored he was so unmanageable Zip was glad to see him gone. A man who enjoyed his work. A psychopath. He was the one who would have broken Terrel's bones.

Then there was Amuuth. The brain. The one who ran the gang, gave the orders. Born in Downwind, barely thirty, Amuuth had worked his way up through the ranks. Cruel, hard, uncompromising, and known to be arbitrary in his decisions. This man was the most feared man in Downwind. And his hands were broken.

Cade couldn't be sure, but it made sense. This man knew of Terrel's fear, because he was one of the original causes. He hadn't made an example of Terrel. His position was too unstable for him to go public. No, he didn't make sure Terrel died of his worst fear for political reasons. He did it for his own pleasure. For fun . . .

There were seven other hard-core members, good fighters all. Twenty auxiliaries rounded out the gang, but only three of these were so loyal that Cade would have to kill them. Twelve. Twelve lives for Terrel's. It wouldn't even begin to balance the scales.

Cade, Raif, and Targ sat at the table in Marissa's house. The guards were on the roof. Marissa was with Sarah. The sun had set. One hour and it would be over. Terrel's death would be avenged.

"Are you sure the whole gang will be at the meet?" Cade asked.

"They always do it that way," Raif answered. "All nine of the insiders at a buy." The boy's voice was happy, and who could blame him? Certainly not Cade. This had been the best week of Raif's short life. Money to have good quarters in Downwind (and to buy his first woman, though he hid that from Cade), all the food he could eat, sword practice with Targ in the hot sun. Gods, his own sword. Though he didn't wear it. Cade and Targ had made it clear he would not be allowed to wear the sword until he knew how to use it. It was all like a dream to Raif, and even all this talk of murder and revenge made no dent in his new world.

Targ watched the youngster, keeping back a frown. Raif was a good boy, and damned smart. But he hero-worshiped Cade, like Toth did. Targ couldn't understand it. Children never feared Cade, always reacted well to him. They missed the madness there, and the years of killing. But then again, whatever Targ thought of Cade, he knew one thing Cade didn't know about himself: for all his self-aggrandizing introspection, Cade had never and would never kill a child.

"I still think I should go with you," Targ said aloud, though he did not look at Cade.

"No." The only light in the room came from the single lantern lying between them. Cade stared at the large shadow Targ cast on the wall behind him, like a giant leaning over to listen to their conversation. "You must get the other three. All must die tonight."

"They're expecting me to be there. The deal is with me. If they see you, they'll know what's up."

"They won't see me"—Cade's voice was firm—"not until I want them to."

"There's nine," Targ insisted, but Cade only answered with a shrug. Targ could think of nothing else to say. Cade insisted on taking on the gang alone. The mercenary didn't like it. But there it was. Cade would do what he wanted, and he explained himself to no one.

"Why not take me?" Raif piped up. Targ just reached for the wine. He knew what Cade's reaction to that would be. "You've seen how good I am with the knife," he insisted. "They expect me to be there, too." His voice trailed off at Cade's dark look.

"Raif, killing a man is not so easy."

"They killed my brother, too, damn them. I want my revenge."

Cade's hand banged on the table. "You're talking like a fool. Do you think this is one of your daydreams? Riding up on a white horse, saving the city to the cheers of men and women alike? Revenge is bitter, boy, and far removed from justice."

"But—" Raif started again, but this time he shut up when he saw the flash in Cade's eyes.

"You've had your revenge, boy. Your information, your help has set this thing up. Now leave it to us to finish it." He turned to Targ, but the mercenary just nodded. Cade could handle himself, and Targ's prey, well, they were as good as dead. Targ could live with this. Cade never asked him to do something his conscience would forbid. Targ's honor would not suffer from this.

Unconsciously, he bared his teeth, the sharp edges of his canines already beginning to show. Too bad it couldn't be a cleaner fight. But he hadn't succumbed to his particular curse in so long, and this night—well, these bastards deserved it.

Cade stood up. He wore leather armor stained black, a bow in one hand, various other weapons strapped on tightly. Targ pushed his chair back and faced the other. He wore only an old faded kilt, his sword strapped to his back. The two clasped arms.

"I'll take the others out," Targ said. "None will escape." Cade gave him a hard smile.

"Good hunting," he said softly. Targ's face twisted for a moment at Cade's choice of words, but the bloodlust was on him and he was eager to go. Neither said anything to Raif as Cade opened the door and they moved into the night. Raif stared at the open doorway for several minutes. Then he, too, got up and walked into the night's embrace.

Cade moved through the shadows to the waterfront district, taking care that no one followed him. The meeting was set up in a large warehouse there. The streets were quiet tonight. The moon was waning and a light cloud cover shielded the starlight. It was a perfect night for death.

There were four of the Sharp Side on outside guard duty, one on the roof, two in front, and one in the back. They were well hidden, but they moved about a lot. Sloppy. They were getting arrogant in their success. It was only a matter of time until someone took them out.

The one on the roof was first and easiest. An arrow through the eye killed him instantly. No one heard the body fall. Cade moved to the roof, looking down on the dark silhouettes of the two guards in front. Another bolt, through the neck, and one was down. The second heard something. He didn't move. Smart.

Cade silently climbed down the side of the building until he was ten feet above his prey. He leaped. The guard was fast, but caught by surprise. Even as he reached for his

weapon, Cade drew a knife across his throat. Cade stared
down at the crumpled body, watching the blood pump
from the neck, staining the ground liquid black. He shook
his head; a waste of talent. This man had once been very
good.

The guard in back was careless. Cade dropped a rope
from the roof, caught the man around the throat, and lifted
him up. His neck broke in the first five feet. Cade an-
chored him to the building. The body dangled ten feet off
the ground. Cade was making an example.

He moved to the inside, through a trap door. The warehouse was full of boxes and crates, which surprised Cade.
Since when did Sanctuary do enough business to fill a
warehouse? There were things in town he did not know
and could not understand. Silently he reconnoitered the
building.

There were five left. Two with bows watched the remaining three. Amuuth, the Beast, and another waited at a
table in the middle of the warehouse, a small lamp on the
table giving the only light in the building. It took Cade ten
minutes to kill both the bowmen; the others were not
alerted.

Cade lay on top of several crates, next to the body of the
second bowman. From this vantage point he studied the
remaining targets.

Amuuth sat at the table, facing the front entrance. His
clothes were fine though dirty. His two gnarled hands
ceaselessly played with the long necklace he wore. His
black hair was worn short, in Rankan fashion; his beard
was well trimmed. Cade could not see his eyes.

To the left of his leader stood the last of the regular
gang members. He was a large man, big-boned and heav-
ily muscled. He wore an expensive chainmail corset and
carried a two-handed sword. From his hiding place Cade
could see the blue eyes reflect the light of the lamp. No

Ilsigi this one. Hired help, and by all appearances well worth whatever his pay was.

The last of the three stood to the right of Amuuth. Cade was surprised at how small the feared Beast was. A little man, all huddled in his stained cloak. The torturer's face was hidden by a cowl; a knife glinted in his pale hands. The Beast ignored the others, his attention on something else. As Cade watched, the torturer began to hum to himself and slowly rock from side to side. Amuuth gave his servant a dirty look, but said nothing.

It was time to move. Cade rolled away from the ledge. From a leather sheath on his side he pulled out three thin black cylinders. Deftly he put the three together, forming one tube six feet long. He placed the object on his right. Reaching into a pouch at his belt he withdrew a three-inch needle. He twisted a bit of fleece about one end of the needle, then lay it beside the tube.

He rolled onto his back and slowly drew his sword, making sure those below him could see no gleam off the blade. Then he checked his bow, placing it and the sword on his right. Once again he moved to the edge of the crates.

He was about eight feet above the men, fifteen feet away. An easy shot. He held the tube to his lips, carefully balancing it. No one noticed the long tube sticking over the edge of a crate. Cade took the fleece side of the needle in his mouth, took a deep breath, and spat the needle through the tube.

The noise he made was covered by Amuuth's reaction. He swatted at his neck, tried to rise, went rigid, and fell over, chair and all. The Beast just stared. The guard turned quickly to his employer then spun to face the sound of the blowgun landing behind him.

The mercenary turned at just the right time for Cade's shot to catch him full in the neck, severing the jugular vein. Cade had time to feel a quick stab of remorse at this.

It was no way to kill a warrior. Even as he thought it, he was leaping down off the crates, his sword now in hand.

The Beast hopped from one foot to the other, apparently at a loss as to what to do. Amuuth lay huddled, unmoving; the guard was dead. What was he supposed to do? He looked at the grinning Cade, tall in the lamplight, his sword held steady and pointing at the Sharp Side's torturer.

"Uh," he said, "uh, guards!" He shouted, "Guards! Attack! Murder! Guards!" Cade let him go on for a while, smiling the whole time, the sword never wavering.

"The guards are all dead," he said finally. The Beast stood to his full height, swinging his thin shoulders back. Cade could still not see his face.

"So," the torturer said, "so. All gone, ah, well." He did a little dance, then moved closer. "All dead. Well, dead." On the second "dead," he moved quickly and a knife appeared out of his long sleeves and spun toward Cade. But Cade was ready and knocked the weapon out of the air with his sword. The Beast just stood there, his other knife still dancing in his hands.

"Uh, so," he said. "Who are you?" he shouted.

"I am Cade."

"So."

"Terrel was my brother."

"Uh, so."

"Terrel was the man you tortured, the man whose bones you broke. All of them." The other was silent for a moment, digesting the information. Then he laughed, a high-pitched squeal.

"Oh, yes. Lovely bit of work, that." The madman's head moved to a song only he heard. "Yes, oh yes. Too bad, though. Only for fun, you realize. There was no information to get or anything. Still, nice bit of work. Spell was a nice touch, I thought." The Beast smiled, showing crooked and browning teeth. "He screamed and

screamed, but the sound didn't carry don't you know.
Magic.'' He snapped his fingers. ''Yes, well, you know—''
   But Cade could hear no more. With a roar he leaped at
the torturer. The other's knife tried to parry his blade, but
it was shoved aside by the power behind Cade's swing.
The sword crashed into the Beast's head, cutting deep into
the skull, splitting it nearly in two. The Beast crashed to
the ground, dead.
   Cade moved closer to see the face. It was hard to
distinguish among the purplish-red remains. The face was
split to the nose. Cade made out watery brown eyes,
quickly filming over, and the face of an old man. He
looked like someone's grandfather, the silver-white hair
now dyed with red streaks. Cade spat on the corpse. This
looked like no beast. Hell was a funny place.
   Cade heard the noise behind him, though few others
would have. He spun in a crouch, his sword held before
him, a throwing dagger already in the palm of the other
hand. Who? All nine were taken care of. Slowly, a slight
form moved out of the shadows and Cade relaxed.
   ''I told you to stay away, Raif.''
   ''I thought you might need some help,'' the boy answered, looking around. He grinned at Cade, though his
face was pale. ''I guess you didn't.''
   ''This is no place for you.''
   Raif bit his lip, darting glimpses at the bodies around
him. He slowly sheathed his knife.
   ''You said you would teach me to be a warrior,'' he
said. He gestured at the dead mercenary. ''I've seen death
before, Cade.''
   Cade's eyes went dark. He grabbed the boy and pushed
him to the ground by the corpse of the Beast. Grabbing the
old man's collar, he pulled the corpse up to face the boy.
   ''This is death,'' he said, ignoring the still warm fluids
sliding down his wrist. ''Look at it, boy, see it for what it
is.'' Raif tried to pull away but Cade held him firm. The

smell of the blood was covered by the horrid stench of the corpse. The bladder and bowels had emptied at death, and their horrid mixture slowly leaked toward Raif's sandaled feet. The split face smiled at him, its dull eyes seeming to search him out.

"No," Raif gasped, pulling away. He got two steps before he vomited. Cade held the boy while Raif emptied his stomach.

"The life of a warrior is the path of death," Cade whispered in Raif's ear. "This is the truth of it, boy: old men's brains spilling at your feet." He turned Raif to face the dead mercenary. Cade pointed. "That's where it ends, boy. An arrow in the dark in a dirty warehouse, in a town all decent people have long ago forgotten about. What is so noble, boy, what is so grand about being a warrior?"

"But you're a warrior."

"No, boy, I am no warrior, because I choose not to be. I kill those who need it, or those who deserve it. I kill those I choose, not those others tell me to. People pay me to kill, Raif. Pay me to do what I was born to do. But don't you realize that I know that I lost my soul because of it?"

Raif said nothing, his voice lost in sobs he tried to hold in. Cade clasped the boy to him for a moment, then let go.

"I will teach you to fight, to protect yourself, nothing more. You needn't see this ever again. I will give you the chance to be free of hell forever." This was the moment: kill the boy now and he would be free. He would find that warm safe world that Cade's mother now danced in. Free him. Free him, his mind chanted.

But Cade could not. It wasn't the risk of being wrong about Raif; he knew the boy was good. It was something else. A chance. Give the boy a chance to lead a life Cade could never have had. The life Targ dreamed of, but his curse kept him from. It was a hard thing to live in hell and dream of heroes.

"Ah, the gentle sounds of lovers' passion," a voice

said. Raif leaped and drew his blade but Cade showed no alarm. He walked over to Amuuth and bent down on one knee.

"So," he said, "starting to come out of it?" He rifled through the other's clothes.

Amuuth glared up at him.

"What did you do to me?"

"Thornneft," Cade answered. "Paralyzes you for about ten minutes." Cade withdrew a knife from the other's clothes. The blade was double-edged and sharp. The handle was abnormally thick, allowing the gang leader to wield the weapon with his crippled fingers. Cade picked up the chair and lifted Amuuth onto it. He moved across the table to stand by Raif.

"You'll come out of it in a moment."

"Why didn't you just kill me?" Amuuth hissed. His face showed no fear. With the black eyes and hawk nose, he looked fierce. Cade could see why this one was the leader.

"I wanted to talk to you."

"About your brother?" came the quick answer. Cade just lifted an eyebrow. "Oh, I know of you, Cade. The local boy made good. I was warned you were dangerous. I misjudged you. I didn't think you'd make the connection between—"

"Between you and Terrel," Cade finished.

"Precisely." Amuuth shifted his shoulders; feeling was beginning to come back, but it was painful. He would not show that. He had lived with the pain in his hands all these years.

"So you've come to avenge your brother?"

"Why did you break his bones?" Cade replied.

"I thought I would finish the job I started so many years ago." Amuuth kept watching the other's eyes; the boy was no threat. Surely some of his own people must still be about. They would hear. He held onto that hope; he knew it was his only chance.

"That's why I didn't kill you."

"What?"

"I wanted to finish the job I started so long ago."

Amuuth gasped. He could not help it. Cade couldn't mean—

"It was me, Amuuth. Sixteen years ago I hunted you and the other three, with my brick and rope." Cade shrugged. "I don't know which one you were. When I caught you, I guess I should have killed you."

"You," Amuuth shouted, "you did this!" He held out his hands, trying to stand up, but his legs wouldn't move yet.

Cade smiled. "The legs take longer."

Amuuth said nothing. He knew there would be no help, no rescue. He was dead. He looked up at Cade, his eyes burning with hate. This is the man. The shadow he still woke up screaming from. The shadow from that night. Unseen, unheard. The whistling noise, the agony in his side, in his head, his legs, and finally his fingers. He wondered that he, himself, had not made the connection between his pain and Terrel's.

"I'm glad then," he hissed, "I'm glad I made him pay."

"No, Amuuth, you did not make him pay. You tortured him out of spite, because even with his ruined hands *he* made it out. Made a life. That's why you did it, for petty reasons. For envy. I have known evil in many faces, Amuuth, but I have never seen it so pathetic."

Amuuth sputtered, his mind refusing to give him words to match his outrage. This one, gods, all along. He could have had him long ago, had his revenge. But now . . .

Cade moved around the table toward him, like a great black cat, and he was the mouse. There was nothing

definable in Cade's eyes or face. Amuuth had no idea how
he would finally die.

"Finish the job," Cade whispered, moving closer, taking his time. Amuuth shuddered. He was frozen, could not
move, and it wasn't the drug that was holding him now.
His broken left hand reached for the right. For the snake
ring. Hitting a latch, long fangs extending. Could he get
Cade with his own poison? Not likely . . . he could kill
himself, before the pain started. Or . . .

Amuuth looked over at Raif. The boy stared at Cade,
his face bloodless, his eyes wide. Amuuth remembered
Raif's brother—he had feared that one. He had tried to
entice Raif into the gang, hoping he could mold him as the
older boy could not be molded. The boy could be dangerous. Amuuth was struck by a memory. Cade had run a
gang for a while: the Demons. They had been terrible,
violent, dangerous. They only ran a block and a half but
they owned it. And Raif looked, looks, so much like the
young gang leader Cade had once been.

Amuuth understood. Cade saw himself in the boy. Wanted
to help. Change it. Vengeance can be sweet.

Amuuth tugged the ring off and looked at Raif.

"I'm dead, boy," he said. "You might as well have
this ring." He threw it to Raif before Cade could react.

"No!" Cade shouted and lunged, but he was too late.
Raif caught the ring, dropping it immediately when he felt
a double sting in one of his fingers.

"What?" he said, but even as he lifted the hand to look,
he stumbled, the air thick, too thick to breathe. The floor
rose up to meet him. He panicked. He could not breathe.
He was surrounded by stone, encased in it.

Cade reached him in time to stop the fall. But he could
feel Raif's flesh already puffing up, the limbs getting
rigid. He spun to face Amuuth, his eyes pinning the gang
leader to his chair.

"The antidote!" he yelled.

"None." Amuuth's voice was harsh. "None. A gift from the finger of a dead fish-eye." Cade said nothing, not taking his eyes off his enemy. His hand reached down to touch the boy. He was already dead. All hope dies in hell's capital, in Sanctuary.

Cade was still for a moment, then slowly he tipped his head back until he stared at the ceiling.

"Mother!" he cried. He was on his feet, his sword cutting the air before he knew what was happening. The sword sliced through Amuuth's neck, the head spinning away. It was so fast that the blood geysered up from between his shoulders.

Cade leaped at the body, chopping and cutting, screaming all the while. His yell was incoherent, but any who heard that sound would never forget the madness in it. Eventually he quit chopping the body, but only when it was no longer recognizably human. For a moment longer Cade stared down. His sword dropped from the red hand.

He collapsed next to Raif, holding the boy's head in his lap, but he could think of nothing. There was nothing to say, nothing to do. He sat, gently rocking the corpse in the warehouse full of corpses, the rats in the shadows the only witnesses to his agony. Rocking back and forth, the vast emptiness around him still seemed to echo with his cries.

Targ went to Sarah's house; he knew Marissa would still be there. The blood was off him. He had swum in the bay to get rid of its sight and scent. But it was bad. The curse had raged through his veins, alive with its deadly passions. Now it was all through, all done. If only the second one hadn't begged so much, if only he hadn't cried . . .

Inside the house Sarah and Marissa sat in the main room as if waiting. He guessed that Marissa must have told her friend that this was the night of Cade's vengeance. It didn't matter. He sat next to them, thankful for their silence, their lack of questions.

Cade came in an hour later. They were all shaken from their private thoughts by the sound of his fist on the door. Sarah went to the door and looked through the grate, her face turning white at what she saw on the other side. She unbarred the door to let her brother-in-law enter.

The smell of the corpse wafted in with the wind. Targ growled at the scent but he said nothing. Sarah stood to one side of the door. The other two sat facing it silently. Facing Cade.

He stood there, holding Raif's body. Behind him the gray night writhed, outlining his powerful form, along with his pitiful burden. The light was not bright, but it was bright enough to show his bloodstained clothes. Bright enough to show the one tear winding its way through the scars and drying blood on his face.

Cade had only cried twice before in his life. This, he swore, was the last time he would, ever . . .

"I'm home."

WAKE OF THE RIDDLER

Janet Morris

Tempus was gone from Sanctuary, taking his Stepsons and the Rankan 3rd Commando with him, leaving only outcasts and dross behind.

In the wake of the Riddler's passing, the town seemed more changed than it should have been because one man (called variously Tempus, the Riddler, the Black, and more scatalogical apellations) had gathered his private army of less than a hundred and departed. Sanctuary seemed emptied, drained, frightened, and confused.

It cowered like a snow rabbit run to barren ground and surrounded by wolves. It shivered and sniffed the breeze, as if undecided as to which way to run. It hunkered in desperate paralysis, seeming to dream of better days while the cold spring wind blew wet promises of life inland from the sea and the wolves skulked closer, red tongues lolling in slavering jaws.

Among fetid streets on this spring evening in question, militias are keeping order, stamping round corners with deliberate tread. Whores whisper rather than croon in their doorways. Drunks slither along whitewashed walls, afraid to stagger boldly in gutters where beggars lurk with ready blades. And the wind comes in off the uneasy ocean with a chuckle on its breath: Tempus, his Stepsons, and the 3rd Commando have left the town to its fate, ridden off in disgust to new adventures capable of resolution, wars winnable, and glory attainable. Sanctuary is not only doomed, but shunned by its last best hope, the Riddler and his fighters.

The wind thinks nothing of whipping the town vacant, of chilling its nobles to the bone, of locking the neutered sorcerers in the Mageguild and the impotent soldiers in their barracks. The wind is Sanctuary's own, wind of chaos, gale of gloom.

Spring has never felt so ominous in the Maze as it does this season, where the first rough gusts blow more detritus than rotting rinds and discarded rags through the streets. The sea wind rattles against the plate armor of the Rankan army regulars, clustered in fours as they police what can't be policed. It flaps the dark cloaks of Jubal the ex-slaver's beggars, his private force of cold enforcers who sell protection now at stalls and bars where Stepsons used to trade. It keens toward uptown and beats on the barred windows of the Mageguild where necromancers fear the unleashing of their dead now that magic has lost its power, more even than they fear the wrath of whores whose youth-and-beauty spells have worn away.

And the wind sneaks uptown, where what is left in Sanctuary that is noble tries to carry on, have its parties amidst the rubble left by warring factions of the various militias, by witches and warlocks, vampires and zombies, ghosts and demons, worshipers and gods.

This wind is of the sort you may remember, coming out of a gray wet sky which makes an end to boundaries and hides horizons. Sounds seem to come from nowhere, go nowhere. There is no distance and no proximity, no future and no past. There is no warmth, even from the one beside you. When you reach out to take a hand for comfort, that hand is clammy as the grave. And the stirring of life these gusts portend is only legend, on such a day, as if the wind itself is here to reconnoiter the very earth and then decide if the world deserves another spring.

Or not.

Down by the docks, alone, Critias ponders that question. Do the beggar armies deserve the warm sun on their face? Do the vampire's undead, over in Shambles Cross, need the kiss of sunlight? Can there be a bright morning for the mages, barricaded inside their fortress where dusk always reigns? Will Zip and his nightcrawlers among the Peoples Front for the Liberation of Sanctuary tip the balance for or against the seasons' change? And does it matter if spring ever comes to this blighted thieves' world again?

For Tempus has gone, turned his back on everything and everyone. No more eloquent an omen could be taken from a dozen slaughtered lambs with jaundiced livers or the birth of twins joined at the lips.

Gone and left . . . what? Left Crit, is what—Crit, in putative charge of the ungovernable, so that Crit's partner, Straton, had turned and walked away without a word. Gone somewhere was Strat, and not to the departed armies, either. No, Strat hadn't gone upcountry with the Riddler, west to meet Niko and then embark on a secret sortie for Theron, emperor of Ranke. Strat, Crit was sure, had gone another way: down to embrace the darkness that was his lover, Ischade the vampire who held sway in Shambles Cross, down to the White Foal River where corpses floated till they waked. Down into hell and this time it wasn't Crit's fault, but Tempus's, who usually had more concern for the faring of his men.

But there'd been no reasoning with Tempus, who'd pulled the Stepsons out en masse, and the 3rd Commando with them, leaving the town to its own devices.

Leaving Crit to take responsibility for fair and all. For *un*fair and all. So there was a new pecking order in beleaguered Sanctuary, and one which was fair only to the extent that it insulted and imperiled everyone, while satisfying no one.

Put it down, Crit told himself, to the foul humor that

caused Tempus to be called "the Black." Crit had the rest of the year to meet Theron's decree of a unified, pacified Sanctuary. If he couldn't manage it, Theron had promised to send the Rankan army here in force, a soldier in every hut and a fist in every face.

Not that Crit cared about the town per se. No, he didn't. But he cared about his reputation, about not failing, about always doing what he was charged to do.

Even though for the first time in his life he'd truly argued, threatened to quit, to mutiny, to bolt, when Tempus had charged him with imposing order where order had never been, Critias couldn't turn away from a job unfinished. No matter what it cost.

In short order it had cost him his only friends here: Straton, his right-side partner and Sacred Band brother; Kama, the Riddler's daughter, abandoned in Sanctuary along with those others who had most displeased her father; Marc, the weaponsmith who'd been his liaison with townies such as Zip; and Zip himself, the PFLS leader and third-shift commander, who now looked on Crit as the enemy because Crit was at the top of Sanctuary's reporting chain.

Where he'd never craved to be, and where Strat had struggled so hard to land.

Shaking his head, Crit started as moisture that had condensed on his unkempt hair spattered his brow and cheeks. In nondescript dockside garb, he was waiting for a contact. Doing what he knew how to do because Crit was a shadow mover, not an empire shaker. Tempus had left him with a shattered infrastructure he needed to fuse, somehow, into a working whole. Or lose. Fail. Crit knew how to do everything required of a soldier but that—he didn't know how to fail. He'd never learned. Was constitutionally incapable of learning, Strat used to say.

Crit missed Strat like food and water. He missed Kama less, but still loved her. And still hated the gutterslime she'd taken up with: Molin Torchholder, the politicized priest of a pantheon unnatural to this Ilsig soil.

All the Rankan conquerors of this Ilsigi town of Sanctuary, and the Beysib invaders who had come after and made an uneasy alliance by marriage with the Rankan governor, Prince Kadakithis, mistook the townspeople here for the sort that were governable. And now Crit was responsible to see that at least the appearance of governance was instilled and maintained here, where the balance between gods and magic had suddenly crumbled and all that was left to do was rule Sanctuary by force of arms.

As commander-in-chief of the policing forces, he was responsible to the prince/governor Kadakithis, who was answerable to Theron and might lose more than his palace if the emperor's demands weren't met; responsible to Kadakithis's Beysib consort, Shupansea, who wasn't even human, but some sort of fish-woman from across a forbidden sea; responsible to Kama because she was the Riddler's daughter and, by all the gods that loved the armies, Crit's woman more than Molin's.

Kama had conceived a child with Crit and they'd lost it on a battlefield. Since then, she'd found whatever man she could to sleep with who'd be most hurtful to Crit when he found out. Which he always did, because she was her father's daughter and thought that women's ways were for lesser creatures, the way her father thought that men's limits applied only to his enemies.

Crit wanted more than anything to find Strat and simply leave, go up to Ranke and plead his case to Theron, get a new commission from the emperor. He was wasted here. Only Tempus knew what he'd done to deserve it.

But here he was, with the rest of the unloved, unvalued, and unwanted—with Strat; with Kama; with Randal, a warrior-mage who was the lesser half of a broken Sacred Band pair; with Gayle, the only 3rd Commando Tempus had told to tarry.

And with those they'd hoped to leave behind: Ischade, the vampire; Janni the Stepson's half-reconstituted ghost; Snapper Jo, the fiend who had tended bar at the Vulgar Unicorn; and, uptown somewhere among the hellish ruins of last winter's incomprehensible war of magic, whatever was left of Haught, the Nisibisi mageling, and of Roxanne, the Nisibisi witch.

Strat had said—the only thing he *had* said about the matter—that Tempus had flat run out of nerve, turned tail and fled, leaving Crit holding the bag. The very bag that Strat wanted so badly in his grip, Crit had thought but hadn't said.

Waiting alone, with no backup (because with Strat gone to Ischade there wasn't a single man he'd trust at his back), down on the slippery dockside hoping his contact would show soon, Crit had had too much time to brood.

He knew it; he knew himself. For the kind of subterranean work he was trained to do, self-knowledge was a prerequisite. If it weren't, his distress over Strat and the horrid triangle of the two of them and the vampire might well have killed him before this. Might kill him yet, if he became too distracted by it.

He had a job to do. Lots of jobs. He'd made sure of that. He couldn't afford too much time for reflection. This task before him wasn't going to be simple, but he needed to occupy his mind with something besides the conundrum of his partner. Tonight, it was finding and restoring Tasfalen, whose entire noble family was missing and had been missing far too long. Torchholder wanted the popinjay found. Or wanted Crit killed in the finding, so that there'd be no rival of consequence for Kama's affections by the time Molin did whatever he was planning about his current wife.

Crit wasn't mistaking Molin Torchholder: in the priest's mind, this was a suicide mission he'd forced on Crit, knowing Crit wouldn't delegate this sort of task to what

men he had available. Zip's half-tame militia wasn't good
for much but swaggering and street fights on their night
shift; Walegrin's barracks of day-soldiers soldiered well
enough, but knew nothing of covert means; and Crit
wouldn't ask at the Mageguild—even with the Stepsons'
mage, Randal, there, the price of magical aid in Sanctuary
was always too high.

So that left only Jubal's thugs, one of whom Crit awaited.
Jubal's faceless horde of enforcers would spit out one with
a face tonight, and that one would lead Crit to Tasfalen.

Once Crit had verified the continued existence of the
noble (or lack of it—a corpse would do), he could get
Torchholder off his back. And see Kama. For Crit was
about ready to force an end to that particular problem:
either bring Kama back with him from the palace, to take
up her rightful place in what was left of the Stepsons'
barracks, or use her affair with Molin to blackmail the
priest.

He wasn't sure which he liked better, but he liked both
alternatives enough to bare his teeth in a humorless smile
as he waited.

And waited. And waited. He stood. He sat. He paced.
He leaned. He heard his horse nickering, then pawing the
cobbles. He checked its tack, stroked its nose. Strat's bay
horse would have evoked the nicker he'd heard, but Crit
didn't see the bay horse anywhere.

Just as well; the bay made him nervous. Made everybody nervous who didn't like reincarnated horses with
spots on their withers through which a man could glimpse
hell itself if the light was right.

Because of the nicker, Crit realized he didn't want to
see Strat right now. Not until he'd solved the problem of
Kama and Torchholder. Not now, when the gray sky and
the gray buildings and the gray dockside melded with the
gray horse Tempus had left him, to take the sting out of
deserting him.

The gray was a prize, one of the best from the Stepsons' stock farm up at Wizardwall. Worth more than a block of the Maze, contents included. Worth more than the whole town, to some men's way of thinking.

But Crit would have given it to Strat gladly if Strat would only renounce the ghost-horse and the vampire woman who'd conjured it for him . . .

"*Psst*," said a voice from behind him and Crit refused to flinch, or jump, or betray the heart-stopping urgency within him that counseled a dive for cover, a drawn sword.

He turned slowly and said, "You're late, hawkmask."

"We aren't hawkmasks any longer," said an oddly accented voice from under a shadowing hooded cloak. "And I never was. We're just freelancing, we are. Just workin' for pay. You like mercs, bein' you was one." A languorous, professional lilt in a northern-accented voice that nevertheless had a deadly, nervous edge to it.

Crit squinted into the gloom but the only thing he saw better for his trouble was the rigging of a small fishing boat bobbing behind the stranger, much farther down the quayside than the cloaked man.

Was it a masking spell, or a trick of the light that veiled this face in gloom? The fellow was out of reach, but just barely. And familiar, but so was half of Sanctuary. Someone he'd rousted long ago, Crit's mind said, and started spinning through the years, seeking to match a face to the voice he recognized.

Crit asked, to hear the voice again, "What do you want, honest work? There isn't any, not here. Prefer my service to Jubal's? Is that what you're getting at?"

"Yours? You've got a service, now? *That's* how come the black man sent me to help you out?"

The hooded man's *s*'s were sibilantly northern and the tension underlying his words was full of satisfaction.

Somebody they'd done something to once, for sure. Somebody the Sacred Band hadn't treated with softest gloves. Somebody who was enjoying this more than he ought, because he feared Crit and his kind more than he'd admit.

"Got a name, friend?" Crit said easily, shifting enough that he could slide his hand onto his belt and his fingers toward his knife's hilt without being either too obvious or too surreptitious. It wasn't a threat so much as a punctuation mark.

The contact saw, and tossed his head. "Vis. Ring a bell, Commander?"

Commander. Crit still couldn't get used to it, not in Sanctuary, not in this context, not with all its current connotations. Did Tempus still hold Crit's affair with Kama against him so venomously that he'd sentence him to years of hard labor here with violent death at the end of it?

For Crit remembered this "Vis" now, and what he recalled didn't put him at ease. Mradhon Vis, a northerner. Thief, malefactor, one-time partner-in-crime of the Nisibisi mageling, Haught. And gods knew of whom or what else. They'd beaten information out of Vis more than once, when the Stepsons were fighting the Nisibisi witch here. Strat, the Stepsons' chief interrogator, had. Crit had been in command of the intelligence unit then. They'd brought this fool up to the Shambles safe house, drawn the iron shutters, and taught him the sort of respect that turns to hatred if left untended.

There were dozens, perhaps scores, of Vises he and Strat had made in Sanctuary. If Crit lived long enough, one of them was going to try to kill him. Perhaps this one. Perhaps tonight.

"Vis," he repeated, his voice low. "Right, I remember. Well, let's go, Vis. Let's see what you've got."

"My pleasure, Commander," said the mercenary, and chuckled nastily. "If you'll follow me into those shadows there, the worst is yet to come."

*   *   *

"I'm telling you," whispered Kama intently to Straton over her beer, "Zip's moving the altar stones uptown to the Street of Temples—moving them *and* what they housed."

Finished, she sat back, eyeing the other patrons of the Vulgar Unicorn surreptitiously. No one had heard, she was certain. She'd been careful of her volume, as well as the drunken slur in her voice. No one human, that is. The fiend who was tending bar late tonight had great gray ears and eyes that looked every which way. His warty countenance was averted, but that meant nothing. In the bronze mirror behind the bar he could be watching them . . .

"So what?" Strat growled, truculent, one arm absently rubbing his damaged shoulder. Perhaps once the best man with weapons among the Stepsons, Strat was doubly wounded now: Ischade either couldn't, or wouldn't, heal his shoulder and there were no Stepsons here for him to be among.

"So, we've got to stop it," she said. Her heart ached for Strat, and for them all, left here where nothing of consequence remained in the wake of her father's leave-taking. She and Strat had something in common now—something more than Crit. They had to shore up the sagging bulwark of command because Tempus might be testing them. None of the others realized it, but Kama did. If her father rode into town of a morning, ready to welcome them back to the fold if only they'd put the town to rights, Kama didn't want to be found wanting.

But the big Stepson was too drunk, or too deeply hurt, to understand what she meant. "Stop it? Why? So Zip's found some sort of pet demon or minor deity—some Ilsig spirit to worship. What difference does it make? The gods fare no better here than magic—or fighters."

Strat believed only in the magic of Ischade, Kama knew. He'd seen too much, too many dead reborn, too many undead abroad in the streets at night. Strat had seen his

doom and embraced it: he was as much the vampire's
creature as any of her slaves.

"C'mon, Straton," she insisted blearily, tugging on the
Stepson's sleeve. "Come with me. I'll show you."

"You and your lovers," Strat grumbled over the screech
of his stool's legs on sawdusted board. "What the frog
you wanna do about it if you find him lickin' his demon's
feet?"

"*Ssh*," Kama warned, and put her small hand to the flat
of Strat's back, pushing him toward the door like a wife
who'd made a nightly trip to the Unicorn to bring her
drunken husband home to bed. Snapper Jo saluted her with
his raffish inhuman grin, dipping his bristly chin in a
gesture of respect.

Great. Homage from a fiend, friends in high places,
estranged from her real friends because of that: because of
Molin, who had another wife, Crit and Gayle and Randal
avoided her like the plague. Only Straton, in similar circumstances, of all the men she'd campaigned with in the
Wizard Wars, acknowledged her. And Zip . . .

As Strat had jibed, Zip was another of her lovers. Men
used their muscle and their sex for intimidation, and no
one thought ill of them for it. Kama was a different sort of
operator, but used what she had to. Whatever worked to
do the job. It stung her to the quick the way the men she'd
fought beside treated her now, simply because she'd let the
high priest wield his influence to help her.

If her father had had a dozen lovers, or a hundred
victims of his holy raping member, no Sanctuarite would
have snickered or presumed to criticize. Maybe she should
strip her next bed partner at knifepoint, prove herself her
father's daughter to one and all. Maybe then Crit would
stop looking past her when they met . . .

Strat stumbled in the doorway, belched, and staggered
down the stairs to the street. The bay horse whickered, its
ears pricked. Kama shivered. The damned thing was dead

as a doornail, just didn't know it. Strat didn't seem to
know it either: he fumbled in his pouch, came up with a
chunk of sugarbeet, and held it out on an open palm.

The ghost-horse's velvet lips delicately snatched the
treat, and it snorted in pleasure.

Well, maybe not quite as dead as a doornail. But unnatural as hell. Unnatural as Sanctuary, a place Kama was
determined to leave completely out of the history she was
writing of her father's exploits. Sanctuary deserved no
chronicler, as it deserved nothing more than the oblitera-
tion it was so obviously seeking.

The town had its own genius, Kama was sure, an Ilsig
spirit that had finally had its fill of interlopers and was
nudging the place itself toward oblivion's precipice. She
wanted only to be quit of it before Sanctuary was razed to
the ground by Rankans, gutted and left to rot by Beysibs,
or torn stone from off of stone by internal strife.

A historian, Kama knew all the signs of a town dying.
Sanctuary didn't lack a one: its gods were impotent; its
magic had lost its power; its populace was polarized by
generations of hatred; its children wanted only to destroy.

"What, Strat?" she said, startled by words undeciphered
but still ringing in her ears. She looked up. The big
Stepson was already mounted, reins in his right hand, his
left arm carefully resting on one thigh.

"I said, finding Zip should be easy—it's his shift, the
dead of night. You want him, let's go up to the command
guardpost."

She shook her head. "Told you, he's moving those
damned stones. And the porking whatever that lives in
'em, tonight. Heard it from a reliable source." The guardpost
was safe for Strat, this time of night—Crit had the day
shift; Strat's erstwhile partner spent his evenings in an old
Shambles Cross safe house the Stepsons used to run.

"So where?" Strat's voice was suddenly uneasy.

"Down to the river, soldier. If you can handle it—the White Foal's banks, I mean, so close to Ischade's."

"Pork what I can handle, woman," said Strat, the booze getting to his tongue. "I've picked that snipe up by his collar more than he's picked up your skirts. You wanted help, you've got it. You change your mind, that's fine, too. But we can't just sit here."

She got her horse, her neck hot though the night was chill with the bone-deep cold of a recalcitrant spring. Her fingers were numb on her slick reins and the roan she rode bucked and danced under her. The wrong horse for this job, too skittish, too green. But the Stepsons had taken their string, leaving only what wasn't held in common. Except, of course, for the single Trôs-bred that should have been hers, but had gone to Critias because Tempus wasn't above that sort of insult.

It wasn't fair, but her father had never been. Didn't want a daughter, didn't care however much Kama tried to make him. A woman wasn't consequential, not to him. And her affair with Torchholder had made things worse, not better.

Was Tempus trying to tell her, by giving Crit the horse and forcing Crit to stay on along with her here, that if she went back with Crit, he'd forgive them both? Was Crit being singled out as an acceptable choice? Or did Tempus just not give a frog's fart?

The latter, most likely. She was going to try to do the same. Try not to care. Try to understand and overcome the trial that was Sanctuary, the punishment of being stationed here. But because she was stationed here, assigned like any of his men to onerous duty, she hadn't had the heart to refuse to tarry. That would have been playing on her blood relationship, asking special favors, admitting that she, a woman, couldn't handle hard duty like the men.

Help the garrison commander and the hierarchy restore some order here, that's your job. You're a good intelli-

gence collector. Collect, her father had said to her, but nothing more. Nothing personal, nothing beyond what was said in that meeting where the rear guard was singled out.

And Crit had stared boldly at her across the table in the safe house, knowing already whom Tempus was intending to name as commander-in-chief of Sanctuary's disparate armed forces. Knowing she'd have to come to him, be under his command.

It stank. She kicked her roan and slapped its poll and, under diverse and punitive instruction, it settled down. Jogging beside the half-drunken Straton toward the river, she wished she was anywhere else, doing anything else. Trying to keep Zip from making this sort of mistake wasn't her job, but Crit's.

Straton knew that, too, but hadn't voiced it. Crit was head of the combined militias, including the fifty grunts that made up Walegrin's regular army barracks, but Zip, like Aye-Gophlan, was an undercommander, responsible for the second and third shifts each day.

Only Crit, or someone from the palace hierarchy, could tell Zip to leave the riverside altar be and make it stick.

But Kama would die before she went to Crit and asked him to solve a problem she couldn't. Bringing Strat into it made the message she was sending the more clear: We who love you won't be treated this way. You've snubbed us both for your precious command, now live with it. But don't expect us to bow and scrape.

Strat had wanted Sanctuary's commission, should have had it. Crit couldn't have wanted it less, so he got it. And that kept the vampire with her hidden agenda out of things, but at a personal cost only Tempus could have decreed. Only Tempus, who had no conscience, could split a Sacred Band pair like he'd split the love-match that had once been Kama and Critias.

Suddenly, she found her eyes blurry. She swiped impatiently at them with the back of her forearm. She couldn't

afford emotion now; it clouded her judgment. Her anticipation of men was generally good. Of Critias, it was
woefully inadequate.

Of Strat, her forewarning was little better. Or maybe it
was just the fact that Strat was drunk and his horse a
numinous creature that caused them to take a shortcut over
the White Foal Bridge and down a road leading past
Ischade's Foalside home.

Zip was transported, in an altered state where every
night noise was new and hostile, down by the White Foal's
edge where he could barely see the eerie lights from
Ischade's house up the bank. He had a wheelbarrow and,
at the bank's crest, a wagon. He had three of his militia
guarding the wagon, but he'd permitted none to come
down here. Not to the shrine.

No one should touch the piled stones but him, the thing
he served had told him. As it had told him to bring it
blood, and worse, it had decreed the time and manner of
its uptown move. It wanted to live on the Street of Temples, with the gods. Zip had found it a place, an alley
behind the Rankan Storm God's temple, and there it swore
it would be content to stay.

And he'd found it a new sacrifice, a special gift that one
of his girls had brought him. The girl wanted a job on the
Street of Lanterns and deliverance from Ratfall. In exchange for what she'd found on the Downwind beach, Zip
was happy to oblige. The red-eyed thing that lived inside
the stones would like its new gift, Zip was sure.

He hunkered down beside the knee-high pile and said,
"Look here, Lord, I've got a present for you, when we're
moved. But now I've got to start on the stones, by myself
if you won't let my boys help."

He waited for a reply, but only a glimpse of a burning
red eye and a sound like shifting weight came to him in
response.

What was it he served here? Most times, it didn't speak. He was prompted without words to do this or that. He'd get a feeling of a presence, and the things he brought it—pieces of human flesh, skins of warm blood, precious baubles—would disappear. Was it inimical only to Rankans, or to everyone? He wanted it to be his friend. He wanted it to be the Ilsigs' friend, guardian of the revolution, since he was bound to have one.

He wanted it to show itself, magnificent and powerful, and help bring down Zip's enemies. So far, all it had done was take the sacrifices, give him bad dreams, and let him know it wanted to move uptown.

So did they all. So did all of Zip's Ratfall movers, everyone trapped in the Maze and policed to wits' end. So did the twelve-year-old mothers and one-legged fathers of Zip's revolution, which he'd never wanted. He might have disavowed the struggle if Tempus hadn't tagged him. But Tempus had.

Zip didn't understand why the Rankan powers wanted Zip's help, or the PFLS on its side. The Rankans wouldn't believe that there really *wasn't* a PFLS when he tried to explain that a score of gang members with lamb's blood and paintbrushes didn't make a political movement.

But since his thieves and mendicants would receive the protection of what police Crit had in Sanctuary if they took the night shift, and Zip took responsibility, his entry into the power structure and polite . . . society . . . had just *happened*.

It wasn't being co-opted by the enemy that bothered him the most. What bothered him the most was that his bad boys and girls were doing exactly what they'd done before— extort, blackmail, roust and roughhouse, burn and plunder— and doing it now with the protection and for the benefit of the state.

It didn't make any sense, until it made all the sense in the world. And when Zip realized what Tempus had done

to him, it had been too late. Zip was already part of the
establishment, a hated enforcer, a dog with a Rankan
collar, and his militia no better than any of the cannon
fodder in Walegrin's demoralized army. They hadn't tri-
umphed over the opposition, they had become it.

They weren't the revolution, they were the sustaining
force behind the injustice that had created them.

When he'd said that—shouted it, actually—to Crit in
fury, the cynical Stepson had flashed white teeth and said,
"The more things change, pud, the more they stay the
same. What's your problem? Not having fun now that
you're legal? It's all your type knows how to do, and this
way you won't end up handless or headless because of it.
You're talent, and we're the talent scouts. Thank your
slime gods you've been discovered and put to work before
you ended up greasing some slaver's wagon wheels."

That was another thing that bothered Zip: Critias seemed
to know more about Zip's affairs than anybody could.
"Slime gods" was an obvious reference to the altar. And
as for the slavers . . . Zip had sold more than one soul
down that river of sighs, to finance the revolution. But
then it had been a matter of conscience. Now it was a
godsdamned state *business*, for pork's sake.

Gayle, the 3rd commando liaison man, had told him not
to mind it, just make his list of expendables. He hated
himself these days, as much as he hated Kama, the twit
who had gotten him mixed up in all this, and her damned
3rd Commando ethos that excused the foulest misdeeds as
exigencies. "Whatever works" might work for the Riddler's daughter and her lot of death dealers, but it didn't
work for Zip.

Especially when, if he wasn't careful, he was going to
become just like them. So here he had this altar, this god
or whatever it was, this eater of sacrifices that never
exactly said it could expiate his sins, wipe him clean, but
surely must mean it. It was the thing in the altar with its

red eyes that was making him believe there was some
method to all his madness. It had a plan. It wanted Zip to
infiltrate the Rankans and the Beysibs, to learn how to
command and the weaknesses of their joint enemies. It was
a living thing in there—or at least a real thing, which other
gods weren't, as far as Zip could tell. It had wants and
needs.

It wanted flesh and it needed blood and it wanted to
move uptown and it needed Zip to be the militia commander to serve it. He had to serve something. He couldn't
justify what he and his little band of rebels were doing
otherwise. He had to have a Cause and the red eyes in the
altar, the slurping sound of fresh blood being drunk and
the godlike belches afterwards, these were his Cause.

And only the river god knew what it wanted of Zip, but
it *did* want him. Nobody had ever wanted him before.
Then came, all at once, Kama and the Riddler and the
river god and . . . No, Kama had come before the god, but
that didn't matter.

It mattered that he got the stones uptown. With a quill he
marked each stone as he lifted it from the pile into his
wheelbarrow. When the barrow was full, he could almost
see into the heart of the altar.

But then he had to wheel the barrow up the slope, no
easy task, and when he'd done that and given the stones to
his boys to load on their ass-drawn wagon, someone came
out of the gloom and hailed him.

"Yo," he called back, while motioning his boys to
cover the stones in the wagon. "Who comes?"

One horse, out of the gloom; a single rider. He walked
toward it, hand on his beltknife, his neck aprickle, back
stiff.

Finally the rider answered, "Zip, it's me."

"*Frog*," Zip cursed under his breath. "Kama, stay
there. The footing's tricky. I'll come up." He turned his
head and said to his rebels, "Get down there, load the rest

of the stones, take 'em where I told you. Careful to mark them and put them back just like they were. I'll catch up.''

But he knew he wouldn't. And he knew the god was going to be angry, though he didn't know what form the god's wrath might take.

But then he thought he did: Kama was beautiful, sliding off her horse in the diffuse light of a hidden moon. She always hit him that way, no matter how he told himself he didn't need the kind of trouble she represented.

And she was trouble, in doeskin boots and leggings, smelling like new-mown hay with trail dust in her hair. And all about her person, as clear in her velvet thighs and firm breasts as in her face or her sweet breath, were the indications of her class: her speech, her bearing, the gulf that was between them and never could be bridged, no matter how he tried.

And he tried then again, wordlessly and desperately, as if laying her on her back in the mud was somehow going to do it. But it didn't. It never did, never would.

She laughed softly and accommodated him until urgency overtook her, too, but it was always the high-born girl with the velvet skin who was slumming, who found him exciting for all the wrong reasons, who played with him casually when touching her was probably worth his life if Crit or Molin found them.

So when she said, as she quivered, her mouth to his ear, ''Strat's here with me, somewhere back there. Don't panic, just be quick,'' all his passion threatened to ebb, then exploded when her nails ran down his back.

''Damn you,'' he said, rolling over and off her, the best rejection he could manage and far too late.

''Stand in line for that,'' she chuckled, her fingers reaching for him, trailing along him, tapping him intrusively with unspeakable truths. ''It's been too long since we've done this.''

He was staring up at the clouds which hid the moon like

a translucent city wall. "Not long enough by half. Not when you're sleeping in with priests and commanders-in-chief. I'm a lowly watch officer, remember? I'm gettin' over you. Got something of my own now."

Like he hadn't, before. He bit his lip and almost looked away from her. But he couldn't. It was her damned body that did this to them both, every time. Riddler's daughter, enemy of the blood, twice his experience and probably twice his brains. What did he think he was doing?

Then he thought he knew what she was doing: "Zip," she said in a seductive tone he wished he'd heard long mintues earlier, "don't move that pile of stones. You don't know what you're disturbing. None of us do."

He sat bolt upright. "Now I get it. You ask nice, and Strat's along to ask nasty if I don't agree, right? Well, it's none of your business, Rankan whore." He jerked to his feet, fumbling with his pants. He couldn't see his fingers clearly and blinked fiercely, trying to lace himself together. "Don't come around me no more, hear? Not on your father's business or because one of your boyfriends thinks I need it. I don't. And I never will, not this way."

She was up, too, calling his name. He couldn't run from her, not from a woman where some of his boys might see. He remembered the time she'd nursed him back from the grave's edge, and the way she'd started all this, kissing him when he was too weak to do the sensible thing and bolt.

She liked 'em helpless, hurt, battle-scared and war-weary, he knew. He couldn't figure what Molin had, but power was a legendary aphrodisiac. And like her father, she spread it around.

He couldn't handle her. He kept wanting to treat her like a Ratfall girl—claim her, claim exclusivity with her. He had a comical vision of himself sitting at some strategy table with her, all silked and leathered and shiny brass-plated in Ranke where her kind moved jade pieces representing armies on marble mapboards. And jammed his hands in his pockets, walking hurriedly away.

"Zip," she called, catching up, reaching out, and he couldn't seem to jerk his elbow away. "We need you. *I* need you. And you owe me this—"

He stopped. He should have known it would come to that. "Right, we're all working together now and anyway, one time you saved my ass so I'm yours to command? No chance, lady. These're Ilsig matters, and you ain't one. Understand, or do I have to say it in Rankene?"

"I understand that you found some sort of talisman on the beach and that if you give it to that . . . *thing* . . . you've been feeding human flesh to, you might not be able to finish what you start. If you've got to move the stones, I'll make a deal with you."

He crossed his arms and looked down at her. At least he had that advantage: he was taller. He said: "Go on, let's hear it."

"I won't tell anyone about the altar, or what's in it, as long as no perceptible trouble comes from it, if you'll give me the talisman you were going to give to it."

"How do you find this crap out?" he blurted. "Is it Randal, your pet mage? You been following me? What?"

She just looked up at him, her eyes full of a surety and power that her little, female body shouldn't have been able to contain, let alone radiate. It was Tempus's blood in her, some more-than-human attribute, he was certain.

He said then, "No. I'm not doing anything like that. Why should I?" and turned to go back down the hill.

And Straton was there, on that freakish bay horse everybody knew about, come from nowhere, out of nothing, leaning on his saddlehorn, cleaning his thumbnail with a glittering blade. There, right between Zip and the path down to the riverbank.

"Going somewhere, pud?" said Strat.

"Strat," said Kama, "I can handle this."

"I was just leaving," Zip replied.

"No you can't," said Strat to both of them. Then: "Zip, what she wants, you give her. What she ordered, you do. Or deal with me. Kama, there's something more important than piffles going on out there. Finish with your boy toy and let's get going."

Kama winced but held out her hand steadily and said to Zip, "Either give me the talisman, or Strat and I are going down there and crush five or six of those stones. Do you want to risk that, and what will follow if the three of us have a falling-out?"

Zip looked from the big fighter to the slight woman and saw a shared purpose there; an implacable, uncaring deadliness common among those sure that their Cause was worth serving. He had to learn to match their spirit. Until then, he'd never win against them.

He reached into his beltpouch and handed her the object a girl had found in the seawrack. It hardly glittered. It wasn't even gold, just bronze. "Here, take it. And take out your lust somewhere else, from now on. I don't want to mess with you no more."

He heard Strat's raw titter as he stalked away, and it scratched blood from his soul. He wondered if the thing in the altar would consider the extenuating circumstances under which he'd lost its gift.

And what would happen if it did not.

Ischade's Foalside home was dimly lit, numinous. When they got there, Kama recognized Crit's gray horse and squeezed her eyes shut. No wonder Strat had come running to get her: Crit at Ischade's was naphtha too close to a torch.

"Gods, Strat, we both still love him, you know?"

"I figure," Strat agreed in an odd tone. "But he doesn't love us. Get him out of there, Kama. If I go in, it's just

more trouble. *She* isn't going to take kindly to him sticking
his nose in where it doesn't belong."

Kama was already off her horse, handing Strat its reins.
"I know. You stay here, there's no use of you two getting
into a brawl over this." Poised to sprint for the door, she
turned back: "Strat, we have to get used to things the way
my father left them. It hurts all of us. Crit didn't want this
command. Not this way."

"That and a soldat will still get you laid at Myrtis's."

Bitterness unanswerable. Kama sprinted for the door
she'd always shunned, behind which was something she
didn't want anything to do with: Ischade.

Through the gate, up the steps, and stop, hearing your
own breathing, wondering what you'll do if *she*'s hurt
him, ensorcelled him, gotten *her* claws into him like Strat,
and Janni, and Stilcho and the rest . . .

Knocking with your heart pounding louder, suddenly
aware of more than one male in there behind that forbid-
ding door, and hoping those other voices aren't undead
voices. You've only seen the undeads at a distance, and
even the memory raises gooseflesh . . . "Ah, Madame
Ischade, I'm here for Crit." Blurted like a fool in a voice
higher than you've heard yourself use since school days.

Inky eyes deeper than any uncursed well, a pale face
whose features are somehow indiscernible, and a hand
cold as anything Kama could remember touching.

"Good," nodded the creature in her cowl. Behind her
were colors, rioting jewel tones, but Ischade was all white
and black. Black. "Come in." Black eyes, so deep you
could sleep in them.

Don't fall into any trap. Don't look at her too long.
"Crit?" On tiptoes. "Crit?" The swathed shape moves
away. "*Crit?*"

There he is, with two men she recognized: Vis, and a
beggar with a stutter, a creature called Mor-am. Wrong
company, wrong place, wrong something going down here.

Kama shivered and felt throwing stars she'd gotten from Niko nestled in her belt. Could you kill anything here? Would it stay dead? Could she take out the beggar, the merc, and Ischade if Crit needed that much help?

She could try, couldn't do less. But then Crit came slowly to the door, his gait telegraphing annoyance, but nothing worse. "Good evening," he said and Kama couldn't figure where the vampire had disappeared to. "What brings you here, Kama?"

He somehow shouldered her outside and then the door was closed, his hands on her shoulders, tight and hard, digging. "Fool," Crit whispered, "don't mix in this. I've got enough troubles." His lips hardly moved when he spoke; the hollows under his cheeks were too deep; his whole bearing was wrong and she was terrified.

"Crit, gods, whatever it is, you can't do it alone. Strat's with me, we're here to—"

"Strat? With you? He bunks here, Kama. Sleeps here. Does whatever he does here. For her. Not us. Go away. I'm finding someone for Torchholder. Special orders."

She tried to shake off his grip. It wouldn't shake. She said defiantly, "Whatever you're doing, I'm doing. Special orders."

He couldn't verify that, not without going to Randal. And Randal might lie for Kama, might say Tempus had sent a message.

The touch of him made her ache and she suddenly wondered whether if, for just one night, every lover in Sanctuary could be in the right bed, things might straighten out.

Critias's usually handsome Syrese face had none of its gentility tonight; it was a fright mask, just shields for eyes and a slash where his mouth should be. He tucked in his chin, bowed his head to stare into her face, then shook his head infinitesimally: "You want in, fine. We're going uptown to the ruined blocks, see if we can't find Tasfalen in one of the houses left standing there. That's where *she* says to look. Me, the two backstreeters she owns, and you. But no Strat.''

''Crit, he—''

''Can't be trusted. Too much *her* creature. Tell him to back off, out of sight till I leave. Tell him if he wants to talk to me, get rid of the horse as a sign of good faith. Or of returning sanity. I don't need a ghost horse, or a ghost rider, which is what he's becoming. Go on. Tell him. Then meet me at the gate.''

He gave her a little push and she wished he felt so strongly about her, even if those feelings were as hard and fierce as what he felt for Strat.

Like a page in court, she ran back to Strat's horse and said, ''He says he's going uptown to find Tasfalen for Torchholder. Doesn't want you involved. We'll talk to you later. You stay with Ischade. If this goes wrong, we need someone on the outside who knows where we went and what happened. And we may need Ischade's—your help.''

''He didn't say that.''

''No, he didn't. I'm going with him, and I'm saying it.''

''I'll come—''

''He *did* say that, Strat. He wants you here, just in case . . .'' It sounded like what it was, a whitewash.

Strat's horse backed a few steps and from there she heard Straton say, ''Go on, then. Ischade's warned him off, told him something. I'll find out what. You need help, you'll get it.'' His voice was thick.

She was glad she couldn't see his face. She ran blindly to her horse, grabbed a handful of mane, vaulted to its back, and urged the skittish roan toward the iron gate where weird flowers bloomed. In her belt, the talisman she'd taken from Zip seemed hot against her leathers, hot enough to make her sweat.

It was the proximity to Ischade's wards, she told herself. Nothing to fret over. She had plenty to worry about without adding the talisman into the bargain.

Crit crossed one leg over his saddle's pommel and lit a smoke, staring at the building across the street. No sign on its steps or to either side of the rubble they'd passed getting here, of the whirlwinds and firestorm of destruction that had ravaged Tasfalen's ancestral home.

This building was intact, its shutters drawn. The vampire had been certain of where to look, but uncertain that looking was wise.

"She said," Crit told Kama, "that Tasfalen's in there, with Haught. You remember Haught."

"I remember," Kama said through clenched teeth.

Mor-am and Vis were off to one side, ordered to accompany them by Ischade, who evidently was in charge of more than her Foalside cottage. Damn Tempus, for putting Crit between sorcerous rocks and political hard places. Vis had brought him to Mor-am, who'd grinned and brought him to Ischade with more satisfaction than Crit liked.

And the vampire had been civil. Both of them had kept Strat's name out the conversation. "Our mutual friend" was what they called Straton, and because of that friend, Ischade was willing to tell Crit where to look.

And to warn him: "There is more, Critias, in that home than just two men in a house. Do not go inside, but merely open the doors—if you can."

This was said for Strat's sake, Crit knew, not his own. He unclenched a fist with difficulty and found he'd dug his nails into his palm, that his fingers were stiff from the clench. "She said," he told Kama, "you'd have the right key for this lock."

"Excuse me?" The woman on the roan kneed her mount closer.

"You heard me. Got anything on you that might do the trick?"

"You're sure she didn't mean that metaphorically?"

And Crit knew what Kama was alluding to: Tempus and an inhuman sprite had coupled before a magically locked door uptown, and things had happened.

"I don't care what she meant, we're not trying anything like that. What have you got that might work?"

"Keys," said Kama with maddening common sense. "Lots of keys. To my place, the guardhouse, the Shambles safe house, Molin's— "

"Spare me the list. Let's try some." He swung first one leg and then the other over his gray's withers, reaching for his crossbow as soon as his feet hit the ground. A bolt might smash the lock, even if it were a stout one.

They drop-tied the horses without a word, a sign both of them were thinking this might not be survivable. Crit cast a look at Kama, wondering how she'd managed to insinuate herself into this so fast, so deftly. And admitting he was glad to have someone there. He was a Sacred Bander, trained to depend on a partner. He wouldn't have tried this alone, and Vis wasn't the sort of man you could trust your right side to.

Not that Kama was any sort of man at all.

Having crossed the street, Crit looked back once because he'd heard Vis's voice—not words, just a tone. And saw a wave of farewell so eloquently hostile and so gloating that he almost shot the merc there and then.

But Kama read his mind and touched his arm. "They're Ischade's. They'll wait. They'll run back with word if we don't come out. We need that."

"Crap," Crit said.

"Agreed," Kama said with a ghost of her father's smile.

Then they climbed the steps and Crit put his back against the stone, crossbow ready, attempting to cover every avenue of attack while Kama tried key after key and cursed like a Nisibisi freeman.

Finally she said, "No luck. Nothing works." And slumped against the doorjamb.

They looked at each other too long, and Crit had to look away. It was in that silence that they heard something move inside, behind the stout wood of the door.

Then they looked at each other again.

"Want to knock?" Kama said lightly.

"I don't think so," Crit replied in the same tone. "We could start digging at the wood with—'"

"Wait," said Kama, simultaneously digging in her belt. "This, maybe." She held out a piece of bronze about half the length of her hand and shaped like a knobbed bar or rod.

"Never fit," he said critically, still holding his cross-bow at the ready, still glancing from shadow to shadow down the quiet street. Still watching Vis and Mor-am as best he could.

"Might not have to. It washed up on the beach. I heard about it from some of my . . . people. Turned a gold coin to lead, and copper to clay, in the finder's purse."

"So?"

"So, let's see if it'll do something to that metal."

"We're here." Crit shrugged, trying to ignore the im-plications. Kama wasn't the finder. Kama had appropri-ated this thing from someone, for her own purposes. And she'd heard about it through some informer of whom Crit was totally ignorant. Nothing was going to work right in Sanctuary unless they all started pulling together. But what he wanted to do to Kama right then wouldn't facilitate anything of the sort.

She shrugged, too, added a sour twist of her thin lips, and bent to the door. He didn't dare look away to watch, but he heard her tap bronze against bronze. And curse. And tap again, and chortle.

"So?" he said when she stood up and carefully put the talisman back in her belt.

"So, do we want to be polite, now that the lock's no problem?"

He took one hand away from the crossbow and, balancing it on his hip, felt for the lock. It was gooey. He brought his fingers to his lips and smelled White Foal mud, rank with rot. He swore and asked her to explain herself.

"I heard," she said, "it might be something like this. That's all."

"Great." He spat over his shoulder. "Next time you 'hear' of something like this, you come to me with it."

"I did."

"*Beforehand*," he said, just as there was a scuffling sound and then a dragging noise behind the door and he and Kama jumped back in unison.

The door opened like a casket's top. And there, behind it, stood something very much like Tasfalen, the popinjay noble who'd been missing so long. "Yessss," said the noble in an entirely horrible voice, a voice that seemed not to have been used for a thousand years.

And behind this shape, Crit could see another: Haught.

And over those two images, he saw superimposed the glowing countenance of Ischade, a slight crease between her eyes, and Ischade was shaking her head, her lips forming a word.

And that word was "Run." In his inner ear, he heard it again: *Run, if you value your soul.*

"Come on, Kama. Sorry to disturb you, Tasfalen," said Crit as he backed down the stairs, Kama's arm in a deathgrip and still holding the loaded crossbow one-handed. "We just needed to verify your whereabouts. Stop by the palace when you can—Molin Torchholder wants to see you."

By the time he'd finished saying all of that, he'd dragged Kama halfway to the street and she was whispering urgently, "What's the matter with you? Lost your mind? Your nerve?"

"Finished, that's all. We're finished here. I have no reason to arrest that man. I only had to find him." His voice was shaking and Kama heard it.

He didn't look at her as they made for their horses. He couldn't stand to see scorn in her eyes. But he saw it in the eyes of Ischade's two waiting minions, and it burned like hellfire.

"What's the matter, Stepson, Tempus take your balls upcountry?" Vis shouted from a safe distance as Crit mounted up.

He got off one quarrel, but his aim was half-hearted. It smashed harmlessly against the brick beside Vis's head.

And then there was Kama to deal with, slouched in her saddle, frowning.

He said, "We have to report this to Torchholder. I need you. Let's go."

She reined her horse after his, either unwilling to dispute his statement or unable.

One way or the other, he'd let the matter of the talisman go if she'd just give him a chance. How he was going to keep Kama with him tonight, Crit couldn't fathom, but he was going to give it a try. Torchholder would have to make do with a written report. It was just too damned cold in Sanctuary to sleep alone tonight.

The sky was beginning to lighten, turning regal above the temple tops. Zip's black sweatband was sopping though the waning night was as chill on the Street of Temples as it had been at the White Foal's edge.

He straightened up from the piled stones in the alleyway, hand to the small of his back. He was alone now. He sent his boys scurrying with a flurry of invective when he'd realized what they'd done.

Or what he'd let them do. They'd touched the stones, because of Kama and Strat. Worse, they'd mismarked the ones they'd touched.

Zip had spent the rest of the night trying to sort out the mess. And all he had to show for his labors was an empty pile of stones that wouldn't sit exactly right, wouldn't form the beehive shape they'd had down at the riverbank.

One more time, he put the stones he was sure of—the top three—in place. And one more time they fell inward, toppled others, and ended in a jumble in the alley beside the Storm God of Ranke's temple.

And again, as the stones rolled and at last came to rest, the ground beneath Zip's feet seemed to tremble. This time, he hardly noticed the earth's tremors over his own.

The rivergod wasn't pleased, he could feel it. Maybe it was gone, or just wouldn't come here because he'd botched it, but Zip had an awful feeling that the red-eyed thing was more than a little miffed about the disarrayed condition of its home. Worse, he wasn't sure any more whether this site was good enough, being not quite *on* the Street of Temples, but somewhat off the thoroughfare.

If only his boys had marked the stones. If only Kama and Strat hadn't interfered. If only the day would stay its coming a little while longer. Zip had been in tight spots before. Given time and calm, he could sort the matter out.

There were thirty-three stones in all. Some of them had Zip's careful marks. It couldn't be impossible to figure out which stones must comprise the bottom row.

But it was. He couldn't do it. He'd tried four times. And now the dawn was threatening to break. First the sky would regain its blueness, eating up the stars. Then royal purple would creep along the temples' walls, then gouts of red and orange flame to eat the darkness. And when the celadon and rose of true dawn came, with them would come the priests and acolytes, padding toward their morning duties.

Zip would be discovered where Ilsigs feared to tread, in the reaches of a Rankan temple. And then the rivergod would have its revenge.

He knew it was that. He was shaking all over, anguished and weak. Too weak to run, too tired to hide. It was as if all his spirit had leeched away with the darkness, as if his soul was as dismantled as the home of stone he couldn't rebuild.

He squatted down beside the tumbled blocks of half-dressed limestone, nearly in tears. He wanted to make amends, he hadn't meant to let the unclean hands of his rebels desecrate the rivergod's temple. He'd tried to do the right thing . . .

And, in extremis like so many men before him over thousands of years, Zip began to pray: *Lord,* he asked wordlessly, eyes closed, hands upon the stone he'd marked himself, the capstone of this puzzle he couldn't solve, *O Lord, forgive thy servant. Evildoing has befallen me. In my foolishness, I have sinned against thee. Forgive thy servant and help me to make things right. Help thy servant to make thy temple and I will bring the blood of a virgin under twelve, the eyes of an ox, the penis of a Rankan noble—whatever thy desire is, just make it known to me and I will do that thing. But help me not fail in the making of thy temple, and give me a sign that this place is acceptable to thee.* Before I get my ass hauled off to jail in the bargain, he added, still silent, eyes yet closed.

For he'd heard a sound that stiffened him as if he were turned to stone as unyielding as the blocks over which he labored: the click of a horse's hoof against a pebble, the scrape of an iron shoe on cobble.

Holding his breath, he heard more: the swish of a long tail, the creak of leather, the jingle of harness. *Frog, I'm porked for good and all.*

Obviously, he told himself, this was the god's wrath come upon him. He was going to open his eyes, turn around, and there would be some palace hotshot, some regular army mover, some Beysib lady fighter, waiting to take him off to the Hall of Justice for screwing around on the grounds of the Storm God's temple. Not even his commission as watch officer could save him now. Not from the penalty for desecrating holy ground when that ground was holy to Rankans.

He opened his eyes and looked straight ahead, at the jumble of altar stones. Well, he'd tried. He wondered what was going to happen to the altar stones, to the god's home, and to the god himself. Would it magically get itself and its stones back to the river where it was safe?

And if it couldn't, what would then befall poor Zip, who'd managed to pork up a god's life as well as his own?

He bit his lip and then, decided, turned from the waist to face his fate.

There, behind him, was a single horseman. The horse loomed in the gloom, its great dark chest seeming to stare at Zip with a panther's eyes, a panther's gaping, toothsome jaws.

Zip blinked, and realized that what faced him was no creature half cat, half horse, but a warhorse wearing a pantherskin shabraque. And the panther who had given its skin to blanket this horse had been large, with glowing eyes, and so magnificent that its head had been not merely skinned, but stuffed so that glassy eyes stared at Zip as angrily as living eyes might have.

The horse was the color of White Foal clay, its mane and tail and stockings black. Its bridle and reins were of woven stuff like swampgrass, and from it wafted a marshy odor. It pawed the ground, neck arched, and only then was Zip's attention drawn to the rider, who was dismounting.

Zip never remembered scrambling to his feet, only the swing of the rider from his saddle, the cloak as dark as the predawn sky, and the feathered helm that inclined toward him as the rider said, "What have we here?"

"Uh, I'm just trying to put this back like it ought to be." Zip waved vaguely behind him, toward the altar stones tumbled there, trying to protect the unassembled shrine with his body.

The rider's helmet turned slowly. His visor was down. He was armored in browns; bronze or hardened leather or some combination, Zip couldn't tell. But armored in the way of well-to-do professionals: arms free and bare but for wrist braces, cuirass and loinguard, greaves below his knees, and all of it fitted custom to his body. Slung at his hip was a cavalryman's sword and equipment belt. Behind, on the saddle, Zip could see two shields, long and short, and a bow and quiver, but in the rider's hand was only a spear.

Coming toward him without another word, the man used the spear as a staff, digging the ground with its butt. And then, when this faceless apparition was nearly upon him and Zip was beginning to wonder if there were really eyes behind the frightful visor, he finally spoke again: "I see your problem."

And he walked right by Zip, whose nose was wrinkled at the salty smell of marsh emanating from him, and on toward the pile of stones.

"No, don't! Please! Nobody's supposed to touch—" Zip lunged unthinkingly toward the armored man and the horse behind him screamed and reared, hooves flailing.

Zip threw up his arms and dived to the dirt as the horse stalked upright toward him.

At the same time, the armored man turned slowly, from the waist, and held up his spear. The horse came down on all fours and bowed its head, snorting.

Zip scrambled to his feet. "Look, like I said, nobody's supposed to touch—"

The armored man's head swiveled toward him and the voice from behind the visor said, "This one first." His spear pointed to a certain stone, then jabbed toward it commandingly when Zip only stared. "*This* one. Now."

Zip found his hands on the stone. And then on another,

the one that the spear touched next. And another, and another. Zip labored there, under the direction of that spear, until the sky was red and gold and he held the final stone in both his hands, chest heaving.

Poised over the pile, afraid that attempting to place the last stone would tumble all the others, Zip blurted breathlessly, ''You're sure?''

The helmeted head nodded once, up and down, and the spear jabbed forward commandingly.

Zip placed the stone atop all the other stones and a spark seemed to jump from the rocks. It bit his hand, crawled up his wrist. It hurt like fire.

He staggered back, squinting at the stones suddenly too bright, as if they'd ignited. He shielded his eyes from the glare. A trick of the dawn light, he told himself when he opened his eyes again and the pile was still there, neither burning nor singed, not even smudged, but squat and sturdy.

Squat! Sturdy! A rough beehive of stones, solid as the temple wall in whose shadow it rested. Success! Relief flooded Zip. Before he knew it, he was on his knees at the low opening, peering inward, trying to see if the rivergod was there.

And he saw something, red and glowing, restless in its appointed dark. And reached out to touch the stones, which were cool and real and snug in place.

He pushed on one. It didn't shift. He pushed on two. They didn't budge. He chuckled and then he grinned. He put his cheek to the cool stone, knowing now that the spark that had seemed to bite him was just some phosphorescent insect and the rest had been illusion, a moment of waking dream.

Because the god was not angry at him—it had come to abide in the temple he had built it!

He gave a wordless shout and then remembered the armored man. He got up from the altar, hand already outstretched to thank the stranger, but there was no one there. No man in fighter's garb. No horse in pantherskin shabraque with panther feet dangling from its back.

Nothing but increasing daylight in an alley where no Ilsig dared be caught, not even Zip, the third shift watch officer of Sanctuary.

"Gotta go, but I'll be back, Lord," he muttered, giving the shrine a final pat before he fled. "I'll be back."

Kama's roan had bolted during the night, found some way to slip its harness and make away. "She does it all the time," Kama said to Crit, who was sure someone had gotten into the barn and stolen the mare. "There's no door that beast can't open, no knot she can't chew through. She'll be out at the Stepsons' barracks, mark my words."

And that stopped all conjecture about the horse, and Kama's attempt to lighten Crit's mood. It wasn't the Stepsons' barracks any longer, not with so few Stepsons left. Nobody stayed there now. It was too lonely. The place was used for storage of gear and extra horses, but Crit stayed here, at the Shambles safe house; Strat stayed . . . where Strat stayed. Randal, who could have claimed the right, was sleeping in the Mageguild, and Kama herself preferred any number of beds with men in them to a solitary one full of unhappy memories.

"I'll go out and check," she said lamely. "You've got to go to work, anyway. See you toni— later?"

"Tonight's fine with me," said Crit gently, and then with more fire in him: "If you want to join me over at Ischade's—I can't let this thing with Strat go on like this. I've got to get him out of there."

"Why?" Strat had been there for them, in his way. When they'd come back to the guardpost to write their report he'd been waiting, full of Ischade's warnings and a more honest concern. But Crit couldn't unbend, wouldn't let Strat have an opening so that amends could be made.

"She says," Strat had offered, using the unadorned pronoun, as they always did, to represent Ischade; "that there's more trouble coming out of that house than you or yours can handle. Leave it to us, all right?"

Crit hadn't said a word to that at first, just stared at Strat in that way he had that made you want to sink into the earth right there and then. And after too long a pause, he'd said what Kama hoped he wouldn't: "*Us,* is it? You and her, you mean? Or some of your soulless zombies under mutual command?"

Strat had been braced for it, by then. Kama wanted to crawl under the table, pretend she didn't understand what was happening and suggest they all go to breakfast—anything but sit there, a mute witness to the rending of a Sacred Band oath.

Strat had said only, "Crit, I signed off on your paperwork, what more do you want? You can't handle this. We won't tell anyone if you don't. Tasfalen's . . . our business. So's Haught. Keep your people away from them, that's all I'm saying." And with that, Strat had left.

There was a time Kama would have taken Crit to her bosom on this sort of rebound and felt like she'd won something. But the comfort he needed wasn't hers, and all the acrobatics he'd put both of them through so that he could finally fall into an exhausted sleep didn't help what was ailing Critias.

Or didn't help enough. Still, she said, "Wait for me tonight," and left him, thinking that, if things were going from bad to worse with Strat, Crit might really need her help. He needed someone's. And Kama knew that, no matter what trouble it caused with Molin or anybody else, whatever Crit needed, she had to try to give him.

Love tends to be like that, even in Sanctuary.

Alone in his office, Critias pretended to work on the duty roster until his eyes started to sting. Then he gave it up, having made little progress, and began to put his papers away, thinking that he'd go down to Caravan Square and see if he could find Kama another horse.

But as he was leaving, Gayle came in, muttering that there was ''some porker outside you'd better take a look at, sir—personal like.''

"I'm not in the mood," Crit snapped, then said: "Sorry, Gayle, it's not you. It's that damned Zip. Anybody report anything odd last night?"

It was Zip's shift, so as to whatever had happened about the stone shrine, Crit didn't expect anything like an honest report from the watch officer. Wouldn't have, even if Zip could write more than his name.

''That's what I'm sayin', Commander: you'd better come have a look at this guy, came in last night to the mercs' hostel, claiming all sorts of privilege. Now he's lookin' for Tempus.'' Gayle shrugged and grimaced, anticipating Crit's next question. "Didn't tell him anything, either way."

"Just where 'outside' is this fellow?"

''Down at the Storm God's temple, like he owned it. Nice horse, nice gear, lots of loose change.''

"Right. I'm on my way." They all knew the type—they *were* the type, before Tempus had welded them into something more usable by Empire.

Gayle was still hovering and Crit understood why: "Somebody's got to watch the shop, friend."

Gayle screwed up his face. "Porking waste, all this porked-up paper work's somethin' any porkin' fool can do."

"Not when it's mine, it isn't. Molin comes by, keep him here, tell him we're making copies and need his signature on something—anything. Try to find out what he's up to on this Tasfalen matter. And let him know that, far as we're concerned, it's closed: we found the man in question, he's not accused of anything, there's nothing more we can do.''

Gayle was nodding intently, trying to memorize all of that, as Crit left.

His gray horse was still where Crit had tethered it, Enlil be praised. If that one disappeared, then it was going to become police business, and fast. But it hadn't. He rubbed its nose and it whickered softly as he mounted up and headed off into the early morning sunlight.

The worst thing about this new duty was getting used to sleeping at night, working in the daytime. For Crit's money, sunlight was something you left to the cattle. In Sanctuary, like most other venues he'd worked, what was worth doing got done at night.

But command made its demands, and when he got to the Storm God's temple he wished he'd commanded his mage, Randal, to come to the Street of Temples with him.

The horse that was tied in front of the temple screamed money and power from every trapping and the pantherskin shabraque it wore was of a style and quality Crit had never seen before.

"Where's the owner of this horse?" he demanded of the temple acolyte who'd obviously been paid to watch over it and was doing that from a distance: the shabraque wasn't the only part of this beast with teeth.

"In back, Commander, down that alley." The acolyte rolled its eunuch's eyes heavenward as if to say, Don't ask me why these warriors do what they do.

Crit looked at the tethered warhorse, whose saddle had hung on it both a large and small shield, and other implements of close and regimented fighting, and blew out a long, slow breath.

Crit's dues to the mercenary's guild were still paid up. He rode, rather than walked, down the alley on the southwest side of the Storm God's temple until he came to a man eating a skewer of lamb and drinking from a wineskin, leaning up against the temple wall near a pile of stones.

"Life to you," Crit said cautiously, keeping rein contact with his horse's mouth with one hand and his other on the crossbow he could shoot without disengaging from its saddle hook.

"And the rest, as follows," said the other man whose helmet, on the pile of stones, was of an ancient style from far to the west. "I'm looking for Tempus."

"You've found his first officer." Old habits died hard. "I'm holding the bag here till he returns." Everything about this fighter screamed trouble; the fact that he was looking for the Riddler didn't mitigate that: whoever Tempus wanted for his sortie, he'd already contacted.

"You'll do, then."

"Thanks. Do for what?"

"I'm offering my services. Tempus needs a little help here, I was told." The man was Crit's height but somewhat heavier, in his middle years, scarred enough by war and wind and sun to prove him mortal. His head was broad and strong and resembled, more than anything else, a human version of the helmet he'd set on the piled stones. The red-brown eyes in that face held Crit's implacably, and the Stepson had the unmistakable impression that he was being judged.

"He's not here, I said."

"But the problems are, and you're short-handed, so they say up at the guild hostel."

"Who sent you?" Bluntly put. If this fighter was a merc, as he said, the guild records could tell him something about the man he was looking at—if Crit needed to know any more.

A quirked smile that showed no teeth. "Your need, for certain—and the Riddler's. The Storm God, if you like."

Crit hated this sort of innuendo. The man he was looking at was of a fighting class not usually under his command, and if the newcomer was staying in Sanctuary, some accommodation between them would have to be made. The last thing he needed was a man like this working against him. And if he was what he seemed—an acquaintance of Tempus—then he might represent a light at the end of Crit's personal tunnel.

The man leaning against the wall merely chewed on his stick of lamb chunks and eyed Crit and the gray horse until Critias knew he must dismount or create an enemy.

When he'd done that, the newcomer threw away his stick of lamb and came toward him. When he reached the pile of stones, he put one foot up on it and retrieved his helmet. "I'm known as Shepherd," he said, and held out his hand.

"I bet you are," Crit replied, taking it. Between them was the pile of stones and, somehow, Crit didn't want to touch it. He remembered what Kama had said about Zip and the stones, but it didn't seem anywhere near as important as the man before him. "Well, Shepherd, I'm not using my war name here, so it's just Critias." He disengaged his hand and unconsciously wiped it against his hip.

Behind Crit, his horse snorted. Duly prompted, the Stepson said, "We've got plenty of work for the right sort of man, but what kind depends on how long you're staying. And what sort of references you can produce. More, I hope, than just evidence of the Storm God's favor."

"More than gods' favor, yes," said Shepherd, tapping his foot on the pile of stones. "Gods: can't live with 'em, can't shoot 'em." He shook his head in mock disgust, to make it clear that the remark was a joke, but it seemed strange to Crit, as strange as this Shepherd come to Sanctuary in the wake of the Riddler.

INHERITOR

David Drake

"You need a dagger, caravan master," said the stranger
to Samlor hil Samt as he began to bring a weapon slowly
out from under his cloak.

The man hadn't spoken loudly, but there were key
words which rang in the air of the Vulgar Unicorn. Weapon
words were almost as sure a way to get attention in this bar
as the mention of money. Conversation stopped or dropped
into a lower key; eyes shifted over beer mugs and dice cups.

Samlor was already in the state of tension which gripped
any sane man when he walked into this bar in the heart of
Sanctuary's Maze district. More than the word "dagger"
shocked him now, so that his right hand slipped to the
brass pommel and hilt—of nondescript hardwood, plain
and serviceable like the man who carried it—of the long
fighting knife in his belt sheath.

At the same time, Samlor's left arm swept behind him
to locate and hold his seven-year-old niece Star. She was
with him in this place because there was no place in the
world safer for her than beside her mother's brother . . .
which was almost another way of saying that there was no
safety at all in this life.

Almost, because for forty-three years, Samlor hil Samt
had managed to do what he thought he had to do, be
damned to the price he paid or the cost to whatever stood
between him and duty.

The stranger shouldn't have called him "caravan master." That's what he was, what he had been ever since he had determined to lift his family from poverty, despite the scorn all his kin heaped on him for dishonoring Cirdonian nobility by going into trade. But no one in Sanctuary should have recognized Samlor; and if they did, he and Star were in trouble much deeper than the general miasma of danger permeating this place.

There were people in Sanctuary who actively wished Samlor dead. That was unusual; not because he'd lived a life free from deadly enemies, but because fate or the Cirdonian caravan master himself had carried off most of those direct threats already.

When he bedded his camels at night on the trail, Samlor walked the circuit of the laager prodding crevices and holes with a cornel-wood staff flexible enough to reach an arm's length down a circuitous burrow.

If there were a hiss or an angry jarring of fangs on the staff, he either blocked the hole or, as the mood struck him, teased the snake into the open to be finished with a whip-swift flick of the staff. That was the only way to prevent beasts and men from being bitten when they rolled in their sleep onto vipers sheltering against mammalian warmth.

The caravan routes were a hard school, but applying the lessons he learned there to human enemies had kept Samlor alive longer than would otherwise have been the case.

Sanctuary, though, was a problem better avoided than solved—and insoluble besides. Samlor had no intention of seeing and *smelling* the foulness of this place ever again, until the messenger arrived with the letter from Samlane.

It could have been a forgery, though the Cirdonian script on the strip of bark-pulp paper was illegible until it had been wound onto a message staff of the precise length and diameter of the ones Samlor's family had adopted when they were ennobled seventeen generations before.

But the hand was right; the message had the right aura of terse presumption that Samlor would do his sister's will in this matter . . .

And the paper was browned enough with age, despite having been locked in a banker's strong room, that the document might well have been written before Samlane died with her brother's knife through her belly and through the thing she carried in her womb.

Samlor couldn't imagine what inheritance could be worth the risk of bringing Star back to Sanctuary, but his sister had been foolishly destructive only of herself. If the legacy which would come to Star at age seven were that important, then it was Samlor's duty as the child's uncle to see that she received it.

It was his duty as the father as well, but that was something he thought about only when he awakened in the bleak darkness.

So he was in Sanctuary again, where no one was safe; and a man he didn't know had just identified him.

Star put a hand on her uncle's elbow, to reassure him with her presence and the fact she understood the tension.

The trio of punks by the door glanced sidelong with greasy eyes. They were street toughs, too young to have an identity beyond the gang membership they proclaimed with matching yellow bandannas and high boots that made sense only for horsemen. They were dangerous, the gods knew, the way a troop of baboons was dangerous. Like baboons, they stank, yammered, and let vicious hostility to outsiders serve in situations where humans would have found intelligence to be useful.

Four soldiers, out of uniform but obvious from the way their hair was cut short to fit beneath a helmet, sat at a table near the bar with a pimp and a woman. The pimp gave Samlor and the situation an appraising look. The woman eyed the caravan master blearily, because he happened to be standing where her eyes were more or less focused.

And the soldiers, after momentary alertness to the possibility of a brawl, resumed their negotiations regarding a price for the woman to go down on all four of them in the alley outside.

There were a dozen other people in the tavern, besides the slope-shouldered tapster and the barmaid—the only other woman present—who slid between tables, too tired to slap at the hands that groped her and too jaded to care. The drinkers, solitary or in pairs, were nondescript though clothed within a fair range of wealth and national origin. They could be identified as criminals only because they chose to gather here.

"I don't need a dagger," said Samlor, releasing Star to free his left hand as his right lifted the wedge of his own belt knife a few inches up in its sheath. "I have my own."

There was nothing fancy about Samlor's weapon. The blade was a foot long with two straight edges. The metal had no ornamentation beyond the unsharpened relief cuts which would permit the user to short-grip the weapon with an index finger over the crosshilt. It was forged of a good grade of steel—though, again, nothing exceptional.

Recently, a few blades of Enlibar steel had appeared. These were forged from iron alloyed with a blue-green ore of copper which had been cursed by earth spirits, kobolds. The ore could be smelted only by magical means, and it was said to give an exceptional toughness to sword blades.

Samlor had been interested in the reports, but he'd survived as long as he had by sticking to what he was sure would work. He left the experiments with kobold steel to others.

"You'll want this anyway," said the stranger, lifting his dagger by its crosshilt so that the pommel was toward Samlor.

Not a threat, only a man with something to sell, thought

the Cirdonian as he sidled away from the stranger to get to the bar. Harmless, almost certainly—but Samlor moved to his left, guiding Star ahead of him so that his body was between her and the weapon that the other man insisted on displaying. The fellow had sized up Samlor as he entered the Vulgar Unicorn, guessing his occupation from his appearance. A con man's trick, perhaps, but not an assassin's.

There was no reason to take chances.

"When are we going to sleep, uncle?" asked Star with a thin whine on the last syllables which meant she was really getting tired. That was understandable, but it meant she was likely to balk when she needed to obey. She might even call him "Uncle Samlor" despite having been warned that Samlor's real name would make both of them targets.

Star was an unusual child, but she was a child nonetheless.

"Two mugs of blue john," said the Cirdonian, loudly enough for the tapster halfway down the bar to hear him. They already had the attention of the fellow, an athlete gone to fat but still powerful. He was balding, and his scars showed that he had been doing this work or work equally rough for many years.

If something had cost him his left thumb during that time—he was still the one walking around to tell the tale, wasn't he?

"*I* want—" Star piped up.

"And two beers to wash it down," Samlor said loudly, cutting her off. As his left hand reached down for his belt purse, he let it linger for a moment where Star's hood covered the whorl of white hair that was the source of her name. She quieted for the moment, though the touch was gentle.

Star's mother had immersed herself in arts that had ultimately killed her—or had led her to need to die. Her child had terrifying powers when necessity and circumstances combined to bring them out.

But Samlor hil Samt had no need of magic to frighten anyone who knew him as well as the child did. He would not cuff her across the room; not here, not ever. His rage was as real as the rock glowing white in the bowels of a volcano. The Cirdonian's anger bubbled beneath a crust of control that split only when he chose that it should, and he would never release its destruction on his kin, blood of his blood . . . his seed.

Star was old enough to recognize the fury, and wise enough to avoid it even when she was fatigued. She patted her protector's hip.

The coin Samlor held between the middle and index finger of his left hand was physically small but minted from gold. It was an indication to the sharp-eyed tapster that his customer wanted more than drink, and a promise that he would pay well for the additional service. The man behind the bar nodded as he scooped clabbered milk from a stoneware jug under the bar.

There was no drink more refreshing than blue john to a dusty traveler, tired and hungry but too dry to bolt solid food. It was a caravaner's drink—and Samlor was a caravaner, obvious to anyone, even before he ordered. He shouldn't have been surprised at the way a stranger had addressed him.

Samlor wore a cloak, pinned up now to half-length as he would wear it for riding. When he slept or stood in a chill breeze, it could cover him head to toe. The fleece from which it was tightly woven had a natural blue-black color, but it had never been washed or dyed. Lanolin remaining in the wool made the garment almost waterproof.

The tunic he wore beneath the cloak was wool also, but dyed a neutral russet color. Starting out before dawn on the caravan road, Samlor would wear as many as three similar tunics over this one, stripping them off and binding them to his saddle as the sun brightened dazzlingly on the high passes.

The bottom layer against his skin was of silk, the only luxury Samlor allowed himself or even desired while he was on the road.

He was a broad-shouldered, deep-chested man even without the added bulk of his cloak, but his wrists would have been thick on a man of half again his size. The skin of his hands and face was roughened by a thousand storms whipping sand or ice crystals across the plains, and it was darkened to an angry red that mimicked the tan his Cirdonian genes did not have the pigment to support.

When Samlor smiled, as he did occasionally, the expression flitted across his face with the diffidence of a visitor sure he's knocking at the wrong address. When he barked orders, whether to men or beasts, his features stayed neutral and nothing but assurance rang in his chill, crisp tones.

When Samlor hil Samt was angry enough to kill, he spoke in soft, bantering tones. The muscles stretched across his cheekbones and pulled themselves into a visage very different from his normal appearance; a visage not altogether human.

He rarely became that angry; and he was not angry now, only cautious and in need of information before he could lead Star and her legacy out of this *damnable* city.

The clabbered milk was served in masars, wooden cups darkened by the sweaty palms of hundreds of previous users. As the tapster paused, midway between reaching for the coin now or drawing the beer first, Samlor said, "I'm trying to find a man in this town, and I'm hoping that you might be able to help me. Business, but not . . . serious business."

That was true, though neither the tapster nor any other man in this dive was likely to believe it.

Not that they'd care, either, so long as they'd been paid in honest coin.

"A regular?" asked the balding man softly as his hand

did, after all, cover the gold which Samlor was not yet willing to release.

"I doubt it," said the Cirdonian with a false, fleeting smile. "His name's Setios. A businessman, perhaps, a banker, as like as not. Or just possibly, he might be, you know . . . someone who deals with magic. I was told he keeps a demon imprisoned in a crystal bottle."

You could never tell how mention of sorcery or a wizard was going to strike people. Some very tough men would blanch and draw away—or try to slit your throat so that they wouldn't have to listen to more.

The tapster only smiled and said, "Somebody may know him. I'll ask around." He turned. The coin disappeared into a pocket of his apron.

"Uncle, I don't *like*—"

"And the beers, friend," Samlor called in a slightly louder voice.

There was little for a child to drink in a place like this. Star didn't have decades of caravan life behind her, the days when anything wet was better than the smile of a goddess. The beer was a better bet than whatever passed for wine, and either would be safer than the water.

"This is a very special knife," said a voice at Samlor's shoulder.

The Cirdonian turned, face flat. He was almost willing to disbelieve the senses that told him that the stranger was pursuing his attempt to sell a dagger. In *this* place, a tavern where unwanted persistence generally led to somebody being killed.

"Get away from me," Samlor said in a clear, clipped voice, "or I'll put you through a window."

He nodded toward the wall facing the street, where wicker lattices screened the large openings to either side of the door. The sides of the room were ventilated by high, horizontal slits that opened onto alleys even more fetid than the interior of the tavern.

Samlor meant exactly what he said, though it would cause trouble that he'd really rather avoid.

Star wasn't the only one whom fatigue had left with a hair trigger.

The man wasn't a threatening figure, only an irritating one. He was shorter than Samlor by an inch or two and fine-boned to an almost feminine degree. He wore a white linen kilt with a scarlet hem, cinched up on a slant by a belt of gorgeous gold brocade. His thigh-length cape was of a thick, soft, blue fabric, but his torso was bare beneath that garment. The skin was coppery brown, and his chest, though hairless, was flat-muscled and clearly male.

The stranger blinked above his smile and backed a half step. Samlor caught the beers that the tapster glided to him across the surface of the bar.

"Here, Star," said the Cirdonian, handing one of the containers down to his charge. "It's what there is, so don't complain. We'll do better another time, all right?"

The beer was in leathern jacks, and the tar used to seal the leather became a major component of the liquid's flavor. It was an acquired taste—and not one Samlor, much less his niece, had ever bothered to acquire. At that, the smoky flavor of the tar might be less unpleasant than the way the brew here would taste without it.

The tapster had crooked a finger toward a dun-colored man at a corner table. Samlor would not have noticed the summons had he not been sure it was coming, but the two men began to talk in low voices at the far end of the bar.

The tavern was lighted by a lantern behind the bar and a trio of lamps hanging from a hoop in the center of the room. The terra-cotta lamps had been molded for good luck into the shape of penises.

There was no sign that the clientele of this place was particularly fortunate, and the *gods* knew they were not well lighted. The cheap lamp oil gave off as much smoke as flame, so that the tavern drifted in a haze as bitter as the faces of its denizens.

"Really, Master Samlor," said the stranger, "you *must* look at this dagger."

The Cirdonian's name made time freeze for him, though no one else in the Vulgar Unicorn appeared to take undue notice. The flat of the weapon was toward Samlor. The slim man held the hilt between thumb and forefinger and balanced the lower edge of the blade near the tip of his other forefinger—not even a razor will cut with no more force than gravity driving it.

Samlor's own belt knife was clear of its sheath, drawn by reflex without need for his conscious mind to reach to the danger. But the stranger was smiling and immobile, and the dagger he held . . .

The dagger was very interesting at that.

Its pommel was faceted with the ruddy luster of copper. The butt itself was flat and narrow, angling wider for a finger's breadth toward the hilt and narrowing again in a smooth concave arc. The effect was that of a coffin, narrow for the corpse's head and wider for his shoulders until it tapered toward his feet again.

The hilt was unusual and perhaps not unattractive, but the true wonder of the weapon was its blade.

Steel becomes more brittle as it becomes harder. The greatest mystery of the swordsmith's art is the tempering that permits blades to strike without shattering while remaining hard enough to cleave armor or an opponent's weapon.

A way around the problem is to weld a billet of soft iron to a billet of steel hardened with the highest possible carbon content. The fused bar can then be hammered flat and folded back on itself, the process repeated until iron and steel are intermingled in thousands of layers thinner than the edge of a razor.

Done correctly, the result is a blade whose hardness is

sandwiched within malleable layers that absorb shock and
give the whole resilience; but the operation requires the
flats to be cleaned before each refolding, lest oxide scale
weaken the core and cause it to split on impact like a wand
of whalebone. Few smiths had the skill and patience to
forge such blades; few purchasers had the wealth to pay
for so much expert labor.

But this stranger seemed to think Samlor fell into the
latter category—as the caravan master indeed did, if he
wanted a thing badly enough.

The blade was beautiful. It was double-edged and a foot
long, with the sharpened surfaces describing flat curves
instead of being straight tapers like those of the knife in
Samlor's hand. The blade sloped toward either edge from
the deep keel in the center which gave it stiffness—and all
along the flat, the surface danced and shimmered with the
polished, acid-etched whorls of the dissimilar metals which
comprised it.

Because of their multiple hammered refoldings, the join
lines between layers of iron and steel were as complex as
the sutures of a human skull. After the bar had been forged
and ground into a blade, the smith polished it and dipped it
into strong acid which he quickly flushed away.

The steel resisted the biting fluid, but some of the softer
iron was eaten by even the brief touch. The iron became a
shadow of incredible delicacy against which the ripples of
bright steel stood out like sunlight on mountain rapids.
Even without its functional purpose, the watermarked blade
would have commanded a high price for its appearance.

Samlor's eyes stung. He blinked, because in the wavering lamplight the spidery lines of iron against steel looked
like writing.

The stranger smiled more broadly.

"Unc—" began Star with a tug on the caravan master's
left sleeve.

The iron shadows in the heart of the blade read "He will

attack'' in Cirdonian script. A moment before they had
been only swirls of metal.

The stranger's hand slid fully onto the hilt he had been
pinching to display. He twisted it in a slashing stroke
toward Samlor's eyes.

Samlor didn't believe the words written on steel. He
didn't even believe he had seen them. But part of his
nervous system— ''mind'' would be too formal a term for
reflex at so primitive a level—reacted to the strangeness
with explosive activity.

The Cirdonian's left hand shot out and crushed the
stranger's fingers against the grip of his weapon, easily
turning the stroke into a harmless upward sweep. The
metal that Samlor touched—the copper buttcap and the
tang to which scales of dark wood were pinned to complete the hilt—were cooler than air temperature despite
having been carried beneath the stranger's cape.

Samlor's right hand slammed his own dagger up and
through the stranger's ribcage till the crosshilt stopped at
the breastbone. The caravan master could have disarmed
his opponent without putting a foot of steel through his
chest, but reflex didn't know that and instinct didn't care.

The stranger—the dead man, now, with steel from his
diaphragm to the back of his throat—lifted at the short,
powerful blow. His head snapped back—his mouth was
still smiling—and hammered the hoop which suspended
the lamps. They sloshed and went out as the heavy oil
doused their wicks.

''Star, keep behind—'' Samlor ordered as the light
dimmed and his right hand jerked down to clear his weapon
from the torso in which he had just imbedded it. The
stranger flopped forward loosely, but the blade remained
stuck.

Somebody's hurled beer mug smashed the lantern behind the bar. The Vulgar Unicorn was as dark as the
bowels of hell.

Samlor ducked and hunched back against the bar while he tugged at his knife hilt with enough strength to have forced a camel to its knees.

There was a grunt and an oak-topped table crashed over. Somebody screamed as if he were being opened from groin to gullet—as may have been the case. Darkness in a place like this was both an opportunity and a source of panic. Either could lead to slaughter.

Samlor's dagger wouldn't come free. He hadn't felt it grate bone as it went in, and it didn't feel now as if the tip were caught on ribs or the stranger's vertebrae. The blade didn't flex at all, the way it should have done if it were held at one point. It was more as if Samlor had thrust the steel into fresh concrete and were coming back a day later in a vain attempt to withdraw it.

One advantage to winning a knife fight is that you have the choice of your opponent's weapon if something's happened to yours. The Cirdonian's left hand snatched the hilt from the unresisting fingers of the man he had just killed, while his right arm swept behind him to gather up his niece.

A thrown weapon plucked his sleeve much the way the child had done a moment before. The point was too blunt to stick in the bar panel against which it crashed like a crossbow bolt.

Star wasn't there. She wasn't anywhere within the sweep of Samlor's arm, and there was no response when he desperately called the child's name.

Steel hit steel across the room with a clang and a shower of angry orange sparks. Someone outside the tavern called a warning, but there was already a murderous scuffle blocking the only door to the street.

That left the door to the alley on the opposite side of the tavern; stairs to the upper floor—which Samlor couldn't locate in the dark and which were probably worth his life to attempt anyway; and a third option which was faster and safer than the other two, though it was neither fast nor safe on any sane scale.

Samlor gripped the body of his victim beneath both armpits and rushed forward, using the corpse as a shield and a battering ram.

His niece might still be inside the Vulgar Unicorn, but he couldn't find her in the darkness if she didn't—or couldn't—answer his call. Star was a level-headed girl who might have screamed but wouldn't have panicked to silence when Samlor shouted for her.

He was much more concerned that she had bolted for the door the instant the lights went out, and that she was now in the arms of someone with a good idea of the price a virgin of her age would fetch in this hellhole.

Somebody brushed Samlor from the side—backed into him—and caromed off, wailing in terror. Samlor did not cut with his new dagger at the contact because Star could still be within reach of his blade . . .

He was willing to be stabbed himself to avoid making that sort of mistake.

Samlor stumbled on an outstretched limb which gave but did not twitch beneath his boot. Then the corpse hit the screen to the right of the door and the Cirdonian used all the strength of his back and shoulders to smash the wicker-work out into the street.

The screen was dry with age, and many of the individual withies were already splitting away from the tiny tre-nails that pinned them to the frame. The wicker still retained a springy strength greater than that of thin board shutters, and Samlor felt a hint of infuriating backthrust against his push.

The frame snapped away from the sash, letting the corpse carry the collapsing wickerwork ahead of it into the street.

There was enough haze to hide the stars and silver moon, but the sky glow was enough to fill the window

sash after the lattice had been torn away. Samlor dived
over the sill, keeping his body as low as possible. He
could have boosted himself with his empty right hand so
that he landed feet first instead of slamming the street with
his shoulder . . .

But if he had done that, the knife that flicked through
the air above his rolling body would instead have punched
between his shoulder blades. Some brawlers, like sharks in
a feeding frenzy, don't need a reason to kill; only a target.

"*Star!*" the caravan master bellowed as he hit, the
shock of impact turning the word into more of a gasp than
he had expected. His cloak and shoulder muscles had to
break the fall, because his left hand, the downside hand,
held the long knife that could be the margin of survival in
the next instants.

The door of the tavern beside Samlor was blocked by
two men, the larger holding the smaller and stabbing with
mindless repetition. The only sound the victim made now
was the *squelch* of his flesh parting before the steel.

A watchman had stepped from a door down the street.
The lantern he raised did not illuminate figures, but
its light wavered from metal in the hands of half a dozen
men scurrying toward the altercation.

Samlor had heard that there were local militias raised
from every few blocks of the Old City. They differed from
street gangs in their expressed determination to keep order
and protect their enclaves—but that didn't mean it would
be healthy for an outsider to fall into their hands after
starting a brawl on their turf. Militiamen rarely saw the
need for a trial when there was already a rope or a sword
handy.

The squad marching toward the noise from the other
direction *was* paid to enforce the law, but the priorities of
the men comprising the unit tended to be more personal.
They were regular army, and the quicker they silenced the
trouble, the quicker they could get the fuck back to the

patrol station where they didn't have to worry about show-
ers of bricks and roofing tiles.

One of the soldiers carried a lantern on a pole. The
glazing was protected by wire mesh, and similar metal
curtains depended stiffly from the brims of the squad's
dented helmets. They carried pole arms, halberds, and
short pikes, and they shuffled forward with such noisy
deliberation that it was obvious they hoped the problem
would go away without any need for them to deal with it.

Samlor was willing enough to do that. The problem was
how.

Star wasn't in the street and wasn't answering him.
He'd find her if he had to wash Sanctuary away in the
blood of its denizens, but first he had to get clear of this
mess into which Fate seemed to have dropped him through
no fault of his own.

Why had that clumsy, suicidal stranger attacked him?
Why had the fellow even accosted him?

But first, survival.

Samlor switched the dagger to his right, master hand,
and dodged into the alley nearest him.

The passageway was scarcely the width of his shoulders, but a door—strapped and studded with metal—gave
onto it from the building on the other side. The Cirdonian
slapped the panel as he dodged past it. Had it opened, he
would have dived in and dealt with those inside in whatever fashion seemed advisable.

But he didn't expect that; and, as he expected, the door
was as solid as the stone to either side of it.

The alley jogged, though Samlor didn't recall an angle
from inside the Vulgar Unicorn's taproom. He slid past the
facet of masonry, into an instant of pitch darkness before
someone within the tavern reignited a lamp.

There were two slit windows serving this side of the
taproom. The grating still covered one, but the light silhouetted the crisp rectangle of the other from which the

wickerwork had been torn since the caravan master last saw it inside.

Even so, the opening was too narrow to pass an adult.

Samlor's mouth opened to call, but the child in the midst of four men was already screaming, "*Uncle Samlor!*"

There were three of them between him and Star, packed into the passageway so that the child's dust-whitened garments were only a shimmer past their legs. They were the punks from the table by the door. Beyond them was a fourth man, tall and hooded, closing Star's escape route.

Light in the passageway was only the ghost filtering through the tavern windows and reflected from the filth-blackened wall opposite, but it was enough for Samlor's business. He drew the push dagger from its sheath under the back of his collar and held it so that its narrow point jutted out between the fourth and middle fingers of his left hand.

Before the caravan master could lunge into action, the hooded man stepped past the cringing Star and held his staff vertically to confront the trio of toughs. Either the hood was flapping loose or something tiny capered on the fellow's shoulder.

"What are you doing with this child?" he demanded in a clear voice. "Begone!"

"Hey," said the nearest thug, doubtful enough to step back and jostle a companion.

The staff glowed pale blue, a hazy color which seemed to hang in the air as the object trembled. The face beneath the hood was set with determination which controlled but did not eliminate the underlying fear. The staff shook because the man holding it was terrified.

Reasonably enough.

Samlor paused. If the toughs *did* turn away in fear of what confronted them, he didn't want to be launched into an attack intended for their backs.

He didn't know what was going on. Sometimes you had

to act anyway—but just now, Star was out of immediate danger, so there was no point in going off half-cocked.

Something—a *man*, there was no damned doubt about it, but he was only a hand span tall—stood on the right shoulder of the man with the glowing staff. The little fellow hopped up and down, then piped, "Do not be afraid to do that in which you are right!"

A thug swore and swung his weapon at the staff.

Instead of blades or ordinary clubs, this trio of street toughs carried weighted chains which Samlor had mistaken in the tavern for items of armor or adornment when they were coiled through an epaulette loop on each youth's shoulder. Each chain was about a yard long, made up of fine links which slipped over one another like drops of water. They were polished glass-smooth and then plated for looks—silver for two of the thugs, gold for the third who now swung his weapon in a glittering arc.

Both ends of the chain were weighted by lead knobs the size of large walnuts, armed with steel spikes. The knobs were heavy enough to stun or kill but still so light that they could be directed handily and with blinding speed. A skilled man in the right situation could pulp an opposing knife artist, and he could do so with the sort of flashy display which on the street counted for more than success.

It was the wrong weapon for an alleyway which even at its widest point was straiter than the span of the chain fully extended, but the hooded man seemed to have no idea of how to defend himself. The weighted end of the chain wrapped itself tight against the staff—it clacked like wood, despite the glow which suggested it was of some eerie material—and the tough jerked it toward him.

The hopping manikin disappeared with a high-pitched shriek of terror. The hooded man staggered forward, managing to keep a hold on his staff only by lurching toward the punk whose weapon had snatched it. The blue glow was snuffed out as if the gold-plated chain had strangled the life from the wood.

The hooded man was a magician, *had* to be with his staff and capering manikin. Samlor—and probably the street toughs as well, though psychotic pride ruled the actions of their leader—expected magical retribution for the attack. A thunderbolt might shatter them, or icy needles from nowhere might lace their bodies into bloody sieves.

Nothing happened except that the leading thug gripped his opponent by the throat and shouted, "*Finish* 'im, dungbrains!" to his fellows as the victim struggled to free his chain-wrapped staff.

The caravan master waded in to do the job that magic wouldn't take care of after all.

One of the three youths hung a half step behind his fellows. Samlor punched the base of his skull left-handed. The steel cap concealed beneath the bright bandanna rapped the knuckle of the Cirdonian's index finger, but the bodkin point of Samlor's push dagger plunged in to its full length.

The youth turned and cried out, pulling clear of the two-inch blade that left a trickle of gore crawling toward the collar of his studded vest. He'd been spinning his chain between the thumb and index finger of his right hand, waiting for an opening to slap the weight into the hooded man. One of the balls gouged Samlor's thigh, but that was accident rather than deliberate counterattack.

The youth dropped his weapon and stumbled off down the alleyway, kicked in passing by the man still struggling for his staff. Star flattened herself against the wall to let him go. Her eyes and the white swirl in her hair were pools of reflected light as she stared at her uncle.

Samlor cut at the neck of the next thug with the watermarked dagger while drops of blood still winked in the air as they flew from the neck of his first target. The hilt of the unfamiliar weapon was slimmer in his hand than

the knife he'd left in the corpse, but the blade's relative
point-heaviness gave heft to the slashing blow. The youth
got his left arm up in time to block the edge with his
forearm while his leader sprayed curses and tried to clear
his chain from the staff which now held *it* rather than the
reverse.

There wasn't enough hilt for Samlor's hands. The shock
threatened to jar the knife away from him as the blade sank
deep into the leading armbone and cracked it through as
the Cirdonian twisted. The youth squealed in hopeless
panic, but luck or practice spun one end of his weighted
chain in a loop around the weapon that had crippled him.

Samlor punched the tough in the chest left-handed, then
jerked down on the butt of his coffin-hilted dagger. The
youth's leather vest was sewn with flat metal washers; the
narrow point in Samlor's left hand scratched across the
face of one before it sank deep enough into unprotected
flesh to prick a lung.

Whether or not the metal in the dagger blade had spelled
Samlor a warning, it served well enough for a fighting
knife. At the Cirdonian's swift tug, the edges sawed through
the silvered chain and freed themselves. The severed knob
spun to the muck on the alley's cobblestones with its bit of
attached chain twitching like a lizard's tail.

The thug lost his footing and fell backward. He should
have tangled himself with his leader, but the youth with
the gilded chain danced clear. On his toes, buttocks flat-
tening against the tavern wall as his fellow sprawled beneath him, he whirled a spiked knob at Samlor in a
downward arc that split the difference between vertical and
horizontal.

The stranger's hood had flopped back and his cape was
twisted so that its broach closure was at his left shoulder
instead of his throat. When the street tough dropped him to
deal with Samlor, the man raised a hand and began to
stutter words in a language the caravan master did not

know. As the spiked chain spun at Samlor's skull in a curve as dangerous as a sword stroke, the stranger stopped talking and prodded the youth between the shoulders with his staff.

Samlor dodged back to avoid the spikes, forgetting the bulge in the wall behind that rocked him to a halt. The knob sparked across the stone and tore the Cirdonian's left ear as the youth tried to recover from the push that sent him off balance.

He didn't get the chance.

The youth wore a necklace strung with the protective charms of at least a dozen faiths, and the front of his vest was strengthened with gilt and silvered studs. None of that helped him when Samlor stabbed upward from the groin level. While the punk thrashed like a gigged frog on the twelve-inch blade, the caravan master punched him repeatedly with the push dagger, aiming at the base of the jaw just below the bandanna and the steel cap it covered.

The youth collapsed. His eyes were open and his lungs were still working well enough to form bubbles in the blood that drooled from the corner of his mouth. A mixture of body fluids and digestive products followed the blade of the long knife as Samlor withdrew it. Their foetor was briefly noticeable even in this alley.

He was probably fourteen years old or so. He looked younger, but bad diet pinched and stunted the faces of those born here into permanent childhood.

"Now the others," chirped a little voice. "Do not kill a snake and leave its tail!"

The caravan master was on his knees. He did not recall closing his eyes, but he opened them now. The man with the staff was on his feet again and straightening his disordered cape. The manikin was back on his shoulder, strutting proudly with hands on hips.

"You," said Samlor very distinctly. "Shit it in or you'll join 'em."

The little figure yelped and disappeared again.

Samlor, Star, and the stranger were alone with the dying youth. The other two toughs had disappeared down the alley, and no one else seemed to have entered the passage behind the caravan master. There were voices from within the taproom, deep and hectoring, but Samlor didn't care enough to try to understand the words.

His niece, shivering also, minced over to him without looking down and put her arms around Samlor's shoulder. "I'm sorry you hurt your ear, uncle," she said in a voice that trembled with the child's attempts to control it. "I shouldn't have—"

She hugged him harder. "But I thought I could climb up from the bench when it was dark and I *didn't* know where you were—" Her words tumbled out like flotsam in the current of the sobs wracking her little body.

"—and the, those *men* came and I couldn't *do* anything!"

"You did fine, darling," the Cirdonian muttered. He encircled the child with his left arm, careful that the point of his push dagger was turned outward. He couldn't put it away until he cleaned it, the way his right hand was wiping the watered steel of the longer knife on the pantaloons of the boy whose breathing had ceased in a pair of great shudders. "But you've gotta listen to me, or really bad things could happen."

The blade of the long dagger showed a nick midway up one edge, but it had come through the struggle at least as well as any other knife was likely to have done. Samlor tried to sheathe it and found the new blade was a trifle too broad near the tip to fit the scabbard meant for the knife it replaced.

He slid it beneath his belt instead; wiped the push dagger; and rose with that miniature weapon in his right hand while his left arm guided Star behind him again.

"Who would you be, my friend?" Samlor asked the

man who was fingering his staff now that his cape was rearranged.

"My name is Khamwas," the fellow said in a cultured voice that tried to be calm. The peak of his hood must have added several inches to his height, because he was clearly shorter than the caravan master as well as much more slightly built. "I'm a stranger here in your city."

The manikin silently reappeared on Khamwas's shoulder. The tiny features were unreadable in the dim light, but the figure's pose was apprehensive.

"Did you have a friend in that tavern?" asked the caravan master softly. When his right thumb turned to indicate the wall of the Vulgar Unicorn, the point of the push dagger winked knowingly toward Khamwas's eyes. There was an ethnic if not familial resemblance between this man and the one who had died in the Vulgar Unicorn.

"I don't know anyone in this city," Khamwas said with cautious dignity. "I'm a scholar from a far country, and I've come to ask a favor here from a man named Setios."

"Uncle, that's—" blurted Star, catching herself before Samlor's free hand could waggle a warning.

"A bird who flies to the nest of another," chirped the manikin sententiously, "will lose a feather."

"What in *hell* is that?" asked the caravan master deliberately, pointing at the manikin with his right index finger. The bodkin-bladed push dagger paralleled the gesturing finger as if by chance.

The manikin eeped and cowered. Khamwas reached across to his right shoulder with his cupped right hand, as if to shield and stroke the little creature simultaneously.

"He does no harm, sir," the self-styled scholar replied calmly. "I—when I was younger, you understand—prayed to certain powers for wisdom. They sent me this little fellow instead. His name is Tjainufi."

The manikin stared balefully at Khamwas, but his own arm reached out to pat the hand protecting him. "A fool who wants to go with a wise man," he said, "is a goose who wants to go with the slaughter knife."

Samlor blinked. He was confused, but that probably didn't matter, not compared to a dozen other things. "You know my name, then?" he said, harshly again, sure that Khamwas had to have some connection with the stranger in the tavern. A sorcerer who knew your name had the first knot in a rope of power to bind you . . .

"Sir, I know *no* one in your city," Khamwas repeated, drawing himself up and planting the staff firmly before him with his hands linked on it. "I have a daughter the age of your niece, so I—tried, I should say, to intervene when she seemed to be in difficulties."

He paused. For an instant his staff glowed again. The grain of the wood made ripples in the phosphorescence, and a haze of light wrapped Khamwas's hands like a real fog.

Star reached past her uncle and touched the staff.

The glow flicked out as Khamwas started, but a tinge of blue clung to the child's fingers as she withdrew them. Samlor did not swear, because words had power—especially at times like these. His left hand caressed his niece's hair, offering human contact when he could not be sure what help, if any, the child required.

If Khamwas's toying had done any harm, he would be fed his liver on the point of a knife.

Star giggled while both men watched her with fear born of uncertainty. She opened her fingers slowly and the glow between their tips grew and paled like the sheen of an expanding soap bubble. Then it popped as if it had never been.

Khamwas let out his breath abruptly. "Sir," he said to the caravan master, "I didn't realize. Forgive me for intruding in your affairs."

Tjainufi, who had disappeared when Star lifted light from the staff, now waggled an arm at Khamwas and said,

"Do not say, 'I am learned.' Set yourself to become wise."

Khamwas would have stepped by and continued up the alley, but Samlor restrained him with a gesture that would have become contact if the scholar had not halted. "You saved Star from a bad time before I got here," he said. "And likely you saved me, besides distracting the little bastards. My name's Samlor hil Samt." He sheathed the little dagger behind his collar. "You and I need to talk."

"All right, Master Samlor," agreed the other man, though the way his lips pursed showed that the suggestion was not one he would have made himself. He gestured up the passageway, the direction from which the Cirdonian had come, and added, "There are more suitable places to discuss matters than here, I'm certain."

"No," said Salmor flatly, "there's not."

It wasn't worth his time to explain that the direction in which Khamwas was headed would be a no-go area for at least the next hour. The passageway was narrow enough to be defended by one man, and both flanks were protected by masonry that would require siege equipment to breach. If their luck were really out, they could be attacked from both directions simultaneously, but that risk was better than being trapped in a cul-de-sac with no bolthole.

Given the nature of Sanctuary, this was probably the safest place within a league in any direction.

"What do you know about Setios?" the caravan master demanded, no more threatening than was implicit in the fact that he had already demonstrated his willingness and ability to kill.

Star was squatting, her skirts lifted and wrapped around her thighs to keep the hem from lying in the muck. A tiny glow spun within the globe of her hands as she cooed. Its color was more nearly yellow than the blue which had washed Khamwas's staff.

The glow was reflected faintly by the eyes of the dead youth.

Khamwas's face worked in something between a grimace and a moue of embarrassment as he watched the child. "Ah," he said to Samlor. "That is, ah—are you. . . ?"

The caravan master shook his head, glad to find that the question amused him rather than arousing any of the other possible emotions. "On a good day," he said, "I might be able to recite a spell without stumbling over the syllables—if somebody wrote 'em out for me really careful." That was an exaggeration, though not a great one.

"My sister, though," he added, embarrassed himself for reasons the other man should not be able to fathom, "that was more her line."

To the extent that anything besides sex was Samlane's line.

"I see," said Khamwas, and he continued to glance down at the child even as he returned to the earlier question. "I don't know Setios at all," he explained, "but I know—I've been told by, well—"

He shrugged. Samlor nodded grimly; but if this fellow called himself scholar rather than wizard, he at least recognized that the latter was a term of reproach to decent men.

"Serve your god, that he may guard you," said Tjainufi, stroking his master's—could Khamwas be called that?—right ear.

"He has," Khamwas went on after the awkward pause, "a stele from my own land, from Napata—"

"Of course," Samlor interrupted, placing the stranger at last. "The Land of the River."

"The river," Khamwas agreed with a nod of approval, "and of the desert. And in the desert, many monuments of former times"—he paused again, gave a gentle smile—"greater times for my people, some would say, though I myself am content."

"You want to . . . retrieve," said Samlor, avoiding the question of means, "a monument that this Setios has. Is he a magician?"

"I don't know," said Khamwas with another shrug. "And I don't need the stele, only a chance to look at it. And, ah, Samlor—?"

The caravan master nodded curtly to indicate that he would not take offense at what he assumed would be a tense question.

"I will pay him well for the look," the Napatan said. "It's of no value to him—not for the purpose I intend it—without other information. It will give me the location of a particular tomb, which is significant to me for other reasons."

The light in Star's hands was growing brighter, throwing the men's shadows onto the wall of the alley. Khamwas's face looked demonically inhuman because it was illuminated from below.

Samlor touched his niece's head. "Not so much, dearest," he murmured. "We don't want anybody noticing us here if we can help it."

"But—" Star began shrilly. She looked up and met her uncle's eyes. The light shrank to the size of a large pearl, too dim to show anything but itself.

"She didn't know how to do that before," said Samlor, as much an explanation to himself as one directed toward the other man. "She picks things up."

"I see," said Khamwas, and maybe he did. "Well."

He shook himself, to settle his cape and to settle himself in his resolve. "Well, Master Samlor," the Napatan continued, "I must be on." He nodded past Samlor toward the head of the alley.

"Not that way," said the caravan master wryly, though he did not move again to block the other man.

"Yes, it is," Khamwas replied with a touch of astringence. He stiffened to his full height. The manikin on his shoulder mimicked the posture, perhaps in irony. "The direction of Setios's house is precisely"—he extended his arm at an angle toward Samlor; hesitated with his eyes turned inward; and corrected the line a little further to the right—"this way. And this passage is the nearest route to the way I need to follow."

"Do not do a thing you have not first considered carefully," Tjainufi suddenly warned.

The caravan master began to chuckle. He clapped a hand in a friendly fashion on Khamwas's left shoulder. "Nearest route to having your head stuck on a pole, I'd judge," he said. The Napatan felt as fine-boned as he looked, but there was a decent layer of muscle between the skeleton and the soft fabric of his cape.

"Look," Samlor continued, "d'ye mean to tell me you don't know where in the city Setios lives, you're just walking through the place in the straightest line your . . . friends, I suppose, tell you is the way to Setios? Are these the same friends who gave you wisdom?" The caravan master nodded toward Tjainufi.

"I think that's my affair, Master Samlor," said Khamwas. He strode forward, gripping his staff vertically before him. His knuckles were white.

The manikin said, " 'What he does insults me,' says the fool when a wise man instructs him."

Khamwas halted. Samlor looked at the little figure with a frown of new surmise. There was no bad advice—only advice that was wrong for a given set of circumstances. And, just possibly, Tjainufi's advice was more appropriate than the Cirdonian had guessed.

"All I meant, friend," Samlor said, touching and then removing his hand from the other man's shoulder, "was that maybe there aren't any good districts in Sanctuary— but your straight line's sure as death taking you through the middle of the worst of what there is."

Star had stood up when Khamwas started to walk away.

The light which now clung to her left palm had put out
tendrils and was fluctuating through a series of pastels
paler than the colors of a noontime rainbow. Impulsively,
she hugged the Napatan's leg and said, "Isn't it *pretty?*
Oh, thank you!"

"It's only a—little thing," Khamwas explained apolo-
getically to the child's uncle. "It—I don't know how she
learned it from seeing what I did."

Samlor noticed that the staff glowed only when Khamwas
could concentrate on it, but that the phosphorescence in
Star's hand continued its complex evolutions of shape and
color even while his niece was hugging and smiling brightly
at the other man.

The light glinted on the bare blade of his new dagger,
harder in reflection than the source hanging in the air
seemed.

The caravan master blinked, touched his tunic over the
silver medallion of the goddess Heqt on his breast, and
only then slid the weapon back from its temporary resting
place in his belt. The twisting phosphorescence gave the
markings a false hint of motion; but they were only swirls
of metal, not the script he thought he had again seen.

Khamwas watched with controlled apprehension. Decid-
ing that it was better to go on with his proposal than to
wonder why Samlor was staring at the knife whose guard
still bore dark stains, the Napatan said, "Master Samlor,
you understand this city as I do not. And you're clearly
able to deal with, ah, with violence, should any be offered. Could I prevail on you to accompany me to the
house of Setios? I'll pay you well."

"Do not walk the road without a stick in your hand,"
Tjainufi said approvingly.

"*We* need to find Setios, Uncle Samlor," said the child
in a voice rising toward shrill. She released Khamwas and
instead tugged insistently on the elbow of her uncle's right
sleeve. "*Please* can we? He's nice."

Cold steel cannot flow, twist, parse out words, thought the caravan master. The nick in the edge was bright and real: this was no thing of enchantment, only a dagger with an awkward hilt and a very good blade.

Star pulled at Samlor's arm with most of her weight. He did not look down at her, nor did his hand drop. That arm had dragged a donkey back up to the trail from which it had stumbled into a gulley a hundred feet deep.

"*Please*," said the child.

"Friend Samlor?" said the Napatan doubtfully. The knife was only that, a knife, so far as he could see.

Go with him, spelled the rippling steel at which Samlor stared.

The words faded as the glow in Star's hand shrank to a point and disappeared.

"I was ready," said the caravan master slowly, "to find a guide in there."

He did not gesture toward the tavern. He was speaking to himself, not to the pair of living humans with him in the alleyway. They stared at Samlor, his niece, and the stranger, as they would have stared at a pet lion who suddenly began to act oddly.

"So I guess," Samlor continued, "we'll find Setios together. After all"—he tapped the blade of the coffin-hilted dagger with a fingernail; the metal gave off a musical ping—"we're all four agreed, aren't we?"

Star leaned toward her uncle and hugged his powerful thigh, but she would not meet his eyes again or look at the knife in his hand. Khamwas nodded cautiously.

"We'll circle out of the Maze, then," said Samlor matter-of-factly. "Come on."

The way down the alley meant stepping over the body of the youth he had just killed.

This was Sanctuary. It wouldn't be the last corpse they saw.

*   *   *

The body sprawled just inside the alley would have passed for a corpse if you didn't listen carefully—or didn't recognize the ragged susurrus of a man breathing while his face lay against slimy cobblestones.

"Mind this," said Samlor, touching first Star, then Khamwas, so that they would notice his gesture toward the obstacle. Human eyes could adapt to scant illumination, but at this end of the alley the dying man's breath was all that made it possible to locate him.

The manikin on Khamwas's shoulder must have been able to sense the situation, because he said, "There is no one who does not die." Tjainufi's voice was as high as a bird's; but, also like a bird's, it had considerable volume behind it.

The Napatan "scholar" reached toward his shoulder with his free hand, a gesture mingled of affection and warning. "Tjainufi," he muttered, "not now . . ."

Samlor doubted that Khamwas had any more control over the manikin than a camel driver did over a pet mouse which lived in a fold of his cloak. Or, for that matter, than Samlor himself had over his niece, who was bright enough to understand any instructions he gave her—but whose response was as likely to be willful as that of any other seven-year-old.

Now, for instance, a ball of phosphorescence bloomed in the cup of the child's hand, lighting her way past the dying man despite the caravan master's warning that illumination—magical or otherwise—would be more risk to them than benefit, at least until they got out of the Maze.

Star put a foot down daintily, just short of the victim's outflung arm, then skipped by in a motion that by its incongruity made the scene all the more horrible. The ball of light she had formed drifted behind her for a moment. Its core shrank and brightened—from will-o'-the-wisp to

firefly intensity—while the whirling periphery formed tendrils like the whorl of silver-white hair on Star's head.

The child turned back, saw the set expression on Samlor's
face, and jerked away as if he had slapped her physically.
The spin of light blanked as if it had never been.

"Is he. . . ?" asked Khamwas as he stepped over his
mind's image of where the body lay. "One of those we
. . . met a moment ago?"

"The gang who came after us with chains, sure," said
the caravan master as he followed with a long stride. The
passageway was wide enough for him to spread his arms
without quite touching the walls to either side; in the
Maze, that made it a street. It held only the normal sounds
of feral animals going about their business and, from
behind shutters, bestial humans. "They're all dead, the
two who ran off as sure as the one who didn't. Turn left
here."

"The House of Setios is more to the—"

"Turn fucking *left*," Samlor whispered in a voice like
stones rubbing.

"Do not be a hindrance, lest you be cursed," said
Tjainufi on the Napatan's shoulder. The manikin bowed
toward Samlor, but the caravan master was too angry to
approve of anything.

Mostly he was angry at himself, because he'd killed
often enough during his life to know that he really didn't
like killing. Especially not kids, even punk kids who'd
have caved his skull in with weighted chains and raped
Star until they sold her to a brothel for the price of a skin
of wine . . .

Sanctuary might be incrementally better off without that
particular trio; but Samlor hil Samt wasn't Justice, wasn't
responsible to his god for the cleansing of this hellhole.

They got out of the Maze with no problem worse than a
pair of thugs—who fled in terror as Khamwas's staff sent a

manlike phantasm of light staggering down the street toward them. Broader pavements made walking easier, and many housefronts were lighted by lanterns in barred niches.

The lanterns weren't an act of charity toward travelers. They were intended to drive lurking footpads into somebody else's doorway.

Khamwas paused, then directed them up one arm of a five-way intersection, past a patrol station. The gate to the internal courtyard was lighted by flaring sconces, and there was a squad on guard outside. An officer took a step into the street as if to halt the trio, but he changed his mind after a pause.

They were in the neighborhood of the palace now, a better section of the city. The residents here stole large sums with parchment and whispered words instead of cutting wayfarers' throats for a few coins.

And the residents expected protection from their lesser brethren in crime. The troops here would check a pair of men, detain them if they had no satisfactory account of their business; kill them if any resistance were offered.

But two men carrying a young child were unlikely burglars. Most probably, they were part of the service industry catering to Sanctuary's wealthy and powerful . . . and the rich did not care to have their nighttime sports delayed by uniformed officiousness. Samlor had no need for the bribe—or the knife—he had ready.

"We're getting close, I think," Khamwas remarked. He lifted his head as if to sniff the air which even here would have been improved by a cloudburst to ram effluvium from the street down into the harbor.

Samlor grimaced and looked around him. He wanted to know how Khamwas found his directions . . . but he didn't want to ask; and anyway, he wouldn't understand if the scholar/magician took the time to explain.

Worse, Star likely *would* understand.

"I wonder what Setios is keeping for her," the caravan

master whispered, so softly that the child could not hear even though Samlor's lips brushed her fine hair as he spoke.

"Is it going to rain?" Star asked sleepily from the cradle of Samlor's arm.

The caravan master glanced at the sky. There were stars, but a scud of high clouds blocked and cleared streaks across them at rapid intervals. There was an edge in the air which might well be harbinger of a storm poised to sweep from the hills to the west of town and wash the air at least briefly clean.

"Perhaps, dearest," the Cirdonian said. "But we'll be all right."

They'd be under cover, he hoped; or, better yet, back in a bolted chamber of the caravansary on the White Foal River before the storm broke.

Khamwas began to mutter something with his fingers interlaced on the top of his staff. Star shook herself into supple alertness and hopped off her uncle's supporting arm. She did not touch the Napatan, but she watched his face closely as he mouthed words in a language the caravan master did not recognize.

Left to his own devices—unwilling to consider what his niece was teaching herself now, and *barely* unwilling to order her to turn away—Samlor surveyed the houses in their immediate neighborhood.

It was an old section of the city, but wealthy and fashionable enough that there had been considerable rebuilding to modify the original Ilsigi character. Directly across from Samlor's vantage place, the front of a house had been demolished and was being replaced by a two-story portico with columns of colored marble. A lamp burned brightly on a shack amid the construction rubble, and a watchman's eyes peered toward the trio from its unglazed window.

The other houses were quiet, though all save the one

against which Samlor's party sheltered guarded their fa-
cades with lamplight. At this hour, business was most
likely to be carried on through back entrances or trap doors
to tunnels that were older than the Ilsigs . . . and possibly
older than humanity.

It might be a bad time to meet Setios; but again, it might
not. He'd been an associate of Star's mother, which meant
at the least that he was used to strange hours and unusual
demands.

He'd see them in now, provide the child with her
legacy—if it were here. If it were portable. If Setios were
willing to meet the terms of an agreement made with a
woman now long dead.

Samlor swore, damning his sister Samlane to a hell
beneath all the hells; and knowing as he recited the words
under his breath that any afterlife in which Samlane found
herself was certain to be worse than her brother could
imagine.

"*This* is the house," said Khamwas with a note of
wonder in his voice. He and the child turned to look at the
facade of the building against which the caravan master
leaned while he surveyed the rest of the neighborhood.

"Looks pretty quiet," said Samlor. The words were less
an understatement than a conversational placeholder while
the Cirdonian considered what might be a real problem.

The building didn't look quiet. It looked abandoned.

It was a blank-faced structure. Its second floor was
corbeled out a foot or so but there was no real front
overhang to match those of the houses to either side. The
stone ashlars had been worn smooth by decades or more of
sidewalk traffic brushing against them; the mortar binding
them could have used tuck pointing, but that was more a
matter of aesthetics than structural necessity.

The only ground-floor window facing the street was a
narrow slit beside the iron-bound door. There was a grate-
protected niche for a lantern on the other side of the door

alcove; the stones were blackened by carbon from the flame, but the lamp within was cold and dark. It had not been lighted this night, and perhaps not for weeks past.

There was no sign of life through the slit intended to give a guard inside a look at whoever was calling.

"Perhaps I'm wrong," said Khamwas uncertainly. "This *should* be the house of Setios, but I—I can't be sure I'm right."

He made as if to bend over his staff again, then straightened and said decisively, "No, I'm sure it must be the house—but perhaps he doesn't live here anymore." The Napatan stepped to the street-level door and raised his staff to rap on the panel.

"Ah . . ." said Samlor.

The caravan master held the long dagger he had taken from the man he killed in the Vulgar Unicorn. The weapon belonged in his hand when they prowled through the Maze, but it wasn't normal practice to knock on a stranger's door with steel bare in your hand.

On the other hand, this was Sanctuary; and anyway, the new knife didn't fit in the sheath of the one Samlor had left in the corpse.

"Go ahead," he said to Khamwas. The Napatan was poised, watching the caravan master and waiting for a suggestion to replace his own intent.

Khamwas nodded, Star mirroring his motion as if hypnotized by tiredness. He rapped twice on the door panel. The sound of wood on wood was sharp and soulless.

"Won't be anybody there," said Samlor. His own eyes were drawn to the watermarked blade of the knife. *His* knife, now; the owner wasn't going to claim it with a foot of steel through his chest. The whorls of blended metals, iron black against polished steel, were only memories in the distant lamplight. There was no way Samlor could see them now, even if they began to spell words as he had watched them do—in defiance of reason—twice before.

The caravan master shook himself out of the clouded reverie into which fatigue was easing him. He needed rest as badly as his niece did, and it looked as though there was no way he was going to clear up his business tonight anyway.

"Look," he said, irritated because Khamwas still faced the door as if there were a chance it would open. "There's nobody here, and—"

Metal clanked as the bar closing the door from inside was withdrawn from its staples. The door leaf opened inward, squealing on bronze pivots set into the lintel and transom instead of hanging from strap hinges.

"No one will see you," said the voice of the figure standing in the doorway. Whatever else the doorkeeper might be, it was not human.

The creature was shorter than Star. Fur clothed its body and long tail in ashen luster, but the frame beneath was skeletally thin. Its features had the pointed sharpness of a fox's muzzle, and there was no intelligence whatever in its beady eyes.

"Wait," said Samlor hil Samt as the doorkeeper began to close the portal again. He set his boot against the iron-strapped lower edge of the door. "Your master holds a trust f-for my niece Star."

"No one will see you," the creature repeated. Behind it was another set of door leaves, reinforced like the first, combining to form a closet-sized anteroom which could probably be flooded with anything from boiling water to molten lead.

If there were anyone alive in the house to do so. The doorkeeper spoke in a thin, breathy voice, but its chest did not rise and fall.

"It isn't real," Khamwas was saying in a universe in which Samlor was not focused in terrified determination on the unhuman—unalive—doorkeeper of this house. "It's a simulacrum like the—"

"No one will see you," the doorkeeper repeated without emphasis. It swung the panel shut, thrusting Samlor violently backward even though he tried to brace himself by stiffening his supporting leg behind him.

"I will *have* Star's legacy!" the caravan master shouted as he hurled himself back against the door, slamming into it with the meat of his left shoulder.

The panel thumped but did not rebound. The bar crashed into place.

"I *will*!" Samlor cried again. "Depend on it!"

His voice echoed, but there was no sound at all from within the house.

"It wasn't really present," said Khamwas, touching the other man's shoulder to calm him.

"It's there enough for me," said Samlor grimly, massaging his bruised shoulder with the faceted knife hilt. "Might've tried t' stop a landslide for all I could do to keep it from slamming the door."

At a venture, he poked his dagger blade through the slit beside the door, in and out quickly like a snake licking the air. Nothing touched the metal, nor was there any other response.

"He who shakes the stone," said—warned?—Tjainufi, "will have it fall on his foot."

"I mean," said Khamwas hastily to deflect possible wrath from his manikin, "that it's no more than a part of the door. A trick only, without volition or consciousness. It's carrying out the last order it was given, the way a bolt lies in its groove when the master releases it. No one may be present."

"If we go in *there*," said Star distinctly, pointing at the door, "we'll be . . . *krrk*." The child cocked her head up as if her neck had been wrung. "Like chickens," she added as she relaxed, grinning.

Samlor's breath wheezed out. He had thought . . .

"Well, Star," said the Napatan scholar, "I might be

able to keep the wraith from moving for a time, long enough for us to get past the . . . zone of which it's a part. I *might*. But I think we'd best not go in by this door until Setios permits us to pass.''

The two of them smiled knowingly at one another.

Samlor restrained his impulse to do something pointlessly violent. He looked at the blade of his knife instead of glaring at his companions and began in a very reasonable tone, ''In that case, we'd best get some sleep and—''

''Actually,'' said Khamwas, not so much interrupting as speaking without being aware that Samlor was in the middle of a statement, ''neither of us have business with Setios himself, only with items in his possession. I wonder . . .''

''*I* want my gift *now*,'' said Star, her face set in the slanting lines of temper. Either she tossed her head slightly, or the whorl of white strands in her curly black hair moved on its own.

GO IN NOW read the iron letters on the blade at which Samlor stared in anger. There was too little light for the markings to be visible, but he saw them nonetheless.

''Heqt take you all to the waters beneath the earth!'' shouted the Cirdonian in fury. He slashed the air with his dagger as if to wipe away the message crawling there in the metal. ''I'm not a burglar, and coming to this *damned* city doesn't make me one.''

''When you are hungry, eat what you despise,'' said the manikin on Khamwas's shoulder. ''When you are full, despise it.''

''Anyway,'' said Star, ''it's going to rain, Uncle Samlor.'' She looked smug at the unanswerable truth of her latest argument.

The caravan master began to laugh.

Khamwas blinked, as frightened by the apparent humor as he had been by the anger that preceded it. Emotional outbursts by a man as dangerous as the caravan master

were like creakings from the dike holding back flood
waters.

"Well," the Napatan said cautiously, "I suppose the
situation may change for the better by daylight. Though of
course neither of us were considering theft. I want to look
at a slab of engraved stone, and you simply wish to
retrieve your niece's legacy from its caretaker—who seems
to be absent."

"We don't know what it *is*," said Star. "My gift."

"Ah," said Khamwas, speaking to the girl but with an
eye cocked toward her uncle. "That shouldn't be an insur-
mountable problem. If we're inside"—he nodded toward
the door—"and the object is there also, I should be able to
locate it for you."

"Will you show *me* how?" Star begged, clasping her
hands together in a mixture of pleading and premature
delight.

"Ah . . ." repeated the Napatan scholar. "I think that
depends on what your uncle says, my dear."

"Her uncle says that we're not inside yet," Samlor
stated without particular emphasis. "And he'll see about
getting there."

Without speaking further to his companions, the Cirdonian
walked to the corner of the building.

Setios's house was two feet away from the building
beside it. There were no ground-floor windows in the
sidewall either, but the second story was ventilated by
barred openings.

Samlor stepped through the gap, too narrow to be called
an alley anywhere but in the Maze. He ignored his companions, though they followed him gingerly in lieu of any
other directions.

The vertical bars of the window above him were thumb-
thick and set with scarcely more room than that between
them. Star might have been able to reach through one of

the spaces, but the caravan master was quite certain that his own big hands would not fit.

"Are there going to be things like that door-monkey waiting by the windows?" Samlor asked the other man quietly. He nodded upward to indicate the opening he had studied.

Khamwas shrugged in darkness relieved only by the strip of clouded sky above them. "I would expect human servants if anything," he said. "They're . . . more trustworthy, in many ways. And from what I've gathered, Setios is a collector the way I'm a scholar. Neither of us, you understand, are magicians of real power."

He paused and tucked his lip under his front teeth in doubt, then added, "The way your niece here appears to be, Master Samlor."

"Yeah," said the caravan master without emotion. His left hand tousled Star's hair gently, but he did not look down at the child. "And he collected a demon in a bottle, among other things."

Samlor grimaced, then went on, "Let's get out t' the street again. You wait, and I'll go talk to the fellow across the way there."

"Ah, Samlor. . . ?" Khamwas said.

"Just wait here," the Cirdonian repeated. "I'm going across the street to talk with the watchman there." He nodded toward the guard shack on the construction site opposite.

"Yes, of course," Khamwas said with enough disinterest to hint at irritation. "But what I wanted to say was— Setios, you see, may not be avoiding you. There's been a recent upheaval in the structure of, you see, magic. He may have become frightened and fled from that."

The Napatan grinned. "He'll have left behind the stele I want to read, surely. Probably his whole collection, if *that* fear is why he left. And, as for this child's legacy"—he touched Star's cheek affectionately—"if we don't find it here, I'll help you locate it. Because you've helped me. And because I am honored to help someone as talented as your niece.''

''The plans of gods are one thing,'' said the manikin on his shoulder. ''The thoughts of men are another.''

''Yeah, well,'' said the caravan master, then strode across the street with a swaggering assurance which immediately set him apart in a city where lone men habitually slunk. The watchman edged back from his window so that his eyes no longer reflected light.

It took five pieces of Rankan gold and ten minutes cajoling the nervous watchman at the construction site before Samlor returned to his companions with the house jack he had borrowed.

''Khamwas,'' he said gruffly, ''come help me with the window.''

Star was curled in the corner of the door alcove, dozing with the Napatan's cape for a pillow. Khamwas stood in front of her, watching the street as well as the caravan master. He was very slim without the bulk of the outer garment, and his bare chest was no garb for this night.

''I, ah,'' he said, looking down at the child. ''I thought it would be good if she got some rest, so . . . She's very like my own daughter, you know.''

''Wish I had more talent for what she needs,'' said the caravan master quietly, staring at the child also. ''Wish I *knew* what she needs, what any kid needs. But you do what you can.''

He grimaced again. ''Bring 'er along, will you? I need you at the side to hand me this jack when I'm ready for it''—he fluffed his cloak open to display the tool—''and I don't want her in plain sight on the street, even though it means getting her up again.''

The sky had closed in above the passage between the two buildings. It was as dark as a narrow cave, and for the time being the air was as motionless as that of a cavern miles below the ground. Samlor found his location by subconscious memory of the six cautious paces which had brought him beneath the window when he could see it.

Samlor climbed to the window by bracing his hands and feet against the closely adjacent buildings. That wasn't hard, but he almost fell when he bent to take the jack which Khamwas raised to him. He was tired, and it was affecting him.

Already.

The window grate might have withstood a battering ram. The screw jack, butted against the stone sash, exerted its pressure sideways across the bars and their frame. The grating crumbled as the Cirdonian inexorably levered the jack through it, ignoring what the effort was doing to his fatigued muscles.

With the last of his strength, Samlor lurched through the opening he had just torn and sprawled onto the floor of the room beyond.

"Praised be Heqt in whom the world lives," murmured Samlor as his senses returned him to the world beyond his own effort and necessities. The marble floor beneath him was cold and slick with water. The glazed windows had not been closed the last time it rained; and that, from idle chatter overheard at the caravansary, had been more than a week ago.

Khamwas called from the alley, his words blurred but the worry in them clear.

"It's all right," the caravan master said, then realized that he wasn't sure he could understand the croaked words himself. He gripped the window ledge, fragments of the grate chiming around his knees.

"It's all right," he repeated, leaning back through the opening by which he had entered. "Just a minute and I'll find"—his hand brushed a tapestry beside the window—

"yeah, just a second and I'll have something for you t' climb by."

He ripped the hangings down and dangled them from the window for his companions. Samlor no longer cared what damage they did to this place—so long as they got out of it soon.

The window was scarcely visible as a rectangle, and the still air smelled of storm.

There was a discussion below. Star came up the tapestry, flailing her legs angrily behind her. There was a pout in her voice as she demanded, "What *is* this old place? I don't like it."

Maybe she felt something about the house—and maybe she was an overtired seven-year-old and therefore cranky.

There wasn't time to worry about it. The caravan master gripped the child beneath the shoulders with his left arm and lifted her into the room. Star yelped as her head brushed the transom, but she should've had sense enough to duck.

"My staff, Master Samlor," said Khamwas.

The Cirdonian leaned forward and caught the vague motion that proved to be the end of an ordinary wooden staff when his fingers enclosed it. Behind him, the room lighted vaguely with pastel blue.

Star shouldn't have done it without asking; but they needed light, and a child *wasn't* a responsible adult. Samlor slid the staff behind him with his left hand while supporting the tapestry with his right hand and his full weight to pin the end to the floor.

The Napatan scholar mounted gracefully and used Samlor's arm like the bar of a trapeze to swing himself over the lintel. Only then did the caravan master turn to see where they were and what his niece was doing.

Star had set swimming through the air a trio of miniature octopuses made of light. A blue one drifted beneath the ceiling frescoed with scenes of anthropomorphic deities; a yellow one prowled beneath the legs of a writing table sumptuous with mother-of-pearl inlays.

The third miniature octopus was of an indigo so pale that it barely showed up against the carven door against which it bobbed feebly.

"Where's . . ." Samlor said as he looked narrowly at Khamwas. "You know, your little friend?"

Tjainufi reappeared on the Napatan's right shoulder. The manikin moved with the silent suddenness of an image in an angled mirror, now here and now not, as the tilt changes. "The warp does not stray far from the woof," he said in cheerful satisfaction.

"Khamwas," the Cirdonian added as he looked around them, "if you can locate what we're after, then get to it. I *really* don't want t' spend any longer here than I need to."

"Look, uncle," Star squealed as she pranced over to the writing desk. "Mommy's *box*!"

Samlor's speed and reflexes were in proper form after his exertions, but his judgment was off. He attempted to spring for the desk before Star got there, and his boots skidded out from under him on the wet marble. Because he'd swept the long dagger from his belt as part of the same unthinking maneuver, he had only his left palm to break his fall. The shock made the back of his hand tingle and the palm burn.

Khamwas had retrieved his staff. He stopped muttering to it when the Cirdonian slapped the floor hard enough to make the loose bars roll and jingle among themselves. "Are you. . . ?" he began, offering a hand to the sprawling bigger man.

"See, Uncle Samlor?" said the child, returning to the caravan master with an ivory box in her hands. "It's got mommy's mark on it."

"No, go on with your business," said Samlor calmly to the Napatan. He felt the prickly warmth of embarrassment painting his skin, but he wouldn't have survived this long if he lashed out in anger every time he'd made a public fool of himself. "Find the stele you're after, and then we'll see what Star's got here."

He took the box from the child as quickly as he could without letting it slip from his numbed fingers. Even if it were just what it seemed—a casket of Samlane's big enough to hold a pair of armlets—it could be extremely dangerous.

Much of what Samlor's sister had owned, and had known, fell into that category, one way or another.

Khamwas's face showed the concern which any sane man would feel under the circumstances, but he resumed his meditation on—or prayers to—his staff.

Star's palm-sized creatures of light continued their slow patrol of the room. The caravan master seemed to have broken into a large study. There was a couch to one side of the door and on the other the writing desk with matching chair. The chair lay on its back, as if its last occupant had jumped up hastily.

"*Open* it, uncle!" Star demanded.

Khamwas still murmured over his staff, so the caravan master got up with caution born of experience and walked over to the writing desk. A triple-wicked oil lamp hung from a crane attached to the desk top. It promised real illumination when Samlor lit it with the brass fire-piston in his wallet.

"There's no oil, Uncle Samlor," said Star with the satisfaction of a child who knows more than an adult. She cupped her hand again and turned it up with a saffron glow in the palm. The creatures of light still drifting about the room dimmed by comparison. "See?"

The bowl of the lamp was empty except for a sheen in its center, oil beyond the touch of the wicks. Only one of the three wicks had been lighted at the lamp's last use. When the flame had consumed all the oil, it reduced the twist of cotton to ash. The other wicks were sharply divided into black and white, ready to function if the fuel supply were renewed.

Setios had really left in a hurry.

"Fine, hold the light were it is, darling," Samlor said to his niece as calmly as if he were asking her to pass the bread at table. The casket wasn't anything which the Cirdonian remembered from his youth, but the family crest—the rampant wyvern of the House of Kodrix—was enameled on the lid. Beneath it was carved in Cirdonian script the motto AN EAGLE DOES NOT SNATCH FLIES.

Samlor's parents had never forgiven him for running high-risk, high-profit caravans like a commoner instead of vegetating in noble poverty. But they'd lived well—drunk well, at least—on the flies he snatched for them, and the money Samlor provided had bought his sister a marriage with a Rankan noble.

Which couldn't save Samlane from herself, but was the best effort possible for a brother who didn't claim to be a god.

The lid did not rise under gentle pressure from his left thumb. There was no visible catch or keyhole, but the little object had to be a box—it didn't weigh enough for a block of solid ivory. Samlor put his dagger down on the desk to free his right hand . . .

And read the superscription on the piece of parchment there, a letter barely begun:

"To Master Samlor hil Samt
 If you are well, it is good. I also am well.
 I enclose w

The script was Cirdonian, and the final letter trailed off in a sweep of ink across the parchment. Following the curve of that motion, Samlor saw a delicate silver pen on the marble floor a few feet to the side of the desk.

Samlor set down the ivory box, and he very deliberately kept the weapon in his hand. From the look of matters,

Setios might have been better off if he'd been holding a blade and not a pen a week or so earlier. Instinctively, the caravan master's left arm encircled Star, locating the child while he turned and said, "Khamwas. This is important. I think I've been doing Setios an injustice, thinking he'd ducked out to avoid me."

The other man was so still that not even his chest moved with the process of breathing. The absolute stillness was camouflaged for a moment by the fact that the octopuses threw slow, vague shadows as they circled the room. The manikin on Khamwas's shoulder was executing some sort of awkward dance with his legs stiff and his arms akimbo.

"Khamwas!" the caravan master repeated sharply. "I think we need to get outta here *now*."

Tjainufi said, "Do not say, 'I will undertake the matter,' if you will not."

Almost simultaneously, the Napatan shook himself like a diver surfacing after a deep plunge and opened his eyes. He stood, wobbling a little and using the staff for support. His face broadened with a smile of bright relief.

"Samlor," he said, obviously ignorant of anything that had happened around him since he dropped into a trance. "I've found it—or at least we need to go down."

"We need to—" began the caravan master angrily. Tjainufi was watching him. The manikin's features were too small to have readable expression in this light, but the creature must think that . . .

"Look," Samlor resumed, speaking to—at—Tjainufi, "I don't mean I want to get out because we found what *I* wanted, I mean—"

"Oh!" said Star. There was a mild implosion, air rushing to fill a small void. "There's nothing inside."

She'd opened the box, Samlor saw as he turned. His emotions had gone flat—they'd only be in the way just now—and his senses gave him frozen images of his surroundings in greater detail than he would be able to imagine when he wasn't geared to kill or run.

A narrow plate on the front of the ivory box slid sideways to expose a spring catch. When the child pressed that—the scale of the mechanism was so small that Samlor would have had to work it with a knifepoint—the lid popped up.

To display the inner surfaces of the ivory as highly polished as the exterior; and nothing whatever within.

Star was looking up at him with a pout of disappointment. She held the box in both hands and the ball of light, detached from her palm, was shrinking in on itself and dimming as its color slipped down through the spectrum.

For an instant—for a timeless period, because the vision was unreal and therefore nothing his eyes could have taken in—Samlor saw blue-white light through a gap in the cosmos where the whorl of white hair on Star's head should have been. It was like looking into the heart of the thunderbolt . . .

And it wasn't there, in the room or his daughter's face—for Star was that, damn Samlane as she surely *was* damned—or even as an afterimage on Samlor's retinas when he blinked. So it hadn't really been there, and the caravan master was back in the world where he had promised to help Khamwas find a stele in exchange for help locating Star's legacy.

Which it appeared they had yet to do, but he'd fulfill his obligations to the Napatan. He shouldn't have needed a reminder from Tjainufi of that.

"Friend Khamwas," Samlor said, "we'll go downstairs if you want that. But"—his left index finger made an arc from the parchment toward the fallen silver pen—"something took Setios away real sudden, and I wouldn't bet it's not still here."

Khamwas caught his lower lip between his front teeth.

He was wearing his cape again, but the caravan master remembered how frail the Napatan had looked without it.

"The man who looks in front of him does not stumble and fall," said the manikin with his usual preternatural clarity of voice.

"Samlor," said the Napatan, "I appreciate what you say . . . but what I seek is here, and I've made a very long—"

"Sure," the caravan master interrupted. "I just mean we be careful, all right?"

"And you, child," Samlor added in a voice as soft as a cat's claws extending. He knelt so that Star could meet his eyes without looking up. "You don't touch anything, do anything. Do you understand? Because if the only way to keep you safe is to tie you up and carry you like a sack of flour—that's what I'll do."

Star nodded, her face scrunched up on the verge of tears. The drifting glows dwindled noticeably.

"Everything's going to be fine, dearest," the caravan master said, giving the child an affectionate pat as he rose.

It bothered him to have to scare his niece in order to get her to obey—while she remembered—but she scared *him* every time she did something innocently dangerous, like opening the ivory box. Better she be frightened than that she swing from his arm, trussed like a hog.

Because Samlor didn't threaten in bluff.

Khamwas said something under his breath. His staff clothed itself in the bluish phosphorescence it held when the caravan master first met him in an alley. With the staff's unshod ferule, the Napatan prodded the study door, lifting the bronze latch. When nothing further happened, he pulled the door open with his free hand and preceded Samlor and Star into the hall beyond.

Samlor touched the latch as he stepped past it. Not a particularly sturdy piece—typical for an inside door, when the occupant is more concerned with privacy than protection. But it *had* been locked, which meant somebody had paused in the hallway to do so with a key after he closed the door.

Otherwise, it would have to have been locked from the inside by somebody who wasn't there any more.

In the old Ilsigi fashion, a balustraded hallway encircled a reception room which pierced the second floor. There was a solid roof overhead rather than the skylight which would have graced a Rankan dwelling of similar quality.

The stairwell to the ground floor was in the corner to the left of the study door. Khamwas's staff, pale enough to be a revenant floating at its own direction, swirled in that direction.

"The, ah," Samlor said, trying to look in all directions and unable to see anything more than a few inches beyond the phosphorescent staff. "The doorkeeper. It's not. . . ?"

"We wouldn't meet it even if we opened the front door ourselves from within," said Khamwas as he stepped briskly down the helical staircase. "It isn't, you see, a *thing*. It's a set of circumstances which have to fit as precisely as the wards of a lock.

"Though it wouldn't," he added a few steps later, "be a good idea for anyone to force the door from the outside. Even if they were a much greater scholar than I. Ah, Setios collected some . . . artifacts . . . that he might more wisely have left behind."

The reception room was chilly. Samlor thought it might have something to do with the glass-smooth ornamental pond in the middle of the room. He tested the water with his boot toe and found it, as expected, no more than an inch deep. It would be fed by rainwater piped from the roof gutters. Barely visible in the shadow beneath the coaming were the flat slots from which overflow drained in turn into a cistern.

Except for the pond, the big room was antiseptically bare. The walls between top and bottom moldings were painted in vertical pastel waves reminiscent of a kelp forest, and the floor was a geometric pattern in varicolored marble.

"Well, which way now?" the caravan master demanded brusquely, his eyes on the doorway to the rear half of the house. Star was shivering despite wrapping her cloak tighter with both hands, and Samlor didn't like the feel of the room a bit either.

"Down still," said Khamwas in puzzlement. He rapped the ferule of his staff on the floor, a sharp sound that contained no information useful—at least—to the caravan master. Perhaps it just seemed like the right thing to do.

"There'll be a cistern below," said Samlor, gesturing with a dripping boot toe toward the pond. "The access hatch'd be in the kitchen, most likely. Not in this room."

He started for a door, ill at ease and angry at himself for that feeling of undirected fear. Part of his mind yammered that the Napatan was a fool who again mistook a direction for a pathway . . . and Samlor had to avoid that, avoid picking excuses to snarl at those closest to him in order to conceal fears he was embarrassed to admit.

Star poked a hand between the edges of her cloak. She did not look up; but when her finger cocked, a bright spark swam rapidly from it and began coasting the lower wall moldings.

"D-dearest," said the caravan master, glancing at the withdrawn, miserable-looking face of his niece, then back to the light source. Star said nothing.

The droplet of light was white and intense by contrast with the vague glows that both—he had to admit the fact—magicians had created earlier in the evening. It might even have looked bright beside a candle, but Samlor had difficulty remembering anything as normal as candlelight while he stood in this chill, stone room.

Pulse and pause; pulse and pause; pulse . . . He'd thought that the creature of light was a minnow, or perhaps no more than a daub of illumination, a cold flame that did not counterfeit life.

But it surely did. A squid rather than a fish, too small to see but identifiable from the way it jetted forward with rhythmic contractions of its mantle.

The marble floor was so highly polished that it mirrored the creature's passage with nearly perfect fidelity, catching even the wispy shadows between the tightly clasped tentacles of light trailing behind. The colors and patterning of the stone segments created the illusion that the reflection really swam through water.

"*Star*," the caravan master demanded in a restrained voice. "Why are you—"

The reflection blurred into a soft ball of light on a slab of black marble, though the tiny creature jetted above it in crystalline purity. The squid pulsed forward and hung momentarily over a wedge of travertine whose dark bands seemed to enfold the sharp outline.

Then source and reflection disappeared as abruptly as they had spurted from the child's gesture.

"What?" said Star, shivering fiercely. She scrunched her eyes shut so that her uncle thought she was about to cry. "What *happened*?"

Samlor patted her, blinking both at the sudden return of darkness and his realization of what he had just seen. Star might not know what she had done or why, but the caravan master did.

"Khamwas, come over here, will you?" he said, amused at the elation he heard in his voice as he strode to the sidewall where the thing of light had disappeared. "You know, I'd about decided we were going t' have t' give up or come back with a real wrecking crew."

"A hundred men are slain through one moment of discouragement," said the manikin on Khamwas's shoulder.

"In this town," the caravan master responded sourly, "you can be slain for less reason 'n that."

"I, ah," said the Napatan scholar. "What would you like me to do?"

"Star, come closer, sweetest," Samlor cajoled when he realized his niece had not followed him. Something was wrong with her, or else she was reacting strongly to the malaise of this house— which affected even the relatively insensitive caravan master.

She obeyed his voice with the halting nervousness of a frequently whipped dog. Her hands were hidden again within her cloak.

Samlor put his arm around her shoulders, all he could do until they'd *left* this accursed place, and said to the other man, "Can you make it lighter down here? By the wall?"

Khamwas squatted and held his staff parallel with the edge molding. The phosphorescence was scarcely any light at all to eyes which had adapted to the spark from Star's finger, but it was sufficient to distinguish the square of black marble from the pieces of travertine to either side of it in the intaglio flooring.

Samlor could not discern a difference in the polish of the black marble from that of the rest, but the way it blurred the light which the others had mirrored proved what would have been uncertain under any other conditions.

He tried the stone with the tip of his right little finger; the rest of the hand continued to grip the hilt of his long knife. The block didn't give to light pressure, neither downward nor on either of its horizontal axes, but it didn't seem to be as solid as stone cemented to a firm base ought to be.

"Is there something the matter with the floor, here?" asked Khamwas, resting easily on his haunches.

Samlor would rather that the Napatan keep an eye out behind them, but perhaps he couldn't do that and also hold the staff where it was useful. The glow was better than nothing.

Besides, he doubted that any danger they faced would be as simple as a man creeping upon them from the darkness.

"This block doesn't have the same sheen as the others," explained Samlor as he stood up slowly. "It's not on any path, particularly, so maybe it's been sliding or, well, *something* different to the rest."

He stepped gingerly on the block, which was only slightly longer in either dimension than his foot. By shifting his weight from toes to heel and then to the edge of his boot, the caravan master hoped he could induce the marble to pivot on a hidden pin. He was poised to jump clear at the first sign of movement.

There was none.

Well, then . . . if he pressed the block toward the wall—

Samlor's hobnails skidded, then bit into the marble enough to grip as he increased the weight on them. The black stone slipped under the molding with the silent grace of mercury flowing.

There was a sigh from behind them. The two men jerked around and saw that the ornamental pond was lifting onto one end. The water, which had dampened Samlor's boot a moment before, did not spill though it hung on edge in the air.

There was a ladder leading down into the opening the pond had covered.

"Collector, you called him," said the caravan master grimly as he watched the reflection in the vertical sheet of water.

"A good trick," responded Khamwas, nettled at the hinted contrast of his knowledge against that of the missing Setios.

The Napatan stood and began muttering in earnest concentration to his staff. Samlor assumed the incantation must have some direct connection with their task and their safety.

When the phosphorescent staff floated out of Khamwas's hands, dipping but not quite falling to the ground, the Cirdonian realized that it was merely a trick—a demonstration to prove that Khamwas was no less of a magician than the owner of the house.

It was the sort of boyish silliness that got people killed when things were as tense as they were just now.

Apparently Tjainufi thought the same thing, because he turned and said acidly into the scholar's ear, "There is a running to which sitting is preferable."

Star's hands wavered briefly from the folds of her cloak; Samlor could not be sure whether or not the child mumbled something as well. Flecks of light shot from her fingers. They grew as they shimmered around the room, gaining definition as they lost intensity—jellyfish of pastel light, and one mauve sea urchin, picking its glowing, transparent way spine by spine across a "bottom" two feet above the marble floor.

The staff clattered and lost its phosphorescence as it fell. Samlor snatched it before it came to rest on the stone. He handed it back to his male companion. "Let's take a look, shall we?" he said, nodding to the ladder. "Guess I'll go first."

"No, I think I should lead," said Khamwas. "I—"

He met the caravan master's eyes. "Master Samlor, I apologize. It'll be safer for me to go first, and I'll spend my efforts on making it safe."

The multicolored jellyfish made the reception room look as if it were illuminated through stained glass. The sea urchin trundled its way forward to the opening in the middle of the floor, then continued downward at the same staccato pace as if the plane on which its spines rested lay in a universe in which sideways was up.

That might be the case.

The two men walked to the opening and looked down while Star hugged herself in silence.

The room beneath the floor was a cube or something near it, ten feet in each dimension. Mauve light filled the volume surprisingly well, though the simulated urchin did not itself seem bright enough to do so. The floor shone with a sullen lambency.

The furnishings were simple. A metal reading stand, high enough for use by a standing man and empty now, waited near the center of the room.

To its right stood an elaborate bronze firebox on four clawed legs, a censer rather than a heating device. The flat sides of the box were covered by columns of incised swirls, more likely a script unknown to the caravan master than mere decoration. The top was smooth except for a trio of depressions—an inch, three inches, and six inches in diameter. Aromatics could be placed there to be released by the heat of charcoal burning in the firebox beneath.

At each corner of the top was a decorative casting. They were miniature beasts of the sort which in larger scale could have modeled the censer's terrible clawed legs. The creatures had catlike heads, the bodies of toads with trian-gular plates rising along the spine for protection, and the forelegs of birds of prey. Serpent tails curled up behind them, suggesting the creatures were intended as handles for the censer; but anyone who attempted to put them to that purpose would have his hands pierced by the hair-thin spikes with which the tails ended.

There was no other furniture in the room, but a pentacle several feet in diameter was painted or inlaid on the con-crete floor to the reading stand's left. It was empty. The floor and white-stuccoed walls were otherwise unmarked.

Khamwas's lips pursed.

"Go ahead," said Samlor with a shrug. "Maybe your stone's on the ceiling where we can't see it."

"Yes," said the Napatan, though there was doubt rather than hope in his tone.

Khamwas thrust his staff as far into the mauve light as it

would go while his hand on the tip remained above floor level.

Nothing happened, but Samlor was not fool enough to think it had been a pointless exercise. His companion was doing what he had promised, concentrating his talents—better, his knowledge—on the task at hand.

Still holding the staff out in his direction of travel, Khamwas backed awkwardly down the ladder. The ferule banged accidentally on the censer as he turned. It made Khamwas jump back but did not concern Samlor, who saw what was about to happen.

But the crash and shattering glass from upstairs spun the caravan master, his teeth bared and his left hand groping for the throwing knife in his boot sheath.

"The wind," murmured Star, the first words she had spoken since the three of them left the study upstairs. She wasn't looking at her uncle or at anything in particular.

But she was right. A door banged shut, muting a further tinkle of glass. One of the window sashes had not been secured properly. A gust had slammed it fiercely enough to shatter the glass.

"Are you all right?" called Khamwas.

The question impressed Samlor, for it sounded sincere—and in similar circumstances, he himself would have been worried more about his own situation than that of his companions.

We're going to get drenched when we leave here," the caravan master said. "Leaving'll still feel good. Any luck yourself?"

The Napatan grimaced. "The room's empty," he said. "The brazier's as clean as if it was never used. I'm not sure it's here at all."

"Do not ask advice of a god and then ignore what he says," snapped Tjainufi, who was rubbing his tiny face on his shoulder like a bird preening.

"Step back," said Samlor. "I'm coming down."

He turned to his niece and said, "Star, dearest? Honey? Will you be all right for a minute?"

She nodded, though nothing in her face suggested that she was listening.

The quicker they found what Khamwas needed, the quicker they—Samlor—could sort out his niece's problem. He jumped into the cubical room without touching the ladder.

Samlor landed in perfect balance, feet spread and his left hand extended slightly farther than the right so that leverage matched the weight of his long dagger. Despite Samlor's care, his hobnails skidded and might have let him fall if Khamwas hadn't clutched the Cirdonian's shoulder. The floor was dusted with sparkly stuff, almost as slick as a coat of oil.

Jumping might not have been the brightest notion, but the caravan master hadn't liked the idea of doing exactly what an intruder was expected to do.

The concealed room had an underwater ambiance which wasn't wholly an effect of the glowing sea urchin trundling across an invisible bottom at waist height. The mauve light had ripples in it, but neither the furniture nor the two men cast distinct shadows on the walls.

"What does your"—Samlor said, making a left-handed gesture to indicate either Khamwas's staff or nothing at all—"your friend say about what you're looking for?"

"That I've found it," Khamwas replied, turning his head to view surroundings which were no less void on this perusal than on earlier ones.

Samlor stamped his foot. Sparkling dust quivered, but the concrete was as solid as the bedrock on which it was probably laid.

Then he kicked the nearest wall.

Stucco blasted away from the hobnails as they raked four short, parallel paths and squealed on the stone beneath.

"Well, I think we know where t' look," said the Cirdonian in satisfaction.

The stucco his boot had scraped was covering two distinct blocks of stone—a slab of polished red granite, and another of marble shadowed with faint streaks of gray. Both stones were inscribed, though on the softer marble the markings had been weathered and were further defaced by Samlor's boot.

He brushed at the stucco with his left hand, flaking away a patch his kick had loosened. The writing on the granite slab was Rankan but of a form so old that the doubled consonants and variant orthography made all but a few words unintelligible to the caravan master.

"Why, this is wonderful, my friend," said the Napatan with a smile brighter than the mauve glow as he bent over the cleared patch.

Tjainufi beamed and added, "There is no good deed save a good deed done for one who has need of it."

"We're not outta the woods yet," said Samlor with a dour glance at the walls around them. If they had to clear all the stucco—or even half, if their luck were average— which it probably wouldn't be—it was going to take a lot longer than the caravan master wanted to spend in this place.

"No, that's all right," explained the Napatan with the uneasy hint of mindreading which he had displayed before. "I'll use a spell of release and the covering will come away at once. He must use the ancient writings because they focus the power with which the years have imbued them."

Maybe that was what Setios used to do with them, Samlor thought as his companion knelt before his upright staff again, but he'd bet Setios hadn't much use for them or anything else in the world just now.

Khamwas was whispering to himself and his gods. Samlor looked at him, looked at the dagger—saw that the watered steel blade was only that, only metal; probably all it ever was, except in his mind.

"Star?" he called toward the rectangular opening. "You all right, sweetest?"

He could barely hear the reply, "All right. . . ," but a couple of the pastel jellyfish were drifting over him in placid unconcern. She'd be fine, Star would.

If any of them were, she'd be fine.

Samlor squatted and squeezed up dust from the floor on the tip of his left index finger. It was colorless (save for the mauve light it reflected) and much too finely ground for him to be able to tell the shape of the individual crystals.

A caravan master has plenty of opportunity to examine decorative stones, jewels and bits of glass cut and stained to look like jewels in the dim light of a bazaar. The dust could be anything, powdered diamond even; but most likely quartz, spread in a smooth layer across all the flat surfaces in the room . . .

Except for streaks—shadows, almost—stretching from the reading stand and the legs of the bronze censer. The dust seemed to have been sprayed violently from the direction of the pentacle in which Khamwas was almost standing.

"K—" Samlor began in sudden surmise.

The Napatan had been whispering, but now his voice rose in a crescendo. Khamwas's eyes lifted also; they were wide open but obviously not fixed on anything in the room.

Stucco shattered away on all sides, raining over Khamwas and the caravan master who reached for the ladder with his left hand and swung his blade at anything which might have slipped behind him as he crouched.

Nothing had. The choking flood of sand and lime dust filling the air as the walls cleared themselves made Samlor pause where the attack he feared would only have driven him to swifter motion.

·The slow tumble of the mauve light source continued, though the mineral-laden air absorbed the illumination. A ball a few feet in diameter glowed in place of the urchin's sharply limned spines and carapace. As dust settled out, the glow spread and paled while the features of the source at its heart slowly regained definition.

"Khamwas," said the caravan master. His eyes were slitted and a fold of his cloak covered his mouth and nose, a response made reflexive by years of dry storms whipping across his caravan routes. "*Where* did Setios keep his demon in a crystal bottle?"

"The gods preserve me from such knowledge, friend!" said the Napatan as his eyes swept the upper levels of the walls which could already be viewed with sufficient clarity. He filtered the air through his cape; a desert-dweller himself, Khamwas must have more experience with dust storms than Samlor did. "Believe me, Setios was mad to keep such a thing by him—and you and I would be even madder to carry it off ourselves."

"That's not what I mean," the caravan master said. He raised his voice so that it could be heard through the muffling cloth— and because he was at a desperate loss to know what he should do next. He would have climbed out of this place at once, except for his fear of what might follow him to where Star stood shivering.

No wonder the child had been terrified into a near coma. She must have known . . .

"Here it is!" cried Khamwas, brushing the reading stand as he swept closer to a wall. "*Here* it is!" he repeated, then sneezed.

The walls of the sunken room were formed entirely of inscribed stones, but the pieces had little commonality beyond that. Some were squared columns, set with one face flush and the other three hidden even now that the stucco had fallen away.

A few bore symbols which were not writing at all. One

of them was a small block of peridotite, polished smooth before a single diagonal was cut across its coarse crystals. The block had marked the victim's place in a temple of Dyareela. Samlor could not imagine anyone removing it from its original location—or being willing to have it close to him thereafter.

The Napatan was brushing his left palm across the face of a slab of gray granite, cleaning it of dust that had settled there after the spell of release. The stele was about three feet high and half that across. Figures—presumably gods— filled the upper portion, and there were about twenty vertical lines of script beneath them.

"—to the blessings of Harsaphes," Khamwas said, his index finger pausing midway down one of the later columns. "*Harsaphes*, not Somptu as I'd always assumed, and the ruins of the temple of Har—"

"Khamwas, *listen* to me!" Samlor shouted. He gripped the scholar with his left hand, though that meant dropping his cloak while there was still dust in the air. "You say something happened to magic a little bit ago. Would that have broken the crystal that held Setios's demon?"

"The townsman," said the manikin who was not in the least affected by the choking atmosphere, "is not the one who is eaten by the crocodile."

And men who leave magic alone, translated Samlor as he whirled toward glimpsed motion, aren't destroyed by its creatures.

A hand was emerging from a slab of limestone on the far wall. It was tenuous enough that the settling dust coexisted with the limb, which was so thin that it would have been skeletal were it not for the gleam of a scaly integument.

The three fingers each bore a claw an inch long and sharp as shattered glass.

"Get up the ladder!" Samlor shouted as he leaped for the apparition behind the watered steel blade of his dagger.

The hilt was adequate for his big hand when he slashed with it, though it was shaped wrong and would have been uncomfortably short had he chosen to thrust . . .

Which would have done as much good; as much, and no more.

The clawed hand twisted to grip the blade while an arm as wire-thin as the hand continued to extend from the wall. Steel parted the limb like smoke, and the claws slipped through the whisking dagger as if it in turn had no substance.

Another hand was reaching through the stone beside the first. The blur above and between them was growing into a narrow reptilian face.

"Get *out!*" the caravan master shouted again with a glance toward the ladder showed him that Khamwas stood where he had. He had crossed the top of his staff with his left forearm.

"No, run!" Khamwas replied. He had been chanting under his breath, and his face spasmed with the effort of breaking back into normal speech. "I released it again, but I can hold it for long enough."

The demon's head and torso had emerged from the wall. One leg was striding forward in slow motion. The creature was half again as tall as Samlor, and it was thinner than anything could be and live.

One hand shot out and snatched the sea urchin which shattered beneath the claws into a cascade of mauve sparks. As the demon's arm withdrew, the sparks formed again into their original shape. The creature of light continued to pick its way through the air.

Samlor was quite sure that if the claws closed on his niece, their effect would be permanent.

"*Run, Star!*" he shouted, afraid to turn from the demon. It continued to pull itself from the stone.

Khamwas hadn't moved, though his mouth resumed its unheard chanting. Maybe Samlor could jump for the ladder himself since the fool Napatan refused to do so. Slam the lid back over this hellish room—if the lid would close without a search for another mechanism. Run out the front door with Star in his arms, praying that he could work the bolts swiftly enough . . . praying that the doorkeeper would ignore them as they left, the way Khamwas had said it would . . .

Samlor stepped forward and swung at the demon again. He wasn't going to abandon Khamwas to the creature unless there were no other choice.

He chopped for a wrist. Instead of slipping through like light in mist, the caravan master's steel clanged as numbingly as if he had slashed an anvil. The demon seized the blade and began to chitter in high-pitched laughter.

All of the demon but its right leg had pulled free of the wall. That leg was still smokily insubstantial, but the claws of the left foot cut triple furrows in the concrete as they strained to drag the creature wholly out of the stone. The left hand—forepaw—was reaching for Samlor's face while the right gripped his knife.

Samlor's mouth had dropped open as he breathed through it, oblivious of the dust that would have made him cough another time. He jerked straight down on the dagger hilt, ducking from the swipe that started slowly as a boulder rolling, then completed its arc at blinding speed.

The blade screeched clear. If a man had held it, his fingers would have been on the floor or dangling from twists of skin.

The demon's paw was uninjured, and its claws had streaked the flat of the blade against which they were set.

Samlor caught the throat-clasp of his cloak. He could throw the garment like a net over the creature and—

—and watch the claws shred it as the demon, steel strong and more than iron hard, leaped free to dispose of the men before it. The creature's eyes had no pupils and glowed orange, a color which owed nothing to the urchin which still tumbled innocently around the room.

"*Khamwas!*" the caravan master shouted, because the demon was already in the air and perhaps Khamwas could get up the ladder while the Cirdonian occupied the creature with the process of being slaughtered . . .

The demon halted in midair, its left foot above the concrete and its right leg, spindly and terrible as that of a giant spider, lifting to deliver a kick that would disembowel Samlor. Dust settled and the urchin of light rolled jerkily forward, one spine at a time, but the creature hung frozen like an idol of ravening destruction.

Its eyes were as bright as tunnels to hell.

Samlor started another cut at the demon. Light reflecting from the triple scratch on his blade reminded him how useless that would be, so he turned instead to Khamwas.

Who had not moved since last Samlor had leisure to glance at him.

Khamwas hunched slightly forward, his left forearm crossing the top of his staff and his eyes fixed on the demon with a reptile's intensity. Tjainufi still perched on his shoulder.

The Napatan's lips had been moving soundlessly, but now he said in a cracked whisper, "Go on . . . quickly."

The demon was not quite frozen. The movements the creature began before Khamwas's spell took effect were still going on. The leg that stretched toward Samlor at a glacial pace quickened noticeably when the Napatan spoke, and the demon's mouth gaped slowly to display arrays of interlocked teeth like needles in the upper and lower jaws.

"But how can you—" the caravan master began as he slipped a step back, beyond the present arc of the claws. The demon bent at its girl-slim waist as it leaped, because otherwise its flat skull would have banged the ten-foot ceiling.

"Samlor," said the Napatan scholar, "get *out*! I brought you here!"

The demon had trembled back to near stasis for a moment. Now it lurched far enough forward in its unsupported motion that it was clear one hand was reaching for Khamwas's head even as the kick extended toward the Cirdonian.

"There is none who abandons his traveling companion whom the gods do not call to account for it," said Tjainufi.

"Fuck your gods," said Samlor, who was already sliding the knife back under his belt to free his hands. He encircled the Napatan's waist, underneath the cape for a firmer grip, with his left arm.

"No—" said Khamwas desperately.

"Do your *job*," Samlor snarled back as he lifted the smaller man. The air swirled with the demon's renewed movement, but the claws now behind the caravan master did not rend him as he stepped with regal determination to the ladder.

Focusing on the creature from the stone was for Khamwas. Samlor hil Samt had the responsibility of getting them both back up the ladder while his companion *did* that job, eyes, arm, and staff locked into their duty.

Khamwas's body was muscular, but weight wasn't the problem. Carrying him upright while Samlor's right hand needed to grip the ladder for balance was brutal punishment, and it reminded him of how badly he had strained himself getting into this *damned* house.

One foot above the other, each step a deliberate one because a jolt at the wrong time might break Khamwas's concentration irrevocably. No way to tell what was happening behind him, nothing to do about it if things weren't well. One foot and then the other.

A gust of wind shocked Samlor as his head lifted above the floor of the reception hall. Fabric, a curtain or a counterpane, had been snatched from a room on the upper floor and was flapping from the railing.

Star was calm as molten glass as she watched her uncle struggle up the ladder with the other man clamped to his side. At his first wild glance, Samlor thought the whorl of white hair on the child's temple was one of the creatures of light which pulsed through the reception hall. It was so bright . . .

He couldn't bend over to balance with his palm on the floor as he neared the top of the ladder, so the caravan master mounted the last three rungs at a quickened pace. Toppling backward would mean the floor killed them if the demon didn't, but if Samlor sprawled on his face the result would be no better. He'd seen the creature start to move; it would be on them in an instant if Khamwas were flung out of his concentration.

Samlor stepped from the top rung to the marble floor, sucking in his lips as he strove to move as smoothly as a duck gliding on water. He set the Napatan down, conscious of the man's weight only after he was free of it, and with the same motion strode for the wall and the latch mechanism.

Khamwas's voice was audible again, breaking with strain as he chanted over and over again a dozen or so words. Sweat from the Napatan's face had splashed Samlor's left forearm as he climbed.

The caravan master's boot skidded when he tried to slide back the piece of marble which was half withdrawn beneath the molding. Instead of trying again with his hobnails, Samlor knelt and scrabbled at the black stone with both sweaty palms. It moved into position with the same greasy certainty with which it had opened.

The pond of mirror-smooth water slipped down to cover the demon soundlessly.

Samlor skidded as he ran from the sidewall to the front door. Hobnails weren't the footgear for these polished stones . . . and this house wasn't a place for humans. Not now, and probably not before Setios's pet got loose.

There was no inside door latch.

"You didn't let them out, Master Khamwas," said Star,

patting the hand of the scholar who had knelt and was
sobbing with exhaustion. "They're playing with us."

"Come on," Samlor shouted. There was certainly a
way to open the inner and outer doors from here, but he
didn't have time to fool with it. "We're leaving the way
we came!"

"There's six of them, Uncle Samlor," said Star. "They're
playing with us."

Something emerged from the pilaster beside the stairs to
the second floor. It was a clawed hand like that of the
demon below. Instead of streaming like smoke from the
stone, it broke free as a chick emerges from an egg. Rock
shattered away from the groping limb, and a section of the
wall started to lift.

Khamwas rose to his feet. His face was blank and his
body swayed with fatigue. He crossed his arm over the
staff again and began a whispered chant.

The wall from which the demon crashed, already formed,
was load-bearing. Tortured roof beams squealed as plaster
in chunks of up to a hundred pounds broke away. A big
piece hit the center of the pond and blasted water out
across the reception hall.

Samlor caught his niece with one arm and Khamwas
with the other. He flung them, all three together, to the
floor against the nearer sidewall. A block of stone, notched
for the butt of a crossbeam, tumbled from the roof to the
rail of the second-floor walkway, then caromed to the floor
in a shower of dust and chips.

"We'll get out through the back!" said the caravan
master who doubted that they would. The wall beside
where they hunched under cover of the walkway was
crumbling as gray claws harder than the stone emerged
from it.

Across the reception room, the other sidewall was disin-
tegrating in a shower of bits and blocks. They hid but did
not disguise the cause of the destruction. One of the

demons was clasping a dismembered human leg. Samlor figured he knew where Setios and his servants had gone.

Six of 'em, Star'd said. Likely five more than they'd need, but you didn't quit just because you couldn't win . . .

The three humans rose and scuttled for the room's back wall and the door there. They were bent over because the walkway's partial roof was no protection against blocks bouncing from the floor at crazy angles.

The front half of the house staggered forward into the street with a roar. The sound did not seem loud until Samlor realized that he could not shout with enough volume to be heard by the two companions he had dragged with him into the temporary safety of the door alcove.

Skeletal, inhumanly tall figures minced toward the trio, shrugging off the tons of rubble that had thundered down on them. There were four, and the mound of stone and timber covering what had been the floor of the reception room heaved as the creature in the room beneath rejoined its fellows.

Sheets of pain flapped across Samlor's body from a center where his right hip had blocked a ricocheting chunk of stone that weighed as much as he did. The crosswall dividing the house was built as solidly as the exterior. It remained essentially undisturbed when the emerging demons had shattered the front of the house. That portion of the building had demolished itself as brittle stone shifted in a vain attempt to find new foundations.

The door in front of Samlor was locked or possibly jammed when ruin made the house twist, but the panel was only thin wood inlaid with horn and ivory in patterns which were probably significant as well as decorative. Khamwas pounded it with the ferule of his staff, breaking off scales of ivory without doing anything to get them through the doorway.

Samlor would have kicked the latchplate, but he was

pretty sure that his right hip would neither support him alone nor lift his boot high enough for the purpose. Wondering how many seconds they had before a demon lunged onto them, he rotated on his left heel and grabbed a torso-sized block from the wreckage that had spilled inward during the collapse.

The demons were advancing with tiny steps, chittering in self-satisfaction. When they chose to, they picked their way over the piled rubble, but one of the four figures strode through the tons of jumbled rock like a man wading in the surf. The fifth of the creatures heaved itself into sight with the ease of a toadstool bursting pavement to reach the open air.

"Care—" cried Samlor, turning with the block in his hands. The movement was so painful that he could feel only his scalp, his palms, and the ball of his left foot.

"—ful!"

The stone splintered the door and carried on, crashing on the floor of the hallway beyond and then bouncing harmlessly from the legs of the sixth demon poised there with its arms spread across the passage.

The air was dead still. The caravan master turned again, no more conscious of his pain than a fox is conscious of the way its lungs burn from its running when the hounds encircle it for the last time.

"The sky," Khamwas said hoarsely. "*Look*."

Samlor drew the long dagger from his belt and lifted Star to his chest with his free arm. The semicircle of demons waited, crouching slightly, with their spindly, steel-strong arms interlocked. They were close enough that if one of the creatures leaned forward, it could rip the caravan master's face away in its pointed teeth.

"*Look!*" Khamwas screamed, and even so his voice was smothered by a sound like the scream of a giant snake.

Samlor looked up. He could see almost a mile into the

sky, up the lightning-lit throat of a descending tornado funnel.

The lower end was shaggy with tentacles of water vapor condensing in the lowered pressure surrounding six separate suction vortices. They extended toward the ruined house.

"Down!" cried the caravan master, but Star twisted like an eel from his arms and stood while the two men tried to flatten themselves.

One of the demons leaped away, covering twenty feet of the distance toward the street before being caught by a suction vortex. The creature reeled upward into the main funnel, like a crab being lifted into an octopus's crushing beak. Blue-white lightning licked soundlessly but with coronal radiance from one side of the void to the other.

The funnel hovered at the level of what remained of Setios's roof. A miniature vortex snaked past Star's erect head, so close that it should have touched her hair but didn't. It was no more than the diameter of a wine jar, spinning widdershins though the main cloud rotated with the sun.

Samlor lay on his back, clutching the medallion of Heqt in his left hand as he watched transfixed. The broken door panel exploded into splinters. They cleared themselves up the shaft of the screaming vortex. The demon flashed out in the grip of the wind, upright and battling momentarily while its hinder claws gouged pieces the size of a man's fist from the stone of the doorjambs. Then the creature was gone, falling upward into the sky in a helix so tight that its limbs had been plucked from the body before it disappeared into the tunnel of lightning.

The tornado was lifting and folding in on itself like a purse whose drawstrings were being tightened. Samlor hadn't seen what happened to the four remaining demons, but they had vanished when he knelt to look around.

"If you are not slack," said Tjainufi in a perfectly audible voice, "then your god will be active for you."

Samlor uncurled his fingers from the amulet of Heqt; but it had not been to the toad goddess that he screamed his prayers in the last instants . . .

"I thought Mommy's box was empty," said Star as her eyes met the caravan master's. "But it wasn't."

The tornado funnel flattened into the overcast almost a mile above Sanctuary. Only then did the normal wind return, a huge gust of it, and with it the start of a cold downpour. It was as dark again as the inside of a tomb.

But the whorl of hair on Star's temple burned for a moment like the heart of the lightning.

A MERCY WORSE THAN NONE

John Brunner

By lamplight, by firelight, on a winter evening, Jarveena of Forgotten Holt sat at dinner with the less-than-man whose foreign agent she had been for these seven years.

In the years since she had served him merely as a scribe-interpreter, Master Melilot had changed but little. He was portlier, admittedly—the satin robe he splashed with grease as he gnawed at the carcass of his third wild duck stretched smooth across his ample paunch—but his suety face was equally innocent of wrinkles and would no doubt remain so till his death.

Most certainly of all, his inner nature had not altered. Though he was a great deal richer than of yore—Jarveena knew that for a fact, having put several immensely profitable deals his way, and having laid the foundations of a fortune for herself—the outward signs of his prosperity were few. He was still reluctant to part with money save when it was unavoidable; food still came to his table from the fire shared between the kitchen and the bindery adjacent to the scriptorium on the entrance floor, and those who clambered up and down the ladderlike stairs with wine jars and full and empty dishes were still the same sort of apprentices, not engaged just now in copying or studying. A thousand others would have flaunted their wealth by buying slaves, or installed one of the hoists of late so popular in Ranke, which delivered food piping-hot by way of a shaft sunk in the wall. Not Melilot. He knew that an excessive display of worldly goods was a sure way to attract the interest of thieves, and he had no wish to be at the expense of hiring armed watchmen. It was cheaper to rely, by day, on the constant vigilance of his staff, and by night on the geese he had installed on the roof, in what formerly had been the nauseous dwelling of the drunken nobleman whose ancestors had built this once fine mansion. He had gone to his repose; now the geese could be trusted to disturb everybody's at a nocturnal shout or footfall, a complaining bolt, or the creaking of a shutter jimmied open.

Besides, here in Sanctuary, what guards were available were as likely as anyone else to rob their employers if they felt they could get away with their loot.

Despite his visibly good appetite, Melilot was uneasy. As well as Jarveena, another guest sat at his table. It was not his custom to admit strangers to his private quarters. Had the fellow not been vouched for by Jarveena personally, he would never have set foot outside the public areas below.

Yet he had been vouched for in a most disturbing fashion. Had he somehow ensnared the girl—*woman*, Melilot corrected himself, remembering how much time had elapsed—perhaps by magic? Was their presence part of some secret plot against him? It was second nature to all in Sanctuary to think in such terms, from lifelong habit.

Keeping up, between mouthfuls, a flow of gossip as entertaining as might be heard anywhere in the city and a sight more trustworthy than most, given that it was based on what he daily gleaned from the documents given him to transcribe or translate, Melilot studied Jarveena from the corner of his eye. She had changed more than he had in the past decade—and small wonder, given the difference in their age and bodily condition—but she still affected mannish garb, boots and breeches and laced jerkin. She was still, moreover, patterned with vicious scars, though they were far less conspicuous than formerly. Therein lay the reason for her annual returns to Sanctuary, and also why she was not already as rich as Melilot. Spells were not cheap, particularly when one must apply to Enas Yorl for them: one of the three greatest wizards in the land.

Under his care, the lash marks on her hands and arms had faded until they were no more than a tracery beneath her tawny skin—and no doubt elsewhere on her body, for her once unequal bosom swelled identically now on left and right, signifying that the old brown keloid had been spirited away and left her form as shapely as that of anyone her age not yet a mother, and more than most thanks to her active way of life. Oddly, though, she had not begun where most young women would have, with her face as being most exposed to public view. Still, when she tossed her head in laughter at some especially extravagant yarn recounted by her host, one might glimpse the hideous cicatrix she could reveal by drawing down her eyebrows, that mark which in the days when she resided here she had used to such effect in cowing disobedient junior apprentices . . .

Oh, she had always been a strange one, this Jarveena! He had been positively glad when she decided to take ship away from Sanctuary after that unpleasant episode involving an enchanted scroll, treachery on the part of a trusted officer, and an attempt to assassinate the Prince.*

Yes, indeed. Life was a great deal more comfortable knowing that this unpredictable person, half loyal employee and half explosive spitfire, was safe at sea or bargaining on his behalf in distant ports. The times when she came back to claim her pay, and spend the greater part

*See ''Sentences of Death,'' in *Thieves' World*.

of it again in a single day, were far from the happiest of
Melilot's existence . . .

And now she had arrived, for the first time ever, with a
companion. Male, at that. Discarding the third duck, belch-
ing unrestrainedly and calling for more wine, he shifted his
attention to this stranger even as he launched into the best
and funniest of the rumors he had lately garnered. It
concerned the plight of a rascally sea captain, Stong by
name, half mariner, half smuggler, who had taken aboard,
all unwitting, both a chestful of silver put long ago by
Mizraith under a geas that sooner or later would compel its
restoration to its rightful owner, and also the victim of a
S'danzo curse designed to drive him away from Sanctuary
for all time. He decorated the tale with all sorts of risible
detail, much of which he invented on the spot, and Jarveena,
relaxed by her good wine, enjoyed it to the full. One of the
changes she had undergone during her extensive travels
was the acquisition of a keen sense of humor. In her teens
she had had little to laugh at, or about.

Her companion, however, made no pretense even of
smiling. His glum face remained as impassive as a stone
idol's except at reference to the S'danzo curse, whereupon
he favored Jarveena with a scowl.

What, Melilot asked himself, could have persuaded her
to bring this boorish fellow here? So far he knew nothing
about him save his name, and that was outlandish and
nearly unpronounceable, something like "Klikitak" except
that it ended with a rasp: Klikitagh?

Of course, a few hints could be deduced from his appearance. His shoulders were broad, his chest deep, his
hands large and sinewy: the figure of a man of action.
Moreover he was of a striking color, for between his fair
beard and bushy fair hair his cheeks and forehead were
windburned to a pale clear red after so many days at sea.

But never in all his life, not even when dealing with
some nobleman's illiterate wife desperate to know whether

letters brought secretly to her husband and intercepted described her infidelities, had Melilot seen such unalloyed misery on a human countenance. Why, even Enas Yorl, sport of a thousand mindless spells that changed his shape, his sex, and now and then his species, contrived to extract a certain wry and resigned humor from his predicament . . .

He ended his story, and Jarveena, hooting with laughter, clapped her hands. The pretty ten-year-old girl who stood silently in one corner beside the wine jug mistook her applause for a signal to replenish their mugs, and made haste to obey. Melilot did not correct her. He had hopes of loosening the stranger's tongue, and in that project liquor was his chiefest ally.

"I note, sir," he said with disapproval that was only partly feigned, "you were not amused by the plight of Captain Stong. Is one to take it that it was because you are unfamiliar with crucial references therein, as to the S'danzo curse and legendary Mizraith's skill as an enchanter? You have the air of a far-traveled man, not acquainted with the ways and notables of Sanctuary."

Klikitagh stirred, and for the first time uttered more than a discourteous grunt; he had not even expressed thanks for the generous repast that had been set before him.

"No, sir," he returned. "Is because in part I can not well to understand your saying."

Hmm! That aroused Melilot's professional instincts. What could this fellow's native language be? The accent was none that he recognized, nor was the curious turn of phrasing. Mayhap Klikitagh was literate in some language lacking from the list posted at the door of his scriptorium, though that was longer by three, possibly four, than the best his rivals had to offer. If only to learn how to recognize a script he hadn't run across before, it would be worth his while to pick the stranger's brains . . .

Before Melilot could formulate any proposal, however, the other had gone on.

"And in other bigger part because is not a matter for make jest, a curse. Speak as pitiably victim knowing well from agony anti-justice, cruelness, of making curse against innocency man, me, self."

That emphatic addition occurs in Yenized, but never at the end of a sentence . . . Oh, I'm really on to something here! Excited, Melilot beckoned the girl back from her corner to pour still more wine.

But Klikitagh refused, covering his mug with a broad palm.

"Tired. I to sleep. Must go, we."

As though taking Jarveena's consent for granted, he gathered the sword belt he had hung on the back of his chair and rose, extending his hand to help her up also.

She ignored it.

A sudden angry flush deepened the color of Klikitagh's cheeks. He said, "You not—"

"I have business to discuss with Melilot," she cut in. "One of the kids will show you to the guest apartment. I'll join you later."

Hastily, for fear of Klikitagh provoking a quarrel that, as surely with Jarveena as with any haughty bladesman of the city, might become a fight, Melilot forced his immense bulk out of his chair.

"That is so, sir," he confirmed. "But I assure you I shall keep our conversation as brief as may be." He hesitated, trying to gauge the depth and cause of Klikitagh's ill temper. "If perchance you fear I may trespass on some right of intimacy the lady has, for the time being, granted to yourself, I pray you consider the—ah—visible signs of my incompetence in that regard."

Klikitagh's face remained blank. Melilot realized he was so nervous that out of habit he had used formal, high-flown terms, incomprehensible to this foreigner. He made hasty amends.

"It is as Jarveena has said. My guest apartment is at

your disposal. During your stay at Sanctuary I look forward to chatting with you about your native country and its
script and language; it would be most interesting, indeed a
positive pleasure, to hear you on the subject. Accordingly,
rather than dismiss you to some flea-ridden tavern like the
Vulgar Unicorn, I suggest you make my home your base
until you have completed whatever business brings you
here. Feel free to come and go . . ."

His words trailed away. Klikitagh was scowling worse
than ever. His hand would have fallen to his sword hilt—he
had refused to be parted from the weapon, bad manners
though it was to bring it into his host's dining room—had
Jarveena not caught his fingers in her own, slimmer but
almost as strong. With a sour grin she said, "You've upset
the poor bastard. Not surprising. I'll take him away and
pacify him, and come back."

"Pacifying" Klikitagh took so long that Melilot, growing drowsy from the fumes of wine, was on the point of
postponing further conversation with Jarveena to the
morrow—the street outside having reached that pitch of
quietness after which almost any noise might set his geese
to cackling—when, silent as a shadow, she returned wearing nothing but her skin and slumped back into her chair.
He noticed that his guess about the keloid on her chest had
been correct.

"Foof!" she exclaimed, though she kept her voice low.
"If I'd known what a handful Klikitagh can be I'd never
have agreed to help him. Still, you can't help feeling sorry
for the poor devil, can you?"

"Personally," Melilot grunted, "I find it the easiest
thing in the world to avoid doing so. What spell has he
cast on you, who never before to my knowledge felt sorry
for anybody save yourself—and maybe Enas Yorl?"

She pantomimed hurling her wine mug at him, but
cancelled the movement with a wry smile at his reflexive

flinch. The mug turned out to be empty. Glancing around, she saw that the little girl in the corner had dozed off. Remembering, perhaps, the days when she, too, had had to wait on Melilot's pleasure after dinner, she went to help herself. Having taken a swig and topped it up a second time, she resumed her place.

"All right." She sighed. "I guess I'd better tell you Klikitagh's story."

"I'd rather hear about the deals with—"

"Tomorrow will do!" she interrupted. "Or more likely the day after."

"I was afraid of that," the master scribe muttered. "On the first full day of each of your visits to Sanctuary, you invariably have urgent business . . . Still, if this time you can afford to have Enas Yorl charm away the scar on your forehead"—brightening—"you'll no longer present such an alarming aspect every time you shake aside your forelock."

"It's true that I intend to wait on Enas Yorl tomorrow, as I always do." Jarveena wasn't looking at him, but at the fading glories of the painted ceiling, on which the lamps and the flames from the dying logs combined to cast curious and intersecting shadows, as though some magician were eavesdropping on them and letting his attention wander now and then from the spell that assured his invisibility. "But this time, not for my own sake."

"For . . . *his*?" Reaching for his own mug, Melilot was so astonished he almost spilled the contents.

"Yes indeed."

After that there was a lengthy silence, broken only by the occasional sputtering of a jet of gas boiled out from the dampest and longest-lasting log across the fire dogs.

Eventually noise drifted from outside: the tramp of booted feet on cobblestones. One of the night patrols was passing, composed of men trained locally to Hell-Hound standards of discipline; yet even they did not dare to venture abroad except in twos, so lawless and unruly was this premier melting pot of cities. The geese were accustomed to the sound of their passage, and the boss gander marked it with no more than an evil-sounding hiss.

Having watched the gleam of the patrol's lantern approach and fade on the curtains that masked his streetward window, Melilot said, "Are you sure he has not cast a spell on you? Last year you said this was to be the time of your final visit to Enas Yorl, at least for personal reasons. You said that after it your face would be restored to the same condition as your"—he coughed behind one plump hand—"the rest of you."

"I'm having second thoughts," Jarveena muttered. "It's sometimes not a bad thing to be able to turn off an unwanted suitor just by doing *this*." And she drew her eyebrows down, glaring at him from beneath their twin graceful arcs. At once Melilot's gaze, against his will, was drawn away from the rest of her face and horribly concentrated on the livid cicatrix that marred her forehead and instantly made her handsome features more repulsive than the worst invention of Sanctuary's hawkmasks.

"You haven't done it to *him*," Melilot suggested.

"Yes. At first. It had no effect. That was what got me interested in Klikitagh." She had perfectly mastered the final sound of the name; Melilot, to his shame, knew that he would have to practice it half a dozen times aloud and in private before he dared address the man directly.

"What, then, followed?"

"The discovery that something worse could happen to a person than what I went through as a child."

For an instant her face reflected memories of long ago and far away. Melilot, knowing what was in her mind, shivered. To have been raped repeatedly, then whipped and left for dead among the ruins of her native village Holt—not for nothing now referred to as Forgotten—when she was no more than nine . . . Was that not sufficient horror to enter into anybody's life?

Yet she had found someone who, in her view, had suffered even more. What monstrous events, then, lay in the past of Klikitagh?

Huskily he said, "Tell me his tale."

"Let it begin," she said after reflection, "with the reason why he took offense at your offer of free lodging. I know you'd not have made it had you not expected *quid pro quo*. It's all, of course, beside the point, but what he might be able to tell you of his mother tongue would be quite useless. Whether he can write I've not inquired; the same applies."

"Still, knowledge of any distant language—"

"Even a dead one? Dead for centuries?"

"*What?*" Melilot jolted forward on his chair, one careless elbow oversetting his mug—but it was empty, and he lacked the energy to rise and fill it for himself.

"Do you not believe there were great magicians in the past?" Jarveena challenged.

"You mean . . ." Melilot sank back slowly into his usual pot-bellied slouch, staring into nowhere.

"Out with it!"

"He's under an immortality spell?"

"That's only the half of it. Don't imagine you should envy him!"—in a sharp tone of warning. "On the contrary! He is the most pitiable creature I have ever met, and in your service I have traveled back and forth across the whole known world. Is that not so?"

Melilot nodded dumbly.

"Then listen." She leaned toward the fire with chin on fists; the flames made patterns of darkness dart across her face and body. "What lies on him is no mere spell, but a tremendous curse. In it consists the reason why he was angry when you offered him lodging. He cannot accept.

Nor will he eat your dinner tomorrow or on any other evening. You see . . ."

She weighed her words with care.

"He is bound never to sleep two nights in the same bed, nor eat a second meal from the same table. And this has been his doom for a thousand years."

Now for a great while Melilot sat motionless, save insofar as the play of fire- and lamplight kept up a constant illusion of movement throughout the room. Finally he had to stifle a yawn. But behind his plump, inscrutable face it seemed his mind had been working hard enough, albeit along lines that were familiar in Sanctuary more than any other place.

"Would this not imply that he cannot be kept in jail?" he suggested.

"Why, you—!" Jarveena leaped to her feet, brandishing her mug as though to brain him with it. Only a warning hiss from the gander beyond the ceiling prevented her. But her face was aglow with fury as she sat down again. "Is that all you can think about? How would you like to be in his shoes?"

"Not at all," the fat one answered candidly. "I'm sorry; I hadn't thought the matter through . . . To what is owed this fearful geas, then?"

"I've no idea. Moreover, nor does he."

"But that's ridiculous!" Melilot stared at her. "You mean he won't admit—"

"I mean precisely what I said! Do you think I haven't pestered him with questions? Do you think I haven't put him under oath? He has sworn by all the gods and goddesses whose names I recognize, plus one or two I never ran across before, that he believes the curse to be unjust. He says, and I've been able to confirm, that he has consulted every magician whom he could afford to pay, and none has given him surcease. What is more, none has contrived to relieve his misery by telling him the curse indeed is warranted. Were he aware of what he is accursed for, he might at least attempt an expiation. Can you think of a crueler fate than his? He is being punished—endlessly, horribly punished—for something he has no memory of having done! Is he not truly to be pitied?''

A shudder plus a vigorous nod made Melilot's gross body wobble under his fine robe.

"But how does he make shift aboard a ship?'' he demanded. "If he may not sleep twice in the same bed—''

"He brought a hammock, and each night slung it from two different posts or hooks. This is permissible.''

"Then: eating twice from the same table?''

"Until this evening I had not seen him eat from a table at all. Aboard ship, he carried his dish to a different spot on deck or in the 'tween-decks, but this stratagem did not entirely serve; our voyage, as you know, was prolonged by a contrary wind, and for the last two days he did not eat at all. In the tavern where I met him, where he had already spent a week, he had to bribe its keeper to move him each night to a different bunk or pallet, and since there were only two tables for the customers he was reduced to eating on the floor, like a dog. He was much mocked in consequence.''

"Has he described what happens when he tries to defy the curse?''

"He cannot. He says he's never had the power to do so. It is, he says, as though he has become a well-trained animal. Though he might sit down to your table tomorrow, be he never so hungry his hands would remain in his lap, refusing to lift food to his lips; though he might fall upon the softest couch in the world, weary to the marrow of his bones, only the first time would he be allowed repose. Thereafter he would toss about all night, unless exhaustion drove him to prefer the floor. He must, he says, avoid the highest and the lowest sorts of lodging: the former because the wealthy often buy antiques, the latter because the poor make shift with what's been handed down or looted from abandoned homes. This carven table might be one he ate from centuries ago, that horsehair pallet might have been in use elsewhere. The curse still holds, even at so remote a reach; he starves, he grows red-eyed with lack of sleep, until he wanders on and falls exhausted.''

"How does he live? What trade is open to him?" Melilot demanded.

Jarveena shrugged. "I think when all else fails he has to rob. But there are tasks even a wanderer may undertake. He goes a lot to sea; sometimes he enlists to guard a caravan; he has hinted at having been a courier, and carried confidential mail. Naturally, though, he can't serve long on any given route.''

"Naturally," Melilot said in a dry tone, and had to hide another yawn. "Well, my dear Jarveena, if it's any consolation, you have indeed elicited my sympathy. Your vivid picture of his unendurable existence must move the stoniest of hearts—which mine, as you're aware, is not. Let us hope for both your sakes that Enas Yorl relieves the curse tomorrow. Go now and tell your friend I wish he may sleep soundly in my guest room, since it may only be this once. And leave me your report and your accounts, so I may peruse them while you're with the wizard.''

"You'll find them all in order."

"Are they not always so?"

"Of course. How otherwise could I have kept on your right side so long?"

Rising with a chuckle, she headed for the door. Passing his chair, she bent to plant a kiss on his shaven pate.

"Thank you for allowing Klikitagh to stay. It can't be often that he enjoys such luxury.''

Said Melilot: "I didn't notice him *enjoying* it . . .''

And his little joke sent him contentedly to bed.

*   *   *

Waking, but with eyes still closed, Jarveena abruptly grew aware of another presence near at hand, apart from Klikitagh. She tensed, sliding her fingers beneath her pillow in search of the knife that never left her reach.

It wasn't there. Come to that, neither was the pillow!

She sat up with a jerk, eyes wide in alarm. Melilot's guest room had vanished. This was another place entirely, a long low-ceilinged stone-walled hall, wherein she found herself on an oblong padded couch, Klikitagh still at her side. The air was pleasantly warm, pervaded with fragrance from dried herbs sprinkled on a brazier.

Looking down on her, clad in a many-layered cape, was a tall and rather handsome youth . . . but where a normal person's eyes would be, there burned two red betraying sparks. She exhaled with a gasp.

"Enas Yorl!" she exclaimed.

Her voice roused Klikitagh. He came together all of a piece, instantly swinging his legs to the floor—which was spread with soft pelts, sable, marten, and sea otter. He cast around for his sword, but there was no sign of it, or of his clothing. Perceiving in the unknown youth a captor and perhaps a rival, he shook sleep from his brain and advanced with both fists clubbed.

Or rather, tried to do so. When he set his foot down a second time, his limbs slowed, as though he were forcing his way through deep water against a fierce contrary current. With vast effort he achieved another step, but that was all; eventually he remained utterly still, balanced absurdly on his left leg, mouth ajar in a face that had become a mask of fury and frustration.

Jarveena knew how he was feeling. Just so had she been trapped at her first unexpected entry into the magician's palace. Guarded by basilisks, it lay beside and beneath Prytanis Street, to the southeast of the Avenue of Temples.

Except, of course, when it was somewhere else . . .

Licking her lips, for even after all these years it awed her to be in the presence of Enas Yorl, especially naked— there was no point in adding "and defenseless," for few there were in all of the known world who could withstand the power of such a wizard—she said, "Sometimes I wonder why you keep basilisks and yet enforce that spell in person. Do they not jest about the man who kept a dog and barked himself?"

"Who told you there was no trace of basilisk in me?" replied the seeming youth in mocking tones. "Welcome back to Sanctuary, Jarveena. You were most royally entertained by Melilot the pinchpenny last night. The flavor of those roasted ducks must have been excellent!"

Even as he spoke, his face was slowly altering. His eyebrow ridges in particular were thickening. Meantime his shoulders gradually hunched. Jarveena knew what such a rapid change betokened.

"You've been engaged in a considerable magic," she deduced. "Were you indeed one of the shadows that played around the fat one's dining room?"

He inclined his head.

"Can you have been that eager to see me again? Did you wish to find out whether I'd added any more scars to my toll, making more work for you in fading them?"

But these gibes were a mere cover for her nervousness. Besides, Enas Yorl was paying them no heed. He was contemplating Klikitagh with a frown. After a moment he touched the man's temples gently and briefly with his forefingers.

He said at length, "I heard his story as you recounted it last night. Now I can tell you one extremely curious fact. He does believe, with all his heart, that the curse upon him is unjust. But in my centuries of life—brief though they be compared to his, of course—I have read, been told, found through experience, that to impose so powerful and durable a spell on an innocent victim is, if not forbidden, self-defeating. It must turn again upon the one who cast it. So say all the best authorities.''

''Might there not have been exceptions in the past?'' Jarveena ventured. ''Could there not have been ancient powers that since have been forgotten?''

''How can that be so, when Klikitagh has trudged from wizard to enchanter to magician for a thousand years, telling them his tale and begging them to strike off the fetters of his life? There's more to this than meets the inward eye . . . Come! Let us start the day with food.''

That was not the usual first engagement she had with the wizard. Puzzled by the change, though not especially dismayed, she ascribed it perhaps to his unwillingness to engage in the lists of love with a third party present—though she was sure he must have rendered Klikitagh blind and deaf and lost to the passage of time.

In her heart of hearts, though, she knew it was because he was interested much more by the stranger than herself.

Turning away, Enas Yorl made a pass in the air and the far end of the immense hall drew obediently closer. There stood a table set with bread and fruit and bowls of steaming broth, along with stoups of fragrant wine. Assuming a high-backed chair, as though by afterthought he said, ''Oh— clothe my visitors.''

Unseen hands wrapped Jarveena in a silken gown, even to the point of fastening its sash. She glanced at Klikitagh; a robe of homespun cloth as harsh as sacking fell around his awkwardly posturing frame.

''You will not let him join us?'' she suggested.

''He is feeling neither hunger nor thirst,'' replied the wizard. ''Besides, I may need to loose his tongue by conventional means, as Melilot essayed to do last night with scant success. How can I, if he has already eaten from my table?''

''But surely . . .'' she began, and bit her lip.

"You were going to say," came the resigned reply, "you have such confidence in my abilities, you fully expect him to be set free by nightfall. Well, if so he will of course be dead—had that point not occurred to you? But the outcome is by no means certain . . . Join me! Sit down! Toast your return beneath my roof!"

She obeyed, having no alternative. The wizard's wine, as ever, was superb. Compared to it the best of Melilot's was sharp as vinegar.

The food, too, was exceptional, but she found she had little appetite, though Enas Yorl ate briskly enough. He had let slip, long ago, that magic was a tiring business, draining the practitioner of energy as much as any normal kind of plain hard work. Jarveena, however, was distracted by the way his face and hidden body kept on changing, changing, as the minutes ebbed away . . .

At last she could contain herself no longer. She burst out, "Old friend—if I may call you so—what drew your interest to Klikitagh?"

"Old friend?" Enas Yorl repeated, wiping lips that now were broader and flatter than before, beneath a broader, flatter nose and beetling brows. "Why, there are few so kindly disposed to me as to call me friend at all—and that, of course, is by design! Nonetheless, I'll not hold your choice of words against you!" He gave a harsh laugh and drained his goblet.

"Know, then, that it was much despite my will. I guard myself from sentimental ties that might bind me to this world, hoping for the day when I myself can be released by death. I would not care to overlook the chance of escape because I regretted leaving anyone, or anything, behind . . ." He seemed oddly reluctant in his speech, as though making a shameful confession.

"Nonetheless I have developed a certain attachment to yourself. There is, admittedly, an element of sensuality involved; that apart, however, I prefer to keep it on the level of—shall we say?—respectful admiration. Few who have so much reason to devote their lives to seeking revenge break away from their obsession; you have done so."

"Because the taste of vengeance was not sweet," Jarveena muttered. "It turned to ashes in my mouth."

"Even so, even so . . . Reverting to the point: when I discerned that you had taken up with a companion, I rejoiced. I watch you sometimes in my scrying glass, you know."

"I didn't!" she said, startled. "I don't know whether to be flattered, or— Never mind! Continue!"

"As I say: I rejoiced, hoping that our attachment would thereby be weakened. Despite my best intentions, though, I grew curious concerning him: what manner of man, I asked myself, could win Jarveena from her wild, her willful ways? Inevitably, in the moment I found out, I was ensnared."

"I don't see— Oh!" Jarveena leaned her elbows on the table, goblet cradled in brown hands. "If he is truly innocent, the curse on him must be stronger than the spells that bind yourself. Break his, and you may find the way to break your own."

"Did I not know you to be ungifted in that area, I might well say you read my mind."

There was silence between them for a while. At last Jarveena looked him straight in his unhuman eyes.

"What are you going to do?"

"I have already begun. You would not know what day it is today; the calendar that counts it has been long disused. But it was necessary that you and he should come here now—not yesterday and not tomorrow. Otherwise one would have had to wait a quarter year."

"You conjured up the wind that delayed our ship!"

"It was imperative."

"Then you must think there's a chance!"

"Of freeing Klikitagh? Perhaps. First, though, I must learn the reason why the curse is on him."

"But you said already that he doesn't know! So how——?"

"Wait." The magician raised one hand which no longer matched his handsome youthful countenance—not that he was so handsome any longer, either. "What I said was that he honestly believes it was put upon him unjustly. That does not mean there was no reason for it. I assure you, even a thousand years ago no one would have undertaken such a work without a reason. Klikitagh may indeed be innocent; if so, there is a great and long-outstanding blame to visit on the perpetrator of a crime against him. Or, more like, descendants of those who benefited by its perpetration."

"But how can he not be innocent, having sworn by——? I waste my breath. You must already know."

"Indeed I do. That is perhaps the most remarkable aspect of the matter."

Enas Yorl rose. "Now I must further the business. Time is wasting."

"May I wait? May I be of assistance?"

"You may not." The wizard's tone was final. "You will go hence about your own affairs. About now Melilot is rising, and he will be eager to discuss your trip. He will display great reluctance to mention Klikitagh, and you yourself will give the fellow not a second thought, save perhaps to hope occasionally that I can rescue him. Until sundown. At the moment when the sun cuts the horizon, you may return. Approach the entrance on Prytanis Street; address the basilisks by name—I'll teach you how—and they will let you by. If the work is not complete by dark, it will have failed."

"But these winter days are so short!" Jarveena cried.

"That is precisely why you must go now. It lacks less

than an hour of dawn. Be on your way! No, wait! There's one thing more.''

"Yes?''—as she turned to obey.

"No need to bring your customary fee. Reserve that for my final onslaught on your scars. It is enough that you have given me my greatest challenge in a hundred years of weary life, the first of all that holds out hope for me . . . Begone!''

And she *was* gone, with further words unspoken on her lips.

All transpired as had been promised. Jarveena spent the morning closeted with Melilot, snatched a brief lunch, and in the afternoon went to the wharf where goods that she had purchased with the money he advanced her had been disposed in tidy piles: here, bales of cloth; there, jars of wine and oil; over there again small chests of spice, ingeniously carpentered, that had a resale value of their own when empty. A certain portion being set aside for her, he paid her due commission on the rest. He might at one time have dreamed of cheating her, as he was used to cheating everybody else; her friendship with the powerful magician Enas Yorl prevented that. Besides, there was an additional advantage. It was *not done* to steal what Jarveena or any other associate of Enas Yorl's left on the wharf before it was transferred to guarded warehouses. Or not done more than once, at any rate . . .

"Well, that concludes our business for the day!'' said the master scribe heartily, handing his compendium and his account scrolls to a boy-in-waiting. "And in good time, what's more; it isn't even sunset, quite. Now I'm athirst. Shall we adjourn to yonder ale house and sample their midwinter brew? Unless, that is, you're eager to rejoin your man and find him different lodging for tonight—''

Klikitagh!

Jarveena clapped hand to forehead. How was it possible? All day, since finding herself back at Melilot's, she had thought of nothing but cargo manifests and market prices and percentages! And the fat one had not even commented on her willingness to spend the time with him, when normally she would have been with the magician . . .

And sundown now impended!

"No! No!" she cried. "Don't hold me back an instant more!"

Incontinently she took to her heels.

The way from the harbor to Prytanis Street had never seemed so long, or so beset with moving obstacles. She lost count of the number of people she jostled against, the number of futile curses that were hurled after her, the times she herself cursed patrolmen shouting to know why she was running, imagining her to be a thief or cutpurse fleeing from her latest victim.

Somehow, though, they realized: she was not running away from, but *toward* . . .

The twin pillars of her destination loomed in the gloaming, accorded a wide berth by the foot passengers on their way to sunset service at the nearby temples. And small wonder. At the foot of each reposed a sleeping basilisk, secured at neck and leg with silver chains. As Jarveena rushed toward them, they became alert. Heads raised, they snuffed the air and listened, pondering in their slow reptilian way whether or not to open their eyes and cast their petrifying glare upon her.

Enas Yorl had said, "I'll teach you how to call them by name . . ."

But he hadn't!

She stopped dead, searching the corridors of memory. No! She had no idea what she must say!

"He forgot!" she moaned, clenching her fists in rage.

And then, suddenly, she heard a groaning, grinding sound that made the pavement shudder underneath her feet. Looking up, she saw that the bronze door of the palace was sliding open, revealing a hall full of luminescent mist. And on its threshold—

"Klikitagh!" she exclaimed.

Still in the homespun robe, barefoot, he seemed to respond to her cry. Shaking his head, he staggered down the five marble stairs that fronted the doorway. He accorded Jarveena a brief glance, but it was vacant, as though she meant no more to him than any chance-met passerby.

"Klikitagh?" she said again, uncertainly.

He struck her aside with violence, and staggered off into the darkness. In a moment the throng of temple-bound worshipers concealed him from Jarveena's view, while their chattering drowned out her shouts.

"Death and *destruction!*" she exploded. She spun on her heel and dashed up the marble steps, desperate to pass the door before it ground shut again.

The basilisks relaxed; lay down; resumed their former immobility.

She was inside the misty hall before she realized what had happened.

A great metallic slam announced the final closure of the door. She was alone, and more terrified than she had ever expected to be again in this life. The mist, though bright, was dense; she could not make out the walls. When she glanced down, she could barely see her own two feet.

Abruptly she was gripped with pure cold rage.

"Enas Yorl!" she shouted. "Damn you! What have you done?"

Her surroundings shifted in unpleasant fashion, as though someone had taken normal space in either hand and given it a spiral twist. She felt she was about to lose her balance, though the weight remained on her soles. Clawing her knife from its scabbard, she prepared for an attack, knowing even as she clasped the hilt that any physical action here must be pointless.

Then the mist cleared, and she recognized the subterranean hall where she had first met Enas Yorl against her will. There was the table so long it could have seated the entire nobility of Sanctuary; there was the caped figure seated at its farther end; and all around her she heard echoes that brought shivers to her spine, as of cantrips which had set the thick stone walls to ringing like a new-struck bell.

She stood as immobile as on that first occasion, this time not by constraint, purely from her mingled fear and anger.

"You failed!" she accused.

Her words, themselves echoing along the monstrous room, drove away the fainter echoes. At long last Enas Yorl bestirred himself.

"No," he said in a thin voice. "I succeeded."

"*What?*" Jarveena took a pace toward him. It seemed not to diminish the distance that separated them; in any case, she had no wish at this moment to be in his presence at all, let alone come closer. "Then why did Klikitagh brush past me without a sign of recognition—worse: shove me out of his way like a persistent streetwalker?" Recollections crowded in. "Besides, you said that if you did succeed, he'd die!"

"Yes, so I did. Nonetheless . . ."

As she stood striving to unriddle the mystery, he heaved a sigh.

"Come hither. I'll explain."

The hall and table contracted to more customary dimensions; in a twinkling she found herself where she had been at daybreak, seated in the same chair. Unseen hands, as ever, had set it behind her knees just as she was about to lose her self-control completely.

Cautiously she returned her knife to its sheath, staring at the magician. But for the emberlike glow underneath his brows one could not have guessed this to be the same personage. His arms, in particular, were far too flexible. His? Might one not better say *its*?

But the voice remained, and was uttering slow words, as though each syllable exacted agonizing effort.

"I did succeed, Jarveena. At what cost I dare not say. Perhaps the cost of every shred of hope left in my inmost heart. I worked a rite such as has not been attempted in living memory—not, certainly, in mine . . . And worked it well."

"With what result?" she whispered.

"I learned the reason for the curse on Klikitagh."

She waited. When she could bear the waiting no longer, she demanded, "Tell me!"

"I shall not. This only will I say: His punishment is just."

"I don't understand!"

"Better you should not. Better that no one should. Had I known what a burden of knowledge I was taking on—no! Condemning myself to!—I'd never have set out to offer help."

Guessing at the meaning behind the words, Jarveena bit her lip. Tears sprang unbidden to her eyes, and yet were welcome, for they disguised the ghastly form that Enas Yorl was melting into.

"Here, then, in brief, is the secret Klikitagh has hidden from everybody in the world, himself included.

"His punishment *is* just. He told me so."

"It cannot be! No one could deserve that fate!"

"Until today I would have said the same," Enas Yorl said solemnly, shifting on his chair as though his new form had grown unsuited to it.

"But how can he have told you so?" Jarveena persisted.

"I chose this of all days rather by enlightened guesswork than by proper knowledge. As it happened, I was right. On one day of the year, in the proper circumstances, he is able to remember why he deserves his curse.''

"Tell me! Tell me!" Jarveena pleaded.

"Though you crept to me on hands and knees, bleeding in the extremity of death, begging to be told before your final breath, I would not let description of such foulness pass my lips!''

Not that, strictly speaking, it was lips he now must use to speak with . . .

"Know only this: after committing it, he bethought himself of his crime and repented. Haunted by self-loathing, he became a court to try himself, and passed the only sentence that was fitting. He wanted so to suffer that no person who had heard about his evil deed, and might be tempted to emulate it, would fail to hear as well about its perpetrator's punishment and change his mind—not considering that the time might come when any such would be long dead and all his victims totally forgotten. Therefore he made the sentence cruel past conceiving—save by one who was evil to the fiber of his nerves.

"He decreed that for all time he would believe, in total honesty and full conviction, that he'd done not a thing to warrant such a doom. Perhaps this affords some insight into the enormity of his misdeed.''

"But what can he have done?" Jarveena shouted.

"You'll never guess. It isn't in your nature to imagine, let alone enact, so foul a crime.''

"Has it tainted you?" She leaned forward accusingly, glad that she could only vaguely see the shape he now endured. "Has it deformed your mind as much as your body?" That was cruel, too, in its way, but she uttered the words regardless. "Have you no mercy? Is not a thousand years enough for even the foulest of villains?''

"Oh, yes.'' Enas Yorl's voice had become like the

sough of wind in bare-branched trees. "More than enough, in my view.

"Not in his."

"You—you mean . . ." Jarveena's mouth was suddenly dry. "You mean you tried to release him from the curse he wished upon himself?"

"I did."

"And he refused to let you, being a more powerful magician?"

"Not exactly."

She threw her hands in the air. "For pity's sake, Enas Yorl! Whether or not you pitied him, pity me who calls you friend! Never in my life before did I find anyone with better reason to hate the world than had I myself at nine years old! Make plain what you have done and not done!"

"I will try . . ." The voice grew fainter all the time. "But words must strain to compass these events. The spells required are half outside the normal universe . . . I did succeed! No other wizard now alive could have accomplished what Enas Yorl achieved today, not even he at Ilsig whom they call most skilled, not he at Ranke who *dis*-serves the court.

"Jarveena: *I gave Klikitagh his freedom.*"

There was a long stunned silence. When it had become more than she could bear, Jarveena husked, "But you said it would have killed him!"

"Which it did."

"*What?*"

"I speak in plain words, do I not? Despite the deformation I endure!" The tone was savage now, and sent new shivers down Jarveena's spine. "Well, maybe your nature fights acceptance. Words plainer then than ever must be tried.

"*I gave him his release! He died! And even dead, so dreadful is the power of that spell, he rose again and*

*said—praise all the gods that no one save myself could
hear those awful words!—'Dead or not dead, I am condemned to walk the world. I may not eat a second time
from the same table, nor may I sleep a second time in the
same bed. It is decreed. By me. It shall continue!'* "

From his recital of the quoted words rang forth a hint,
an echo, of the force that had endowed the curse on
Klikitagh with its original power. It was unbearable. Crying
aloud, her brain assailed by hideous visions, Jarveena
slumped fainting from her chair.

In the light of torches, both her cheeks gleamed wet.

She woke, once more at dawn, and found herself alone
at Melilot's, as had often happened to her in the past. Not
this time, however, was her frame pervaded by the truly
magic skill of Enas Yorl's caresses. Only a dull sense of
deprivation filled her mind as she kicked aside the covers
and moved to use her chamber pot, then douse herself with
the contents of the ewer on the nightstand. Then, uncon-
cerned as ever about nakedness, she dragged the curtains
back and threw the shutters wide to the new day.

Cold air combined with cold water to bring her back to
full alertness. She reached for her clothes—and checked,
catching sight of her reflection in the tall and expensive
mirror that hung beside the window.

There was no trace of any scar upon her body. Not the
faintest, lacelike, weblike hint beneath the skin could be
discerned. She was as perfect as though no wire-lashed
whip had ever whistled through the air to break blood from
her tender flesh.

Amazed, then astounded, she flicked back her forelock.
Surely the cicatrix her forehead bore—?

Gone as well.

"But I told him!" she said aloud. "I mean, I told
Melilot, and he was listening! I said I wanted to keep that
for when it came in useful . . ."

The words died away. She let her hands fall to her sides.

"Oh, you're in there, aren't you, Enas Yorl? You've sown a counterpart of yourself inside my brain! It's the same trick that taught me the names of your basilisks! Maybe you have too much on your mind to hear me at the moment, but I'm damned well going to treat your projection the same as I would yourself! Now answer me! Why did you take my forehead scar away before I gave you leave?"

The reply came, not in speech, but in a sense of warm and private intercourse, reaching below the deepest level of her mind. If it resembled anything at all, it might be likened to the impact of hot spiced wine on a cold day.

"Not me," said the mental duplicate of Enas Yorl in words that were not words. "Not by my intention, anyway. Listen, Jarveena, and remember all your life!

"Not to recall what he had done was for Klikitagh a mercy. I state this on the basis of what I have found out. To live with recollection of such horror . . . ! You must concede this."

She nodded, participating in this nonexistent dialogue.

"However, it became exacerbation of his punishment. It made his sentence unendurable. Indeed it was a mercy worse than none. He knew it, and condemned himself regardless."

Again a nod, tinged this time with terror.

"Yet you took pity on him!"

"Yes, I did!"—defiantly. "And I still feel the same!"

"You were the first to do so in a thousand years."

For an instant she stood rigid. Then:

"I can't have been!"

"He told me so when I interrogated him, invoking a power greater than any god's. Not once, till he met you, had anyone felt pity for his plight."

"Then I weep for our sick world!" Jarveena cried—and abruptly it was true. Tears that had so long been unfamiliar to her flowed as freely down her face as they had last night.

"And well you may," the illusory Enas Yorl confirmed. There was a pause.

"For you have worked a miracle."

"I don't understand." Snuffling, fighting to regain control, Jarveena resumed the donning of her clothes.

"How are your scars today?"

"Why ask? You cleared them, didn't you? And took away the one I'd thought of keeping!"

"Not I, Jarveena, but yourself."

She froze in midmovement, bending to strap her boots.

"Go forth, as soon as you are dressed, into the street. Do not ask why; you will at once find out. I worked a greater magic than I knew. For the moment, then: goodbye. Don't try to call on me until I send for you. The names I give my basilisks are daily changed. Sometimes I cannot give them names pronounceable by human tongues. That's why I have not spoken words to you this morning . . ."

The contact faded in a garble of discomfort that left Jarveena imagining for several seconds that she had four stomachs and a mouthful of regurgitated hay.

The sensation passed. The laces of her jerkin still unfastened, she dashed down the slanting ladders that served this house for stairs and cuffed aside a sleepy apprentice who tried to stop her unbarring the main door on the grounds that Master Melilot was still asleep. Beyond, in the wan gray light of dawn, she saw a form upon the cobblestones, face turned aside, one arm outflung, chest smeared with blood still red thanks to the sharp cold: victim, presumably, of some chance robber's knife . . .

"Klikitagh!" she whispered, dropping on one knee beside the . . . corpse?

It was indeed. No pulse was to be felt. A rime of frost had formed upon its hair, its beard, its hands . . .

Slowly she straightened, gazing down in wonder.

"So your journey ended here, in Sanctuary," she murmured. "Well, death was what you most desired. And . . ."

A thought occurred, as wonderful as it was terrifying.

"If I'm to believe what Enas Yorl asserts—and who but him should I believe in such a matter?—it follows that the worst crime in the history of the world has been committed. It was yours, my Klikitagh. And yours alone."

It was going to snow any moment. The air was so cold, the lips she licked were numb. She half expected to taste ice.

"But even you have reached the last stage of your pilgrimage in search of expiation. What now becomes of you will be no matter. Let your shroud be snow. Let dogs and thieves assail your body—you won't care. Perhaps you should have come to Sanctuary sooner. It cannot just have been because of meeting me that you were saved! I won't believe it!"

So saying, she spun on her heel and marched back into the scriptorium. Much relieved, the apprentice slammed and barred the door behind her. White flakes swirled down outside as she went to seek a breakfast of hot broth and dumplings.

By nightfall—for such had been the will of Enas Yorl—she cared no more for Klikitagh save in the sense that all misfortune must be pitied, and he had been least fortunate of all. He lingered in her memory as myth and symbol; meantime she had a life to lead herself.

"Mayhap," thought the wizard who sprawled across stone flags in guise but ill adapted to such human artifacts as chairs, "that snow enshrouding Klikitagh, by his own verdict foulest villain of all time, will cover me in turn. Let it be soon!"

Whereafter he composed himself to patient meditation, tinged with regret that for the duration of their present encounter he and Jarveena would be unable to make love.

SEEING IS BELIEVING
(BUT LOVE IS BLIND)

Lynn Abbey

Illyra awoke to the sound of an infant's crying and a sudden stiffening of the muscles in her neck and shoulders. She stayed that way, tense—almost cringing—until she heard the wet nurse shove her blankets aside then stumble across the night-dark room. The crying changed to contented sucking sounds; Illyra closed her eyes and shrank back into Dubro's arms. He hugged her reflexively but the infant had not interrupted his sleep. Why should it? Children were women's work and this child was not even his.

The S'danzo seeress matched her breathing to her husband's and waited for sleep to touch her again. She listened to the wet nurse tuck the infant back into her cradle and return to her own bed where she swiftly resumed her gentle snoring. Dubro's strong arms were no longer comforting but had become an encircling trap from which she could not free herself—tangible symbols of the weight she had felt since summer when her half-brother, Walegrin, had appeared with the newborn girl-child in his arms.

It had never seemed like a good idea. Three years ago Illyra had borne twins: a boy-child and a girl. Now they were both gone. The boy, Arton, had been taken from the mortal world. Caught up in the influence of the demigod, Gyskouras, he had sailed for the Bandaran Islands this past spring and if he returned at all, it would not be as her son, but as a wargod stranger. Worse, Lillis, her blue-eyed daughter, had been hacked into pieces by ravening street gangs during the Plague Riots at about the same time. Illyra had tried to protect her daughter with her own body—with her own life—but fate had denied her sacrifice. There was a purple scar running across her belly but it went not nearly so deep as the scars mourning had left on her heart.

She had nurtured her grief and had wanted nothing to do with living or joy. She had hated that squirming bundle Walegrin had thrust into her arms. Had wanted to dash its head against the doorposts because it lived and Lillis did not. But it had wrapped its fragile fingers around hers and stared into her eyes. And Illyra had Seen that this child would remain at her side.

Strange how the S'danzo Sight worked. It rarely focused on the self, family, or loved ones but brought the abstract, the uncared-for, into clarity. Illyra did not love—would not allow herself to care for—this not-daughter they called Trevya and so the infant flashed constantly in her mind's eye where the Seeing visions grew.

Had not Trevya's legs been crippled in the prolonged birthing that had claimed her blood-mother's life? Had not Illyra Seen, superimposed over every other vision she commanded, a construct of baleen and leather guiding the infant's soft bones into a healthy alignment? Had not Dubro made such a brace, following her precise instructions, and was not that twisted little leg already growing straighter as the Sight had foretold?

Illyra had wrought a miracle for Trevya, who was not her daughter and whom she did not love. She had given Trevya freedom and built an unyielding trap for herself. Hot tears squeezed out from her eyes and puddled in the crook of Dubro's arm. The young woman who had once been a mother prayed that they would not awaken him and

waited the long hours until dawn when she would be
released.

This not-daughter consumed more of Dubro and Illyra's
time and money than their own children had, for they kept
Trevya with them in the Bazaar rather than send her
behind the fortress walls of the Aphrodisia House where
working merchants often kept their precious children. So
they had had to hire a wet nurse, a woman—scarcely
more than a child herself—whose baby had been stillborn
and who had come to live with them alongside Dubro's
forge. But there wasn't enough room for them, Trevya and
the waiflike Suyan, so they'd hired workmen to make their
home larger. And, of course, Suyan must have food, and
clothes, and medicine when she grew sick.

Fortunately there was plenty of work to be had in Sanctuary these days. The new city walls were being made
from cut and dressed stone; there were picks and mauls in
need of constant repair and replacement. Dubro had both a
journeyman and an apprentice working beside him at the
forge these days, and he talked of building a larger furnace
beyond the rising walls. Verily, a fortune could be made
these days in Sanctuary, but the pump needed priming and
it seemed to Illyra that their coin hoard shrank rather than
increased.

She was half S'danzo, fully gifted with their preternatural clairvoyance but bereft of their tolerance for haphazard
poverty. She was half Rankan, through her father's blood,
and craved the material security that was the heritage of
that empire's middle class. And, of course, her S'danzo
Sight could offer no assurances to her Rankan anxieties.
Even without Trevya, Illyra would have lost many a night's
sleep this season.

As it was, she balanced on the edge between dreaming
and waking, and her thoughts spiraled far beyond her
control. Trevya's face drifted toward her, like a leaf on the
wind or driftwood with the tide. Illyra called her mind's

eye back, but it did not come and the face grew into a full Seeing of a child running through a neat flower garden, arms outstretched, silently laughing and singing a single word over and over again.

Illyra cried out, breaking the thrall of the Seeing but not disturbing her husband who, in truth, was accustomed to her cries in the night. The seeress, still bound in Dubro's protection, stared into the night determined now to remain fully awake. The vision would not be denied and inserted itself into her thoughts, demanding interpretation.

That was easy enough. If Trevya ran, then her legs grew straight and strong. If she ran through a garden, then she became a child in a place where beauty was an affordable luxury. If she sang as she ran, then she was happy. If that word was *Mother* . . .

But no, Illyra would not acknowledge that part of her Seeing—though it could have told her she would have the material security she craved. She preferred the loneliness of her anxiety and clutched its darkness tight around her until slits of dawn light came through the shutters.

Dubro stirred, freeing her as he did. The soul of routine and regularity, the smith rose with the first dawn light year around and had his forge ready when the sun peeked over the horizon. Usually the sight of his broad shoulders as they vanished beneath his worn leather tunic was enough to banish Illyra's night-born doubts, but not today—nor did she share any aspect of her visions with him. She remained huddled in the bed until Suyan had the baby at her breast and even then Illyra gathered her brightly colored garments as if in a trance.

"Feel you poorly?" Suyan asked with sincere concern.

Illyra shook her head and laced a rose-colored bodice tightly over her own breasts. The girl's voice—her odd, but lilting, syntax—grated with extra harshness this morning, and Illyra was, without forethought, determined to ignore her.

"Herself cried but once in the night, though if that come at a bad time, it's enough to keep you waking until dawn?"

Always a curl to her voice. Everything was a question that needed—no, *demanded*—an answer. But this time it would not work.

"There's herbs left from Masha zil-Ineel—from Herself's congestion—that could be brewed up?"

"I'm fine, Suyan," Illyra said at last. "I slept fine. The baby didn't bother me. You didn't bother me. And I don't need any herbs—just . . ." She inhaled a pause and wondered what she did need. "I'm going uptown today. What I need is a change of scenery."

Suyan nodded. She did not know her mistress well enough to sense how little Illyra needed change of any kind—and would not have done any different if she had.

Shunning her pots of kohl, Illyra brushed her hair into a thick chignon and wrapped a concealing, drab-colored shawl around her shoulders. She would never be mistaken for a woman who followed any of Sanctuary's fast-changing fashions but neither would she be taken for a S'danzo.

"You'll be wanting breakfast?" Suyan asked from the corner, the lilt making her maternal and chastising.

"No, no breakfast," Illyra replied, meeting the other woman's eyes for the first time, and watching them grow fragile with self-doubt. "I've got a craving for the little tarts Haakon sells; I'll get some on my way."

Those huge eyes grew bright and knowledgeable. "Aye, *cravings* . . ."

Illyra found her fist clenching into a warding sign. Suyan had her own need for security, and security for a wet nurse was her mistress's pregnancy. Not a day went by that somehow, buried in the lilting questions, the subject of Illyra's barrenness was not raised. As Illyra forced herself to relax, the unfairness of it all swept over her and she knew if she remained one more moment she would dissolve into tears that would only make her world worse.

"I'm going now," she muttered in a voice that sounded almost as bad as she felt.

Dubro was instructing the new apprentice in the finer arts of squeezing the bellows. His voice was deep and even with hard-held patience; there was nothing to be gained by interrupting him so Illyra gripped her shawl against the chill harbor wind and hoped to slip away.

"Madame . . . Madame Illyra. Seeress!"

Illyra shrank against the walls, unable to pretend that she had not seen or could not hear the young woman racing through the market-day crowd.

"Oh, wait, Seeress Illyra. Please wait!"

And she did, while the other woman caught her breath and pressed a filthy, battered copper coin into her hand.

"Help me, please. I've got to find him. I've looked everywhere. You're my last hope. You've got to help me."

Numbly Illyra nodded and retreated the few steps to the anteroom where she kept her cards and the other paraphernalia of the S'danzo trade. She could not refuse—though not because of the coin as the *suvesh* commonly believed. It was not payment that compelled the Sight but, sometimes, the contact of their flesh with her flesh. Already she was growing dizzy with the emergence of another reality. It would be a hazard to her if she attempted to deny the vision.

She pushed the deck across the table as she half collapsed onto her stool. "Make three piles of them," she commanded; there was no time to shuffle them.

The visitor's hand shook as she separated the deck. "Find my Jimny before it's too late!"

Illyra swallowed the notion that it was already too late, then surrendered herself to the emerging images: the Lance of Air, Seven of Ships, Five of Ores, reversed—the Whirlwind, the Warfleet and the Iron Key transformed into a lock. The lock wound through a chain and the chain grew from the belly of a dank, swaying ship—not an anchor chain, but a galley chain from keel to ankle, from ankle to wrist, from wrist to oar. The air reeked of drugged wine and echoed with a whip's crack.

It was too late. Illyra Saw slaves' faces, one clearly, the rest wrapped in fog, and heard—as was the way with her gift—Jimny speak out his own name. She separated herself from the Seeing and sought words to blunt the despair her answer must contain.

"Another card," she heard herself whisper. "Seek beneath the Whirlwind."

The *suvesh*, the ordinary non-S'danzo folk of the world, might not know any of the Seeing rituals but they knew the way things were supposed to go after they'd put their coin in a seeress's palm—and any deviation was certain to mean bad news. Illyra's visitor was sobbing openly as she reached for the first pile.

Two—not one—cards slipped free: the light-and-dark tunnel of the Three of Flames and the dark-faced portrait of the Lord of the Earth. Illyra absorbed them both and grew no wiser.

"He's been taken onto a boat," she said slowly, gathering the now lifeless chips of vellum into a single stack. "His leaving was not of his choosing," she continued, putting a high gloss over his enslavement before adding, without much conviction, "nor will he choose the time or manner of his return." Illyra could not bring herself to say that the best Jimny would likely get out of his future was a grave under the soil rather than the waves.

"Is there no hope? There must be something I can do. Something, anything. Which temple should I go to? Which gods should I pray to?"

Illyra shook her head, then spoke as a woman rather than a seeress. "There is always hope—but hope doesn't come from a handful of S'danzo cards."

Her visitor shuffled awkwardly to her feet. Illyra con-

firmed her suspicion that she was a few months shy of
giving birth and poorer than Suyan had been when they'd
found her.

"Take back your coin."

"Will it change things?"

"No, but it will buy you today's food and tomorrow's,
too."

"I won't need food tomorrow," the girl shouted through
her sobs as she ran from the room.

But she will, Illyra thought, weighed down by the Sight
of a pale woman and a scrawny child. *There's no death for
her. And no life either*.

The clanging of three hammers brought her out of her
visions. Dubro was tapping the cadence and the other two
were beating the red-hot iron. One of them had it right—
tap, *bang*; tap, *bang*—but the other, probably the apprentice, was off the mark and stuttered against the metal. The
forge reverberated with an unnatural rhythm that pene-
trated deep behind Illyra's weary eyes.

"Can't you get it right!" Illyra snarled, thrusting head
and shoulders through the anteroom drapes.

The percussive chorus came to an immediate halt with
an aghast look on the faces of the younger men and a
knowing, concerned one on Dubro's.

"Learning's not easy," her husband said cautiously, his
blue eyes narrowed to unreadable slits.

"What, then, is he learning? How to give me a
headache?"

Dubro nodded twice, once to his men who laid down
their hammers and the second time to his wife as he
approached her. He wrapped his arm gently around her
and brought her into the anteroom beside him. Just as the
forge was his true home—a place built to his scale and
comfort—so the scrying chamber was Illyra's true home
and it made him seem an unwelcome giant scraping his
head on the rafters, yet unable to sit, as the visitor's chair

would not take his weight.

" 'Lyra, I'll send them home, if you want, but I think it's not the hammering that's wrong. What ails you, 'Lyra?"

Illyra on her scrying stool had taken command of the room. She would have had to arch her neck to see Dubro's face, but she had no intention of meeting her husband's eyes. She spoke to the table instead, in a soft voice that emphasized the smith's awkwardness. Yet she was no more comfortable than Dubro; her hands sought the scrying deck and her fingers riffled through the cards.

"Everything and nothing, husband. I do not know what ails me—and I'm almost past caring." The cards broke free of her nervous fingers to scatter across the green cloth.

Heaving a sigh as he moved, Dubro dropped to one knee; he could look into Illyra's eyes and force her to look into his. "Read the cards for me, then. Ask them what I must do to make you happy."

Illyra avoided him, watching the cards as she gathered them into a rough-sided stack. "You know I cannot. I love you. I cannot See what I love."

She raised her eyes, thinking to shame him but was herself shamed by what she read, without Sight, in his face. He doubted her love and, now that the notion flowed within her thoughts, he had a right to, because she doubted it as well. The worst pain Illyra had ever known shuddered along her spine. The cards spilled onto the table when she hid her face behind her hands. She never imagined Dubro would study and remember each image in the moment before he reached across the table to massage her neck and shoulders.

"Had we rich relations or a hidden villa surrounded by lakes and trees, I'd send you away. It's Sanctuary herself who's hurt you," Dubro said with an eloquence few others knew he possessed.

Illyra imagined the villa and recognized it from her

predawn vision of Trevya. Fresh sobs came loose within her as she shook herself free of the villa and her husband.

"What, then?" Dubro asked, a trifle less understanding.

"I don't know. I don't know . . ." but then, though she still could not discern the nature of, much less the solution to, her problems, Illyra stumbled across something that could, under different circumstances, have accounted for her despair. At least to Dubro.

"I woke this morning with a foreboding around me," she admitted, not yet lying but working herself up to the sort of half-truths she routinely fed her visitors. "I thought to escape, but that woman came and the foreboding became a Seeing. She wanted to know where her lover had gone and I found him—in chains in the belly of a ship somewhere. And though I only Saw his face clearly, I saw as well that he was not alone and that many men had been pressed into slavery."

Dubro grew thoughtful, as she had known he would. Chains were made from iron, and Dubro knew every man in Sanctuary who knew that metal—in any of its forms— against his flesh. The blue eyes grew unfocused as he, like any other ungifted *suvesh*, ordered and made sense of his thoughts.

Illyra watched his pupils move as each mote of knowledge fell into place. Her sense of guilt lessened; she had tricked him into thinking about something else—but a good issue might yet come of it. She gathered her cards and wrapped them in a square of silk, never noting which ones had lain exposed.

"This is something for your brother, Walegrin," Dubro decided with a firm nod of his head.

"You tell him then. I'm going for a walk, maybe I'll find a garden somewhere. I don't want to go to the barracks."

Dubro grunted and Illyra suppressed a sigh. A year ago, less even, and her husband would have gone into a rage at the mention of Walegrin's name. He had blamed all their misfortunes on her straw-haired brother. Now, since Walegrin had deposited Trevya in her arms, the commander was welcome in their house and the two men often spent the evening in a tavern. Dubro had even gone so far as to share the cost of posting the child to citizenship in the increasingly meaningless Rankan Empire.

Illyra couldn't imagine conversation, let alone friendship, between the two taciturn men, had never really tried, then realized they talked about her. She had pushed them together with the wall she had built around herself. But the understanding brought no desire for reform.

"Talk to him then. Maybe eat with him as well. I don't think I'll be back until after sundown."

She straightened her shawl and eased past him to the door, never touching him, even with her skirts. The journeyman and the apprentice were gone. Trevya was squalling despite Suyan's best efforts to sing her quiet. None of it caught Illyra's heart. She was into the market-day crowd without a backward glance.

There were perhaps two dozen S'danzo in Sanctuary, counting the female children. The men and the children moved unnoticed through the city—especially now that it had become the workplace of the empire with strangers still arriving each day. But the women, the seeresses true and false, put down their roots in the Bazaar and rarely left its confines. Illyra recognized many of the faces she passed, but none recognized hers. As free as she felt, she was also very much alone and shrinking with each step farther from the Bazaar and the forge.

She was all but invisible when she reached the main gate of the palace. She was known here, and recognized, from the many visits she had made to her son when he lived in the royal nursery with the god-child, Gyskouras. She was not greeted, as she passed into the interior corridors, for much the same reason.

There were others here who knew her, who mumbled a greeting with their eyes averted from hers as they picked up their pace to be gone from her shadow as quickly as possible. It was, perhaps, a great honor to be the mother of a godling. Certainly the slave-dancer who'd been the mother of the other child did well by her servants, suite, and jewels, but such motherhood did not inspire mortal friendship. In truth, though, Seylalha, with her lithe beauty, would have found her nest of luxury without Gyskouras's help and Illyra, confidante to half of Sanctuary, had never had any friends.

Aside from Dubro and Walegrin, whose relationship to her was defined in ways other than friendship, there was only one to whom Illyra could bare her soul: Molin Torchholder. And it was a sorry state when a godless S'danzo claimed counsel with a Rankan priest.

At that moment, however, Illyra wore her isolation like armor and strode by the stairway that would have taken her to Molin's cluttered suite. She had her destination clearly in mind: a sheltered cloister that caught the sun without the chill wind. A place certain to have flowers even this late in the year.

The little courtyard was empty—deserted for considerable time and given over to weeds. Two hardy roses held onto brown-edged blooms, their scent all the stronger for the frost that had doomed them. The rest was yellow-top, white lace, and, in the most sheltered corner, a patch of fiery demons-eyes. Illyra was grateful she had no allergies as she gathered an armful of the blooms and settled onto a sunlit stone bench to weave them into a garland.

She'd learned the flower braiding in a vision once. Her mother had certainly never taught her, nor Dubro, nor Moonflower, who'd told her what she'd needed to know about womanhood and her gift. She'd learned other things as well: bits of song and poetry, snippets of lovemaking, tricks for killing with a knife or sword. She knew too much to be just one person—and she'd loved Lillis because she yearned to share herself with someone, anyone, who would understand.

Trevya could never understand.

The sun warmed her shoulders, finally loosening the knots that had been there since that late winter day when she'd last held a living daughter of her own blood in her arms. Illyra turned her face upward, eyes closed, imagining an ageless Lillis: child, woman, and friend. She took that predawn vision and changed it until it was her own daughter and she could hear the laughter and the single word: *mother, mother, mother . . .*

But the laughter, Illyra realized after a blissful moment, was real—echoing within the cloister—not in her imagination. She opened her eyes and gazed upon the passel of children who had invaded her retreat with their games. There were none that she recognized from her visits to the nursery—save that two were clearly Beysib. Both were girls and, by their apparent ages, immigrants like their parents.

"It's your turn now!"

"And no peeking!"

The designated child, the younger of the Beysib pair, separated reluctantly from the group. Her arms and legs, which extended well beyond her fine but dirty and shapeless tunic, were still pudgy with baby fat; her gait was still flat-footed, after the manner of toddlers, rather than rolling. Her face pulled back into a near-bawling grimace as the distance between herself and the others increased but none of the children had as yet noticed Illyra sitting still and quiet on her bench.

The little girl squared her shoulders and put her hands over her eyes.

"Out loud. Count out loud, Cha-bos!" the other Beysib girl commanded.

"One . . . two . . . th-th-three . . ."

By the count of four the other children had vanished, squealing and shouting and quickly dispersing through the tangle of rooms and hallways of their home. The little girl, Cha-bos, heard the silence and lowered her hands from her tear-streaked face. She noticed Illyra for the first time.

The nictating membrane that distinguished the exile community from the continental norm flicked over the child's amber eyes and she *stared*. Illyra, despite her best efforts, started backward just as reflexively. But Cha-bos was apparently immune to that gesture—or at least already able to conceal her own reactions.

"I can't count to one hundred," Cha-bos declared, confident that she had explained everything, and Illyra learned that Beysibs could cry while they were staring.

"Neither can I," Illyra admitted—not that she had ever had need to count so many things.

Cha-bos wilted. What use was an adult who knew no more than she did? "It doesn't matter," she told herself and Illyra. "They don't want me to play anyway."

Caught up in those huge, fixed eyes, Illyra Saw that Cha-bos was right. The older children had not continued with the simple game but were, even now, regrouping for a greater adventure.

"I'm sorry. You'll grow up soon enough."

"They won't ever grow *down*."

Illyra felt herself squirming to get free of the child's endless eyes. She realized why the other gifted S'danzo women stayed so close to their families—where familiarity, if not love, inhibited the curse of Sight and the scrying table turned vision into a cold business. She especially did not want to know that Cha-bos was no ordinary child— even for a Beysib—but the daughter of the Beysa Shupansea, and already her blood was laced with potent poison.

"You can't have any friends, can you?" she blurted.

Cha-bos went solemn and shook her head in a slow arc,

but the membrane flicked back and she blinked. "Vanda. She takes care of me."

Vanda was a name Illyra recognized from before. An Ilsigi girl who had somehow gotten herself made nurse-maid to the polyglot menagerie of the palace nursery. Illyra had not seen her since Arton had been sent away and had, for no good reason, assumed the young woman had been swallowed back into the city.

"Is Vanda still here?"

"Course she's here. I need her."

Cha-bos's faith in Vanda was as strong as her gut-level certainty that the world—in the proper order of things—revolved around her personal needs. She was willing to lead Illyra through the palatial maze to an interior chamber which by its chaotic condition and the size of its beds had to be the current location of the nursery.

Vanda sat with her needle and thread amid heaps of children's ravaged clothing. Her face glowed with genuine welcome when Cha-bos announced herself but cooled and became mature when she saw Illyra.

"It's been a long time," she explained, shaking the mending from her lap and bowing slightly—as was proper in the presence of one who was the mother of a potential god. "Fare you well?"

Illyra nodded and was at a loss for words, wondering what she had hoped to accomplish by visiting. "Well enough," she stammered politely.

Living with children had preserved some of Vanda's audacity and forthrightness. "What brings you here?" she asked, taking up the mending again.

Illyra felt her mind carom wildly from one mote of knowledge to the next. Vanda was the daughter of Gilla and Lalo the Limner. Gilla had watched as her children embarked on the journey of adulthood, and had buried one who had not at the same time Illyra's Lillis had been laid in her grave. Gilla had also nursed Illyra through the bleak

weeks of their mutual mourning. Vanda would know what
her mother knew, and Vanda knew children. . . .

"I have a child," Illyra began from somewhere deep in
her heart.

Surprise and suspicion flickered across Vanda's face.
"Oh." she sighed as a calm mask formed over her features. "How fortunate for you." It was a voice to quiet the
insane.

The S'danzo couldn't help but feel the emotional distance Vanda hurriedly created between them. But her despair was a throbbing, emotional aneurysm and, having
finally found its voice, it would not be stilled. She described how Trevya had been literally dumped in her arms
and how the child gave her no peace. She spoke of Trevya's
twisted leg and the psychic intrusions that had led to the
construction of the baleen splint which, though it was
straightening her bones, chafed her skin and made her cry
for hours at a time.

Then Illyra told herself and Vanda about the changes
that had come over Dubro since Trevya's arrival. Come
over him and between them as if children were inter-
changeable and a woman's love flowed to any infant that
squirmed in her arms. Not, of course, that it was just one
child; there was also Suyan who was little more than a
child herself. And the new apprentice who, though he still
lived with his family in the town, *expected* that she would
care for him . . . about him.

And through it all Vanda sat attentive and blank, polite,
and growing more reserved with each syllable the S'danzo
uttered. Until Cha-bos, who had gotten infinitely bored
very early in Illyra's oration, inserted herself into their
attention.

The child had unearthed one of her *ti-cosa*, the miniature
version of the Beysib court costume, padded and embroi-
dered so it bulked as much as Cha-bos herself.

"Fix it!" she demanded as she began a run across the room.

Ribbons trailed from the robe's seams and edges, imitating the poisonous Beynit vipers that dwelt with the older female members of the Beysa's intimate family.

"Cha-*bos*-tu!" Vanda shouted the child's full name as the impending catastrophe came closer.

Emerald and ruby silk serpentined around the child's legs. Cha-bos lurched forward, unaware at first that she was no longer in control of her unbalanced burden. She shrieked as she tumbled forward, becoming a confused mass of cloth and child. The nursery was frozen and quiet when her motion ceased. For a moment Illyra and Vanda believed no harm had been done, then a wail of heartrending terror erupted from the tangled embroidery.

Vanda reached her first, fairly shouting her reassurances as she separated Cha-bos from the *cosa*. A splinter as long as the child's finger protruded from her forearm. (The floors, this high up in the palace, were constructed of wooden planking that had seen better days.) Chabostu, second daughter of Shupansea and witness to all that had driven her mother into exile in Sanctuary, was transfixed by the sight of her own blood. Her whole body stared in the rigid Beysib way; her only movement came during her spasmodic gasps between screams.

Vanda could not relax the child's arm and when she yanked the splinter free the blood followed in bright red spurts.

"Dear Shipri preserve me," the nursemaid intoned as Cha-bos's wide-open eyes went completely white. "Hold her!"

The child was thrust into Illyra's unwilling arms as Vanda shouted for the palace guards and crawled toward the unmended clothing to tear a compress. Illyra rocked back on her heels and went almost as rigid as Cha-bos herself as the warm blood trickled along her fingers.

This was no ordinary child—no ordinary blood. That was foul and potent venom gathering in the crevice between her thumb and forefinger. Illyra gulped, shuddered, and nearly fainted as the fluid streamed over her wrist and out of sight beneath her cuff. There was nothing she wanted to do more than heave the little girl across the room and get as far from her as mortally possible. But Vanda was back, ripping strips of cloth with her teeth, and the corridor resounded with approaching guards.

Illyra could do nothing but contain her revulsion as Vanda tended the wound and Cha-bos twitched and shuddered in her arms. The nursery shimmered with surreal absurdity: what manner of contagion could possibly take root in a child whose very blood was poison? Then the visions came.

She was in the Beysib Empire, Seeing a nightmare world with a child's eyes. Giants stormed from living shadows with red-dripping steel in their hands. Cold, unyielding hands held her from behind and made the world go wild as they moved her from the familiar to the horrible.

A face swam before her: a face half her mother and half hard, grimacing giant—and the other part, the part that was not her mother, was in control. But mostly there was blood as the last fortress loyal to Shupansea fell to their enemies and the noblest individuals of the empire scrambled for their lives like lowly peasants.

Illyra, whose childish memory held scenes no less graphic, shared Chabostu's terror—and an unhealable outrage that not one of those giants who habitually controlled her world took notice of her. Worse, her mother, Shupansea, seemed herself to have been reduced to gibbering.

In the starkly judgmental mind of young Cha-bos, Shupansea had usurped the attention and comforting that belonged to her. Cha-bos was unable to comprehend this inversion of the universe and so had transformed it into something she could understand: She had never felt like this before and she'd never seen so much blood before, so blood must cause the feeling. Must lead to the feeling inevitably.

And blood became the ultimate terror in her world.

Vanda worked furiously to cleanse and conceal the child's wound, well aware of the child's progressive fears if not of their cause. Though the guards had been assured that the injury was neither serious nor the result of any malfeasance, they raised a racket in the nearby corridors—primarily designed to prove to Shupansea (who had also been summoned) that they were diligent in their duties. Illyra watched the commotion from a greater distance. She had freed herself from the child's visions, thereby insulating herself somewhat from her own fear of the poisonous fluids still staining her arm. She had wisely resisted returning completely to the world of the frantic nursery.

The seeress remained detached from her surroundings until Shupansea crossed the threshold with Prince Kadakithis and a dozen courtiers in her wake. The Beysa dropped gracefully to her knees and attempted to take her daughter into her arms. Chabostu would have none of it and fought like a little demon to avoid her mother's attention.

"Your Serenity . . . ?" Vanda interjected cautiously, cocking a finger ever so slightly to the bandage.

Knowing what would happen if the wound bled again, Shupansea withdrew her arms. "It has been very difficult for her," she explained softly and quickly to Illyra, speaking like any mother who had been shamed or rejected by her offspring rather than as the de facto ruler of Sanctuary.

Illyra, though she was the mother of a probable god, had no idea how to speak to one who was personally both goddess and queen. She cast a furtive glance toward Vanda whose nod, she assumed, meant she should treat Shupansea with the same calculated familiarity she accorded her paying visitors. "Children have their own minds," she said with a trace of a smile.

The Beysa had the good manners not to *stare*, but her pet viper chose that moment to rustle through her undergarments and poke its jewel-colored head above her collar. It tasted the air, revealing its crimson maw and ivory fangs, then, while the women held motionless, it lowered itself onto Illyra's sleeve.

"Don't move," Shupansea cautioned unnecessarily.

The immense *NO* remained imprisoned until the beynit investigated the clotted blood on Illyra's sleeve with its darting tongue. Any thoughts of instant death were insignificant compared to the reality of the serpent's touch. With a stifled gasp, Illyra propelled herself out of the circle, flinging the serpent and the child in opposite directions.

Cha-bos cried, the snake disappeared, and Illyra was surrounded by a mixed cohort of palace guards. Rankan, Ilsigi, and Beysib by the look of them, they were united by the steadiness with which they kept their well-sharpened spears pointed at her throat.

The guards saw their duty; no one would blame them for not following procedure when the child of an avatar of one goddess was bounced on the floor by the mother of another. For once Sanctuary proved itself a place of law and due process. Not even the protests of the prince and the Beysa combined could free the S'danzo from the ordeal of reporting to the watch commander.

"There's nothing to worry about," the prince assured Illyra as he joined the bristling circle escorting her from the nursery. (Shupansea remained behind, watching her daughter and looking for her snake.) "It's just a formality. Sign your name a few times and it will all be over."

This brought little comfort to the seeress who signed her name with an X like almost everyone else in Sanctuary.

It might have been different if Dubro had accompanied his wife—for he had begun life destined to be a scribe, not a blacksmith, and remembered what he now had little use for. Unfortunately Dubro wasn't even at the forge when a liveried palace servitor made his appearance there, and Suyan was awed into incoherence.

Not that Dubro had told her where he was going when he banked the fire and lowered the leather awning that separated the entrance to his workplace from the entrance to Illyra's. He could hardly admit to himself that he was going to the back wall where the other S'danzo seeresses made camp, to ask their advice.

He thought of Moonflower and was not the only person in Sanctuary that day or any other to gently mourn her untimely death. She'd been barely taller than Illyra but in all other respects she was built on Dubro's scale and he'd felt comfortable around her.

He reconsidered his whole plan as he entered the incense-rich, S'danzo quarter. He had decided to turn around and retreat to his own familiar world, when he was caught in the appraising glare of the woman who had replaced Moonflower as most indomitable among the seeresses.

"Greetings, blacksmith," the tall stick of a woman called. "What brings you up here?"

It was not done to walk away from the Termagant. She was the living embodiment of every tale ever whispered in the dark about the S'danzo. No sane man doubted that she would and could curse anything that crossed her path in the wrong light.

Dubro crumpled the lower edge of his tunic in his fists and took a step in her direction. "I have a question to ask—about the cards."

She looked him up and down, which took a moment or two, then pulled aside the curtain to her scrying room. "Then come, by all means, and ask it."

The Termagant lived alone. No one dared ask or remember if she'd ever had a family. As far as the other S'danzo and all the rest of Sanctuary were concerned she had always been exactly as she was. An aura of timelessness hung over her—by gaudy S'danzo standards—austere chambers. Her wooden table was worn black and shiny from years of use.

Her cards were tattered at the edges, their images both faded and stained. She was a seeress who let no one but herself touch the *amashkiki*: the cards, the Guideposts of Vision. They cascaded from one knobby hand to the other as she settled on her stool.

"Tell me where to stop. Choose your first significance."

Dubro thrust his hands, palms outward, between himself and the flittering paper. "No," he stammered. "I do not choose cards. Illyra chose them."

The cascade came to an abrupt halt. "If she chose, what is your question?" she inquired, though surely she suspected the answer.

"She cannot read for those she loves. She would not lay down the cards—but certain ones fell from her hands. I believe that she cannot read for us—but I do not believe she cannot choose."

"For an overly large man, you are not without perception," the Termagant said between self-satisfied cackles. Dubro folded his hands and said nothing. "Very well, describe the cards you saw."

"There were five. I've heard her name them Orb, Quicksilver, Acorn, Ocean, and Emptiness."

For ten or more years Dubro had stood outside Illyra's workroom, pointedly ignoring the wherewithal of her craft. Yet he had absorbed something despite the banging of his hammer. His eyes met hers and were not put off by the disbelief that grew there.

"Prime cards each and all," he averred.

Not to be outdone, the seeress set her own cards back in their silken nest with imperturbably steady hands. "I don't suppose you noticed the relation of the cards one to another as they lay? Reversed or covering?"

"They *fell* from her hands," he repeated.

"I see." A lengthy pause between them. "Well, then, I suppose it's safe to assume the simplest message: all images erect and alone. It will be easiest that way. You do want the *simplest* interpretation, don't you?"

Dubro nodded, unfazed by her sarcasm. They'd had dealings with this woman before. Her acid was as normal a part of her as a smile was to Illyra—or had been to Illyra.

"I take it you know that among the *amashkiki* there are five families: fire, ore, wood, water, and air, as correspond to the five elements from which the universe was made. Each family is led by its Prime and defended by its Lance. There are, of course, cards which do not fall into the families but they are of no concern here for you described only Prime cards. Every Prime card."

Again Dubro nodded. He had known that. The *amashkiki* had been generally adapted by the larger society around the S'danzo, though only *they* preserved its arcane functions. A gaming hand showing five Primes was worth a heavy bet.

"The Lances defend. They are rigid, sharp-edged, defined. The Primes, though, are the start of things." The gray-haired woman grinned. "And also the ends. Magicians like the Prime cards because they mean everything, you know. The appearance of a Prime simplifies the reading, she may have told you this; two Primes and it practically shouts. Five Primes is absurd—and you, blacksmith, I think, know that."

This time he grunted, but it meant the same as a nod.

"Perhaps she had just ordered the *amashkiki* and merely dropped the end cards?"

"She'd just sent out a visitor. If I thought it were an accident, I'd not have come here."

"Then you and she stand on the cusp. All has already been revealed to you. It wants only your feet upon the path."

Dubro nodded to himself, letting her statements shore up his own convictions. The old S'danzo's eyes narrowed. At her age, Sight was a secondary gift. Her chiefmost asset was her long knowledge of mortal behavior. The Termagant could read as much in a gesture as the S'danzo Sight might have revealed in her cards.

"If she waits much longer," the crusty woman admitted, "that path may well rise up to bite her feet. It is not to be denied."

"But she *will* deny it, amoushka"—a S'danzo diminutive for grandmother or elder seeress. "She *sees* Trevya wherever she turns, but her heart only grows harder."

The Termagant snorted. "She is a little fool who should by now know what happens when children get tangled up in the Sight and fate."

Even swollen with strong-backed workers from every corner of the empire, Sanctuary was still a small place where no one was by more than three or four degrees a stranger to anyone else. It took a determined insularity to live in rumorless ignorance; it was utterly impossible to live in privacy. The entire city had known about Illyra's first children and the Termagant was informed about her well-cared-for but unwelcome not-daughter.

"The longer your wife denies what her Sight has shown her, the more inevitable it becomes, blacksmith. Glimpsed once, fate is a weak thing subject to change and uncertainty—especially for the young. But repeatedly glimpsed and denied, as Illyra has done . . ." The Termagant shook her head and chortled softly to herself. "Ah, nothing in this life is accidental. Perhaps she knows what she's doing; not even Illyra is stronger than fate."

The interview had come to an end. There was another visitor hovering beyond the curtained doorway. Dubro scrunched down to pass under the lintel.

"Mind you," the old S'danzo added as the curtain slid

across his back, "if you and yours are pawns in fate's game, you will not feel its hand upon your back."

Dubro shook his head and kept moving. He was *suvesh*; he expected clear answers when he went to an oracle and he ignored the ones that weren't. Visiting the S'danzo quarter had been a long shot at best: a rare submission to the gambling urge. He was satisfied that he had not lost anything by the inquiry and was not unduly distressed that he went away no wiser than he'd arrived.

It was about midday. The crowds were thick and his two assistants were gone for the day. He could go back to his forge and do a few hours of business in the old way—by himself—or he, like everyone else in his extended family, could take the rest of the day off. And, as it seemed a day for impulses, Dubro decided against the forge for once. He made his way through the town to the palace.

Walegrin and his men had the first of three great watches these days, coming on duty in the cold, predawn hours, then relieved at just about this time. Even if the man hadn't been his brother-in-law, Dubro wold have chosen him over the other two watch-commanders, the eminently corruptible Aye-Gophlan or the murdering Zip, to tell about Illyra's visions.

And lately, as Illyra suspected, they'd found a comfortable subject of conversation in their concerns for her. A hearty meal and a few mugs of ale in the all-male taproom of the Tinker's Knob might be just the cure for his own irksome malaise. The market-day crowds parted before him once his destination, the palace barracks, was fixed in his mind.

"There, you see, I told you it was nothing," Prince Kadakithis said with rather too much surprise in his voice to be entirely convincing.

Illyra nodded weakly. They might have at least warned her that her examiner would be none other than her own half-brother—and whatever other flaw Walegrin might have, his sense of family loyalty was above reproach. He'd made it plain that it was reasonable to panic when one of those infernal snakes was around.

"I'm certain the kitchens have got more than enough food. Shall I have the guards escort you there? I'd go myself, but . . ." The prince cast his eyes upward—in the general direction of not only the nursery but the Hall of Justice and Torchholder's suite of exchequer and registry. Neither husband nor ruler, yet somewhat more than a decorative figurehead, Kadakithis showed his adolescence more these days than he had seven years ago when he had first arrived as a naive puppet. He was growing but not yet grown.

"Thank you, I can find it myself," Illyra assured him.

He seemed genuinely relieved and took off at a decidedly unregal trot. Illyra had a flash vision of him seated on a steel-colored stallion, then nothing, as her thoughts turned to the aromas wafting out of the beehive-roofed kitchen. They'd recognize her there and accord her the same distant politeness the other palace retainers did: they knew they were better than some S'danzo wench from down in the Bazaar even if she did have the ear of royalty and the gods.

With a tightly woven basket, worth more than the food it contained, slung in her shawl, Illyra strolled into the bright forecourt. She might wander along the general's road to the hills where the trees had turned a hundred shades of red, gold, and orange. Or she might go to the Promise of Heaven which was usually deserted by daylight. Or she might . . .

Illyra's musings stopped short when she caught sight of a familiar figure passing under the West Gate. Dubro—and though she herself had told him to seek out Walegrin her heart began to pound. Once or twice—when she'd been a child and the blacksmith her protector, not her husband—

she'd run away from him, but never in recent years. Until now. She scooted behind a water cart, crouching over her basket, pretending to examine its contents.

She waited, cried, and thought of Cha-bos who hadn't known how to count to one hundred. When her tears had dried she decided it was safe. She headed in the direction she was now facing—to the back corner of the palace, past the ornate gate where priests and gods made their communion with temporal authority.

The palace stoneyard was here, ready for the next round of palatial repairs, and the huge water cisterns to sustain the inner fortress in times of siege. Though far from lost—she could still see the water cart—Illyra had entered unfamiliar territory and did not know the name of the little gate she discovered there. Or even if it was a deliberate gate and not one of Molin Torchholder's bright ideas. It seemed, judging by the dust, to be the main conduit between the work gangs and the palace.

"Hey, sweetheart, got anything in there for me?" a half-naked roustabout called from farther down the path.

"No, just my own meal."

"You're sure? A pretty little piece like you shouldn't be out here eating alone. . . ."

Illyra understood, then, what he had in mind. She blushed radiantly; he laughed heartily and she ran through the nameless gate into the jumbled red sandstones piled beyond it. Indignation got the better of her; she wished all manner of minor disasters upon the workman who had not recognized her as a happily married matron and implied propositions never suggested to a S'danzo seeress.

She ate the creamy cheese without tasting it. The fire of her shame burned inwardly now, illuminating the misunderstanding with which the world treated her. It wasn't as if she asked for so much, Illyra reminded herself. It was pure selfishness and stubbornness that kept those who claimed to love her from understanding that her world—

her promise of happiness—had ended when Lillis died. If they really loved her they would commiserate with her and cease their meaningless efforts to jolly her out of mourning.

Her life was a tragedy: a slow dirge relentlessly playing between Lillis's death and her own. She'd become a martyr—and was comfortable with that identity.

"You should not scowl so."

Illyra sent the basket flying and stared into the sun, unable to recognize the man who spoke so familiarly to her.

"And you should be more careful where and how you make your personal storms."

Not about to be scolded by a stranger—or anyone else, for that matter—Illyra was tempted to break her private vows and launch a full-fledged S'danzo curse in his direction. But something she did not understand restrained her. She clambered down from her perch and gathered her scattered meal instead.

From this angle, away from the sun, he was easier to see but no more recognizable. Not that there weren't a dozen incomprehensible languages spoken these days along the walls—but this one wasn't a stoneworker. Even Tempus, silhouetted by a bloody setting sun, was not so timeless and out of place as this man seemed to be. Moreover, she could not *See* him or his shadow which boded ill when Sanctuary itself was remarkably free of magic.

"I'm a free woman," she said petulantly, climbing onto a different stone where the light was better and she could look straight into his eyes.

"Not here you're not."

He was calm, not threatening; speaking simple facts as if there were something obvious she had overlooked. But what could be overlooked sitting on forgotten rubble with her back to the main path?

"Look down," he suggested in a bemused and paternal manner.

Down. The dirt was red where years of storms had had their way with the sandstone. Nothing grew there. Nothing was buried there. She couldn't See anything.

"Where you're sitting. Where you've been sitting this past hour."

Well, *that*. It was rubble, after all. These stones had been dressed and shaped into a building once, a long time ago. Not as if these were the only rocks around with little chips and bumps of some forgotten language on their sides. Lords and frogs, it could be Rankene for all she would know, wind-blasted as it was and illiterate as she was.

She took a mean-tempered bite out of her fruit and jawed it pointedly. "So?"

"Are you blind, child?"

This stranger with his beaten, bronze-colored armor and his probing, dark eyes deserved nothing less than a S'danzo curse, Illyra decided. His stare was worse than a Beysib's and his high-and-mighty attitude worse than that. He'd be less arrogant when the S'danzo were through with him. She wrapped her thoughts in the ancient forms, then dug deep in her memory to find the ritual words that would merge her desire with the Sight.

He sprang at her, though she prepared her curse in silence, and wrestled her from the stone with his hand locked firmly over her mouth.

"You fool," he exclaimed, dropping her to the ground. "You blind, hopeless fool. How many times has Sanctuary been damned by petty curses uttered in ignorance by petty fools who don't recognize sanctity when they see it?"

Illyra swept the dust from her skirt as she stood. He was too sincere in his protests, too secure to challenge directly. "Who are you to scold me?" she muttered, watching the ground. "Who made you the guardian of Sanctuary? You're just another stranger come to work on the walls. It's my home and I'll send it to hell and back if I want to."

"You're more the fool than I thought, Illyra the Seeress."

"All right, I don't want to damn it to hell. I'd love to see a Sanctuary where flowers bloomed along the streets and honest people didn't have to hide after sundown. I'd love to see a Sanctuary where men loved their wives, wives loved their children, and children had a chance to grow up with food in their bellies.

"Who wouldn't want Sanctuary like that? But Sanctuary's Sanctuary and it never changes."

She raised her eyes to glower at him and to make him think better of whatever he had meant to say next.

"If you could bring yourself to take care of it, it might change into something better. Maybe even something you could love."

"That'd be the day. Who are you, anyway?"

"Call me a shepherd."

Illyra cocked her head at him. Whatever he was, the only sheep he saw were dead, cooked, and served to him on a platter. Some errant warrior, more likely. She noticed he'd left a horse drop-tied back on the path, and noticed that no one was coming or going on the path, either. It was not really a good idea to argue with one whose saddle and weapon belt bristled with a dozen modes of death.

"All right, I give Sanctuary my blessing—"

"From the rock."

She seated herself on the first stone and made a show of clearing her throat. "I give Sanctuary my blessing," she repeated. A gust of wind carried dust into her eyes; that, and the back-lighting sun made it impossible to see him clearly. "Let its people live in peace. Let its governors rule wisely. Let its walls be strong and its stewpots full.

"There, is that more like it?" she demanded, squinting into the sun.

"You forgot love."

"Right, husbands love wives; wives love children; children . . . oh, children love whoever they want."

"It's a start," the unlikely shepherd confirmed. "Mighty trees and the like. Are you thirsty?"

He unslung a wineskin and offered it to her. Thinking he meant to embarrass her, Illyra took it. Not that many townswomen could aim the bladder and catch the stream without covering themselves with wine. She could. She'd learned to drink from a skin—and not from a borrowed vision, either. It was one of the very few things her father had taught her. The wine wasn't half bad: a bit tannic, perhaps, but not local. She caught a last drop and handed the skin back to him, smiling like a well-fed cat.

"Thank you," she said and noted with some satisfaction that she'd surprised him with her skill.

He tipped the wineskin up and maneuvered himself beneath it so his back was almost touching her and he, too, faced the sun. Illyra couldn't imagine why he twisted around that way, when it was apt to make him miss his aim. Wine spurted past his ear, landing on the red stone.

"Watch what you're doing," she snapped, hastily lifting her skirt out of the way as she spoke.

But he squeezed the skin again and left a goodly stain across the worn inscription before adjusting his arms and getting a decent mouthful of wine. Odd that a warrior, or a shepherd for that matter, would be so clumsy with the wine. Hard, even, to believe it had been an accident—especially when she caught him looking back at her and grinning.

"Out of practice," he said, and she did not believe him at all.

"I'd best be leaving. It's getting late. I live . . ."

Illyra hesitated and thought better of telling him where she lived, not that her heart believed it would help her if this stranger took it into his head to pay her and Dubro a visit. She slid carefully from the stone, avoiding him as much as the wine, and put the substantial remains of her lunch in the shawl-sling. It seemed prudent to back away from the stone. He was still grinning when her heel touched the path, then he laughed and she shot through the gate.

In truth it wasn't that late, barely past midafternoon, and she hadn't intended to return to the Bazaar before sundown. The day was still pleasantly warm, and there wouldn't be many more like this until the next spring. She might still wander along the General's Road and headed that way—back through the forecourt and along the Governor's Walk.

Haakon the vendor was prowling his afternoon route, singing a song of nutmeats and pastry. Despite the food she'd eaten and the food she carried, they made her mouth water.

"Copper bit," the vendor said when she started to approach him, then, when he finally recognized her, added in a much softer voice, "for two."

Illyra smiled and gave him the battered coin she'd received in the morning. Because she'd bought two, he wrapped the second one in a scrap of translucent parchment and tucked it into the folds of her shawl.

"Delicious," she confirmed, biting into the sweet and savory confection.

"Best to share."

He meant to share with Dubro but the face that came into her mind was Suyan. She wondered if the wet nurse had ever even tasted one of these uptown luxuries. Not likely. Suyan claimed she had grown up Downwind, though Walegrin had found her in a Shambles house. Illyra imagined the look on Suyan's face when she bit through the still-warm pastry shell to the nutmeats within. She changed direction and hurried along the street to the Bazaar.

The forge was empty but before Illyra could become concerned she heard Trevya crying and ran the last little way.

"I brought you a pastry," she announced as she pushed through the curtain.

Suyan smiled but it was almost lost amid her unsuccessful efforts to quiet the infant.

"Here, I'll hold her. They really taste best when they're warm."

She picked the child up and found, not surprisingly, that she fit snugly into the crook of her arm and that she remembered how to rock her arms a bit and wiggle a finger or two as a distraction. And as Illyra's fingers were shiny with butter and nutmeats, Trevya found them fascinating. She pulled them into her mouth and sucked contentedly. Illyra felt the sharp ridge of the tooth that had caused this latest round of wailing.

"She's getting her milk teeth."

Suyan gulped a mouthful of pastry. "Not milk teeth, I'll warrant?" Another of her lilting questions, but this one came with a furtive smile.

"Not milk teeth then. She'll soon be ready for gruel and a bit of porridge in the morning. I used to like to make porridge—especially in winter."

The happiness in Suyan's face wavered. Illyra could almost see her thinking of where she'd been before they'd brought her to the forge.

"We'll still need someone to take care of her. I'm S'danzo, not . . ." Illyra hesitated, wondering why she'd been about to say she wasn't Trevya's mother. Neither was Suyan, for that matter. And other S'danzo women had children underfoot all the time. "Well, Trevya should have someone watching her all the time," she decided after a puzzling moment. "It's dangerous here, with the forge. Not like some other places where the worst that could happen is a bumped knee."

The tension left Suyan in a great sigh. She ate the rest of her pastry but left the baby in Illyra's arms. They talked then, in the afternoon light, as they had never talked before, though not about anything of importance. They talked about the foods Dubro liked, and the ones he didn't;

and the bolts of brightly colored cloth that had just arrived
in a caravan from Croy; and whether the journeyman had a
wife in his future.

Illyra stole a look at the future, then shook her head. "I
can't See a thing," she murmured and remembered what
she had said out on the rock. For a heartbeat her blood
went cold. He had tricked her. That strange man who was
not a shepherd had tricked her into casting an unprece-
dented curse over Sanctuary: a S'danzo blessing. Not that
there was such a thing as a S'danzo blessing. "Everyone's
a child, one way or another—"

"I didn't hear you?"

Suyan leaned closer but Illyra did not repeat herself. She
was, after all, only one S'danzo and Sanctuary *was* Sanctuary and not likely to change very much no matter what
she did. But she would have to, if she ever saw him again,
thank the shepherd for setting her free, at least.

HOMECOMING

Andrew Offutt

Someone is always awake in Sanctuary . . . especially when others are sleeping.

—*Universal absolute*

When she saw that he had wakened, she returned to the bed, mostly dressed but not quite. She bent down, exotically pale hair streaming long, to brush the tip of his nose with her lips.

"We fell asleep," she told him. "I've got to go! It's terribly late."

Lazily, muzzily, he lifted a hand to try to capture a dangling lobe of her chest as she bent. She straightened swiftly with a little chuckle and finished closing her latch-front tunic.

"Awww . . ." he began, lazy-muzzy, and the sound slid off into a yawn.

She started for the door. He saw her pause, lift a hand to her temple, up under the newly silvered hair she had combed partially free of the tangles the two of them had put in it. She turned back. Moonlight admitted by the open window let him see that she was frowning.

"My earrings," she murmured, hurrying back to the little table beside the bed.

A moment later: "Darling? Didn't I put my earrings right here? They're—they're gone!"

"Muss've dropped 'em on th' floor," he said without concern, and yawned again.

Watching her, smiling a little, remembering. Watching her go to her knees beside the bed in her search was fun, and he entertained a little fantasy about that.

"They're not here, Cusher! Please get up and help me. Could you light the lamp? Those are good eardrops!"

Eight or nine minutes later the bedclothes were on the floor and they had even searched his abandoned clothing, lest her missing dangles of gold and jade and topaz had somehow gotten entangled in the attire he had hurriedly dropped to the floor, hours ago. By then she was sobbing and babbling about how the baubles had been gifts from her grandmother, years and *years* ago.

At last Imaya—the lady Imaya Rennsdaughter, if truth must be told—gave it up and left. By now fully as awake as she, Cusharlain latched the door after her.

A better man would escort her home, he mused. *Down to the street, at least.* Absently scratching his thigh, he realized that he was still naked. He regarded his clothes, forlornly strewing the floor. Then, one eyebrow up, he looked at the window. Of course it was open, but after all! It wasn't as if this room was on the first floor!

Naked, he padded to the window and looked out. He saw nothing; only other buildings and the dark alleys and streets among them; only Sanctuary, tired and snoozing in the moonlight. He looked down, then, down three flights, leaning out a bit with his hands on the sill, and then up. A little shiver ran over him and he ignored it. He twisted his head to cast thoughtful glances to either side.

Cusharlain straightened, sighing. "Damn," he muttered aloud.

This room was inaccessible save by the locked door, and it had still been locked when she'd thought to check it while he shook the bedsheet for the third time. He remembered the same as she did. After one of those pretty earrings had pricked his arm during their horizontal embrace, she had removed them both. He had watched because he liked the way her bare breasts moved when she lifted her arms to her ears. He had seen her: she had laid them on the little table right there, just beside her side of the bed.

And we made love, and drifted off, he mused, staring at the open window. *And while we were sleeping someone came in that window and took those earrings, not to mention what I chose not to tell her: the moneypouch sewn into my leggings! Except that no one in Sanctuary could possibly do such a thing. No one's good enough.*

One man was able; one man had both the climbing skill and the stealth to have accomplished this impossibility. He could have done it, but he's gone; left quite a while back. Over a year? Yes, by all the gods; well over a year ago.

Nevertheless someone came in that window and took her earrings and my purse, while we were right here sleeping!

Damn! The little bastard's back in town!

"I'm a carpenter, Spellmaster. Was." The man with the hound-dog face held up his hand to display its severely restricted use, especially to a carpenter.

Strick showed the fellow a compassionate expression. All his recent weight loss accounted for the droopy aspect of his face; long-stretched skin still hung in the memory of former jowls and "plump" cheeks.

"Wints told me before you came in that you are a better than good carpenter, Abohorr, and that you've recently lost fifty or so pounds. He did not say that you had also lost your thumb."

"Want to hear how I lost it?"

"No," Strick said, regarding the still upraised hand and its thumbless state. He knew of the occupational hazards of carpenters and woodcutters, and was not interested in

particulars doubtless both gory and overlong in the telling.
"That is, telling me would be of no value to either of us.
And I have to tell you at once that I can't do a thing about
that thumb, Abohorr."

Abohorr heaved a big sigh. He nodded. "Figured that.
The—the point is, Spellmaster . . . I don't want to carpenter no more. Tired of it. I mean I was even afore this
happent to m'thumb, I swear by Anen's beard I was. I
know you have a lot of contacts and a real name for
helping people, and so . . ."

The formerly fat Maze-dweller waved that maimed hand
while he looked sadly yet hopefully at the very big man
behind the desk draped in rich blue. The man who had
already made such a change in Sanctuary and its troubled,
surely damned people. A foreigner with an odd accent,
come here from up north somewhere!

"My abilities don't extend to—to . . . hmm. I'm not
sure what it is you want of me, Abohorr." Strick's pro-
nunciation of "want" rhymed with "font" or his extreme
shortening of the *o* in "lost."

His visitor rose swiftly. Even standing, he maintained
his deferential aspect, so that he didn't *seem* to be looking
down upon the seated man in his plain blue tunic.

"I'd do anything for you, Spellmaster. I'll pay you for
yer time, too, 'f I'm wasting it. Just—well, just let me
know if you hear of anything; a job I might fill. I'm big,
and strong, and a damned good worker, Spellmaster. I'm
used to a lot of work. You've got a lot of contacts and
everybody's talkin' about all the people you've helped,
Spellmaster. If you hear of anything . . . well, Wints—yer
helper Wintsenay, I mean—knows where to find me."

Strick nodded. "Wintsenay suggested that you come?"

"I don't want to get him in no trouble ner nothing,
Spellmaster. We was talking, an' he sort of did, just sort of."

"Um." The spellwright's expression did not change,
which took effort.

"Uh, well, anyhow, uh—what do I owe you, Spell-master?"

Strick showed his visitor a very small smile and a small shake of the big head that was covered to midforehead, midcheek on each side, and the base of his nape by the snug cap of leather dyed dark blue. No one had seen this man's bare head, or a sign of hair. They saw the cap, and the strangeness of deep blue tunic over matching leggings. Strange, and dull. The medallion, a plugged gold piece he always wore, did little to alleviate the severity of his attire. Oddly, the medallion nearly matched his large and droopy mustache.

"I've done nothing for you, Abohorr. You owe me nothing. You're sure that you don't want to fight back and cope—to be the best one-thumbed carpenter Sanctuary ever saw or heard of? That I can help you with!"

"I just don't want to go back to carpenterin', Spell-master," the poor fellow said, and with several expressions of thanks and apologies, he left the office of the man from Firaqa.

Strick waited a minute or so to allow him time to get down the steps and to the door of what he referred to as "my shop" before shouting, "Wints!"

The man formerly described as "an overage street urchin" was much less than a minute in making an appearance. Wintsenay was a changed man, now, with good steady employment and the blue livery of Strick ti' Firaqa.

"Sir!"

"You suggested to your friend Abohorr that he come see me," Strick said grimly, fixing the other man with a stern face and a pointing finger bigger than any of those of the carpenter or ex-carpenter who had just departed. "You know bloody well I can't do anything about a lost thumb, Wints! I wish you'd never learned my curse—that I *have* to help or try; can't *not* help or try, especially when I'm asked."

Wintsenay started to expostulate, to deny. He broke that off and looked down at the nice carpet someone of wealth had recently presented his master. Like the medallion, it was another expression of gratitude for another of the white wizard's services.

"I'm sorry, master. He's a good man, Ab is. Used to be so fat and strong and jolly all the time, you know. Now he looks like somebody's huntin' dog that's been run hard for a solid week of nights. He sure needs and deserves somebody's help."

"You play tricks with me, sirrah Wintsenay, and so will you need somebody's help. Now get your treacherous butt out of here and take the rest of that ugly corpus with it."

Wints understood the first part well enough, and acted on it. He was setting his slow brain to the working out of the rest of his master's meaning as he departed, louting at speed.

Strick sighed, shook his head, and slapped an inordinately big hand down on the fine cloth covering his desk: a large piece of deep blue velvet that trailed gold tassels on the side facing the visitors' chair. After a moment he spoke, loudly but not shouting as before.

"Avneh?"

A girl in her teens bustled in, also in the distinctive blue of Croy: Strick's color. Former streetgirl, former hanger-out at the low drive called Sly's Place, former alcoholic, former aspiring whore. Now she was receptionist and devoted servant of the man who had rescued her. Servant, as in acolyte of a god. He called her niece and enforced her calling him "uncle" in self-defense: the grateful teenager had wanted to give herself to him in every way. She had also just outgrown one tunic of Croyite blue and had to have a new one to accommodate her steadily plumpening body.

"What can I get you, Uncle StrieeEEEE!"

She was staring past him when she broke off to emit that

loud, prolonged *e* sound. Her seated "uncle" astonished her by the speed with which he rose, pounced three feet sidewise, and whirled. An obscenely long knife had appeared in his hand. He and Avenestra stared at the intruder while the latter stared at the big man and the ready blade nearly as long as a sword.

He was dark, lean and rangy at medium height. Jet black of hair and the eyebrows that almost met above a falcate nose. His eyes were nearly as black as his hair. He wore a plain green tunic, nicely tanned leather leggings, short buskins, and several knives. They included one that was a mate to Strick's outsized blade. Lifting his gaze to Strick's blue eyes, he elevated his arms a bit as well.

"Mother Shipri have mercy, Hanse!" Avenestra said. "Only you could have gotten in here 'thout being seen by Frax 'n' Wints 'n' me! But when did you get back in town? I thought maybe you was dead!"

" 'Were' dead, Avenestra, damn it," Strick said without turning or looking at all away from the intruder, "and get out of here. Tell Frax and Wintsenay to be still, and hold visitors for a few minutes."

"That's really Avenestra?" the intruder said a few seconds later. "She sure looks better'n she used to. Even working on getting fat! Yours?"

"My 'niece,' assistant, and sometime cook, and that's all. I told Ahdio what you said: that you hadn't taken the red cat, but that it followed you, even out on the desert."

"You've got a good memory, Strick of Firaqa."

"Umm. Come on around to the proper side of the desk. Yes, I remembered to pass on to Ahdio the message you gave me when we met on the road to Firaqa, and I recognized you too—once Avenestra called you by name. I've heard it rather more than once since I came to Sanctuary. You aren't exactly unknown in this town."

Wiry and youthful, walking almost catlike on the balls of his feet rather than the heels, the dark, youthful-looking man rounded the desk and stood beside the chair set there for clients; supplicants.

"Neither are you, Strick. Didn't take you long to gain a reputation in my town. And that day in the forest I thought you were a weapon-man on the run! You came to help my town—so're you going to get rid of those fish-eyed snake-turds from oversea?"

"Afraid not, Hanse. The Beys are here to stay."

"Heard that. Sure going to take some getting used to. Is it true about you?"

"How would I know?"

Hanse came very close to smiling. "That you deal in white magic only—"

"Yes."

"*That's* a switch, in Sanctuary! And is it true that every blessing from you also comes with some sort of curse?"

"Of sorts. The Price, in addition to the payment in coin or goods. Avenestra, for instance, no longer needs or wants to get drunk every night—but developed a rather grievous craving for sweets."

"Which explains her new, uh, plumpness," Hanse said, nodding.

"And you, Hanse. We met only briefly, long ago. Have you come here on business?"

"No. Just wanted to say hello. I mean, we did meet, however briefly that day months and months ago, and gave each other a little information about Firaqa and Sanctuary—carefully." Hanse chuckled.

"I remember that each of us was very wary indeed of the other, yes, that day on the road up in Maidenhead Wood. You had a young woman with you, I remember—and of course the singularly large cat. Red."

Hanse nodded. "Aye. Name's Notable. First cat I ever liked. First cat I ever didn't dislike! As soon as I came here—"

"From Firaqa?"

"Uh, well, aye, along with a, uh, stopover along the way. As soon as I got here I went to Sly's. I left Notable with goodole Ahdio, who told me about you. Hearing alot more about you from other people was easy. You responsible for this ridiculous silver hair so many people have broken out in?"

"I suppose."

"Not the bare-jigglies fashion though, hmm? That came from the snake-eyed fish-faces."

"Um. You might try to stop calling them names, Hanse. Fact is fact, and the fact of their continuing presence in Sanctuary has to be accepted."

"I'll work on it," Hanse said without enthusiasm. "Lots of other changes since I left. Lots of construction work—*re*construction work. Noticed repairs to this building and the new paint job outside, too; really like blue, don't you! You were wearing mostly dust last time I saw you—first and last time. And liveried guards, too. Even Avenestra in matching blue. Pretty place, your 'shop.' Handsome cover on that table; handsome carpet, too."

Strick continued to gaze at him from those large blue eyes above the droopy, yellowish-russet mustache. He shrugged.

"I'm also hearing about mysterious disappearances in town, and rumors of slavers, operating right here in Sanctuary?"

"A lot of people are trying to learn more about that, Hanse. It appears to be fact, aye. Be careful, should you chance to be out after dark."

Hanse laughed aloud. After a few moments Strick's big mustache twitched in his small smile.

"I'm sure I'd be interested in your impressions of Firaqa, Hanse, and how you fared there. But I do have some visitors waiting, downstairs."

"You'll be interested in hearing a few things, all right,"

Hanse assured him. "Do these names mean much to you: Thuvarandis, and Corstic, and Arcala?"

Strick blinked. Slowly, he sat. He gazed expectantly across his desk at the younger man. The names of those three men meant plenty to him, as Hanse had assumed.

Briefly, he outlined his activities and adventures in Firaqa. He ended the abbreviated narrative with the ghastly happenings in the wizard's manse, and the outcome.

Strick sat staring. "He is dead?"

"Very."

Strick slapped the blue-draped desk he called his worktable. "Dead! About time! You've rendered Firaqa a great service then, Hanse. That was a genuinely wicked man."

"That," Hanse said in a voice dry as the desert, "I know."

After a silent moment he said, "And you've rendered good service in Sanctuary, too. Just a pair of do-gooders to each other's towns, aren't we!"

"Um." Strick made muttering noises about having to go back and forth from his fancy villa every day, ending with "I'm a man of the people who'd rather live in town."

"Why, I can help you with that," Hanse assured him, all wide-eyed. "Be happy to accept the villa as a gift, Strick."

With a wry smile, Strick asked who owned the Vulgar Unicorn.

At last Hanse let his wiry form slide down into the chair across the desk from the master of white spells. "Old Earrings! You've asked me something I know. Unless the place has changed hands since I left, the owner's the physician Nadeesh, on the Street of Goldsmiths. Can't miss him. He wears moonstones." Hanse held up two fingers. "Two. Earrings. Stones black as a tax collector's heart."

"Nadeesh the physician," the big man repeated. "Thanks, Hanse. Oh—where are you staying?

Hanse's expression became bland and blank, the business face of the thief called Shadowspawn. "I . . . get around, Strick. If you should want me for anything, just leave word at the Vulgar U or at Sly's."

Strick nodded. "Oh, and your young woman—I gave her my amulet . . ."

"Which served her, me, and Firaqa mighty well," Hanse assured him. "Let's, uh, talk about that some other time, all right? I have *a* young woman with me. Odd that you mentioned Old Earrings, or asked about him—I picked up a nice pair of earrings just last night, as a present for her. Silky. Well, actually her name is Vivispor, but who cares— just a girl I, uh, picked up in Suma."

"You . . . 'picked . . . up' . . . a pair of earrings."

"Right," Hanse said equably, and was hasty to cut off further comment or queries with "And I'm fresh out of a cat. You know, I really got accustomed to havin' that damned cat with me. I hate to admit it, but I already miss—oh, *No!*"

For the second time within a half hour or so, Strick sat gazing at a person on the other side of his worktable who was staring past him in surprise unto shock. Since Hanse did not shriek or reach for one or more of his several weapons, however, Strick refrained from giving another demonstration of his swiftness and the fact that he was armed.

Besides, this visitor soon announced its presence in its own voice; a very low and sweet voice at that:

"*mew.*"

"Damn it, Notable, you sneaked out of Sly's and followed me again! Up the side of the building next door, even!"

So that's how he accomplished his not-so-impossible surprise entry!

"I'm sorry, Strick. C'mere, you dam' cat. He always makes that sickeningly sweet li'l kitten sound when he hears aggravation in my voice and he thinks he deserves a tongue-lashing. Come . . . Here, Note . . . able!''

"*mew?*"

Strick sat very still while the red cat—unduly, unequivocally, and almost unconscionably *large*—trotted tippytoe past him and, an instant after Hanse said ''No, Notable!'' and started to duck, precipitately appeared on the lap of the seated young man's tunic. Hanse grunted and gave the spellwright an unusually, unconditionally, and decidedly unwontedly subdued and guilty look.

"I'm, uh, sorry, Strick.''

"It looks very much as if Notable has decided he is your cat, Hanse, not Ahdio's.''

"Aye, I know," Hanse said. His voice was sad, though his face was not.

"Once a cat makes up its mind . . .''

"Alleged mind. Aye, I know. It's just that Ahdio's so damned big . . .''

"Um. Let's hope he's big about understanding, too. Hanse . . . listen, I need a favor. Two.''

"Uh.''

"Take Frax and Wints out and show them how you got in here. Tell them I want them to make any changes necessary to make sure no one can do it again.''

"Strick, I swear: no one else could.''

Strick sat staring at him in silence until Hanse had to exert his strength to keep from looking down. The expression of wide-eyed innocence that had long served him well with others didn't work with this man. This maker of spells was different. Strick was like . . . like no one.

At last Hanse asked, "What's the second favor?''

"Don't ever come in that way again.''

"Strick, I swear I won't.''

"Good. Thanks. Otherwise, Hanse, good to see you and thanks for the information about this Nadeesh. We must get together and talk again. After hours, and normally.''

"Uh." After a time Hanse said, "Damn! You just dismissed me, didn't you?"

"I work days, Hanse. People are waiting."

Hanse gazed at him, his mouth slowly widening. "Strick, you're really something! Let's go, Notable, you dam' cat."

On the way out he saw that Strick hadn't exaggerated: two others sat in the downstairs waiting room. One had the look of a Rankan of substance. *Strick sure is doing well by doing good here*, Hanse mused, and winked at the icily staring blue-uniformed man with the sword and dagger. Ex-palace guard, Hanse was sure. He recognized Wints, too, but pretended not to notice. A shaking sight, Wints decently dressed, shaved, and looking as if he knew who he was!

A few steps down the street called Straight, Notable pacing at his side, he saw still another woman with silver hair. Strick had started this craze? *Damn, why? A man never knows whether a woman's dyed, prematurely gray, or extraordinarily well preserved!*

Avenestra ushered in a well-dressed Rankan noble.

Strick swiftly learned that Noble Abadas was new in Sanctuary; he was cousin to Theron, the new emperor-by-his-own-hand. Noble Abadas was of medium height, perhaps ten pounds overweight, with receding light brown hair and reddish mustache, big ears, and stubby fingers. Superb eyes the color of doeskin met Strick's directly, which was impressive. Abadas was just arrived from Ranke with his daughter and, unusually, a single servant. He wanted a good place to live, he said, and planned to staff with Ilsigi; locals.

Odd Rankan, Strick thought. *Seems to be a liberal who wants to show what a good fellow a Rankan can be; particularly the . . . agent?—spy?—of the new emperor!*

"I have deposited funds with a local banker. You know Renn."

Strick nodded. Renn was one of the two men he banked with, both Ilsigi.

"He showed me around a bit," Abadas said. "I have to say that I saw two places I love, Spellmaster. One, a villa, turns out to be yours!"

"Ah."

By the time Noble Abadas departed Strick's place of business, the two foreigners to Sanctuary had made a business arrangement. Strick was happy to have leased the villa he bought from Izamel (since old Izamel and other wealthy, old-money Ilsigi kindly loaned him the money) to Abadas for an amount that was a shade more than Strick's loan payments and taxes. The current inflation helped; Strick had recently bought the place at what were now called "old rates"; prereconstruction rates! Their deal made both men happy.

Strick called in his man-of-all-tasks.

"Wints, go to Cusharlain. Tell him I am looking for a large place in town, preferably a house I can also use as a shop. All right?"

"Yes sir. Oh, are you—"

"Good. Then go to Gilla Lalo'swife. Ask that good woman whether any of her children or relatives would like good employment with a decent Rankan noble. All right?"

"Yes sir. Sir, I—"

"Aye, I am sure that you know of some prospective servants for the household of the lord Abadas, Wints. Just go on about my business my way, for now."

Wintsenay went.

In the next hour Strick saw four people. He refused to do anything at all for the one who wanted vengeance on a landlord, used a minor spell and an unnecessary foul-tasting concoction to get rid of the really ugly warts on another's face, told a third sadly that he could do nothing about the long-twisted leg but secretly made a spell to make the poor woman more accepting, at least, and told a

sufferer of persistently upset stomach that he needed to
go to a physician, at once. It wasn't as if anyone was
going to cure the rampant malignant growth Strick *saw* in
the too-young man's upper intestine, but at least he could
go through his final weeks of life in a drugged state. For
all this the spellwright took in three pieces of silver and a
nice bolt of cloth of a color he did not desire. Well, he
could trade it, or use it as gift goods.

Avenestra came in, chewing.

"No one else is waiting, Uncle. I hung out the 'closed'
sign as you said."

"Good!" He rose and stretched.

"Ooooh! What a beautiful bolt of cloth!"

"You like that, Avneh?"

"It's just beautiful, Uncle! I *love* paisley!"

"Hmm. We may not be able to do anything about your
craving for sweets, poor baby. But show me that you can
come in here without chewing on something and we'll see
what we can have made for you from this."

"Oh I'm sorry, Uncle. Mother Shipri make me strong!"

Strick patted her shoulder, turning a little sidewise to
avoid being hugged (with hands one of which he saw was
sticky from some pastry), and hurried downstairs to collect
Fulcris. Leaving Avenestra "in charge" and Frax on guard,
Strick and his other aide headed for the Street of Goldsmiths.

Nadeesh the leech had heard of the foreign spellwright
who had come here to be of such value to Sanctuary, both
physically and psychologically. His sad-looking servant
ushered the visitors in to his master. Nadeesh the leech
was a cadaverously thin man with hair that began at about
the midpoint atop his skull and dangled stringily in long
ugly strands of corpse-gray. He looked to be seventy or
more. He also, Strick and Fulcris discovered, wore only
one earring. Attired in a paradoxically bright tunic that
appeared to be draped over mere bone, he sat weakly in a

chamber made dim by drawn drapes. Strick saw at once that he was in bad shape, and not just from the healed wound that showed his left earring had been torn from him. The fellow looked far too old for his age, which he said was "about fifty."

"What do you think is wrong with you, sir?"

"Can't find a cause, sir. Just last night a friend—a fellow physician—suggested that it might be . . . a spell."

Strick saw the little shiver that went through this too-thin man as he spoke those words. Showing confidence and making sure to project it, Strick suggested that he look. Nadeesh agreed, nervously.

"What—what do you need to do?"

"I need for you to give me something of value, and then just lie back and try hard not to think of anything at all. I will have my hands on your shoulders, that's all."

The physician snorted. "Only the gods know how many patients I've said that to—and all of us knowing all the while that it's completely impossible!"

With a little smile, Strick accepted the proffered coin and set his hands on shoulders that might have been mere bone covered by the other man's yellow tunic. The Firaqi wizard was quite able to stare at nothing.

It took him only seconds to discover the cause of Nadeesh's malaise.

"Your friend was right, leech. Someone has set a dark spell on you."

Nadeesh moaned.

"Hmm. And left a barrier. Perhaps you would think of an opening gate, opening doors, a cave with a wide open mouth . . . no no, please be still but not stiff . . . hmm."

A little work discovered the impossible: the spell came from a dead man. One Marype, the son of a mage named Mizraith and long apprenticed to a shadowy mage named Markmor. The problem was that everyone knew Marype was dead! *Except that this spell is not that old. Marype is vehemently alive! Furthermore he's past the apprentice stage—past journeyman, by the Flame!* Strick concentrated, began to sweat—and soon realized that the severity of Nadeesh's affliction was because Marype had gained possession of something belonging to the physician.

"Ah, the earring, and thus a bit of blood!"

"Wh-what?" The wizened physician's voice quavered.

Strick released those frighteningly bony shoulders and sat beside the man who looked far too old for the age he claimed. The spellmaker would have bet that before this malignant spell the physician had looked fifteen years younger.

"How did you lose your earring?"

"Late one night about two months ago I was set upon by footpads and—by the gods! *This* began about then! I have lost very much weight in these past two months, Strick, and of course strength as well."

"Um. Those were not footpads, Nadeesh, but men hired for a definite assignment. A dark mage who hates you used them to gain possession not only of your earring but, since it was torn from your ear, a bit of your blood as well. It has enabled him to make a powerful spell indeed."

"How do you know this?"

"Do you answer your patients when they ask you such a question?"

"No. And usually I cannot answer this one: What is to happen to me?"

"You already know. You are wasting away; no one would know that it's the result of an inimical spell. I'd say this sorcerer intends your death."

Nadeesh surprised his visitor with a string of words concerning the unnamed mage, his sexual activities, and his mother. Then:

"Who is it? Who has done this, Spellmaster?"

"That I cannot say," Strick said, as perfectly capable of

lying when he deemed it wise as any physician. "What mage hates you so much?"

"None! I mean—I've no idea."

"You've never treated a sorcerer?"

"Not knowingly."

"Um. In that case, have you *refused* treatment to a sorcerer?"

"Not knowingly," Nadeesh repeated. After a few seconds he added, "But now one is going to murder me."

"Is *murdering* you," Strick said, staring at nothing. "Unless we can do something about it."

Nadeesh lurched up, gasping with effort. "You think you can?"

"One can always try. In this case, one must."

"I don't understand."

"Never mind. You are too good a man to be murdered this way without my trying to stop it."

A long sigh escaped the pitifully wizened man, and Strick heard the rattle in his scrawny throat.

"Bearing in mind that I am a spellwright, not a physician, let us discuss the bill in advance."

Nadeesh's smile was hideous, but genuine. "You certainly have me, sir. Name the price and I shall agree. Understand that if the patient dies, however, he cannot pay."

Despite the gravity of the complaint of his "patient," Strick laughed aloud.

They discussed his bill.

Hanse noted more construction/reconstruction on his way to pay a visit to Mignureal's widowed father. It was not something Hanse wanted to do. He had loved Moonflower, Mignue's gross diviner of a mother; he was able to admit that to himself, now. Ahdio and a couple of others at Sly's Place last night had already observed that the dark, youthful man called Shadowspawn was "different." They were right. Events on the desert and up in Maidenhead Wood had changed him a bit; the Mignureal experience had enforced responsibility and changed him accordingly; the constant dark shadow of sorcery and ghastly events in Firaqa had changed and matured him; and so had more recent experiences in Suma.

The presence of the outsized red cat strolling along at his side, tail high, attracted plenty of looks. Hanse's eyes and the presence of so many sharp blades worn openly here and there about his person persuaded people to keep their comments to themselves or low-voiced. Once he did hear a scornful laugh and knew it for a deliberate attempt at provocation. He didn't even turn. Shadowspawn was "different," yes.

At the shop where Mignureal's father Teretaff sold this and that . . . item, he was admitted by one of Mignureal's dark-haired and dark-eyed younger sisters. Since their number was several and Hanse had never been interested in children, he wasn't sure of this one's name. Odd, how she had bloomed in so short a time. Girls had a way of doing that, and the S'danzo did seem to bloom earlier than others.

He entered into warmth made heavy by a fragrant mix of odors, aromas, smells, scents of foods and leather and spices and perfumes and other herbal . . . things. The shop had always been cluttered. It was more so now, with Moonflower dead.

"Does your father have a, uh, woman friend?" he asked, feeling sneaky, and was not displeased by the shaking of a large-eyed head. What was this girl, about thirteen? That meant that the next one—the boy Cormentaff—was fourteen. Another member of the family was pushing sixteen too, as he recalled. The one with red hair, or almost red. What was her name, anyhow?

This one made girlish noises over Notable, who eluded her attempts to pet him. The cat disappeared behind a counter.

"He, uh, he's a one-man cat," Hanse explained. "Notable, if you knock anything over or get into anything it will go hard with you!"

"Mraow."

Hanse was not happy to discover that Teretaff already had a visitor. The aged S'danzo "chief" with he implacable eyes and straight mouth and the usual multicolored, modestly cut garb barely acknowledged Hanse's presence. Hanse was determinedly respectful. The Termagant was not visiting Teretaff, he realized; she was interested in the almost-sixteen-year-old. Now both stared at Hanse, Jileel from huge round eyes the color of walnut wood flanked by a great deal of hair the color of a roan horse. Her blouse was striped yellow and green and was unaccountably stuffed; under a multiprint apron, her skirts showed six or nine other colors and hues.

"You left here with my daughter," Teretaff said, but it was a question rather than an accusation.

"Precipitately," the Termagant said, straight-mouthed and flat-eyed.

Suddenly Hanse has to tell them, no matter the consequences: "Yes. When I found Moonflower I went wild. I started running, ran into a fish— a, uh, Beysib, and killed it. Her. I think it was the one who ki— who . . ."

"Oh, I do hope it was!" the almost-sixteen-year-old said ferociously, in a rather throaty voice.

"Jileel!" the Termagant snapped, inadvertently helping Hanse by providing the girl's name.

Teretaff glanced at her, and back to Hanse. "I hope so too, Hanse. She did like you, my wife."

Hanse was surprised to hear himself say, "I loved her, Teretaff."

All three of the others blinked. At last the old woman said, "You have changed, young man."

Hanse nodded. "We endured much. We even accomplished much, up in Firaqa."

"Firaqa?"

"A city far north. Strange people with a strange religion. Ruled by a sort of council of sorcerers. The chief was also the most evil and I suppose the most powerful. He's dead, now. Teretaff, Termagant . . . Mignureal's powers soared, in Firaqa. She was glad to find a small colony of S'danzo. They were unwelcome in Firaqa; S'danzo, I mean. That's no longer true. She . . . Mignureal has remained there, Teretaff. She's an accomplished Seer, now, an *amoushem*. Did I say that right?"

"Yes!" the Termagant said, astonishing Hanse by the sudden happy light in her eyes. "So! She flowered, then, and is respected, with the Ability."

"Yes. She Sees, Termagant, Teretaff; Mignue Sees beyond anyone else in Firaqa."

"She will do well there, then," Teretaff said, with some happiness and pride mingled with sadness. Tears had appeared in the walnut eyes of the girl beside the old woman, to hear that her sister was not coming back. "But—you are here and she there?"

Hanse nodded. "It was not easy. Oh, we had our troubles—probably mainly because we were under the shadow of sorcery all the time. But I think we will always love each other. It's just that I *had* to come back, and she felt she had to remain there. She is happy there. Established."

"I am glad for her," Jileel said but her voice quavered and she sniffed.

"*I* am de*light*ed!" the Termagant said, and again she astonished Hanse, by proving that grim mouth could smile.

Hanse wondered whether Teretaff might have been less equable about this news had the Termagant not been present, and so enthusiastic. Almost he wished that Jileel were not present. She kept staring at him, staring with those huge dark brown eyes. She always had, he remembered, when he had come to see Moonflower and then Mignureal,

but now it seemed different. She was older, with the cusp
of womanhood newly sealed upon her. And . . . could that
be she in there, rather than the family laundry or a couple
of smuggled melons, making her blouse stand out and
strain so? Mignureal had not been constructed so! Of
course her mother had been, but Moonflower had been
huge everywhere, a truly obese woman whose size had
made walking difficult for her. (She also remained the
most beautiful woman Hanse had ever known. It was she
who taught him, just by being, that beauty was not something a person wore, like clothing or skin, but was inside;
it was something a person *was*.)

He produced the bag and handed it to a surprised Teretaff.
It jingled.

"From Mignureal," Hanse told him.

"From . . . Mignureal?" Now it was Teretaff's eyes
that glistened wetly.

Hanse pretended not to notice. He nodded. "She insisted.
She is doing well. That is for you and her sisters and
brother, she said. It is, uh, considerable Firaqi gold, Teretaff.
Gold because that way I had fewer coins to carry. Be sure
to go to a decent bank to get a fair exchange on those
flame-marked coins, now."

Teretaff smiled, then laughed, and embarrassed himself
when laughter became sobs. In manner womanly, his daughter Jileel went to embrace him. Uncomfortable, Hanse
began backing.

"I have to go now." He swallowed. "Got an appoint-
ment, you know."

"Young man."

Hanse swallowed again. "Name's Hanse, ma'am."

"Hanse, then. And I am called the Termagant. You
know that I am the senior amoushem; first among the
S'danzo with the Ability. Moonflower liked you, I know,
and Mignureal . . . well. I admit that I never had much—I

never had any use for you. That has changed. You may consider me friend, Hanse."

Still again Hanse swallowed. It was his way not to act honored, but he could not escape the feeling that this was like being acknowledged friend by the Prince-Governor, as he had been. Suddenly his stance changed, and his grin was the old cocky one.

"My occupation hasn't changed, Termagant."

She blinked. "I do not hear you. A friend entrusted a bag of money to you for her father, and you brought it this long way."

Damn! "Uh . . . well, that's different. You won't tell anyone, will you?"

"What?"

Hanse shrugged. "I've got my reputation to think of."

"But young ma— *Hanse,* it is a *bad* reputation!"

Hanse nodded. "It's *mine,* Termagant."

Between the old woman and her father, with her arm around him, Jileel giggled.

The Termagant shook her head. "I, however, have spoken. You are to consider me friend, Hanse."

"I'll remember. I have to go now."

As he left, he heard the Termagant's voice: "Very well now, Jileel, let's test you again to see if that really was the Sight . . ."

Hanse hurried on, clucking to Notable, thinking of the considerable amount of money he had secretly left with that banker in Firaqa for Mignue, dear Mignue . . .

He found a decent place to live, in Red Court in the Maze, and delighted the proprietor by laying down a few coins in advance. Silky the ever supple and ever ready was for testing the bed; this soon after leaving Mignureal's family, Hanse just couldn't. He also couldn't admit that. He pointed out the need to find her employment, and they wandered. Sometime that afternoon he realized that he had no intention of living with the tan-haired girl he and his loneliness had *acquired* up in Suma. All right, he could handle that; he was not stuck with her and besides she was obviously not charmed with the Maze, Hanse's natural habitat.

He did succumb to Silky's importunings to buy a melon. As he cut it, he noticed that the wooden handle of his favorite knife was loose.

"Damn!"

Next he noticed that she was talking animatedly with another of the pedlar's customers, a Rankan. *Good,* he thought, and without any compunctions at all he walked away. Silky was just Silky, a passing fancy, but a defective knife was serious business. Using this cut-through and that, he was soon on the Street of Tanners. Three blocks down from Sly's Place was Zandulas's Tannery; one had only to follow one's nose to find it and the busy establishment of Zandulas's next door neighbor, Cholly. Cholly the Gluemaker was the man to see. Oh, his real name was Chollander, but only his wife called him that. Cholly performed a number of important services for Sanctuary, including the making of glue. In a town where bodies tended to appear with the morning sun and tended never to be claimed by anyone, a man who had use for them and thus rendered a free corpse-collection service was valuable. Come to think, "rendered" was the right word for the main part of Cholly's activities.

The bear-sized man with the barrel belly greeted Hanse heartily and with surprise. "Why haven't I seen you for so long, Hanse? Must be a year or more."

Cholly was alone in his smelly, cluttered place of business, meaning that his two assistants were out on this errand or that. Taking orders for or delivering glue, probably, or the ancillary products of Cholly's trade. Selling jewelry, perhaps, or slightly used clothing. A bone or two, maybe. Or nice long hair, perhaps, to make nice wigs.

Briefly and without much patience, Hanse told Cholly where he had been.

"I had no idea, Hanse! Oh—I guess you left before that sexy Rankan gladiator came to town, didn't you?"

"How can a gladiator be s— oh. You mean Chenaya Nutcracker? We, uh, met, Cholly."

"Oh? Surprised you don't grin when you say that, Shadowspawn. Surely Milady Swagger either insulted you, tried to kill you, or bedded you. Or all three."

Hanse clamped his teeth. "She bedded me, Cholly. That's the way it was, too—she collected me, took me home, and bedded me. She's good-looking and she's cat-supple, I'll give her that. Bed is another matter. I didn't enjoy it with her and we will *not* be doing it again. I prefer women."

Cholly saw the expression and heard the tone. Considerately and wisely, he nodded and said nothing at all. Then his visitor laid the wounded knife on his counter and the huge man shifted to his business demeanor. He picked it up in a big meaty hand, examined it, said "hmm" twice, and shrugged.

"Easily fixed, Hanse. Let's just make repairing this a welcome-home gift," Cholly said, already starting to work. "We'll use dry-tack. It's a special sort of glue I made up; sticks by pressure." He grunted softly; a man the size of Chollander the Gluemaker seldom found tasks large enough to require large grunts. "There. Now we apply the dry-tack wet, so, and allow it to dry. We don't have to wait long. I remember this old knife from years back. A really superior blade! Oh—you, ah, pick up any new knives up in Furakka?"

Hanse showed him a couple, knowing this lover of knives would consider both of them exotic because they were of foreign manufacture. "The really fancy one was a gift from the head mage up in Firaqa, a man named Arcala."

"Hmp! Never knew you to stay around a mage long

enough to receive a gift! Hard to imagine, from a fellow who hates sorcery worse than anybody!'' Cholly said, admiring it and the other knife Hanse handed him, a normal enough sticker. He examined both with the respect and care of a man who knew knives. "Nice," he said, laying them down. "Here, look at this pretty thing while I finish the job on your old knife." He placed in Hanse's hand a dagger whose blade was inlaid with silver.

Sensing trade negotiations, Hanse naturally found it necessary to demean the seeming treasure. "Uh. Pretty," he said casually. "I'll bet this fancy inlay weakens the blade, though."

Sensing an impending trade, Cholly snorted and made a chuckling noise to show Hanse how silly that was. It was also subject-changing time:

"Ah yes, this is good now, Hanse. Dry-tack's a really good bonder. I'm proud of it. It won't stick to slippery surfaces, see, like wax or grease. Or soap. On the other hand it's easy to peel it off smooth, polished surfaces."

"In that case how can it be strong enough for a knife I need to trust?"

"I said 'peel' it off, Hanse. *Pulling* it off, breaking the bond—that's another matter. Believe me, I could glue a handle onto a horse's back and lift him by it. If I could lift a horse, I mean. It's *strong*."

That triggered a thought, but Hanse was careful to sound casual when he asked how one got the stuff off.

Cholly gestured. "Oh, I have a remover for it! Had to come up with that!"

"Uh. I guess," Hanse said, and decided it was time to swing back to the potential trade: "How strong d'you think this silvered blade is?"

"It's a dagger, Hanse. I mean, it isn't as if you're going to try throwing it or chopping trees, is it?"

The ritual of leading up to a transaction had begun. The dickering had to come first, of course, and the deliberate

dropping of the subject for friendly converse before returning to another offer or "suggestion" of offer. This time
the process took only fifteen or eighteen minutes. When
Hanse left, Cholly had both Firaqi knives in exchange for
the inlaid dagger and a pot of the dry-tack Hanse called
"Cholly's Dry Stickum." The gluemaker threw in the
remover as a courtesy. Their deal made both men happy.

Hanse returned to the area where he had left Silky. The
melon pedlar had gone on, and apparently so had Silky.
A little asking around apprised him that the tan-haired
Sumese girl had departed, with that blond Rankan. While
Hanse's pride was wounded a bit, he was not unhappy. He
did seem to be stuck with the big red cat. By that evening
he had left Notable with Ahdio twice. The moment a door
was opened, Notable hastened to use it and seek out
Hanse.

"All right, you damn' cat, let's go home and drop off
my new pot of glue! You'll need to sniff out the place
anyhow."

Notable swerved sharply to bang his flank into Hanse's
leg. "Maowr!"

"No."

"mew?"

"No, damn it, Notable, we will *not* stop and get you a
beer *now!*"

Strick's rule was that people came to him; he went to no
one. For this interview he had long wanted, however, he
would have gone to the palace. Prince-Governor Kadakithis would not hear of it. Instead, secretly, in disguise and
terribly early on a Fourday morning as agreed for his
convenience and security, he arrived in Strick's "shop."
In this absolute privacy and confidence, the handsome
young Rankan of about Hanse's age and size astonished
Strick: he admitted that he was less than he wished to be

and had decided that it was because he was too indecisive; fearful of what the Ilsigi would think of him.

"The young half-brother of the emperor," he said quietly, tapping his chest while studiously not-looking at the spellwright, "always had to be careful not to offend or even be very visible, you see. Abakithis—the emperor— was that sort of man. In time, though, he decided that I wasn't invisible enough. He shipped me out here. The goal was not to do anything for Sanctuary or for me, but to get me out of Ranke!" Kadakithis sighed. "So, I felt the need to prove something, to do well. Trying too terribly hard, I was overzealous in trying to clean up this town. In taxing the Red Lantern Houses and . . . other things."

Strick sat very still. He said absolutely nothing and more, he made no sound.

Embarrassedly looking at the wall to his right, Kadakithis went on in that sadly quiet voice: "This morning Lord Abadas, the new emperor's cousin, visited to present himself formally. I disgusted me. I was positively ingratiating."

After a time he turned his head to look at Strick from pale blue eyes.

"Your efforts and actions were understandable," Strick said just as quietly. "And with Lord Abadas as well. The man is surely here to keep an eye on you for his cousin, isn't he. After all, you're half-brother to . . . Emperor Theron's predecessor in the imperial chair."

Kadakithis shook his head. "No, Strick; I have come to like this town, both from sympathy and feeling a part of it. If I'm to amount to anyth— if I'm to help these people in anything approaching the way you have, I'll need . . ." The Prince-Governor broke off in embarrassment.

Strick didn't need to hear the words. "I like Sanctuary and its sorely stressed people, too, lord Prince, and . . . I *must* help. I have no choice."

"I have heard that mysteriousness before, Spellmaster,

but I will not pry. I believe you. If it is pain, then I am sorry. Both of us know pain."

"And so am I sorry, lord Prince, so am I. Now I must warn my lord Prince about the Price."

Kadakithis nodded. "Naturally I have heard about that, too. I want that help you've given so many others, Strick."

"The Price is the Price, Prince Kadakithis. It is beyond my control. Sometimes it is severe and sometimes it is readily bearable. I have no control over it."

"I know these things, Strick. I said I want that help you've given so many others. While I am called Kittycat, you are being called Hero of the People. Is a prince of the people not a person? Shall a prince be treated as less? Shall a prince be fearful of the Price? I know about it, Strick. Must a prince cajole?"

Strick rose and bowed. "Noble Lord Prince! I have desired this meeting for months. These people deserve more of their gods and their rulers. Now you embarrass me; I have *wanted* to be of aid to you, as you know. The warning, believe me, is something I give to everyone who comes here. I must."

Kadakithis nodded. And sat looking expectant. Waiting.

Strick called Avenestra, but met her at the door. She knew that she was not to enter as usual and not even to see this visitor, and was able not to try. He let the prince hear him bid her prepare "Saksarabooninga." She already had the drink's revolting but harmless ingredients ready, except for a bit more stirring to mix the vegetable colors of purple and green. She hurried to do so. Strick waited at the door; Kadakithis sat very still, staring at nothing past the Firaqi's empty chair. Avenestra reappeared from the other room to hand her savior a silver goblet. Strick paced over to set it on his worktable before his visitor. Kadakithis stiffened, bent forward to peer into the cup, stiffened the more, and tensed his face. Then, as if accepting a mandated cup of poison, he bravely reached for it.

"A moment, my lord Prince. Give me something of value."

First Kadakithis gave him a look. "I suppose the ritual bans the use of the word 'please'?"

Strick stood gazing at him. He said nothing. True, this was a prince royal of Ranke and governor of this city—co-governor, at least, with his alien companion. Torezalan Strick tiFiraqa, however, was Torezalan Strick tiFiraqa, Spellmaster and Hero of the People.

From within his pillow-stuffed brown tunic the disguised prince slid a tiny, beautifully carven box. He set it on the desk and opened it to reveal a single pearl. As if ritually, Strick only touched it. And looked expectant.

With obvious misgivings and distaste for the concoction Strick had been at pains to make unpleasant in appearance, odor, and flavor, Prince Kadakithis drank it down. All of it, without lowering the cup. The man did know, Strick mused, how to take medicine!

Lowering the drained goblet, Kadakithis shook his head. "And people think it's easy being a royal! By all gods, Strick, what's in that stuff!"

"Nothing to harm you, Lord Prince. A secret formula I have of a Zimmanabuniga wizard far to the west."

With hands on the lean blond's shoulders, Strick told him that he was decisive, charismatic, and had no need to lack confidence, "for charisma and more importantly your intelligence will carry you through, to the benefit of Sanctuary. You must think much on this, particularly before sleep and before rising."

The Rankan Prince-Governor of Sanctuary stood and gripped the far bigger man's hand. Strick noted that the young man stood more erect than when he had entered. For a few moments they stood gazing into each other's eyes. Then Kadakithis swung, drew his hooded cloak again about himself and his padded tunic, and left. With, Strick noted, a firmer and more confident tread than when he had entered.

Strick sighed. *Charlatan,* he grumbled at himself, hardly for the first time. *That handsome young man was already charismatic and decisive! It's just that now he* Believes!

Then the spellwright sent Wintsenay to pass the word: Strick needed to see Hanse.

Kadakithis paid the Price. That same Fourday afternoon he received word that Taya had fled the palace.

Shupansea was amused: "Well after all, she came here as your concubine, my love. And, however pampered, she's had nothing to do for a long, long while now!" Then: "On the other hand, I would recommend—"

"Never mind," Kadakithis said with cool decisiveness. "I have already decided to take no action whatsoever. This cannot reflect badly on me, but will serve as further proof of how truly you and I love each other."

Shu-sea blinked. "Well. How very clever—no, how very *intelligent* of you, my love!"

Yes, he thought. *And the point is, this is obviously the Price I must pay for Strick's help, even if it costs me face.*

An hour later a bank messenger arrived to tell Strick that someone had just deposited sixty unshaved golden Imperials to his account, each coin bearing the face of the previous emperor. Strick smiled and nodded. He knew who it was from, and wondered what other Price Kadakithis was paying.

A short time later, Hanse responded to Strick's request to visit. He met the young Lady Esaria on her way out. Neither recognized the other because neither knew the other.

Somewhere, the goddess Eshi smiled.

"Hanse," Strick said without any preamble at all, "a man needs your help. A client needs a service only you can perform."

Hanse put on his face of sweet innocence. "I can't imagine what you mean."

Strick's smile was cursory; dutiful. "A wall or two needs to be scaled. A house and a room or two need to be entered. An item needs to be fetched."

"Ah! I've heard of just the roach you need. He's called Shadowspawn, I believe."

"Do you think he will perform this service?"

"Probably. He usually works for himself. But, if the price is right . . ." Hanse gestured eloquently. "Tell me about this . . . mission."

"The price is right," Strick said, and told him about the mission.

"Oh, no! Not a *sorcerer!*"

"Hanse! After your experiences with the real thing up in Firaqa, this *boy* will pose you no problem. True, he was apprentice to Markmor the Archmage, but Markmor was found dead even before I came here. A lot of mages have come and gone, Hanse."

Hanse nodded. "I remember that big one with the blue star on his forehead . . ."

"Lythande," Strick said.

"Lythande! Odd name for a man!"

"That one will not be back, Hanse. Lythande does *not* like this town at all, and will *never* be back."

"You know a lot, Strick, for a newcomer who's been here only a few months."

Strick nodded. "Yes. I make it my business to learn things. Sanctuary is my business, now. And I, believe me, am here to stay. And we were discussing a certain venture concerning a roach and one Marype."

"Oh but Father Ils, how I hate sorcery!"

Strick stared. "Perhaps you will refer me to a brave *professional,* then."

"Bastard!" The professional thief made a show of his sigh. "What does he have that you want . . . acquired?"

Strick held out his hand. An earring gleamed brightly in his palm: a glowing black stone caged in good gold. "The mate to this. It was torn from its wearer's ear and now that swinish mage is using it to harm him."

"Nadeesh," Hanse murmured, and sighed. He nodded, gestured.

Strick told him a bit more. Reluctantly, Hanse named a price. Disconcertingly, Strick did not even bother to dicker. He rose, placed the earring in Hanse's hand, bade him grip it and try to visualize its mate, and laid hands on the best cat-thief in Sanctuary.

"Now. You will be able to find it, once you're in its proximity. If it is in a container, bring it that way. This is important."

Once more Hanse sighed. "A sorcerer! Gods, how I hate sorcery!"

Strick merely gazed at him.

The younger man rose. "It will be done, Strick," Shadowspawn said casually, on his way out.

Strick surprised him with the standard benison on a thief: "May the night-dark cloak cover you and your actions this night." Meanwhile the spellwright was think-ing: *How interesting. He keeps company with an ensorceled cat and wears a dagger that's the product of sorcery. Hates it, hmm?*

Hanse wandered his town, thinking and working to relax as he preferred to do before an important roaching venture. He noted reconstruction, a purse-cutting, the painting of various buildings, the large number of foreigners imported to handle the work. Occasionally he returned—or ignored—a startled greeting. He saw Beysib mingling with Ilsigi and Rankans. Near the marketplace he was surprised to see large dark eyes peeping at him; the girl he had thought of only as Mignue's little sister. He pretended not to notice. Beard of Ils! Jileel! All grown up and seemingly smug-gling watermelons—and still staring!

Noise at a walls reconstruction site attracted him. He ambled that way, seeing that it was a real uprising. While disgruntled Ilsigi laborers mutter-muttered, refusing to work, a big fellow harangued them. He was ranting loudly about the *way* these walls were wrecked, among other destruction and deaths, and how the gods were angry at Sanctuary, and why should "we fix and put back a wall for those damned oversea Beys occupying *our* palace!" Imported workers meanwhile stood away. Uninvolved, they performed that act known as honoring the strike, meaning they stood or sat around enjoying the break.

Some of the bully's words made sense to Hanse. *Things were bad here when I left, and obviously got a lot worse. I hate these loudmouthed rabble-rousers, but . . .*

Suddenly a lean, blond young man appeared, wearing a leather apron over his well-made blue tunic. He commenced working. Stone dust flew. *Brave fellow*, Hanse thought. *Brave fool!* Then he frowned, seeing the ranter pick up a jagged chunk of stone and take aim at the sole worker . . .

Almost out of sight, the three Beys sent by Shupansea to watch over her beloved drew bowstrings to slay the rabble-rouser in defense of Kada—

And Hanse threw. His flat lozenge of knife rushed to slice across the back of the big fellow's hand so that he dropped the stone with a scream. Another scream followed: he had dropped it on his own foot. Laughter rose as he danced, simultaneously squealing and cursing.

The Beysibs lowered their bows and went back to looking invisible while everyone watched the dark, wiry young man who came running into the work area, wearing a good green tunic and nice doeskin leggings. The daring young worker in the leather apron, having retrieved the thrown knife, stared while the newcomer faced the loudmouth.

"Go away, Tarkle," Hanse shouted. "All that babble

you've been giving out is just that—everybody knows you just don't like to work."

The big rabble-rouser with the bloody hand, once again discovering that bullying was becoming a more and more hazardous pastime, glowered and made surly noises. He also noticed the deadly eyes and several other knives on the person of a known expert he had thought was long gone from Sanctuary. Tarkle backed off—limping. Suddenly Hanse and leather-apron were exchanging stares of recognition:

"Prince!"

"Hanse!"

Excited noises went through the assemblage along with the usual rumble-rumble as they watched the prince-governor himself pounce onto a high spot and extend a hand to Hanse.

"See who works on the walls of Sanctuary?" Kadakithis called, in a loud clear voice. "A *Rankan!* See who saves him from a murderous bully who knows not what he's doing?—an Ilsig . . . my *friend.*"

Hanse's eyes rolled. *Oh blast! There goes my credibility!*

Kadakithis spoke on, startling all of them with his confidence and charismatic eloquence. They cheered! *His people* went back to work—with Kadakithis.

Damn, Hanse thought cheerlessly, stooping to grasp a big cut slab of stone. *I'm stuck! I can't just walk off and leave the Prince-Gov working like a Downwinder! But . . . damn! Work! Me!*

Since Markmor's death, Hanse learned the following Eshday afternoon from one of the fixture/characters of the Maze, the street cleaner and trash picker called Old Thumpfoot, the quite young Marype had secretly set himself up in Lastel's villa, whether legally or otherwise.

"How nice," Shadowspawn murmured, meandering along the Serpentine. He knew that well-appointed villa, and the late Lastel/One-Thumb's secret. All he had to do was use the tunnel connecting the house with a House; the brothel called Lily Garden. True, he had an idea about Cholly's dry-tack, but he'd try that another time. Cheered by that prospect, he dropped in to the Vulgar Unicorn for a piece of cheese and an apple. He'd eat a proper meal afterward, if his stomach agreed. He tarried, more than civil and almost loquacious to the surprise of a couple of old acquaintances. He left their company at sunset, taking a small pail of beer home to his new second-floor room. Notable was happy to see him and more than happy with the beer. He lapped with gusto while Hanse stretched out to rest and think.

No question about it, entry will be like slicing pie. Now what am I likely to need? he thought, and his smile faded. *Blast.* Here previously, and up in Firaqa, he had grown accustomed to Mignue's warnings and directions!

Suppose I'm in and it turns out that I should have brought a brown crossed pot, or a copper kettle, or . . .

"Gulp," he said aloud, trying to shame himself out of unwonted nervousness that was as uncharacteristic as his affability in the Vulg.

Notable looked up from his whisker-grooming. " 'rr-aow?''

"I said cats aren't supposed to belch, you beer-guzzling greedbag."

Hanse directed his thoughts to Nadeesh, and from that unfortunate man to Strick. *That man's going to make a Difference*, he reflected. *Already has!* Twice he shocked Notable by lurching up into a sitting position and snapping a throw. He had not told his landlord why he had grunted up here to his room with the old wooden wheel. It was inordinately thick and joined by pegs rather than nails. Braced against the wall farthest from the bed with the iron rim removed, it made a nice target. The throwing star he sent straight into the hub; the slender wafer of a knife from its sheath on his right upper arm missed by an inch.

"Must be getting old," he muttered, swinging off the bed to retrieve both missiles. Pacing back to the bed, he whirled and threw. The flat, hiltless and guardless knife appeared in the hub. Tired of the violent nonsense, Notable said "rrrawwrr!" and pounced.

"Ouch! How'd you like to become my favorite target, Notable you dam' cat?"

A couple of hours later he rose again and stripped, to change into his blacks; his work clothes. Notable seemed already to understand this ritual, whether or not cats saw colors: the big red animal pounced up onto the shelf under the window and looked from it to his human.

"You're right," Shadowspawn said, double checking the lock on his door. "That's the way we go out tonight, m'friend."

They did.

An hour later, both of them had easily gained silent entry to the large house formerly occupied by one Lastel/One-Thumb and now the lair of a young mage many thought dead. Hanse was sure they were wrong, although by now he had heard tales of the legions of walking and indeed wandering dead who had plagued Sanctuary's streets during his absence. No. Marype was alive. A look in the kitchen provided evidence of occupancy and recent cooking. A bed on the second floor had been used recently. In fact that bed looked as if Marype had lately entertained company. The tall cabinet-like press contained clothing. Not that of the departed Lastel, surely; expert eyes found membranous black gloves and noted that the thumbs of both were expanded by wear. On the point of keeping those nice thin gloves, the silent intruder decided against it. He'd steal nothing from the lair of a sorcerer; only that property of another which he was here to retrieve. He departed the bedroom without searching further, remembering the spellwright's words that he would know when he was nigh Nadeesh's earring.

Soft-soled buskins as silent on good carpet as Notable's pads, a living shadow roamed dim corridors and stepped briefly into well-furnished chambers. Some had been long closed, he saw; he passed them without opening their doors. Man and cat saw no one and heard no sound. Notable gave no indication that he scented any. Once he paused, head and one foot uplifted, and his companion went to the corridor wall like a shadow. A dark knife had materialized in his hand even as he squatted. Notable ambled over. Shadowspawn didn't touch the animal, waiting for any further indication of danger. Notable gave none. After several silent moments his human tapped his back with the knife.

"Dumbhead," Shadowspawn whispered, and Notable immediately commenced purring. "Shhh!" He rose and ghosted on, purring cat pacing close by.

At last they came to a room containing a worktable and things that made the hair twitch on Shadowspawn's nape and writhe under his working blacks. Notable's purring stopped as if sliced. *O gods, how I hate sorce—*

Abruptly he *knew* that the earring was in that nice little mahogany casket. *Nice work, Strick.* On the point of opening the box, he paused, cocked his head, and stepped to one side. From there he flipped up the lid with the point of one of his knives. He heard the concealed trigger and watched the slender dart fling itself straight up into the ceiling with a tiny *thunk* of impact. Notable went into a low crouch while Shadowspawn nodded at sight of the little box's contents. Bloodstains, too. Still using the knife, he tipped the lid and waited alertly. Nothing happened save that the lid dropped almost noiselessly back into place. On the point of snatching it and departing this silent chamber whose contents made him horripilate, he spotted several strands of hair on the table. He popped them into the box, wrapped it in a nice strip of scarlet cloth off the table, and slipped it into his black upper garment. With rather unseemly haste, he vacated the chamber of Marype's sorceries.

Easy as slicing pie, he reflected as he hurried down to the concealed entry to the old tunnel. *Just as good as ever, without any help from Mignureal or anyone else!*

In that musty old tunnel he heard a rat and saw another and then he saw ghastly eeriness. Ghost images seemed frozen, locked in eternal combat. It looked like—*could that be old One-Thumb? Surely not*, he thought, and that was when the rat pounced.

It was big, a rat the size of a normal cat, which Notable was not. Shadowspawn was only just able to duck, flailing. The cat had already pounced at the rat with a long ugly "Rrawwwww," and Hanse smiled in anticipation of a swift squeaky massacre. A flurry of action wiped away his smile and brought a grunt from his throat; a big red shape went hurtling backward to flop loosely on hard-packed earth.

"Notable!"

Shadowspawn slammed a throwing knife into the rat, then another. His eyes went wide and he felt his nape hairs stir again at sight of both blades passing through the creature, bloodlessly. Shock immobilized him long enough for the rat to leap upon him and sink its fangs into his arm. Hanse groaned and bit his lip while he clamped the unnaturally heavy beast with his right hand. The rat felt just as strong as he. Its fangs were like thick needles and the pain was awful when he tried to pull the huge rodent away. Sweat coated him in seconds. Despite the fact that the other knives had accomplished nothing against what was obviously sorcery, he could not give it up. Even as the rat-thing gnawed him and his brain began to stagger in a red haze of pain, a terrified Shadowspawn drew Cholly's dagger and stabbed, slashed.

With a shriek and a horrid jolt that made him cry out, the sorcerous *thing* vanished. So did the pain in Hanse's

arm and the mark there. Yet his glance showed him a
satisfying smear of blood on the dagger's silver-inlaid
blade. Pouncing to take up the unconscious Notable,
Shadowspawn ran.

I didn't name Strick a high enough price!

Emerging like the shadow of a ghost into the Lily
Garden, he ducked an amorously entwined couple who
never saw him. A downward glance showed him that the
big heavy cat in his arms had one eye slitted open. It gazed
greenly up at him.

"Oh, Notable, you ornery faker! See who gets the beer
after *this* night's work!"

Notable made a distinctly unpleasant remark. Hanse
tarried to be cute with the Lily Garden's proprietor, Amoli,
but not for long.

A few minutes after his departure, Amoli was bustling
along the tunnel to tell Marype a few things . . .

Early Anenday morning Strick himself arrived at the
home of Nadeesh the leech. Using the earring with its
brown-stained post, Strick easily "cured" the physician.
Nadeesh upheld his bargain: he agreed to sell the Vulgar
Unicorn (which he wanted to get rid of anyhow!) to Strick
tiFiraqa. Strick kept the sorcerer's box and the few strands
of human hair. Marype's hair.

"There, Snapper Jo. Do you have any further doubts
that I have power over you?"

The cowering demon shook its hideous head.

"Good," the new owner of the Vulgar Unicorn said.
"You've just been replaced. Go find other employment."

By the following night a native Ilsigi had been installed
as night barman at the Vulg; seeing that former carpenter
Abohorr had lost a digit, everyone immediately delighted
in calling him One-Thumb. Later that evening those same
patrons were astonished and proud to see in their favorite

haunt here in the very heart of the Maze: the white spellmaster Strick and Lady Esaria (with two bodyguards, of course). They seemed to have a nice time. Even drunks were sensible enough to say nothing untoward to the spellmaster's lady.

No one knew that Strick owned the place. As a matter of fact hardly anyone knew that Nadeesh had owned it. Most patrons did like the new serving girl, Silky, with her odd accent.

That same Moondy night Hanse ambled along, richer by quite a bit and actually trying not to swagger. As he passed an alley he was hit by a stagger spell, grabbed by three large toughs, punched, drugged, bound, gagged, and popped into a big cloth bag. Callous men hurried him to the waterfront. Their bagged burden thought of the stories he'd heard of slavers, right here in Sanctuary. Groggily he recognized one voice among the three: Tarkle. In the rope-bound sack, Hanse was boosted onto the ship *Asienta* and tumbled into the hold with a mild splash. He listened to the hatch being screwed down tightly. Groggily he heard that the ship sailed tomorrow for the far Bandaran Islands.

MURDER, MAYHEM, SKULDUGGERY... AND A CAST OF CHARACTERS YOU'LL NEVER FORGET!

THIEVES' WORLD™

EDITED BY
ROBERT LYNN ASPRIN and LYNN ABBEY

. . . .

FANTASTICAL ADVENTURES

One Thumb, the crooked bartender at the Vulgar Unicorn...
Enas Yorl, magician and shape changer...*Jubal,* ex-gladiator and
crime lord...*Lythande the Star-browed,* master swordsman
and would-be wizard...these are just a few of the players you will
meet in a mystical place called Sanctuary™. This is *Thieves' World.*
Enter with care.

__80591-4	THIEVES' WORLD	$3.50
__80590-6	TALES FROM THE VULGAR UNICORN	$3.50
__80586-8	SHADOWS OF SANCTUARY	$3.50
__78713-4	STORM SEASON	$3.50
__80587-6	THE FACE OF CHAOS	$3.50
__80596-6	WINGS OF OMEN	$3.50
__14089-0	THE DEAD OF WINTER	$3.50
__77581-0	SOUL OF THE CITY	$2.95
__80598-1	BLOOD TIES	$3.50